HUMAN

WILLIAM R. HUMBLE

Copyright © 2021, Version 2.0 2024 Castle Humble Publications+ LLC

Hardcover Print ISBN: 978-1-953172-12-9

Trade Paperback ISBN: 978-1-953172-10-5

E-book ISBN: 978-1-953172-09-9

Cover art by
J. Kathleen Cheney
www.bookcoverinsanity.com

Interior book design by
Lisa Bell (Radical Women)
www.bylisabell.com

CONTENTS

ALSO AVAILABLE

Short Story Collections

Tales from the Veil: Volume 1*

Novels

The Barrington Job
Anders Cohagen: The Cure
Anders Cohagen: The Fleet*
Rose Smyth—Vampire Sorceress*

Published by Fawkes Press
The Shield of the Vanir

*Forthcoming

PROLOGUE

M y name's Ethan Shaw. Ever feel out of place? Like you and the world are out of sync?

If so, we have something in common.

For starters, my school is weird. Freemont High averages one new teacher a week. Where do the old teachers go? No idea. *Why* do they go? Yeah, no idea there, either. Heck, even the date is weird. Us being in the year 2021 just doesn't feel right. It's not something I can put my finger on, but it feels *wrong*.

Also, I don't take meds, but since my ninth birthday, I'm always happy. Stub my toe? Happy. Leg cramps or growing pains? Happy. I was even happy both the times I got sick. I mean really, who's happy worshiping the porcelain altar? I used to have normal emotions. Not anymore.

So farkin' strange.

Speaking of strange, since I was little, I've dreamed of a voice making proclamations about Zones One, Two, and Three. Zone One, clear for decontamination. Zone Two, data transfer commencing. Zone Three, all non-Simulation personnel evacuate immediately. That sort of thing.

Yeah, and those aren't even the weirdest of my dreams. Not even close.

But all that is just part of why I don't belong.

Yesterday was my seventeenth birthday....

CHAPTER 1

HOW I'M GONNA GET IN TROUBLE ON MY BIRTHDAY

B irthday parties and Mondays. Never been a fan of either. When combined....

Le sigh.

My parents and my few friends have conspired to throw me a party.

While not my thing, I really do understand that they put time and effort into the preparation, and it shows they care about me. So, I force a brief smile.

"Thanks," I say to day mom as I cheerfully over-pepper my breakfast eggs and bacon. Between bites, I ask, "Who all's coming over? And when?"

"Tonight, at seven. Your father, night mother, and I *knew* you'd love it."

I'm quite sure that if I look up "to know" in the dictionary, it will say nothing about delusion or hope.

Opening my mouth to say this, I shovel in the last of the eggs instead.

When Mom's not looking, I frown. Not about the party or eggs. No, there's this really annoying sound—a constant, unwavering tone that started the other day.

Yeah. It started right after that minor earthquake. Coincidence?

Coincidence or not, there's a bigger issue. Two of 'em, really. One, it's not actually a sound at all. And two, no one can "hear" it but me.

While there's a lot of strangeness in my life, this is impressive even for me.

Grabbing my backpack and the last of the bacon, I head to the door. "I'm off, Mom! Love ya!"

"Love you, too. Have a good day at school."

Like that's gonna happen.

I cross the street heading to the next house down, the one with all the vibrantly colored flowers instead of a lawn. My best friend, Gabby Kwan, lives here. Unfortunately, she and all three of her parents are yelling at each other. She wants them to mind their own business, and they want her to fess up to something.

Doesn't sound like they'll be winding down soon.

Gabby wouldn't appreciate me getting in the middle of her family drama, so I keep walking and eat the slice of bacon I saved for her.

It's only a three-block walk to school. Two blocks away, the annoying not-sound becomes a little clearer. My interest in school plunges as hope surges. I might yet find the source of this obnoxious noise.

After the minor earthquake, I put in earplugs. No change. For three days, I've been putting up with this annoying, mysterious tone.

Maybe I can finally shut it off. Yeah, I really like the sound of that.

I cut between two houses and drop into the drainage ditch. This leads me to a quietly burbling creek, which I follow to the nearby wooded hills.

Reaching the first hill, the "sound" is a little clearer still.

Sounds like progress. Wait, *doesn't* sound like progress?

Whatever. I'm closer to the source.

The ruins of Old Town sit directly ahead. Old, ridiculously large city is more like it. Some of the ruin mounds are taller than this hill. Old Town extends dozens of kilometers to the north and east.

To my left is our actual town. Unlike Old Town, it's tiny—home to a little less than a thousand people—which seems like a good size. Despite being a little berg in the middle of BFE, our town's got a cool, kinda retro-fifties vibe to it. The people are, if not always friendly, at least interesting.

And, when they figure out I've ditched, most of them will be even less friendly.

My mood sours slightly, though as always, I'm still happy. They'll send the cops after me. Again. They *really* dislike it when a student bails on school. I can practically hear Principal Gates lecturing me on how I should be more responsible.

But… a chance to find the source of the not-noise and potentially stop it—definitely worth the risk.

Since time is running out before the search for me begins, I run. I'm athletic and enjoy running. It's something I do well.

Usually.

On the way down the hill, a rock turns under my foot. I lose my balance.

As I'm falling, my face is heading directly for a spiky dead tree branch. Adrenaline blazes through me. Just before the branch turns my face into meatloaf, there's a weird twitch in my mind and the branch snaps off before I hit it. Skidding down the rocky trail on my hands, I slide nearly four meters before my momentum plays out.

Standing, I absently dust myself off and stare at the branch. It's laying there to the side of the trail, as though I somehow knocked it away.

Freaky.

Like something out of my other dreams. Not the audio dreams of the Simulation. The other dreams….

No. Dreams becoming real… this is a level of weird I'm not ready to even consider.

I turn over my well-tanned hands to check my palms. No scratches. Ditto for my knees. My hands and knees, parts I used to scratch and scrape fairly often as a kid, have been growing tougher of late. My black jeans? Not so lucky. There're holes in the knees of both legs.

Giving myself a shake, I run again.

Five minutes later, I'm panting lightly as I top another hill. This gives me a great, panoramic view of this part of Old Town.

They say the earthquake that took it down was big—nine plus on the Richter scale. But that was decades ago. Despite the time lapse, there's little growing there in the way of trees or even scrub brush. Almost like God or the Devil smote the place and salted the earth.

Descending the hill brings me to the faded yellow metal panels of the caution wall.

It's covered in repeating warnings.

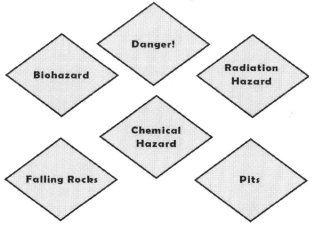

So far as I've been able to tell, they're all bogus except for the occasional bit of falling rubble. Pits would at least be interesting and give me something to rappel or free-climb into.

There's a tree growing near the wall, but I don't need it. With a running start and a leap, I grab the top of the four-meter-high wall. As I'm pulling myself up, Gabby calls from the top of the hill I was just on. Despite having hearing that's far, far above average, I can't make out what she's saying.

What in the world is she doing here?

Straddling the wall, I wait for her.

I don't have a long wait. When she wants to run, Gabby's fast. Maybe not as fast as me, but she's pretty quick. With her short blue hair, brown eyes, and cute little nose, she's pretty, pretty, too.

More and more, I wish I could tell her that. But, since that time in the second grade when I asked Lori Sangler to be my girlfriend and she barfed on my shoes, I've learned to be more cautious about such things. Especially after the reinforcing lesson two years later when I asked Elissa Goreman the same question and she ran away screaming. Yeah. Next day, her parents came and dis-enrolled her from school then moved to coastal Mongolia.

Talk about curb stomping the ego.

You'd think from those incidents that I must look like some sort of deformed buffalo with a severe hygiene problem, but I honestly don't. My build is athletic and I'm fairly tall. I've got short brown hair, my eyes are medium blue with purplish dots, and my features seem reasonably normal. If my nose was a little smaller, it wouldn't upset me, but it's not nearly as large as my friend Julian's, so I don't complain. I'm not mean and like to think I've got a decent sense of humor.

I don't get it.

Panting, Gabby reaches the wall below me. She's wearing a white blouse with a blue patterned vest and black knee skirt.

"What are you doing?" she demands, glancing around as though to make sure no one's followed us. "You can't just bail on school."

I take a moment to dramatically look around. "Evidently, I can."

"Ethan, they'll just send the police after you. Again."

Since the tone continues to sound, I just shrug. A thought pops into my head. "Wanna come with?"

"Dammit, Ethan. You're gonna get me in trouble."

I snort. "*You* never get in trouble. It's always me on the receiving end of that."

"Yeah, well this time, it looks like you're earning it."

"Okay," I say, swinging around to drop to the other side. "See you later."

"Wait!"

Holding on with my feet hanging over open air, I raise an eyebrow.

"I'll come with you," Gabby says with an aggravated frown. She runs to that tree near the wall and quickly climbs it.

I drop and go 'round a sizable pile of rubble to join her as she slides down a tilted piece of ceracrete on this side of the wall.

Dusting off her backside, she throws me a sour look. "You probably ate my slice of bacon, too."

By way of reply, I give her my best I'm-totally-innocent look.

"I thought as much. Stupid parents. Always wanting to argue when bacon's on the line."

"Sorry. That's a lousy way to start the day."

Gabs throws me a look which clearly suggests I'm the biggest moron on the planet. "Not as lousy as getting in trouble on your *birthday*. Speaking of which, if we're not dead or in jail, are you looking forward to your party?"

"No." I think Gabby appreciates that I don't lie to her. Or maybe she just tolerates me.

Hard to tell.

Her laugh is almost musical. "Didn't think you would be. Still, we got you a piñata and everything."

"Everything?"

"Sure. Ice cream, chocolate bunnies, and a few presents even. Everything."

Well, one thing about feeling happy all the time, guilt is muted. And while I feel a tad guilty about skipping school and the upset to follow, it's not enough to change my mind. Especially since the not-noise has grown a tad louder.

"So," Gabby begins, "where are we going?"

"That way," I say, pointing east by south-east.

She tries but fails to summon a smile. "Oh. Into the heart of Old Town."

CHAPTER 2

GABBY BRINGS CONFUSION LIKE HURRICANES BRING RAIN

G abby and I have been walking deeper into Old Town for roughly fifteen minutes. It feels like we're passing through a winding canyon made up of shattered ceracrete. Coming in all varieties of color—though black is dominant—it's beneath our feet and everywhere we look. There's a strange beauty to it, like a monster shattered the Rainbow Bridge of Norse mythology, and we're walking through its wreckage.

The tone's louder. We're close.

I abruptly stop and face Gabs. "How were you able to follow me?"

Her surprise quickly gives way to annoyance. "How'd you know to eat my bacon?"

"Truth?"

She nods.

"I heard you and your parents arguing."

Her expression switches to skeptical.

"Young lady," I say, doing a terrible job of mimicking her father, "whatever it is you've been up to, it's time for you to admit it. This is an honorable house, and we will not have you dishonoring it."

"Oh. Right."

"Yes," I agree, turning my hands from me to her.

9

Gabby bites her lip. "You can keep a secret, right?"

"Of course."

"Big time secret."

"Gabs, I can keep a secret."

Her eyes dart around before meeting mine. "I followed your scent."

I blink. "Was that a joke? Maybe a crack about my bathing habits?"

"No," she whispers. "I have a better than usual sense of smell. You, my aggravating friend, smell amazing."

Oh.

Unsure how to respond to that, I abruptly walk towards one of the large rubble mounds and slide under a big grey ceracrete slab with crystalline spikes protruding from the edges.

"Ethan!" Gabby calls, hurrying to catch up. "What the hell are you doing?"

"It's called exploring. You should try it sometime."

She mutters a curse and follows me.

In here is an open area the size of our favorite hamburger joint. Maybe three stories above, the ceracrete slabs, with their crystal spikes protruding from the broken ends, have interlocked. A little daylight filters down from somewhere much higher. I eye the mishmash of broken building parts skeptically.

If it hasn't fallen in this long, it's not likely to suddenly do so.

With some difficulty, I swallow.

Yeah.

Gabby's staring at it too.

"It's held for all these years," I say, repeating my thought and trying to sound reassuring. "I'm sure it'll last a few more minutes."

She throws me a doubtful look. As her gaze moves past me, her eyes widen.

I turn to see what's caught her attention. The wall behind me has an actual, *intact* door.

A small surge of excitement flares and almost immediately fades. I grab her hand and pull her over to it. Worried that I'm sending the wrong, but right signal, I regretfully release her hand.

"A door?" she whispers in awe.

"Sure," I say brightly. "They're brilliant devices that allow you to pass from one side of a wall to another without involving any messy particle physics."

Gabby delivers unto me a droll look. "Thank you for clearing that up. I've been wondering what doors were for since I was young."

"Yeah, I'm just a fount of knowledge."

"You're certainly a fount of *some*thing," she says with a little smile tugging at her lips before putting her hand on the lockplate.

Nothing happens.

"Well," she begins, relief permeating her tone, "we tried, and it didn't work. Now, let's go—"

I put my hand on the lockplate. The edge surrounding it flares green and the door irises open with a faint groan that ends in an ear-splitting squeal.

"—home." Gabby winces and mutters another curse.

"Yeah, that was unpleasant. Something I've gotta know... do you kiss your mothers with that mouth?" I tease.

She unloads her bag of expletives and rains insults on me. "Cat piss gargling sheep molester" tops out my amusement scale.

"Guess you do," I say with a smirk.

Though she tries to hold it in, Gabby laughs.

Slowly, concern enters her eyes. "It's dark in there."

Turning to look through the doorway, I nod. The annoying noise is considerably louder now. Not painful by a longshot, but far more aggravating than before.

"Well," I begin, "shall we?"

"Step inside and stop," she says, making a little shooing motion with her hand.

I do so then turn to her with a questioning look.

Gabby shrugs. "I was hoping the lights might come on. No such luck, huh?"

"Guess not."

She sighs and pulls an almost-flat box from a hidden skirt pocket. From the box, she takes out a peculiar pair of glasses, which she puts on. There're a few other gadgets I don't get a good look at before she closes the box and puts it away.

"What are those?"

Turning a fresh frown on me, Gabby says, "They're part of an emergency kit I've been assembling. Like my enhanced sense of smell, please don't tell anyone, okay?"

"Sure."

She puts a hand on my chest. "I'm serious, Ethan. This is important. Don't. Tell. Anyone."

"Gabs, I won't say a word. I promise."

"Okay."

We stand there a moment before she seems to suddenly realize her hand's still on my chest and yanks it back as though I'm a hot stove.

It's weird being happy when I want to sigh.

Guess asking her out to a movie, or something is out of the question.

Forcing a tiny smile, I change the topic. "What teacher do you think will be gone this week?"

"Hmm," she says, relaxing as her lips scrunch up. "I'm gonna have to guess Mrs. Henneman." Gabs sees the question on my face. "She seems weak to me. I really don't think teaching is her forte."

"Umm, hasn't she been teaching at Freemont High like twenty or thirty years now?"

"Some people are just slow learners."

I don't have a response for this beyond breaking out a fresh smirk.

My happiness has seeped back in past the sadness of her rejection, so I'm reasonably sure it's safe to get back on topic. "So, what's with the glasses?" They're very thin, with a weird little tube where the center of the lens would normally be.

"They're dark glasses."

"Never heard of 'em. Some sort of night-vision?"

"Yeah, that."

An awkward silence falls.

"Uh," I say, "Shall we?"

Gabby waves for me to lead, and I do.

This new chamber is tiny but clean. Strangely clean for old ruins. A stairway descends into darkness. We exchange looks, then start down at the same time.

"Okay, I've gotta admit, this is *sooo* cool!" she declares just before she races down the stairs.

The deeper we go, the darker it gets.

Ten flights down, all color has vanished.

Twenty flights down, we reach the bottom. Everything looks strangely grainy, but I can still see. It's noticeably cooler down here. Gabby's stopped by another door, hands on her thighs as she continues breathing hard. When I reach her, she takes my hand and gently pulls me towards the door.

"Wonder what this place is?" I ask. There's a vague sense of familiarity to all this that's bordering on *DeJa'Vu*. This familiarity should feel super weird. It doesn't.

Which, you know, *is* weird.

I'm close enough that even in the darkness, I can see Gabby frown as she pants, "There's rubble to the left. I think there was... a passageway there. Gone now. Right in front... of you is another door. Plate's on the... right side."

"It was kinda silly of you to run all the way down here."

"What's the sound..."—she flips me off—"...of a bird flying?"

I can't help but laugh.

Once she can breathe normally again, Gabby says, "My legs are gonna be sore tomorrow."

"Just wait 'til we climb back up."

She groans. "Open the door, Ethan." Without waiting, she grabs my hand again then slides it over the lockplate. Green light flashes and the door irises open.

Like the last time Gabby touched me, she maintains contact longer than normal. But unlike then, she's slow to release my hand, taking it in both of hers before finally letting me go.

Incredibly distracted by this, I say the first thing that pops into my head. "Why didn't you open the door yourself?"

She waves airily. "I'm much too important for such menial tasks. As the future queen of the Earth, I'm getting an early start on delegating."

I chuckle and look around, despite the lack of light.

The room is roughly the size of my house, so long as you don't count the second floor. Shelves form five aisles on the left side of the room. Most of the shelves look full, but I can't quite make out what's on them from here. At the back sits an enormous desk surrounded by monitors.

"You bring a flashlight in that kit of yours?"

"Nope," Gabby replies, tapping one arm of her weird glasses. "Don't need it since I've got dark glasses."

"That's *super* helpful for me," I complain. But even as the words leave my lips, I spot a small greenish glow. Walking to it, I find an orb with a green light on it that's about the size of a pencil tip. I turn the orb with the toe of my shoe. "*This* is the source of the damned noise."

"Noise?" Gabby asks. "What noise?"

"I've been hearing this blasted thing since that last tremor. Maybe it fell off the shelf and activated. I don't know. Anyway, that's another secret for *you* to keep."

She's close enough I can just barely make out her skeptically raised eyebrow. "Are we exchanging secrets like hostages or something?"

"I don't know. Something like that, I suppose. Sure."

Gabby curses again and pulls out her datapad. She types in a long code before it does a retinal scan and a DNA scan.

"Uh, that's beyond the normal security precautions for your average high school student."

She raises her shoulder in an elegant shrug. "I'm far beyond average."

"True that."

I think despite herself, Gabby smiles, but her eyes remain focused on the datapad as she types with one hand on some sort of holographic keyboard that's suddenly floating over it. A file opens and I spot the phrase Top Secret before she whirls away.

Top secret? Is my best friend some sort of spy? Also, what kind of tech was that? I heard her fingertips touching the holo-freakin'-graphic keyboard. That's not supposed to be possible. Is it?

"Son of a diseased mutant whore!" she snarls.

Startling at her sudden outburst, I ingeniously ask, "What? Me?"

"No, this place!"

"Um, yeah. It's old and intact, which *is* unusual for Old Town ruins. Despite that, I haven't noticed any health or moral problems."

Gabby whips her hair around as she violently shakes her head. "It's not that. I mean, it's not just that this place is intact. This is.... I was supposed to.... Dammit, it's complicated."

"So, start explaining."

She compresses her datapad back into its case and drops it into a skirt pocket. "It's not that simple."

"Okay," I bend down to pick up the orb at my feet. "Do you know anything about—"

"Ethan!" I sense more than see her leaping towards me. "Don't touch tha—"

As I grab the orb, her voice fades away and I feel something new in my head. There's... almost a vibration. The image of a flower opening leaves me with a weird floral scent I've never encountered. The flower fades, replaced by a butterfly chrysalis which bulges from within.

Deep in my head, there's a shudder.

Darkness sweeps in.

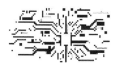

I'm on the floor.

Gabby's holding me. Though muted, I feel her concern for me. I know it with the same certainty I see her, hear her breathing and her heart beating, feel her warmth soaking in as she supports me.

Speaking of breathing, mine has sped up, as has the thundering of my heart. There's an urgency in my mind. Surging blood pulses in my head with each heartbeat. Each breath blasts oxygen into my brain.

The orb remains locked within my tightly clenched grip.

The chrysalis image remains as well, like a hologram I see everywhere I look, but it's slowly fading. It's replaced by a man in ancient clothing. As the last piece of his huge brass telescope assembles itself, he looks through it and I look through it with him.

Stars.

They whirl and spin around me in a dance of unimaginable beauty. But they're not stars. They're people. So very many people.

Slowly, they fade, taking the sense of urgency with them.

Normalcy returns accompanied by a peculiar sense of having accomplished something. I'm also strangely tired, though not physically, which is even more peculiar.

My mind drifts before settling on a memory.

Four or five years ago, my family went on a picnic trip to Lake Royer. While I ran around a lot, mostly I swam. Day Mom swam with me while Night Mom and Dad called encouragement from the shore. At the end of the day, I was so tired my knees shook as we walked ashore. I stretched my arms, back and legs, and shared a smile with my parents. As soon as we got in the car, I promptly fell asle—

"Ethan!"

Startled, I rouse from the memory-dream. "Wha...?"

"Oh, thank goodness." Gabby heaves an enormous sigh of relief.

I'm still on the floor in the dark, underground room. Gabby's holding my head in her lap. I blink fuzzily. "Hey. What's up, Buttercup?"

"Buttercup? I've never heard that word before. Did you just make it up?"

"Dunno." I'm pretty sure I can get up if I want to, but Gabs and the floor feel really comfy.

Gabby sighs and picks up the orb I evidently dropped. "This complicates things."

"Huh? How? What do you mean?"

She pushes a button on the orb. The green light winks out, as does the annoying not-noise.

Her lips compress into a flat line. "This is a psychic induction orb."

"Uh, okay." After a silence-filled pause, I add, "I don't know what that means either."

Eyes closing, Gabby's expression turns sad. "It means virtually everyone on the planet will want to kill you."

Chapter 3

GLORIOUS AUTHORITY & A NON-EXPLODING PIÑATA

A while later, as Gabby's resting at the top of the stairs, I ask, "What did you mean about everyone wanting to kill me? Was that figurative or—"

She stashes the case with her weird glasses back in the skirt pocket. "Oh no, that was literal. 100% non-figurative."

Gabby's mostly got her breath back from the climb, which means we'll be leaving soon. Time for this conversation is running out. "Okay. Why will everyone want to kill *me*? And does that include my parents? Our friends? You?"

"No, of course not," she says, looking at me like I'm some sort of idiot.

"Well, that's a relief. So, what's the deal?"

"Ethan, it's...."

"Complicated?" I guess, giving her my best sardonic expression.

"It most certainly is," Gabby agrees with a sigh as she runs her fingers through her blue hair.

I meet her eyes and raise an eyebrow.

She mutters a curse. "Look, this isn't just complicated, it's super-complicated. I.... I need time to think about it and consider what moves are open to us. You've got to keep this secret for a few days. Do that, and I'll figure a way out of this mess. For all of us."

"Gabs, you're not making any sense."

"Things aren't as they seem," she snaps, "and I need time to think." She stalks away from the stairwell and across the diner-sized open area.

Frustrated to my core, I follow her.

After we low crawl out from under the rubble, Gabby grabs my arm to stop me. "We can't talk about what happened. You get that, right?"

"Which parts? Your high-tech tools, the orbs, the ruins, or everyone wanting to kill me?

"Quiet!"

Frustrated, I turn up my hands and give her my best WTH look.

"It's... everything's all snarled up," she whispers as her eyes turn hard. "And dangerous. Seriously dangerous. For all of us. And I mean exactly *all* of us."

I repeat the gesture and look.

Gabby glances around before turning back to me. Voice even quieter, she says, "Trust me. *Please!* I'll tell you everything when I can. Right now.... Right now, we've got to come up with an excuse that will explain us being out here. Keep them from searching the ruins we've been in."

A dark smirk crosses my face. "We could tell people I brought you out here to make out with you, but you were repulsed by me."

Salt meet fresh wound.

"That's silly," she replies with a flick of her hand. "No one would believe that."

My brain does a hard break, sliding to a full stop at the implications.

"Maybe the opposite...." she mutters, staring at the debris and tapping her lip with a finger. "It's not bad. Bit of squirmy embarrassment. Far from the surveillance net in town for a little *real* privacy. I think people could understand that. Yeah, this might work."

"Uh... you're *not* repulsed by me?"

"Goodness, no," Gabby says, before lifting up on her toes to give me a quick kiss on the lips. "You're the sexiest man in the galaxy."

She doesn't seem to be teasing or joking.

My brain does another hard stop.

"Okay, here's what we're going to do," Gabby says. "We're gonna tell anyone who asks that we came out here to do it."

That we came out to...? Oh!

With my confusion surging, I again blurt out the first thing that pops into my head. "But you're not even my girlfriend."

"I know!" she says with a glare before lowering her voice again. She takes a deep, apparently calming breath. "Despite that, we've been friends forever. Nobody will question that we've taken the next step, so relax. Just tell anyone who asks that we came out here for some privacy and that I chickened out at the last second."

When I don't immediately agree, she pokes me in the chest.

"If I tell people anything, it will be with great reluctance."

She smiles. "That's perfect."

It's a long way from perfect.

I sigh and we start back towards home.

Sexiest man in the galaxy? I mean, who wouldn't like the sound of that, but... is it real or just words? And, she kissed me. Was that real, or just to shut me up?

So many questions. *Sooo* much confusion.

As we near the Yellow Wall of Many Cautions, I hear soft footfalls up ahead. Acting on inspiration, I take Gabby's hand and intertwine our fingers. "Hey, you know even if we didn't do the deed, I still love you, right?"

Surprised, her gaze meets mine. I give my eyes a momentary flick to the right before returning to hers.

"I know," she says with a nod and a blush, sounding so sincere I doubt everything all over again. "I'm just sorry I chickened out on you. It was supposed to be a special birthday present. Instead, it was a big birthday nothing."

I snort. "I got to spend the day with my best friend, who also happens to be my dream girl. That's about as far from nothing as you can get."

The realization hits me like a two-ton hammer.

Gabby really is my dream girl. Why am I just now figuring this out now?

"You're so sweet," she says, squeezing my hand. "You're the best boyfriend, ever."

If only us being a couple was really true.

Half a dozen police officers step around a pile of rubble not three meters away. The police chief, who I still think looks like the model from the Mega Cola commercials, says, "There you are."

Gabby and I freeze in unison.

"Oh," I say cleverly. "Umm... hey Chief."

Sergeant Lawton gets on her radio and says, "We found them. Section 418. Coming to you now." She gives us a stern look, then jerks her thumb back over her shoulder.

We all start walking that way.

Sounding pained, the Chief asks, "Ethan, why can't you just stay out of Old Town?"

I start to spout off the first thing that comes to mind, but I haven't exactly had outstanding success with doing that. Instead, I think about it. I can give an honest answer without saying anything about the noisy orb. "The unknown."

"Come again?"

"Everything on our side of the wall is a known quantity. It's all clean and sanitized. Maybe too much so. I mean, it's nice, but sometimes it's also boring. *This* side of the wall may be dirty and a little dangerous, but it's also new and exciting. Yes, I know it's actually old, but it's new to me. I think the exploration calls me."

Lawton snorts in derision. "Admit it, Mr. Shaw. You were mostly wanting to explore Miss Kwan."

My ears burn and my cheeks grow hot, but I admit nothing.

A few steps later, I realize maybe my silence and blush still count as an admission. What's even more aggravating is that this *is* our perfect cover story. And it's working. Still, when Gabby said it would be squirmy, I thought that part was for other folks.

We finally reach the wall of warnings. A team of technicians has used a crane to remove one of the wall sections. As soon as we cross, they lower it back into position.

The Chief leads us over to where the Mayor and Principal Gates stand with crossed arms.

Oh, this is going to be fun—like having your appendix pulled out through your nose.

The mayor turns to us and just stares for several uncomfortable seconds. His cybernetic left eye doesn't twitch the way the right one does. "How'd you cross the wall, Ethan?"

Prolly best not to tell 'em I just jumped to the top and pulled myself over.

Hoping I'm even half as good an actor as Gabby evidently is, I say, "There's a tree." I wave towards the south. "That way, I think."

Wait. Did Gabby see me jump to the top of the wall? If so, she didn't say anything. Even if she didn't see that, she definitely saw me sitting on top of the wall.

Again, Gabby effortlessly confounds me.

The mayor slowly turns and scowls at the tech guys. Expressions increasingly uncomfortable, they fidget. The mayor's scowl switches to us. "Why can't you stay on this side of the damn wall?"

Sergeant Lawton thumps a hand on my shoulder. "Ethan here's an explorer."

"Lawton," the Chief warns.

"No," the mayor says. "It's alright. I want to hear this."

"You see, Mister Mayor," Lawton continues, sliding over to clap her other hand on Gabby's shoulder, "Ethan's real keen on topographical geography. In particular, he's interested in exploring Miss Kwan's peaks and curves. Oh yeah. Why, I bet he was especially looking forward to spending some time down in the valley."

Someone just shoot me. Please.

"That's quite enough, Sergeant," the Chief says.

Lawton pats us both on the shoulders again, then walks over to her squad car.

"Bitch," Gabby snarls.

Except... her lips didn't move. Was that some sort of ventriloquism? Maybe my imagination? Despite her less than quiet volume, none of the others are telling her not to be rude and that she must be respectful of authority.

Which is weirder? That they didn't hear... or that they're ignoring her comment?

Either way, I'm not gonna argue with the sentiment.

The mayor turns a disturbing shade of red. "Is this true, Mister Shaw? Did you come out here with the express purpose of,"—he makes air quotes—"'exploring' Miss Kwan?"

"I... uh...."

"It was my idea," Gabby says, giving my hand a squeeze.

Looking at Gabs as if she's grown an extra head, the mayor asked, "What?"

"It was gonna be a special birthday present," she says, blushing bright red. "But I changed my mind. Ethan was super cool about it."

The Chief says, "Mister Mayor, their families are at the station. We should reunite them."

"I'll ride with you," Principal Gates says, looking Gabby and me in the eyes. "It appears we need to reinforce our previous talks on responsibility."

The two of us groan in unison.

Several hours later, uncomfortable silence fills the car as Dad drives my moms and I home from the police station.

Night Mom is fuming so much I'm worried her dark hair will catch fire. Day Mom's practically radiating disappointment. Only Dad's kept a neutral expression.

I'm just praying there's not gonna be another lecture on responsibility. My mind is still numb after Principal Gate's and I'm worried that just a little more will set me bleeding from my ears.

On the other hand, if my ears fill up with blood, I won't be able to hear....

As we pull into the driveway, Day Mom asks, "Do we cancel the party?"

Dad's lips purse, then he shakes his head. "I don't think so. The party's a show of love and support. What better time?"

"Maybe some time," Night Mom begins sourly, "when our son hasn't spent the day breaking the rules? When he doesn't need time to reflect on his actions and how they affect those around him? Also, maybe on a day when he hasn't been trying to bang the neighbors' kid?"

"They're driven by hormones," Day Mom says. "It's only natural. We were young once, too."

Night Mom snorts, then turns to me. "Did you at least have protection?"

"Protection from what?" No, I'm not really that naive, but my mind isn't quite on the same track as hers and I'm thinking about all the bogus warnings on the big yellow wall.

She throws up her hands. "Pregnancy. Disease."

"Wait, you think Gabby's diseased?"

"No, of course I don't."

"Then why would you say that?"

"Because that's part of what protection protects *against*. At least certain forms."

Dad holds up his hands. "We will discuss this later, but not tonight. Right now, we're all going to relax. We've still got a couple of hours before our guests arrive." He hands me my datapad, which they picked up with my keys and such at the police station. "The school forwarded your homework. While you're taking care of that, the three of us will finish preparations for the party."

"Okay," I mutter and trudge upstairs to my room.

Sprawling on my bed, I stare at the ceiling. This has certainly been a memorable day. Gabby, the super spy. Gabby, who said I'm the sexiest man in the galaxy. That branch breaking. Weird visions from that orb thing. Everyone supposedly wanting to kill me because I touched it. The surveillance net around town. Thanks to my abnormally good hearing, I've suspected something like that existed for years. I've just never been able to confirm those suspicions. Oh, let's not forget about Gabby's weird ventriloquism trick that no one noticed.

Could the orb stuff be some sort of joke at my expense? Gabby's got a delightful sense of humor, but a mean-spirited "joke" isn't her thing.

Sitting up, I scrub my hands over my face.

If I finish my homework, maybe Night Mom will chill. Hopefully, this too won't bite me in the arse.

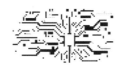

The ringing doorbell startles me awake. Out front, a bus shifts gears as it pulls away. This gives me a pretty good idea of who's here.

A glance at the datapad shows I've done two out of fifteen pages of schoolwork. One and three-quarters, really.

Oh yeah, *this* is sure to make everyone happy.

I stop by the bathroom to comb my hair and brush my teeth as Day Mom lets in two of my friends.

Might as well get this over with.

Downstairs, I find my friends Embry and Carmen. They're both a head shorter than me. Embry typically wears dark clothes that go well with his dark skin. Carmen's skin tones are exactly midway between ours. She almost always wears blue jeans with a brightly colored top. Tonight is no exception. From the way Carmen's eyes light up when she sees me, she's heard enough about today's festivities to pique her interest.

Dammit.

Forcing a smile, I greet them then lead us out to the back porch. It's a clear evening and the stars are already out.

Carmen begins intensely, "So tell us—"

Day Mom slides open the glass door and steps out with a tray of raspberry lemonade.

"Oh, that's so sweet, Mrs. Shaw," Carmen says instead, all traces of her previous intensity gone. After Day Mom sets the tray down, Carmen takes a drink. "Thank you, so much!"

"You're welcome, dear." Day Mom smiles, then steps back inside.

Out front, a car pulls up and stops. This falls into a questionable hearing range for me. Since neither of my friends reacts, I keep it to myself.

Carmen's head snaps back around to me, her expression suddenly serious. "Spill. I want *all* the juicy details."

I mentally flip through my collection of cuss words and grossly inappropriate phrases. Since Gabby's refresher earlier, I have a great selection to choose from. Maybe "substitute dog's arse licker...."

Before I choose one for sharing, the doorbell rings.

"This does *not* get you off the hook," Carmen says, her eyes locking onto me like a hawk on a mouse. "Fate is only delaying the inevitable."

If you were to (unfairly) limit a description of me and my friends to just one word, for me, that word would probably be "clueless." I'd say "adventurous" or maybe "fearless" for Gabby but there's so much more to her....

Ahem.

Anyway, that one word for Carmen would be "stubborn." *Sooo* much stubborn.

Embry absently adjusts his glasses and quietly says, "Should be a good story."

As usual, he's standing a meter farther back than Carmen. His personal space is much larger than any of my other friends. For him, I'm torn between "quiet" and "invisible." Still, he's a nice guy. Always polite. A good listener. Hmm. "Underappreciated" might be good, too.

I step over and open the sliding door just as Dad ushers Julian into the living room along with his parents. Julian's a big guy, but not very athletic. I've always wondered if he was adopted because, like my dad, he's two meters tall. Unlike my dad, he looks vaguely Samoan. This is also unlike his parents, who stand a good half-meter shorter than him. Regardless, his quirky sense of humor amuses me.

Catching his eye, I wave him over.

For him, I want to say "nerd," but to some extent or another, I think we're all nerds. Maybe "ubernerd."

"Hey, guys," he says, closing the door behind him. "Ooh, drinks! Also, happy birthday, Ethan."

"Thanks. Here," I say, handing him a cold glass that's already sweating. "Let's sit."

Carmen nods. "Ethan was just about to tell us *everything*."

"Will Gabby be here?" Julian asks as he takes a seat.

We follow his example and sit. I shrug. "Dunno. Hope so."

"Dude!" Julian begins. He then takes a moment to drain half his drink. "Dang, these are good." Ignoring Carmen's exaggerated look of aggravation and her follow-up eyeroll, he continues, "School freaked out once they figured out you and Gabby ditched. Principal Gates ran out along with the entire coaching staff. The teachers were all quiet and lost looking. It was *strange*."

Carmen glares at him. "Is this an *appropriate* conversation to be having?"

He tips his head to the side in a little shrug and takes another drink.

Appropriate? What's up with that?

I shake my head and take a sip. The sweetness of the raspberry juice nicely buffers the sourness of the lemons. Yum. "That definitely sounds weirder than normal."

Embry nods. "It was."

Carmen throws him a frustrated "you, too?" sort of look before turning back to me. "So? Where'd you go?"

Is everyone keeping secrets? It's beginning to feel like it. I glance towards Gabby's house. Even me.

Heh. Maybe especially me.

"Gabs and I went to Old Town."

Embry gives me a puzzled look. "Again? How'd you get over the wall this time?"

"There's a tree growing right next to it. We climbed it, then crossed right over the wall," I lie. I'd prefer to tell them the truth, but right now, at least according to Gabby, the truth will get me in more trouble than I'm already in.

"How'd you avoid the drones?" Julian asks.

"Drones?"

"Drones," he confirms. "I heard they had over a hundred searching the area."

"Aerial drones?"

Everyone else nods, though Carmen throws Julian a quick scowl accompanied by a what-the-hell look.

Why would drones searching for me be a secret?

"Never saw any drones. Maybe the one in our area flew over while we were exploring debris."

Carmen leans forward. "That's what you did? Explore Old Town?"

"Yep," I reply. And this isn't a lie. It's just nowhere close to the whole truth.

"There's more to it," she says, critically eyeing me.

Crap, is she a mind-reader?

"Umm... what makes you think that?"

"That 'umm' for starters. It's a dead giveaway you're nervous about something."

"What? I don't...." I'm not really sure how to finish that sentence.

Julian and Embry give me simultaneous "sorry to say" looks, followed by synchronized nods.

"Oh. Well, crap."

"Anyway," Carmen says, sitting back in her chair. "You're just part of it. Gabby's been squirrelly for days. She planned this, didn't she?" Mistaking my surprise for confirmation, she nods. "Yeah, I thought so. But why? What's her motive?"

Excellent questions.

I'm saved from having to try and answer by the back door sliding open.

All the parentals come trooping out. Speaking of drones, Night Mom's carrying one. Dad has the piñata. She sets the drone to hovering, and they connect a line to the piñata. Grinning, she starts the drone on a quick test run in a drunken course around the backyard. This year's piñata is a winged unicorn in white and electric blue.

Day Mom sets the bat down on the table meeting my eyes to be sure I'm not tempted to pick it up. When I was twelve, I delivered a two-handed, overhead death blow to a piñata that blew the thing up and trashed the BBQ grill it'd been flying over. That got me permanently banned from piñata bashing duty.

Shame. I rather enjoyed it.

She also sets out a dozen chocolate bunnies on the serving tray before winking at me and stepping away to speak with Julian's moms and dad.

A door opens somewhere across the street open.

Gabby?

"Ooh!" Julian says, grabbing the bat. "I love your birthday parties. At everyone else's, they get to break their own piñatas. At yours, I get piñata-slaying duty for a second time in the same year."

I grin. "Thanks. Just rub it in."

His expression turns upset, then he sees my smile. "Hey, at least you know when *I* slay the piñata that the candy inside isn't gonna get disintegrated."

Embry and Carmen snicker, and she gives several exaggerated nods.

"Yeah, yeah," I say with a twisted grin, standing up. "I think I heard Gabby. Be right back." I walk behind our over-tall hedge, pop-out near the backyard gate, and open it.

Gabby's crossing the street, heading this way. Over her shoulder, I can't help but see her father. He's standing on their front porch, arms crossed with a stern expression fixed to his face. The moment I step out, his eyes latch onto me and stay there.

Oh.

"He doesn't look happy," I whisper when Gabs is close.

She shrugs. "Law of unintended consequences. Sorry, but I can't stay. Had to do some serious wheedling just to deliver this." She hands me a small box.

"Thanks. What is it?"

"It's a present, dumbass." A wicked grin puts in a too brief appearance.

Lord, she has a beautiful smile.

"Ethan!" Day Mom calls. "We're about to start the piñata battle."

"Go ahead. I'll be there for the candy pickup."

The piñata battle begins with whoops, encouragements, and catcalls. Julian chases the piñata around as Night Mom maneuvers the drone to keep it just out of bat range.

I turn back to Gabby. "Thanks for the present. I'll save you some candy from the piñata." I lean closer to whisper a question, but stop when her eyes widen then dart to the side.

"Umm, what? Oh. It looks like.... Uh.... So, your dad's gonna freak out if I kiss you?"

"Yes," she says with an emphatic nod. "And ground me for the next three-years."

"Dammit."

Gabby's eyes light up. "I've gotta go. Happy birthday."

"Just a sec," I say before running back to the porch and grabbing a couple of chocolate rabbits for her. The piñata battle has shifted, so I duck behind the hedge to get around the spectators. Popping out from behind the hedge, the piñata flits by, almost hitting me.

There's a hint of movement, then stars explode in my head.

Chapter 4

DREAMS OF NOT-ME

I dream.

Like most of my dreams, the world is different. There's a moon in the sky, but not a huge one. Or rather, not a particularly close one. It's weird looking up and seeing a moon, but at the same time it's perfectly natural.

Yeah, "dichotomy" is my word of the year.

There're also more people. A *lot* more. Most are in uniforms of charcoal grey and black. These folks all walk with a purpose—like they've got somewhere to be, and what they're doing is important.

Far as the eye can see, there are buildings. Most are huge, reaching hundreds of stories into the sky. Bridges and transit ways form a web between buildings. Some high, some low, and too many to count in between. Above, all manner of ships fly in orderly rows and columns.

The place I need to go today is deep underground.

While walking into a transit station, I tell my keeper, "Transport to Whiskey Kilo X-ray Training facility."

My keeper flashes an acknowledgment and orders a pod.

A pod parked to the right gains a green halo. I stroll over and the door opens. Before I step in, something hits my back, knocking me inside. I roll awkwardly, but still pop up ready for battle.

There's a cute teen about my age standing in the pod's doorway. She's got kinky hair, dark skin, and amazing brown eyes. Wearing the same black and grey uniform as me, her perfect fighting stance is marred only by her challenging grin. As soon as I see her, it feels like another part of my brain wakes up. I know exactly where I am and what I'm doing. What's more, I recognize the girl.

Kendra, one of my fellow students.

"Oh," I say, grinning back at her, anticipation for our fight lighting me up like an overcharged LED. "It's on!"

"No, it's not!" Professor Gillam declares as she gently pushes Kendra into the pod. "You two save that for training."

"But—" I start to say.

"Training *in* the training facility."

"*Awww*," Kendra and I say at the same time. This sparks a laugh from all three of us.

The halo around the pod switches to yellow and starts flashing. We take seats. Twenty seconds later, the halo turns red and the doors seal. The halo vanishes, and the pod moves.

"Any news?" I ask the Professor.

Her expression turns hard. "Yes. The enemy is now scouting planets Arkam and Kameline."

Kendra curses. "They've found every single outpost and colony. If they win this war, the human species will be nothing but a memory. Worse, we'll be nothing but one of *their* memories."

"Enough of that negativity!" Professor Gillam snaps.

"Sorry, ma'am," Kendra replies immediately as she sits up straight. "It won't happen again, ma'am."

The professor waves the apology away, the hardness in her eyes fading as her gaze covers us both. "It's a natural reaction to bad news. But, so is running away or hiding in the corner. We must overcome our natural reactions so we can act as *we* want."

"Yes, ma'am," we reply in unison.

Professor Gillam's eyes flick to the side—probably to something her keeper's showing—then back to us. "What has you two up so early?"

Kendra grins. "Today is boost day."

"Ah," the professor replies with an answering smile. "Which one is this?"

"Psychokinesis Two," I reply. I reach out with my mind and gently lift Kendra so she's floating a third of a meter above the floor. "I've been looking forward to this one for months."

Kendra raises a hand, and flames appear around it. She smiles again, but this smile is much less friendly. "Unless you want to be called Barbecue Boy, you'd best put me back down."

In the Training Center, I'd take that as a challenge. My eyes cut to Professor Gillam. Yeah, we're not there. I drop Kendra and she thumps back into her padded seat.

"Jackass." Her flames vanish.

I shrug and nod. "That's fair."

She eyes me. Kendra's telepathic shields are strong, so I can't hear her thoughts, but thanks to her body language, I don't need to. If we were in the Training Center, she'd already be trying to melt or pound my face off. Since she started it with that push, I'm a bit regretful we're not gonna have a chance to really mix it up.

Professor Gillam's head tilts to the side. "Are you two sex buddies?"

Stunned, Kendra and I share a horrified look.

The professor gets a case of the giggles that lasts until we exit the car at the WKX Training Center.

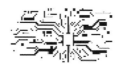

Sirens seep through my consciousness.

Panic surges through me. I'm late. I shouldn't have napped. Sitting up, there's resistance—a strap across my chest. I tear it in half and sit up. "Are we at the Training Center? I don't want to miss the boost."

My vision is blurry, but someone moves close.

Night Mom places a hand on my shoulder. "Relax, honey. It's okay, you're safe."

I really notice the siren this time.

We're in the back of an ambulance.

"Oh. Hey, Mom." Some of my confusion fades, as do the details of my dream. "Why wouldn't I be safe?"

She hugs me. "I'm *so* sorry, sweetheart. I flew that drone right by you and Julian was already swinging." She's not crying, but she sounds close to it. A first.

Someone attaches to my other side. I can't see her face, but I'd know Gabby's scent anywhere.

I spare an arm for each and hug them close.

After a while, I let them go. I realize there's a male med-tech in here with us. His eyes are huge and scared, and he's standing as far from us as he can. I shift on the gurney enough to keep him within sight.

"So, I got hit in the head, right?" I ask. I feel more than see Gabby's nod. "Okay. How's Julian? He's a big softy. Bet he's probably really upset."

"He is," Gabby confirms.

Night Mom says, "The poor boy was crying his eyes out. His parents and your friends were trying to tell him it wasn't his fault."

"I need to call him. Let him know I'm alright and that it really wasn't his fault."

"After we get to the hospital," Night Mom says.

The idea of going to the hospital is thoroughly unappealing, but I suppose I did just get knocked out.

"Where're Dad and Day Mom?"

Night Mom kisses me on the forehead. "There wasn't room in here, so they're meeting us at the hospital."

"Okay, I don't want them worrying either."

She smiles, one of her few smiles that doesn't seem strained. "Worrying is part of our job, honey."

I hug her again. "Love you, Mom."

"Love you too."

A couple of minutes later, Gabby, who's been rubbing her hand along my back, stops doing so. "What did you mean when you asked—" She cuts off suddenly, and I catch her eyes darting to the med-tech. "... When you wanted me to get you a berry cobbler? Did you want me to make one from scratch, or just buy one from the bakery?"

Since I've never asked her about a berry cobbler, I assume this means she doesn't want the med-tech hearing her real question.

The side of my head is suddenly throbbing. I don't know if this headache sprang up out of nowhere, or if it was there since I awoke and I simply didn't notice.

Since she's supposed to be my girlfriend now, at least until enough time has passed that she can tell the world we've broken up, I shift Gabby around and lean the undamaged side of my head against her shoulder. "Homemade, please."

"Okay," she says. "It's a deal. We can work out the details later."

I pull her a little closer and give Night Mom's hand a squeeze. Real girlfriend or not, she's still my best friend. It's nice knowing I've got people who care about me.

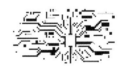

I'm running through an underground obstacle course. It's a circular track around a lake, and I've got to make two passes as fast as possible. As I near the three-story climbing wall, I leap. Reaching back and down, I shove out with my telekinesis. It pushes me high enough that I'm able to skip off the top of the wall. On the way down, I reverse the push to soften my landing. I could probably land from three floors up without hurting myself, but I don't want to risk twisting an ankle during our annual evaluation day.

Sprinting across the balance beam is easy, but when I'm halfway across the water hazard it spans, a pair of combat androids rise out of the water at the far end.

Damn, that's a new twist.

Reaching out with my telekinesis, I grab one and hammer it into the other. There's a splash and a loud metallic crash.

Sparks flash as I sprint past.

I'm coming up on the crawlway, a half-meter deep pit filled with mud. Evenly spaced within are wooden supports holding up coils of razor-wire mesh. It's a *long* thirty meters to crawl when you're going for speed, as I am. If I get top score on the course, that'll put me first in line for one of the new psychic assault mods.

I *want* one.

With one of those mods, I'll be able to do some serious damage. Really help in the war once my training's over. Make a difference.

Maybe save my friends and family from extinction.

A year ago, after receiving the Psychokinesis One boost, I could shove behind me just as I jumped. This carried me over the crawl's auto-stunners, which was good since they were constantly blazing away to ensure folks crawling through the pit didn't raise their heads too high.

Rounding a bend, the crawl comes into view. It looks like it did last time, save that a wall of auto-stunners on the left fire, covering a full ninety-degree arc in bolts of blazing energy.

They adapted. Leaping won't work.

On top of that, small thin prongs are poking up out of the mud. Each set forms a 'V' and I spot over a dozen of 'em. Freaking stun mines.

As I race towards the obstacle, I spot a clear path. It's on the far-right edge. Problem is, it'll take me close to two of the mines.

It's worth the risk.

Diving, I use my telekinesis to augment my momentum. Hitting the mud, I bounce, and my head rises too high, striking one of the wooden crossbeams. It cracks and I see stars, but I keep pushing.

Squirting up out of the mud, I stumble and launch back into a sprint. Blood drips down into my right eye and I wipe it away.

The thought that I don't have time to bleed tugs at my sense of humor, but I ignore it.

I've got a race to win.

Rushing through the other obstacles, I telekinetically yank a gold glove out of a tiny box in the remarkably high ceiling. It's worth five seconds off my time. Pyrokinetically setting a lake buoy on fire takes off another five seconds, as does using cryokinesis to freeze a burning torch by the starting line. Despite this, as I come back around to the climbing wall, I'm behind the lead time by four seconds.

No!

Pouring my sudden fury into a massive telekinetic strike, I lash out at the climbing wall.

It explodes.

Not slowing, I sprint through the pieces of the wall as they rain down across the area.

Crossing the balance beam, I'm not surprised when the two damaged androids rise out of the water. I reach out as though grabbing their heads and squeeze, clenching my hands into fists. Roaring in response to their challenge, I crush them with telekinesis. Metal and plastics crunch, and there's a screech of dying electronics as I race past.

I've closed to within two seconds of the lead.

Ahead, the crawl comes into view. My eyes automatically go to the path I took. There're mines there now.

In fact, there's a mine every square meter of the crawl.

Reaching out with my power, I hammer the wall of stunners. Once.

The wall shudders, and one stunner stops firing.

Twice.

The wall tilts forward and sparks erupt as half a dozen stunners have the power cables ripped out of them.

Thrice.

Even as the wall is falling into the mud, I leap.

One of the stun bolts hits my foot and my entire left leg goes numb.

No! I will not fail!

Instead of landing, I touch down briefly with my good foot before launching myself again. This is mostly telekinesis, which is bad because the mental strain is building fast. I've pushed myself harder than ever before and I'm in danger of seriously hurting myself.

Push too hard and I can permanently damage my psychokinetic abilities.

I'm in the lead!

I "run" for three more steps, each one taking me six meters, before my course time flashes red again on my keeper. I'm falling behind again.

No!

Reaching far ahead, I grab a pair of trees. Rather than pulling them to me, I fling myself to them—rather, between them.

This is so much like flying that for a moment, a wild joy overtakes my determination. Flying is above what's supposed to be within range of the Psychokinesis Two boost, but this is *my* talent. This is where I truly excel.

Despite that, the pain in my head is quickly growing towards agony. I taste blood from a nosebleed.

Hopefully, that's just strain and not a cerebral hemorrhage.

Focusing with all my might, I reach out around me. With a minor adjustment to my course, I fling myself through the air, aiming just beyond the finish line.

I cross the line. My keeper still shows green on the course time. After bouncing a couple of times, I tumble and roll to a stop.

Now I have time to bleed.

A tired laugh escapes me as I release my psychokinetic center.

My training commander walks over to meet me. "I suppose I should say 'well done'. You've set a new course record." She looks down at me with a critical eye. "But it also appears you took some unnecessary risks."

"I'm still trying to figure out where my limits and boundaries are, ma'am."

"And there are ways of finding that out that don't involve risking your life."

I sit up and wipe blood off my lip. "Ma'am, I'm not sure that's how boundaries get tested."

"Maybe not," she admits with a smile as she helps me to my feet. Pulling my arm over her shoulder, she helps me limp towards the nearby med station. "But there are ways of pushing your boundaries that don't involve *foolish* risks."

Reaching up to my aching forehead, I again pull back bloody fingers. "You raise a good point, ma'am."

She pats my shoulder. "Then you may not be a tiger after all, but a young dragon." Her look becomes speculative. "Time will tell."

Chapter 5

LEARNING THE WAYS OF FRYING PANS AND FIRES

I wake up in a hospital bed.

After a good stretch, I rub the crud out of my eyes. Sunshine streaming in through the window draws my attention. Sunny and clear outside. Nice.

Nic*er* if I was running around out in it.

Speaking of running... damn. Those were some weirdly cool dreams. These are the ones I like, and there've been a lot of them. They usually fade quickly, but this last one seems to be staying with me so far. Some details of the other dreams come back to me. My mother and father. My sisters, Keit and Peigi. Kendra and dozens, probably hundreds of other people.

Looking back on them, the dreams almost form... a pattern. I can almost see—

Day Mom walks in holding a cup of coffee. Her face lights up in a smile as she sees me seeing her. "Hey, hon," she says, giving me a not-so-quick hug. "How you feelin'?"

"Good. Got a little headache, but it's not bad." I frown and ask, "I called Julian last night and reassured him I'm okay, right?"

"You did," she confirms, sitting next to me.

"Okay, just wanted to be sure." I look around but don't see my clothes. "I'd kinda like my clothes. I don't know why someone designed these gowns without a back, but I'd feel really odd wearing one of these out into the parking lot."

"About that...."

41

My heart sinks as my expression sours.

"Sorry," she says. "They wanna keep you here for observation. It's just one day."

I scowl, but my persistent happiness slides in to buoy my spirits.

Day Mom leans over, wraps an arm around me, and kisses my temple. "You scared us," she whispers. "You were lying there, motionless, blood spreading through your hair...." She sniffs back tears. "Please? For me?"

Scowl fading, I mumble something that might have been an "Okay."

"Thanks, hon," she says, hugging me again.

Holding back complaints, I press my cheek against her hair and remind myself to be thankful I have a family who loves me.

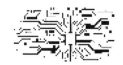

The following afternoon finds me leaning back in the comfy hospital bed. I'm absently working on homework when a fast set of footsteps from the hall distracts me. I sit up and listen. Ooh, that sounds like Gabby's gait.

Before rounding the corner, she slows to a more sedate pace.

Gabby stops at my open door, knocks, and steps inside. She gives me a beautiful smile, one that lights up not just her face, but the entire area. Rushing over, she wraps her arms around me.

I know it's gonna hurt when she stops pretending to be my girlfriend, but for the moment, I enjoy the hug and the feeling that Gabby considers me special. Today, her hair smells faintly of vanilla. She normally smells like one of her mother's flowers, so this is an interesting change.

Should I mention it?

She leans back and pulls out her datapad. "Before I forget, I've got your schoolwork." Gabby makes a tossing motion to my datapad, and it beeps.

"Oh, thank you *sooo* much," I reply sourly, thoughts of compliments vanishing like chili-cheese dogs near Julian.

She grins. "I *knew* you'd want that as soon as possible. Wouldn't wanna fall behind."

"Yeah. Strangely enough, that reminds me of this weird dream I—"

Gabby's eyes grow wide in alarm.

She darts in and kisses me. Hard.

My shock and surprise erase all thought. Closing my eyes, my hand slides up to the back of her head as I kiss her back.

"Mmm," she purrs. Her left hand is on my neck, her right on my hip.

Gabby is an amazing actress.

"Who's acting?" she whispers before diving back in for another kiss.

Once the kiss ends, which happens just before a nurse pokes his head in to make sure I'm okay, Gabs and I talk about homework. This morphs into working on homework. As we're proceeding through algebra equations, it occurs to me that I didn't say anything out loud about her being an actress.

Hmm. Psychic induction orb. An orb to induce psychic abilities? That sounds crazy. But is it any crazier than what's been happening?

In the dream....

I glance at Gabby's stylus. When she reaches for it, I give it a bump like from the dreams, only much more gently.

The stylus bounces to the floor as her hand hits the datapad.

Clearly annoyed, Gabby hops off my bed and picks it up. Retaking her seat, she throws me a suspicious glance.

I try on a mask of innocence.

Her suspicious look changes to a suspicious frown.

Evidently, my mask doesn't fit. "Don't look at me with that tone of voice," I say, still pushing the innocence thing. "It's not my fault you're clumsy."

Voice light and playful, she says, "It's so cute when you try to be funny. I could just eat you up. Unfortunately, there's not enough privacy here."

Contrary to her voice, Gabby's eyes are serious. Then she laughs, and that hardness in her gaze slowly dissolves.

Not enough....

Surveillance net.

Hmm. Okay.

I force myself to grin. Yeah, I *really* freakin' wish I knew what was going on.

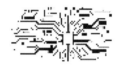

Stepping back into the house later in the day brings a surprising amount of relief. There's just something about home.

Up in my room, I'm reminded of a dream I had the other night. By comparison, it was only a little strange.

Within the dream, darkness surrounded night mom and dad. Night mom said, "Darling, my shoulder's completely frozen. I can't move my arm at all. I need to have my shoulder actuator replaced."

"I'm sorry to hear that," Dad replied. "I'll notify Maintenance immediately. We'll take care of things here until you return."

Thing is, the morning after the "dream," night mom was gone. Left on a surprise business trip.

Hmm. She's puttering around downstairs....

No. No need to bring it up. I just got home. Let's go for a bit of normality for a change. I don't need any new strangeness in my day.

With that decision made, I settle in at my desk and turn to my homework. About halfway through, I spot a file I haven't seen before.

Oh.

So much for not adding any fresh weirdness.

I stand and stretch. Time for a walk coz I really don't wanna open the file here.

Like the hospital, there's probably not enough privacy.

It doesn't take long for me to reach the center of town.

Our town has a cool vibe to it. There's a square surrounding an old courthouse. On one corner, the drugstore has an ice-cream bar. Yeah, that's always popular with the school crowd. Just down the street, Embry's dad runs the video rental store. We exchange waves as I walk by. They've got over thirty-thousand clips in stock. I prefer the sci-fi and fantasy section, but Gabs has kinda brought me over to action movies. Julian likes rom-coms and Carmen cop shows. Embry likes 'em all, so long as they're well made.

The police department's robot meter maid rolls by. Why a town this small needs a meter maid, robotic or not, I'll never understand.

A few doors down, I pause in front of the big window at the electronics store.

The owner is unrolling a new two-meter-wide vid. It's got something that's causing it to adhere to the back of the window display as it's rolled out. With a tap, it levels itself and powers on. There's a moment of static, then President Owens appears. She's giving a speech about why she should be elected to her third term in the 2021 elections.

With a shrug, I resume walking. The vid's cool, but ours isn't that much smaller. Also, politics just isn't my thing.

Continuing on, I stroll by the robot pet store. Inside, a woman and her eight- or nine-year-old son look at displays while the kindly old proprietress points out features and varying levels of customization. I probably shouldn't be able to hear them with the door closed, so I don't react. Nor do I react when one of them says, "It's okay. We're in the clear, he's passed us by."

I should probably be more paranoid.

The mayor drives by in his white and baby blue T-bird. Oh, that's such a sweet ride! Passing me by, he takes the time to slow down and frown at me before driving on. That's my dream car right there, though ironically, I've never actually dreamed about it.

Outside of town, I turn down the road that will eventually lead me to the grain mill. It's quiet there at this time of year, and it's a nice, scenic walk with all the hills and such.

As I walk, I open the file Gabby sent.

*** Classified TOP SECRET ***
To: All Project Simulation Personnel

Due to the recent breach in security protocols, the TACOB has voted to audit the entire program for viability and is exploring all options for future containment. Simultaneous to this, we'll be running an updated Cost / Benefit analysis.
Please send any security recommendations as well as proposals for cost-cutting measures and potential profit streams.
Remember, galactic security is our responsibility.

*** Classified TOP SECRET ***

Project Simulation. Just like in my early dreams.

Is this some sort of bizarre joke?

After pondering this, I reach the same conclusion as before. While Gabby sometimes has an odd sense of humor, I don't think she's joking about this anymore than she was about my life being in danger.

What is it about Old Town that these Taco-B people are so worried about? How can a couple of high school kids pose such a threat to their secret program? And that line about galactic security being our responsibility? It reminds me uncomfortably of those dreams in which I want to fight for exactly that.

These questions and more tumble wildly around my head as I reach the top of the hill. The grain mill is only a few meters away. The mill is big and needs a fresh coat of paint. Best of all, it's quiet.

Just me and the breeze.

To not arouse suspicion, I find a spot with a view of town and take care of most of today's homework. What I really need is some private time with Gabby. *She* knows what's going on. But, how to arrange it now that I'm out of the hospital? Me being in the hospital was the only reason her parents allowed her to visit. Despite me being whacked in the head, I doubt her dad's forgiven me for "dragging his only daughter into dangerous ruins."

Had Gabs denied it? She hadn't specifically said, but probably.

When she digs her heels in, Gabby can give Carmen a run for the money when it comes to being stubborn.

An hour later and mostly caught up on my schoolwork, I head home. Despite my slow pace, the four-kilometer trip goes fast. Stepping off the sidewalk and into our yard, I pause and stare at Gabby's house. I don't hear her and vaguely recall something about her visiting Carmen.

Inside, I kiss Day Mom on the cheek in passing and proceed up to my room. There, I finish not just today's homework, but tomorrow's too. I'm not comfortable with my answers to the history quiz, but I'm not worried about it. Mrs. Henneman usually allows us to do a make-up test. Also, Gabs might be right, and she may be our next vanishing teacher. If so, we usually get a few easy weeks while the replacement's brought up to speed.

Flopping onto my bed, I stare up at the ceiling.

Dad and Night Mom come home. Across the street, Gabby returns to her house. Hmm. With almost no effort at all, I could hurdle her back fence. From there, it would be an easy climb up to her window....

After putting on some running clothes, I go downstairs. "Guys, I'm gonna go for a run. Blow off a little excess energy."

Dad's already changed out of his work clothes. He looks away from the vid and meets my eyes. "Just make sure your run takes you nowhere *near* Old Town. *Or* Gabby's house. The Kwans are upset enough as is."

"Especially Mr. Kwan," Day Mom mutters sourly.

"Right. No problem."

So much for a clandestine visit with Gabby.

Still, as I step out into the early evening, I gotta admit, running really sounds like a good idea. Without consciously deciding, I jog back towards the grain mill. After maybe a kilometer, I pick up the pace to a run.

The wind in my hair, my heart pounding—feels like freedom.

Reaching the big facility, I slow to a walk. The sun has set, and the stars are out. It's crisp enough that the light breeze will become unpleasantly chilly if I walk far enough to cool off.

Evidently, this is one of my favorite places.

Can't beat the view.

Sadly, I've gotta get up early for school tomorrow.

As I'm about to take that first running step towards home, I catch sight of a different colored rock in the gravel. Stopping, I pick it up and hold it close to my face for a better look. I can't see what color it might be beyond dark.

Rolling the smooth stone between my fingertips, my thoughts drift back to the dream and recent events. I hold my palm out and try lifting the stone out of my hand.

There's a weird, stretching feeling in my head.

The stone lifts a few centimeters.

Before I have a chance to celebrate, the stretching sensation turns to a sharp pain. The stone drops back into my palm.

Farking ouch.

Dropping the stone into a pocket, I run towards home.

By the time I get back to the neighborhood, the pain's passed.

Hmm. The light's on in Gabby's room. Maybe I could still—

Night Mom jogs over to join me. "Hi!" she says a little too loudly and with a bit too much enthusiasm. Her smile is broad and knowing.

"Hey, Mom," I reply, trying not to look guilty. "Care for a couple of laps around the block?"

"Sure. Let's run."

She sets a fast pace but slows down after half a block.

Eventually, she says, "I presume you have questions?"

"Lots. So many that my questions have questions."

"Fire away. I'll see what I can clear up."

"Why'd everyone freak out when we went into Old Town?"

She throws me a droll look. "You mean aside from all the posted hazards, and the danger posed by rubble falling if there's an earthquake or high wind?"

I return her look in kind. "Sure. Aside from the posted warnings—none of which seem to have any evidence to support them—why would so many people drop what they were doing to come look for a couple of students wandering around a bunch of dusty ruins? And at the time, no one even knew *where* we were, just that we weren't in school. I guess I kinda get Principal Gates coming out. But the coaching staff? The entire police department? The fleet of drones? Seems like overkill."

"Honey, you and Gabby are part of our community and as a community, we look out for one another."

"Uh, huh."

"Okay, it appears I've failed on that question. Ask me another."

"How's the new shoulder actuator?"

"It's—" Night Mom stops.

I circle around back to her.

"Where did you hear about that?"

"A dream."

She nods. "When I was about your age, I was in a car accident. A bad one. Doctors had to replace my entire shoulder. It's been bothering me more and more over the last few months. The other day, it locked up completely, so your father took me to the hospital."

She's wearing a tank top. I look over her shoulder but can't see any scars. "What'd they do?"

"They injected some sort of lubricant into the joint, then helped me work it around. It's a temporary fix, though. In another year or two, I'll need the shoulder replaced again."

I hug her. "That sucks, Mom."

She hugs me back, then gives me a little push. "It does, but I still want to run tonight, so move it!"

We run.

As we near the house after our first lap, lights in the sky draw my attention upward and my stride falters before I stop completely. A star explodes. Then a second.

"What tha hell?"

Night Mom grabs my arm and pulls me towards the house with surprising strength. "Inside. Hurry, Ethan."

"What's going on?" I ask as she opens the door and pushes me inside.

Following me, she turns to Day Mom and Dad and opens her mouth. Instead of words, a weird electronic buzz erupts from her.

I stare.

Day Mom and Dad both look alarmed. Dad presses several buttons on the entertainment remote. The vid slides down the wall revealing a compartment with three white, high-tech looking rifles. There's other stuff, but the rifles have my attention. Day Mom tosses one to Dad, then a second to Night Mom before taking the third for herself. She then does the same for matching wrist bracelets and heavy-looking, segmented belts.

"Guys, what's going on?"

After donning the wrist thing and belt, Night Mom runs a hand down the side of my face in a caress. Any other week, it would be a rather unusual display of affection for her. "Some people may be trying to steal you away from us. We won't let them."

From outside sounds the voice from my Simulation dreams. "All personnel, all personnel, perimeter defenses have been breached. Defense teams, move to your assigned posts. All others, seek cover immediately. This is not a drill. Seek co—"

The announcement cuts off. The night goes eerily silent.

I'm trying to make sense of all of this when approaching footsteps running towards the house snag my attention.

A staccato burst of knocking presages Gabby sticking her head inside. "Are you seeing this?" When she sees how my parents are outfitted, she relaxes a bit. "Oh, good."

Good? How is any of this...?

"What's going on?" I demand, raising my voice slightly. "Perimeter breach?"

Gabby steps inside and looks to my parents. There's a strange urgency in her expression.

Day Mom sighs and nods. Dad's lips scrunch up, then he nods as well. A tear slides down Night Mom's cheek, which shocks me to my core. She closes her eyes for a moment, then nods, too.

"Ethan," Gabby says, "they're after you. Whoever is in those ships is after you."

Ships? There're no lakes, rivers, or oceans near town. That leaves one alternative—which lines up disturbingly well with the lights in the sky.

I blink at her a few times before I ask, "Why?"

Easier to ask about motive than what's happening in orbit.

"Because you're so awesome." Seeing my expression, she says, "No, seriously. It really is because you're awesome. You're stronger than practically anyone else, faster, and your mind is a fortress the psychic community has never dreamed of."

Psychic community?

She looks to my parents and winces. "Since that last trip to the ruins, his psychic abilities have been unlocked."

Day Mom surprises me with a snarled expletive.

But Gabby's wound up and continues, "Ethan, you've defied all expectations. Society expected you to be like a super-warmonger or something. An uncontrollable force of rampant destruction. Instead, you're just about the sweetest person on the planet, and I should know, because I'm a psychic too, and I'm really good at reading people."

Why would...? What?

I open my mouth, but my words and thoughts tangle.

Night Mom orders, "Ethan, pack a bag. Fast." She gives me a little push to get me moving.

Still unable to speak, I run upstairs and start throwing clothes into a backpack. Gabby steps into the bathroom and returns with a small bag containing my toiletries.

"This makes no sense," I finally say as we reach the bottom of the stairs.

Gabby gives my hand a squeeze.

"Son," Dad says as he leans to the side and looks out the front door. "There're other possible scenarios at play. Bad ones."

"Worse than lights in the sky coming to kidnap me?"

He meets my eyes. "They may be coming to kill you."

Oh.

Day Mom adds, "They may also want to harvest your DNA for some sort of illegal weapons program. Right now, their motives are unclear, but odds are, these people do *not* have your best interests at heart."

Harvest my DNA?

Damn, I'm getting tired of asking "why" all the time.

"Uh," I manage to say. "In that case, shouldn't I have a space rifle, too?"

My parents exchange glances. Then they open their mouths and those weird buzzing noises come out.

HUMAN

What the fark is going on? I'm fairly sure I'm not dreaming, because no matter how strange my dreams are, they've never been *this* weird.

Night Mom looks to me and shakes her head. "We just ran through sims of the fifty-five most likely scenarios. None of them benefited by you being armed. In fact, most of them turned bad because of that."

...Through the fifty-five most likely....

My brain skips that for the moment and my eyebrows lift again. "Worse than me being killed or used for DNA harvesting?"

"Those are... extreme... possibilities." Night Mom tries to sound firm, but she looks conflicted. And worried.

I give her a skeptical glance, but a change in the lighting focuses my attention on the window over Day Mom's shoulder. A massive fireball falls from the sky and crashes somewhere in the mill's direction. A moment later, the ground shakes, and a family picture falls off the wall. Car alarms sound all around the neighborhood.

"Was that a weapon?" I ask. "Some sort of bomb?" Strangely, I'm not scared. I'm excited. And happy.

Always with the happy.

Yeah, I'm every bit as weird as my friends. I glance at my parents. And family.

I feel more than see Gabby shake her head. "No, orbital defenses took out a ship. We just saw the remains impact. Hopefully, whoever it was ejected their engine core somewhere far, far away."

Engine core? Orbital defenses?

And I thought I'd been clueless before.

Chapter 6

A Night of Rampant Change

"If spaceships are falling out of the sky," I say, glancing around at the people I love, "and the perimeter, wherever that might be, has been breached, shouldn't we find shelter? I don't think the house is going to fare well if something like *that* drops onto it."

Dad says, "The city storm shelter isn't any better equipped to handle an attack of this nature than the house."

I look to Gabby. "We know a place. In Old Town."

She closes her eyes, then nods. "Ethan's right."

"What kind of place?" Night Mom asks, eyebrow rising.

"A sort of basement," I explain. "It's twenty stories below ground."

"How big is it?"

"Roughly the size of our ground floor."

My parents exchange looks. Reluctant nods follow.

"Okay," I begin, "we gonna run or drive?"

Dad says, "Drive. That way we can use the car to help climb the wall."

"Wait," Gabby says. "What about our friends?"

I ask, "What about *your* parents?"

She flicks her hand dismissively. "Those aren't my parents, they're just minders. My family's off-world, in a different quadrant." As we all rush towards the side door and the carport, Gabby adds, "If possible, we *should* pick up Julian. I don't think we can help the others. Carmen will have gone after Embry, which means they'll be way over on the wrong side of town."

Off world. In a different quadrant.

What. The. Hell?

As we open the car doors, Gabby's dad skids to a stop in the middle of the street.

Her not-dad. Whatever.

"Gabby, we're leaving!" he yells, holding out a hand for her.

"Go ahead," she says, pushing me into the car. "I'm going with them." Her conviction is like a huge, unshakable stone.

"Young lady—" he's cut off by a string of small explosions that race down the street.

"Son of a bitch!" Gabby gasps as she jumps in halfway on top of me. "If someone's strafing us, they got past the defense net. This is *not* good!"

Strafing - Discharging automatic or continuous fire weapons from an aerial vehicle against surface targets.

That strangely familiar yet alien thought bubbles up from out of the blue. I haven't learned it in school or read about it. It probably comes from the same place as my dreams. If I have to guess. Which I do.

Just another grain in this massive sandstorm of weirdness.

Night Mom pops in beside me as Gabby twists around and closes her door. Dad backs us out of the driveway, near Mr. Kwan, who's struggling to his feet. Her not-father has a large hole in his right thigh, which is sparking. Within the wound, I see the shine of metal and strange tubing. He's bleeding around the outer edges of the wound where the fake-flesh ends. Huh, not as much blood as I would have expected.

Dad turns and looks at Gabby.

"Was that some sort of cybernetic limb?" I ask.

Why would I expect a fake leg to bleed at all?

Ignoring me, Gabby says, "He'll be fine. Let's go."

We race away.

Bang!

A fresh puff of smoke appears high in the sky. A second later, more puffs arrive—these are lower and form an almost perfect circular pattern.

Gabby curses. "Cluster munitions. They're attacking the town."

Not-so-distant explosions erupt across the area. Houses blow apart. The entryway to the high school vanishes in a fireball. Cars fly about like unwanted toys.

"Oh, no," I whisper, unable to tear my eyes away from the unfolding disaster.

Several somethings dart across the sky as they strafe the far-side of town.

Hope Carmen and Embry are okay.

"Fighters?" I ask.

Eyes hard, Gabby gives a single nod. "Or drones. Either way, it's bad."

Dad slams on the brakes and we skid to a stop in front of Julian's house. Julian peeks out through a window and his eyes widen. He and his parents rush outside.

"Oh," he says, "it's *sooo* good to see you guys!"

Sitting beside me, Night Mom waves him towards the back of the car.

Julian's dad and moms hurry him back there. They open the hatch and look inside. There's barely enough room for Julian's big frame back there. His day mom asks, "Take care of our boy?"

Night mom nods. "We'll do our best, we promise."

Without warning, his parents shove Julian into the back, and slam the hatch closed. They shout, "We love you!"

Dad stomps on the accelerator and the car peels out.

Over town, one fighter explodes, crashes into the water tower, and explodes again.

Oh damn.

"Where do we cross?" Dad asks. "Section 418?"

"South of town," Gabby confirms. "Take a left on the service road. The tree we climbed is there."

"I can't believe they just— Wait, what? Cross?" Julian asks, tearing his gaze away from his parents, who are watching us depart.

Meeting his worried eyes, I nod. "We're crossing the wall. We'll hide in the Old Town ruins where Gabby and I went the other day."

Instead of easing the worry in his eyes, this magnifies it.

"Sorry. We think it's the safest place."

Something near the center of town explodes in a fireball, emphasizing my point.

Swallowing with clear difficulty, Julian opens his mouth, closes it, and gives an unconvincing brief smile.

Maybe five minutes later, we skid to a near stop. Dad parks next to the wall over an area covered with sawdust.

"So much for our crossing tree," I mutter.

Gabby climbs onto the car, then springs up on top of the wall. "Right here, guys," she whispers. "There's a big slab on this side you can slide right down."

Night Mom says, "I'll secure the other side." She vaults over the wall.

Julian and I stare, then exchange amazed glances.

"Up," Day Mom orders.

"Uh," Julian begins, "I don't think I can climb that."

I jump up to the car roof. "You can. I'll help."

Day Mom points at Julian. "Up!" Day Mom is usually the 'nice' mother, but her tone is 100% pure, no-nonsense iron.

He gulps and climbs clumsily onto the car before giving me a lost, nearly panicked look.

I form a stirrup with my hands. "Step here. I'll lift you up."

Though doubt fills his eyes, Julian steps. I lift. He struggles. I lift more, then give him a little throw. With a string of muffled curses, he falls over the wall.

"At least he's on the other side," Dad mutters.

He, Day Mom, and I leap to the top of the wall, then over.

Night Mom has torn off the bottom edge of her shirt and is wrapping it around Julian's bleeding arm. Gabby's crouched maybe twenty meters away, near some of the ever-present rubble. She waves for me to join her.

I tap each of my parents on the shoulder, and nod towards Gabby before hurrying to her.

She's wearing her dark glasses. Leaning close, she whispers, "We went that way, right? Past the rubble with that big slab sticking way out, we took a... left?"

Behind us, the others are ready to go.

Instead of saying anything, I squeeze her shoulder.

Gabby leads the way with me right behind her.

As she's looking over the path forward, a gasp from Julian turns me around.

A massive bank of lights is approaching from high in the sky. With a roar of braking jets, the spaceship coasts in to hover over town. It's big. Bigger than Freemont High.

Night Mom ushers us right up next to one of the ruin mounds before quietly saying, "Keep rubble between us and it. Debris like this combined with the ship's current location gives us a sizable sensor shadow. Let's use it."

"But hurry," Dad adds. "Soon, it'll pop drones, launch scouts, or both."

With an acknowledging nod, Gabby takes off again, this time staying low and close to the ruins.

Four blocks later, Julian is huffing and puffing.

"Sorry, buddy," I say, picking him up in a fireman's carry. "Hope this isn't too uncomfortable."

He makes a noise that's hard to interpret.

Roughly ten minutes later, we reach the building.

Gabby ducks under the 'entrance' slab. Before I have time to worry, she calls, "It's clear."

The rest of us crawl under and into the open area with the rubble ceiling.

Voice disapproving, Night Mom says, "This isn't as secure as I'd hoped."

"This way," I whisper and move to the still open door. Yeah, considering the way it squealed before, I'm not surprised it never closed.

Night Mom follows me. Up ahead, Gabby heads down the stairwell.

"I can't see a thing," Julian whispers.

Day Mom and Dad each grab an arm and guide him towards us.

"How are you guys seeing?" Julian asks as we start down the stairs.

I reply, "I've got excellent night vision." I exchange smirks with my parents and add, "I think it runs in the family. Gabby's got a pair of dark glasses."

"You mean night vision glasses?"

"Nope."

"Oh. Never heard of 'em."

"Buddy, these are great times for things never heard of."

We pause our descent three times for Julian to catch his breath. After the last rest, he gasps, "I'm wishing I'd taken that whole athletics thing more seriously."

"Never too late to start," I say.

"Yeah, just keep in mind I'm not some superhuman like you." He winces at Day Mom, but they don't slow down.

Superhuman?

Wait. Are they saying that all this mess is because I've been genetically engineered or something? Is there some sort of weird super-science thing going on? The clues kinda back that up....

Yeah, I'm gonna need more information before jumping to a conclusion this strange.

At the bottom, Gabby's panting next to the closed door. The rubble to the left doesn't seem to have shifted any, which suggests this really is a secure area.

"Gabs, why didn't you open the door?"

Still gasping for breath, she throws me a glare and the bird. Women.

The lockplate lights up green when I touch it, and the door opens. Once everyone's inside, Dad touches the lockplate, but nothing happens. He meets my eyes and gives a sideways nod towards it. I touch the plate, closing the door.

Why won't the doors work for Gabby or Dad?

Day Mom pulls a small glow light from her pocket and powers it on.

Night Mom turns to Gabby. "Young lady, there's been a few too many coincidences concerning you and recent events. Time to explain."

"Well...." Gabby begins, shifting around, looking uncomfortable. "Umm... you see...."

I lean forward. "Yes?"

Avoiding my eyes, she admits, "I'm kinda working for an outside agency."

CHAPTER 7

CONFESSIONS IN THE DARK

"What do you mean 'outside agency'?" Julian asks. He turns to look at her and his jaw drops. "Wait, did you bring the attack?"

"No!" Gabby snaps. Deflating, she groans. "At least... I don't *think* I did."

"Who do you work for?" Day Mom asks.

"The Pan-galactic Life Keepers."

My parents simultaneously relax.

Pan-galactic?

What's even stranger is that *none* of them so much as bat an eye at this. Confused, bordering on bewildered, I ask, "Umm, what does that mean?"

Day Mom sits and leans back against the wall. "Gabby didn't cause the attack."

"Gabby," Night Mom says, "please explain. The whole story, if you please."

With a sigh, Gabby sits with her back to a shelf and leans her head into her hands. Without looking up, she says, "I've been giving reports about Ethan since I was little. I guess we all have. He's a great guy." She glances at me. "You are, Ethan. But that's never what's given out to the galactic news agencies."

Everyone's been giving reports. About me? Again, with the galactic. Again, with them all acting like this is normal.

I should have been more paranoid.

Day Mom nods. "Yes, the lack of positive reporting has been most frustrating."

61

What the... Is *everyone* in on this but me?

"That," Gabby continues, "led me to believe that those at the very heart of the Simulation don't have a bright future in mind for Ethan. Rather, the opposite."

"You've been mirroring our fears," Night Mom whispers.

"Before I went on vacation last March, I snuck into the mayor's office, and copied as many reports as I could. Back home, I got my cousin to deliver those reports to the Life Keepers. They were as dismayed as me by the disparity between our reports and what the official press releases say."

"Back... home?" I ask. I didn't know Gabby had any cousins, but that seems like small potatoes compared against all the other stuff I plainly don't know.

"Aklansic."

"Bless you."

She doesn't look up, but one corner of her lips tilts up almost in a smile. "Aklansic is my homeworld. It's a long way from here, but it's a beautiful water world with only a little land. I... I hope I can show it to you one day."

Home. World.

Closing my eyes, I scrub my hands over my face.

"So, you're actually from another planet," I say, before glancing at Gabby and Julian. "Both of you?"

Expression as sad as I've ever seen on him, Julian nods.

"Yeah," Gabby whispers. "There.... There's more to it, but that should probably wait until after we've... escaped."

She was gonna say "survived."

I'm not sure how I know this, but I do.

"Other worlds. That's the sort of thing I've only read about." But, as soon as I say it, I realize it's not true. I've *dreamed* about other worlds since I was young. Strangely real dreams, as opposed to the more... expected... dreams of getting to school only to discover I've forgotten my clothes or pulling the nose off a bear because he refused to give me the proper number of sugar cubes for my tea.

Though details remain hazy, when I look back at those dreams—the ones in which I can move stuff with my mind and hear other people's thoughts—they coalesce into a living vision of six worlds. My mind is running like never before as I assemble all the pieces. The vision that's suddenly laid out before me is breathtaking. These six worlds contain huge, glorious cities—technological marvels of ceracrete and crystal that extend for dozens if not hundreds of kilometers. Worlds where urban life and the splendor of nature intertwine through cities that blend in and out of massive nature preserves.

Something shifts.

Something unspeakably bad.

Those worlds burn. Destroyed by enormous ships and the giants of darkness and hate who drive them.

The vision ends. My hands are shaking. That shift from that bright vision to one so dark was too abrupt.

Abrupt and horrifyingly new.

Gabby slides over and holds my hand between hers. "Your mental walls are really strong, Ethan, but I felt your shock bleed through. This must all be very... weird."

Still reeling from the vision, I pinch the bridge of my nose with my other hand. For a moment, I feel a vague sense of concern for me from Gabby. Kinda like she's underwater or something. There's a pushing sensation in my mind, which is weird, because I'm doing the pushing. Then Gabby's completely out of my head.

Day Mom leans over and rests a hand on my shoulder. "We know this is a lot to take in. Are you okay, honey?"

I swallow with difficulty before mumbling, "Yeah."

Actually, I'm pretty far from okay. I want to ask them all about the reports, homeworlds, and the galactic stuff, but the end of that vision.... Those giants of darkness and hate weren't figures of speech. They were *very* real and by far the most awful thing I've ever seen. Could my dreams... that vision... could they somehow be real? Was that a glimpse of the future? Some sort of waking nightmare? Or maybe a movie I saw as a child and I'm only just now remembering? I've had a few nightmares before, but not for years.

Leaning towards me, Julian says, "You look paler than usual, dude. Sure you're okay?"

"Julian's right," Night Mom agrees, looking me over with a critical eye.

"Lot to take in."

Day Mom asks the room, "So, what brought the attack on town?"

Dad says, "I suspect word leaked of the Life Keepers' intentions." He looks to Gabby. "Speaking of which, just what were *your* intentions?"

Gabby reaches over, pulls an orb off the shelf, and hands it to Dad. "Step One was to activate Ethan's psychic powers with one of these."

"What is it?" Julian asks.

"A psychic induction orb," Dad replies. "So much of the galaxy's psychic tech originated from these—" He turns back to Gabby. "How did you know where to find this? This room?"

"Wait a second," I say, reclaiming my hand from Gabby as I try to chop up my confusion into bite-sized bits. Monstrous giants are just too much for now. Fortunately, I have tons of other stuff I need to get a handle on to distract me from them. "So, you're *all* part of some inter-galactic something or another? Everyone?"

"Intra-galactic," Night Mom says. "And yes, we all are. Everyone on the planet but you."

Dad kneels in front of me. "I know you've got a lot of questions. And you deserve answers. Answers we've all been wanting to give you for years." His gaze lifts to the ceiling before returning to me. "Right now, we need to find out as much about the attack as possible. Our lives may depend on it."

My usual happiness is having a tough time keeping up with the seemingly unending stream of life-altering revelations and horrifying visions. I give a vague "whatever" sort of wave. It's not like I don't already have enough to process as it is.

Turning back to Gabby, Dad says, "You were saying?"

Gabs gives me a look, filled to the brim with concern, before shifting her focus to Dad and then everyone else. "Ethan led me here. Evidently, one of the induction orbs got activated by that brief tremor the other day. He somehow heard it and followed it here." She flips her palms up. "*This* was the real reason we visited Old Town, again. That said, I had planned to bring him here, soon. The Life Keepers were on their way. They thought that with his psychic abilities active, Ethan would have a better chance of defending himself until they arrived."

Julian raises an eyebrow. "How did *they* know about this place? Whatever it is?"

"One of the original survey teams discovered this storage facility, but never reported the find. Later, when the Simulation started, they informed the Life Keepers. The Life Keepers passed that information to me."

Shaking his head, Julian asks, "Why would they do that?"

"Let's not get side-tracked," Dad says.

Day Mom catches Gabby's eye. "What was the next step?"

"Help Ethan train up. Get scans of him having hu—" She chokes, and I get a flash of something in her mind she's not ready to give up. "Scans of him using his abilities for something other than war and destruction." Gabby's blushing. "Umm," she says, looking at her lap. "Right. The last step was gonna start with extracting him from the Simulation. Then, we'd leak the scans and the reports that got suppressed. Prove that those in charge of the Simulation were hiding the true results from the public. After that, try to get Ethan galactic citizenship."

I have so many questions bouncing through my mind, it's impossible to settle on one to ask. However, one thing stands out above the others.

Everyone here has spent a *long* time deceiving me.

Gabby hugs me and kisses my cheek.

I throw her a hard look.

Her expression falls, and she sits back with a sigh.

Night Mom leans forward and takes Gabby's hand. "You two are going to have to have a *talk*. Soon. You know the one."

Dread rips through Gabby like a blast-wave from a high-yield warhead.

"What the heck was that?" I ask, turning back to her.

"*Please* don't ask me about that right now. And please, please, please, don't pry into my thoughts."

Pry into....

"I wouldn't do that," I say, but realize that I *am* getting a very faint sense of... something from her and Julian. While I truly can't read their minds, even with my eyes closed, I can point straight to them.

Is it odd that I can't do that with my parents?

Definitely.

But... is it stranger than anything else?

The urge to snort tangles with the urge to cry, which loses the battle to a resurgence of my constant and bizarre happiness.

Eyes sad, Day Mom whispers, "That's a conversation we *all* need to have."

"Which conversation is that?" I ask. "It feels like I'm drowning in conversations we're not having."

"Later," Dad says quietly, resting a hand on my shoulder. "Right now, you need to process what you've learned, and we *all* need rest." He glances up at the ceiling again. "I suspect that soon, things are going to become active. Disturbingly active."

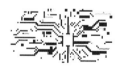

"Who are you?" echoes through my dreams. "Who *are* you?"

I have no answer, but I know it's important that I find one. Maybe more than one.

Later, my dreams take on more form.

Mom and Dad are here with my older sister Keit and my younger sister Peigi. We're home for the evening, but still in uniform as we sit down to eat. The sense of family runs deep as we hold a low-level telepathic connection to each other. This is part of our routine. Part of our bond.

Dad got home early and baked potatoes and grilled steaks. The smell from the resting meat makes my mouth water. Mom stopped by a specialty shop for a variety pack of cheeses. Keit picked up salad fixin's while Peigi and I met up after classes and eventually decided on a carton of citrus explosion ice-cream for dessert.

The meal is fantastic, but it's cut by an undercurrent of Peigi's upset. Keit will go out on deployment next week. It's a dangerous assignment and—

Like Peigi, I force my thoughts back to enjoying the food and the company.

My dreams fade not away, but into the background. I'm neither awake nor sleeping.

A voice whispers, "*Oh gods of my ancestors, I hope he still loves me once he finds out.*"

A girl? A woman? I keep listening.

"*We've hidden so much.*

"*I've wanted to tell him for so long.*

"*Now that the time's come, I'm terrified.*

"*Gods of the deep, grant me strength.*"

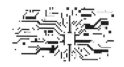

I sit up in the dark and look around. Everyone else appears to be asleep. I'm too restless to sleep. But, at the same time, I feel sleep deprived.

Picking an orb off the shelf, I look it over. There's just not much to it. Somewhere between baseball and softball size, it's got a metallic finish somewhere between brass and bronze, and is slightly cool to the touch. There's a fine texture formed by hundreds of hexagons that were stamped or maybe engraved into the surface. A lack of texture differentiates the button. I press it and a yellow light fills a tiny hex and starts blinking. When it turns green, I 'hear' the noise and get a slightly better feel for Gabby and Julian. I'm pretty sure they're sleeping, but not deeply.

Opening my palm flat, I lift the orb with my mind. This is *much* easier with the orb active. I move it around the room, being careful to remain in complete control of the orb. For some reason, I think doing so is a lesson that's carried over from my dreams.

Pulling another couple of orbs off the shelf, I juggle the three around, still using only my mind. After maybe five minutes of this, the first hints of a headache manifest. Not wanting to push it, I set the orbs on the shelf, though I leave the one active. The noise is every bit as annoying and distracting as before, but I feel more... connected. I'm not sure if that's the right word, but it will do for now.

My gaze aimlessly drifts to my bag. Ah. A fresh change of clothes sounds good, so I swap out what I'm wearing. Fresh clothes aren't as good as a shower, but they're better than nothing.

For a while, I sit in the dark listening to our quiet breathing.

Some people might find this relaxing.

Evidently, that would be someone else.

Quietly, so as not to wake anyone, I walk to the back of the room and the ginormous desk there. Last time Gabby and I were here, we never got around to checking it out.

Definitely an oversight worth correcting.

It's hard to tell given the lack of light and all, but the desk looks to be made of ceracrete, which seems like a weird building material for a desk. A bank of monitors almost surrounds the desk. Behind it sits a high-back chair.

Looks comfy.

Almost certainly better than the floor.

Smirking at the thought, I step around and plop myself down.

Ooh. The chair *is* still comfy after all these decades.

The thought tickles something in my mind. Something that doesn't quite add—

The monitors light up.

Ooh!

One screen shows an inventory control system. According to another, the link to the transport system has critically failed. The others indicate links to various computer networks and communications systems can't be established.

Once I get some high-quality staring out of my system, I shrug to myself and bring up the local inventory.

Oh, nice!

This facility primarily warehouses Tier One and Two psychic equipment. All that's out on display are the induction orbs, but there's a lot more here. Keepers and every mod for them. There's also implant frames for augmentation chips—like the one I was so desperate to win in the dream. Oh, not just the frames, but all the chips for those as well, including the Tier One and Two boosts.

Feeling like a kid in a candy store, I order one of everything. Wow. Unable to keep a smile at bay, I order a thin, backpack-like carryall to put everything in. After a few minutes, the carryall slides out of the wall. I check inside.

It's full.

As I'm gazing lovingly at all this psychic goodness, my elation fades. The keeper and the implant frame both require surgery. Specialized surgery.

With a sigh, I close the carryall, lock it, and wear it like a backpack.

My dreams are merging with reality.

It's deeply disturbing how weird this doesn't feel.

A couple of hours later, we're eating protein bars Day Mom thankfully had the foresight to bring. Well, Julian, Gabby, and I are eating. My parents have concerned expressions plastered across their faces. I'm in the corner to the left of the door. Julian's to my left, wedged up against a shelf. Gabby's on my right and my parents are in the middle of the floor, forming a sort of boomerang with Dad in the middle.

Slowly, my waning happiness returns.

Lord, but I'm weird.

"It's time," Dad says quietly.

"For...?" I ask. There's a weird vibration in the floor. It's not much. Maybe a prelude to another—

"To explain it all. The Simulation. Your part in it. Our part in it. Everything."

All thoughts of weird vibrations vanish.

Gabby sniffs and a tear slides down her cheek. "I'm scared."

My jaw drops.

Gabriella Kwan is afraid of something? Anything?

Day Mom holds out her arms. Gabby goes to her. After a hug, she sits beside Day Mom. Mom holds her close and runs a hand through her hair.

I look to Julian, but his eyes are round as he stares at Gabby. Exactly.

Dad says, "We all know this won't be easy for any of us." He meets my eyes. "Especially you, Ethan."

"Uh... why is that?"

"Because what we have to say will change—"

Something heavy hammers on the door three times.

"Open up!" a faint voice calls. "Or we'll blow the door."

Chapter 8

THE HAMMER OF TRUTH

"I think the desk is ceracrete," I say to no one in particular as I wave towards the back of the room. "We can take cover there."

Dad shakes his head. "There's insufficient venting in this room. An explosion big enough to take out the door would likely cause an over-pressure event. Ethan, our family would probably survive, but I doubt Gabby or Julian would."

Oh. Damn.

"Then what do we do?"

He points to Gabby and Julian. "Get behind the desk. Ethan, you step against the wall and open the door when I give you the signal. Let's find out who's out there."

My parents fiddle with their wrist things and the belts. Suddenly, shimmering blue auras cover all three of them.

"Is that a...?" I'm not sure how to finish my sentence.

"Deflection field," Night Mom says before moving close to me. She takes a knee and aims her rifle at the door.

Day Mom raises her rifle to her shoulder and stands behind Night Mom and a bit to the side. They seem to take care to keep their deflection fields from overlapping. Dad moves to the wall between me and the door.

Outside, someone hammers the door again. "You have to the count of three!"

Dad glances back at me and nods before lifting his own rifle.

I touch the lockplate and lean back out of the way as the door irises open.

Wearing a suit of over-sized, thick white armor, Sergeant Lawton bends down and steps through the door. Each of her footsteps connects with a heavy thud. She was the source of those weird vibrations in the floor. Her armored fists are bigger than my head. Only her face is visible behind a clear screen. "Well, well, well, look who brought out the good toys. Up and out, everyone. We're leaving this miserable chunk of rock."

"Whose ship was that?" Dad asks.

Lawton snorts. "Which one? There're ships everywhere now that the defense grid's down. Whole thing's blowing up and it keeps getting worse. Time to get out while we can." While my parents exchange looks, she thumps over to a shelf and picks up an orb. "Huh. Ancient Terran induction orbs. Collectors will pay well for these. You lot," she calls to people out in the hall. "Get in here and bag these."

My parents move to stand around me. They're not quite pointing their rifles at Lawton or the people who come running in to bag up the orbs, but it's a near thing.

"You four," Lawton snaps. "Out and up. Let's move."

Trying to watch everyone, we exit the room.

Lawton raises her hand. "Wait. Where's Gabriella Kwan?"

Before I can come up with a suitable lie, Gabby stands. A second later, Julian does, too.

"Figures." Lawton jerks her thumb towards us. "Hurry. As I said, we're leaving."

We wait for Gabby and Julian before Night Mom starts up the stairs. The rest of us follow her with Dad and Day Mom bringing up the rear. Dad and Day Mom seem to be more concerned with those behind us than what we'll find up top.

Gabby and Julian are breathing too fast, and their eyes are huge.

"Take deep, even breaths," I tell them quietly. "And whatever happens, stay close to me."

They nod, but it doesn't appear I've done much to relieve their anxiety.

Lawton's lagging. Evidently, her heavy armor doesn't navigate stairs very well.

Halfway up, I pick up the panting and wheezing Julian again.

"This really isn't very comfortable," he gasps, but I detect a thread of humor behind the statement."

"Cheer up, buddy. Think of how great it's going to feel once you've embraced athleticism and can run up and down stairs like these on your own."

He lets out an overly dramatic, piteous groan.

Gabby snorts out a surprised laugh.

At the top, we exit the stair room and enter the rubble-domed chamber where more of Lawton's people await. I've never seen any of them before.

Holding out my hand, I tell the nearest guy, "Hello, I'm Ethan Shaw."

He jerks back as though I took a swing at him, and his hand drops to a pistol at his side.

Not particularly friendly.

Two of the people who've been looting the induction orbs join us. One of them passes out a few orbs from a bag. They turn them on, their expressions full of surprise and wonder.

The noise from multiple orbs on at the same time is thoroughly annoying. However, maybe because so many are active, I'm 'hearing' weird thought echoes.

"...joyous price in money for these...."

"...here with creature, not tolerable...."

"...the Dark Union has accomplished! We'll take our prize and flee...."

"...once we sell monster, we receive hulking bonus!"

I take Gabby's hand, lean in, and whisper into her ear, "Tell me about the Dark Union."

Gabby's eyes turn to me in surprise, which immediately fades to nonchalance. But inside, she's anything but indifferent. I can feel her roiling emotions, which is much weirder than the new usual.

On her tiptoes, she hugs me tight and whispers, "Remember when we said there was a group who wanted to weaponize you via DNA extraction? The Dark Union is at the top of that list."

Not the good guys. Check.

I can feel Gabby's reluctance as I pull away from her. Additionally, I get a sense of her love, which makes me feel better about... well, everything.

"Dude," I say, addressing the closest of the unknown people waiting with us. "Where's your spaceship?"

"Kamezzei tok. Koap raggaizz."

"Bless you," I reply, because I have a true talent for beating my own jokes to death.

One of the others steps over. "He isn't speaking this linguistic."

"So, I gathered. Where's your spaceship?"

"Near the tall school. We wait the Commander before breaking cover."

Tall school? Oh, the high school.

"Moms, Dad, remember that little discussion we recently had about DNA? These are the folks you were talking about."

Without hesitation, my parents open fire. Scarily fast and accurate, their rifles blaze, sending out bolts of intense blue light, each shot accompanied by a high-pitched whine.

Just that fast, all the Dark Union people are down.

Since they seem to still be breathing, I assume they're stunned.

"What the hell is going on up there?" Lawton demands, the rhythmic thumping of her armored footfalls slowly growing closer.

Night Mom turns off her deflection field and leads the way out into the night.

Why... oh. Probably because the glow would give away her position.

I dump Julian and roll him out under the ceracrete slab and into the brisk night air. Bear crawling out, I follow him, and pick him up again before he gets a good start on complaining about the rough treatment.

As the others join us, I ask, "How hard is it to steal a spaceship?"

"Without the right codes?" Dad says, "Very. But... we might have a bit of an advantage there. For now, it's as good a plan as any." He nods to Night Mom. "Escape Protocol 2. Move out."

She does, and the rest of us follow.

Escape Protocol 2?

Gabby doesn't react to the protocol being enacted, and I can't see Julian's expression.

As we reach the wall-of-many-warnings, I complain, "I should have grabbed one of those guys' pistols."

"Nope," Day Mom says before shooting out a large hole in the wall.

So, not just stunners. Good to know.

Once back on the other side, we find our car. Someone blasted it to pieces, and the rest burned.

"That doesn't seem very friendly," Julian mumbles quietly.

"No," I agree, "it doesn't."

The lot of us exchange concerned looks and run to the woods before starting up the tallest of the nearby hills. My legs burn from carrying Julian. I don't complain, despite a rather powerful temptation to do so. Complaining and whining are so closely tied together. Nope, not my style. When we reach the top, I set Julian down and sigh in relief.

Gabby creeps to the edge of the woods and looks out across the town from behind a tree. I move to a tree large enough to provide me with cover and do the same.

Town's a mess. Fires and wreckage are everywhere. More interestingly, there're two spaceships: Lawton's by the school and another near the hospital. Flashes of brilliant red and blue light and the snaps and bangs of distant weapons' fire suggest there's a raging battle right in the center of our small town.

With a nod towards the hospital ship, I ask, "Who do you think that ship belongs—"

"Attention Simulation personnel," Lawton's voice booms out, magnified beyond reason. "The human is on the loose. Yet again. You know how strong he is. You've seen the holo of how easily he tore off the restraint while being transported to the hospital. He could just as easily do that with one of your limbs."

Gabby and I exchange WTH looks.

"Ethan Shaw," Lawton continues, "you've been lied to your entire life, but I'm going to do you a huge favor. *I'm* going to tell you the truth, that no one else will.

"You are human. You know this."

I turn a she's-off-her-rocker/what-the-hell look to Gabby, but rather than returning the look, Gabs has gone pale in the moonlight.

She looks like she might throw up.

I hear the smile in Lawton's voice when she says, "What you don't know is that you're the *only* human. The only one here. The only one *any*where. You're probably looking at your parents or Gabby and thinking what a foolish lie I'm telling you. But it's not a lie. Your parents are robots. Your little snuggle bunny is a shapeshifter. Your friends are aliens. Hell, everyone but the robots are aliens. Some of us are in meat-suits, others were surgically altered."

It's like an audio version of a train wreck. I want to stop listening but can't. My heart is pounding, and my hands have gone sweaty.

"Again, you're probably thinking this is a lie. Well, let me ask you a question: how old is Old Town? You've been told it's decades old. Destroyed in an earthquake. But that didn't happen. Humanity wiped itself out in a civil war that spanned over a hundred worlds and lasted over three-hundred years.

"Ethan, you'll love this next part."

Oh, I doubt that very much.

"That war happened over *fifty-thousand years* ago. Yeah, that's right, your entire warmongering species was dead as dust. Extinct. But Operation Simulation changed that. Our archaeologists found a corpse that was less moldy than the others and grew a clone. And here you are."

Nausea churns my stomach. I close my eyes.

"We found these ruins—yeah, these right here in town—some of the most intact structures and artifacts our archaeologists have found anywhere. So, it seemed like a good place to do a little restoration. We built the world around you one lie at a time. And that's exactly how we re-created a town on a world you and your people destroyed.

"Ethan Shaw," she says, her voice quiet and sincere, "you are human. A monster. Come with me so I can protect the galaxy from you.

"As for the rest of you, take off the meat suits. The Simulation's over. Time to complete Ethan's introduction to reality."

Silence falls. Maybe ten seconds later, distant weapons' fire resumes.

Lawton's right.

Maybe not about everything. I mean, I don't think I'm a monster. But what she said fits the clues I've been collecting. I lean my head against the rough tree bark, close my eyes, and try to wrap my mind around... everything.

From close behind me, Day Mom says, "Lawton's trying to drive us apart. Maybe even send you into a rage. That way, you'll be easier to capture, and she'll have 'proof' that you're so dangerous you don't deserve citizenship."

There's no way I'll be able to swallow this mess whole. I need to slice it up. "*Are* you robots?" I ask without turning around.

"We're cybernetic beings," Dad says. "We had these bodies formed to human specifications."

Night Mom adds, "We're a lot of things, but we're *not* robots. And yes, before you ask, we *are* capable of love, and we *do* love you. Very much. We may not be the same species, but you *are* our son."

My only response is to wipe away a tear. My mind's stuck at a rolling boil.

So is my heart.

"When you turned one," Gabby says quietly but clearly, "they proceeded with Operation Simulation. Until then, they considered it an exercise in reconstructive archaeology. That's when they brought me in. I was about to turn seven. For my people, that's a special time. We find a species that calls to us, and we study and emulate them. On our seventh birthday, we shapeshift to match them.

"The archaeology people had millions of hours of holographs showing all aspects of human life, so I immersed myself. Me and forty-nine other six-year-old metamorphs. Only the best would join the program, and I was the smartest—had the highest psychic potential, too. And, since I don't want to lie to you anymore—not even by omission—I'll tell you, I also had the least fear. That was important, because humans had... have... a bad reputation."

I wipe away another tear.

"So," Gabby continues after swallowing with some evident difficulty, "on my seventh birthday, I met you. Your parents had just picked you up. The archaeologists who'd been taking care of you were amazed at how quiet you'd become. They'd been telling us metamorphs for months about how you'd cry and scream for hours on end, but there you were, in your Day Mom's arms, quiet as could be. When I walked over, you met my eyes. At that moment, I felt something shift inside my head. You stopped being the object of my studies and became a person. The notion that you were an alien vanished, erased by your laughter. You were a baby—warm, happy and in need of friends.

"I had no reservations about touching you and becoming as I am today. About becoming your friend. I believed then that I was born to be by your side.

"I still believe it... with all my heart."

It was Gabby's dream or prayer last night.

While it's a small piece of the puzzle, it's nice to have something... *anything*... that fits into my strange, puzzle-like life.

An explosion downtown yanks my attention back to the here and now.

I sniff back tears and wipe my face before turning around. My parents... yeah, I still think of them as my parents... are on lookout duty, each facing a different direction, but they each throw a concerned glance my way. Gabby's still pale and her cheeks are wet with tears. Julian's watching me with big, concerned eyes.

"What about you?" I ask.

"They paid my family a lot. Figuring out you weren't actually some sort of bone-gnawing monster came as a huge relief. Eventually, I decided you're a surprisingly good guy. Also, your sense of humor amuses me."

"Yeah, that's what I was thinking about you the other day."

"That I'm a bone-gnawing monster?"

"Exactly."

Julian nods, his expression sad. "Yeah, I get that a lot."

Get a grip, Ethan. Later, you can process all the emotions that are surging and straining against the weird happiness. Survive now.

Yeah.

Not looking at any of them, I say, "Lawton's hoping to delay us. Is there still any chance of us getting to her ship and stealing it before she gets there?"

Night Mom says, "She's likely called for pickup. We've been trooping through the woods and climbing. Odds don't look good."

"What about the other ship?"

My parents step closer to the edge of the woods and stare into town.

They exchange glances and my moms nod.

"There might be a way," Dad says. "Follow me."

CHAPTER 9
EPICENTER OF A CHAOS VORTEX

Dad leads us on a convoluted route through town. Seemingly all around us, the pops and snaps of weapons fire come and go. A distant scream suddenly cuts off. It sounds less like a pitched battle, and more like half a dozen running gunfights. As if the dark of night wasn't hindrance enough, smoke from countless fires makes it hard to see. My eyes burn and water. Truth be told, I'm not sure if that's the smoke or too many Earth-shattering revelations.

Speaking of which, some of my confusion and heartache are slowly slipping towards anger. I usually only feel it in small bursts before my happiness slides back over it. But this... this is... different. New.

My anger is combining with my happiness.

Strange though it may be, I'm having the time of my life.

Behind the movie theater, we find eight dead people. They're all marked by deep, fist-sized burns.

"Weapon's fire?" Julian whispers.

Night Mom nods once.

Judging by their uniforms, three were Lawton's Dark Union, one was a city maintenance guy, and four are wearing dark blue uniforms, which is new.

"Pan-galactic Life Keepers," Day Mom says. "Probably their ship we're headed towards."

Gabs forces a half smile. "Things might be looking up."

I pick up a dead guy's rifle. Shrugging to myself, I pick up two more and hand one apiece to Gabby and Julian. Turning to my parents, I ask, "How do these work?"

Despite their unhappy expressions, they show us.

"I've never held a rifle before," Julian whispers as we once more follow Dad through town.

"You'll never be able to truthfully say that again," I reply. I've always had a hard time staying angry at Julian. It's like trying to stay angry with a puppy.

But angry or not, all is not well. Not between me and him.

Not between me and anyone.

The closer we get to the hospital and the nearby spaceship, the louder the sounds of fighting become.

"Ethan," Gabby whispers in a voice so quiet even I barely hear her. "Tell me something reassuring. Something to take my mind off the fear."

We walk half a block down a deserted residential street before I finally say, "Just keep breathing. It's going to be alright. We'll get through this." Yeah, it's not exactly Grand Admiral Otizen addressing the fleet before the battle of Kurney 5, but I'm distracted and hurt and confused and trying not to get any angrier.

Gabby throws me a worried look and a weak smile.

"Movement, right," Night Mom whispers.

We crouch behind a wrecked car. Day Mom pulls Julian down with us. Dad slips over to support Night Mom while Day Mom covers our left. After a few whispers too quiet even for me to hear, Dad creeps off into the darkness.

As the seconds drag out into minutes, worry inexorably pushes aside most of my anger.

Easing up beside me, Gabby leans towards me until her shoulder's touching my side. When I don't flinch or move away, a sense of relief radiates out of her, like sunshine from the middle of a thunderstorm.

Before I know what I'm doing, I'm pulling her closer and kissing her temple.

Annoyed with myself, I pick her up and set her down by Day Mom.

Gabby throws me a confused, hurt look before focusing her attention back on the darkness.

A few minutes later, I note a soft, repeating crunch that's slowly growing louder. Distant footsteps.

I whisper, "Someone's approaching from my ten."

Night Mom turns slightly, then pushes down the barrel of Julian's rifle. "It's your father and someone else."

Dad returns with a female nurse I've seen at the hospital.

"This way," he whispers, and the two of them lead us into an alley between two rows of houses.

Gabby reaches out as though to take my hand, then pulls back. Leaning close, she whispers, "We're close to Carmen and Embry's homes."

With a nod, I move ahead.

Gabby's little sigh highlights that I'm not the only one who's emotionally fragile.

I lightly touch Night Mom's shoulder. "Carmen? Embry? Their homes are only three blocks away."

She frowns, nods, and moves up to whisper to Dad.

The nurse, Night Mom, and Dad pause, and we stop a few meters behind them. They wave Day Mom up and have a quick, quiet conversation.

Day Mom rejoins us as Dad and Night Mom vanish into the darkness. "We're proceeding to the ship with nurse Kabbix. It *is* a Life Keeper ship. We'll meet up with the others there."

"I don't like splitting up."

She caresses my cheek. "I don't either, sweetheart, but small groups will attract less attention. Follow us."

I glance back. Gabby and Julian throw me worried looks, but nod.

We follow Day Mom and nurse Kabbix.

Yeah, for some strange reason I suspect Kabbix wasn't her name earlier today.

Change is in the air—like a freaking tornado.

It feels like it takes hours, but I suspect it's closer to thirty minutes to work our way around the hospital into the damaged office building closest to the spaceship. We creep through hallways filled with fallen ceiling tiles, debris, and puddles from the fire suppression system. The sprinkler heads are still dripping. We reach a broken window facing the ship.

Five gun emplacements surround the ship. The glowing blue dome of a deflection field encircles each.

The ship itself sits oriented so the engines are facing us. There're four large, wing-like landing arms, two on each side at the extreme front and rear that have pressed into the ground. Those wing/arms are holding the bulk of the ship a good two to three stories above the ground. It's hard to tell from here, but I'd guess the ship has somewhere between three and five decks. The underside is well lit, and there's one especially bright area towards the front.

Kabbix steps to the window and puts a small device up to one of the many holes. She begins rapidly clicking a switch on the device.

A moment later, a light on the underside of the ship flashes.

"Oh," I mutter. "It's a code."

Julian whispers, "It's CGT or Common Galactic Trade. Virtually all species can use the code for basic communications."

"Meaning most people can translate what Kabbix and the ship are saying? Easily?"

He shrugs. "The lights look pretty directionalized to me."

"Weren't you the one telling me there are lots of drones available around town?"

Expression suddenly worried, he shuffles around.

Kabbix grabs a brick and knocks out the window's remaining glass. With a quick, "Follow me," she awkwardly climbs outside.

Day Mom and I look to Julian at the same time.

Seeing this, Julian groans and gives us a weak smile. He then kinda flops out onto the window ledge, flails around awkwardly, then falls out of the building.

"Gee, why wasn't he on the gymnastics team?" Gabby asks before springing out after him.

"I know, right?" I agree before jumping through.

Day Mom follows me, and we all follow Kabbix across the field at a slow run.

Halfway across, a blast of red light from the nearby woods hits Kabbix in the leg.

I step up, throw the nurse over one shoulder, Julian over the other, and sprint for the ship. The rifle slung across my shoulder thumps rhythmically against my back. Julian's holding his rifle by the sling, which allows the rifle butt to bounce against my ribs repeatedly. This probably should hurt, but it doesn't.

Around the field, the gun emplacements turn and open fire with roaring shrieks. Thanks to Julian's bulk, I can't see the trees being shredded, but the ongoing destruction sounds like someone's tossing trees into a giant blender.

"The light," Kabbix groans. "Run into the bright white light beneath the ship."

I sprint that way with Gabby and Day Mom hot on my heels.

Another shot barely misses us.

The gun emplacements whip around and scream as they blast out incandescent bolts of blue destruction into a small store. Pieces of the building explode across the road and that end of the field before the remaining structure collapses.

I run into the light.

Losing my balance, I start to fall, but I'm not falling down, I'm falling *up*. As we rise into the ship, I release Julian and shift to a more secure hold on Kabbix. A fellow who looks to be a bipedal lizard wearing a blue uniform pulls Julian to him and out of the light. I'm next, and it's a relief to have my feet back on something solid. Gabby and Day Mom are soon flanking me.

Part of me thinks I should have more trouble with a lizard guy standing right in front of me, but all things being equal, it's just not that odd.

Mouth clamped tightly shut, Kabbix pats my chest and points down a hallway.

The lizard guy says, "Izzit shassh rees dozzta." Before I have a chance to say, 'bless you,' a voice from his suit says, "This way to personal repair center."

Personal repair—

As the scorched meat smell from Kabbix's wounded leg reaches me, so does understanding. Personal repair. Maybe personnel repair. I suppose either works.

At my nod, the lizard guy turns and quickly leads the way down the hallway Kabbix pointed to.

As I follow, I can't help but notice what looks like a blood trail leading in the same direction—you know, if blood was green. There's the occasional splash of dark blue fluid, too.

No, this isn't weird or creepy at all.

The medical bay has maybe three-dozen variously sized cradles sticking up from the floor at about waist height. I'm not talking baby cradles. These are more like young adult to large adult-size cupped beds on some sort of support post. Maybe twenty of them have someone in them. The lizard guy moves to an empty one and pantomimes putting Kabbix in it, so I do. Numerous panels rise out of the floor, and holographs appear over the wounded nurse. There're all sorts of graphs as well as a closeup of the injury. Shifting text floats over the nurse in no language I've ever seen.

A couple of aliens... people... wearing green slashed versions of the blue uniforms rush over from other patients. Kabbix is the only patient who appears human.

Lizard guy ushers us out of the way. The medical staff begins a rapid conversation full of clicks and almost burp-like exhalations as they remove tools from various panels and begin working the controls.

A faint but deep hum starts up somewhere towards the back of the ship. A slight vibration runs through the floor.

Before I can ask, rapidly approaching footsteps draw my attention to the hallway. Dad rushes in carrying Embry.

Gasping for breath, Carmen staggers in behind him.

Passing us, Dad sets Embry in a cradle and leans back. There're half a dozen pieces of wood and metal sticking out of my quiet friend. More medical staff run over and begin frantically working on him. Seeing his injuries, Julian sucks in a too-quick breath and covers his mouth with both hands. Gabby groans, then hugs the smokey-smelling Carmen. Still panting and gasping for breath, Carmen clutches her tight.

I realize someone's missing and listen. No one else is running this way.

"Dad, where's Mom?"

He walks over, covered in an orangish substance from Embry, much as I've got blotches of light-bluish goo from Kabbix on my shirt and jeans. "We got your night mother to the ship in time for her to upload."

"She's dead?" I whisper, horror echoing through me.

"No. But they damaged her body to the point of non-sustainability. We got her to the ship, and she uploaded to the Nexus. When we get somewhere with a high-capacity link and a grade seven or better fabricator, we'll make her a new body to download into."

I'm staring and can't stop.

Day Mom grabs my shoulder and turns me to face her. "She's *not* dead. She's back in the Nexus. It's where our people are born and spend most of our lives. When we get somewhere more... civilized, we'll get her back."

I swallow with difficulty and nod. Alive, just not here.

"Dad, what happened?"

"Lawton," he spits, his eyes narrowing and lips compressing into a thin line. "Embry was already injured. Lawton set up an ambush outside the remains of his house. She and her people attacked as we were leaving."

"She used Embry as bait." I glance over to where the doctors are frantically working to keep him alive. Lawton had the power to help him, but chose not to. My hands curl into fists as a white-hot fury boils up from deep within me.

For the first time in years, my weird happiness is completely gone.

Before I can so much as step towards the door, Gabby attaches herself to me with a hug. She stretches to whisper into my ear, "Please don't. Please let my love be enough to counter your hate for that awful woman. We *need* to leave this world and we're about to, but if you jump off the ship and go after her, we'll stay. This world has become a battlefield and we all may die, and I don't want to die without knowing you've forgiven me for not telling you the truth."

Her love?

Surprise derails a sizable chunk of my anger as my arms automatically wrap around her.

Day Mom and Dad step over and envelope us both in hugs. Joining us, Carmen hugs Dad, her hand latching back onto Gabby's arm as Julian hugs me and Day Mom.

Slowly, my anger fades.

After a while, the lizard guy leads us through the ship to a suite of rooms surrounding a small common area. They specifically reserved this area for us, and it's nice. There's a large window on the left.

Outside, there's nothing but darkness and stars.

Chapter 10

Culture Shock via Electric Chair

G rossly understating the obvious, life on the ship is different. For instance, there's a clothes recycler in our suite. You put your old, dirty clothes in it—much like I just did—and they're broken down into base components. Then, you print new clothes from a huge menu of styles, materials, and colors, or design your own. At least you do if your measurements are in the system. While pondering this, a peculiar rattling draws my attention to a small door at the bottom edge of the machine. Opening it, I find a small red rock.

"Now where in the world...? Oh! I picked you up at the mill."

Fortunately, the stone doesn't reply. Pleased to find this bit of Earth, I stick it in my pants pocket.

Unfortunately, our suite doesn't have a scanner to provide all those pesky measurements and such so I can get some clean new clothes.

Day Mom joins me and gently elbows me aside with an amused grin. She enters body type "bipedal" lists my appendages and where they're located.

"I coulda done that," I mutter, feeling rather dumb.

"True. But you probably would have had trouble with this part." She enters my measurements into the system. She winks and goes off to do Day Mom things.

Umm... okay. So, I guess there's the occasional unexpected perk to having a mother who's sorta an android.

Gabby steps out of her room, sees me, and walks over.

"Oh, you're picking clothes." Leaning against me, she flips through the design menu. She smells good, like oranges and cinnamon. I'm still annoyed with her. Confused by her, too. But right now, the comfort of her presence far outweighs any of that. So, working together, we pick out and print several pairs of clothes for me, then for her—because naturally, she's already got *her* size information. Once that's done, we stash our clothes in our tiny-but-functional bedrooms, then return to the common area and sit on a long, semi-circular white leather couch surrounding a three-meter-wide vid.

I start to put my arm around her but change my mind as some of my aggravation with being lied to for practically all my life resurfaces.

Gabby leans towards me, then stops awkwardly when I pull back. She feigns indifference.

As the awkwardness from that slowly fades, we talk about life in space. What to do in case of different emergencies on the ship. How to open the bloody doors—there's a scanner on the right side that's strangely similar to the lockplates on the doors in Old Town. Don't go into "crew only" areas. And since I'm the galaxy's only human and most people think I'm a monster, be extra polite to anyone I encounter.

Being thought of as a monster is gonna take some getting used to.

Then again, it does explain a few odd reactions back in the ol' hometown. No wonder my shoes got barfed on.

For our next order of business, Gabby and I move to the fold-out dining table and the machine in the wall beside it. Getting food is surprisingly... disturbingly... like ordering clothes. You enter dietary parameters and restrictions, and the machine gives you a menu of food-like substances to choose from.

"You'll need a chip," Gabby says, holding up the back of her wrist in front of a black spot on the food machine that's evidently some sort of scanner. "I'm already set for a human diet, so we can order together. Still, probably best you get a chip. Just in case we... get separated." I feel thrills of fear and dismay run through her as subtle traces of those emotions flicker across her face.

Feeling other people's emotions and thoughts, even someone as familiar as Gabby, is still a new brand of strange. I suppose the "new" will wear off after a while. Dream-me filters thoughts and emotions from dozens of people at once without a second thought. For him/me, it's like walking or breathing.

Maybe I'll get to that point. Someday.

There's a tightness around Gabby's eyes I don't like seeing.

Whether I'm aggravated with her or not, she's still my best friend. Reaching out, I take her hand and give it a squeeze before leaning forward for a better view of the menu screens.

Gabs returns my squeeze and relaxes. A mild frown spreads across her lips as she gently raps a couple of knuckles against the machine. "The chip stores... call them recipes. The machine reads them. Then, when you make your selection, it prints out the results. If this was a better model, we could order steaks, or pizza, or pretty much anything. As is, looks like meal-bars or drinks."

With expectations about as low as possible, I say, "I guess I'll try a chocolate meal bar and a strawberry drink."

Gabby shrugs, then nods. "I'll try the strawberry bar and the chocolate drink." She punches in our orders. Twenty seconds later, we carry our kinda-food to a table.

Chewing, Gabby and I exchange pleasantly surprised looks.

"Not bad," I admit.

She nods again and takes another bite.

After... lunch? Dinner? I have no idea what time it is anymore. Anyway, once we've finished eating, Julian joins us. He fidgets and doesn't meet our eyes.

"What's up?" I ask.

"I... uh...."

Though we don't look at one another, Gabby and I share a surge of concern. She crosses her arms. "Out with it."

"Um, should I... uh. Should I get rid of my meat-suit?"

Oh. Wow. Yeah. He's an alien.

Everyone's an alien.

"If you want to," I say, pinching the bridge of my nose, "then do it. Whatever makes you comfortable."

He slowly nods. "I *am* kinda tired of always being the best-looking human. Everyone always staring, hoping to go out with me, or wanting my autograph. I think I'd like to go back to living the quiet life of just being the smartest person in the room."

"Right," I agree, keeping a straight face. "I can see how that would become a burden after a while. So, what's the drill? You just shuck out of it like pants, or what?"

"Naw, it's a medical procedure. The suit's lightly tied into my sensory organs, but it's mostly focused around my digestive system. Just for the record, human food is disgusting." He glances around, before leaning forward and whispering, "Also, I have this growing concern."

Gabby glances around. "About what?"

"That they'll take my meat suit and toss it into the food recycler."

Gabs and I make faces.

"Yeah!" Julian says, laughing and pointing at us. "Woo! On that note, I'm off to medical. Catch you pathetic lower life forms later."

Gabby double flips him off. "Julian! What's the sound of two birds flying?"

He's still laughing when the door closes behind him.

Looking me in the eyes, she says, "Let us agree to never, *ever* mention the meat-suit in the food recycler again."

"Hells yes."

The two of us return to the semi-circular white couch. We sit close enough together that I can feel her body heat even though we aren't touching.

Part of me wants things to go back to the way it used to be between us. But normal was us being just friends. I'm pretty sure I don't want to go back to that now that I know she loves me. On the other hand, I'm still conflicted. How do I forgive the people I love for lying to me for practically my entire life? A lifetime of trust dashed to the ground like a lousy Christmas snow globe. How do I put the pieces of that trust back together? Do I want to?

Gabby did say she didn't want to lie to me anymore. Not even by omission.

"There's a lot of learning you'll need to catch up on," she says into the silence.

"Yeah." After gathering my courage, I ask, "Gabs, back in town, what would have happened if you told me the truth?"

Gabby leans back and puts a hand over her eyes. Though she looks like she's in pain, her voice sounds coolly precise. Professional, even. "You'd have inadvertently shown signs you knew the truth. Part and parcel to that, you'd have stared at people for no apparent reason. Then, you would have acted strange. Tried to find the surveillance devices in your house. In my house. In the whole damn town."

"Uh—"

"Once that happened, project personnel would have sounded a silent alarm. You would have been drugged unconscious. Then they would have taken you to the hospital and induced a coma. The Simulation's executive board would have convened an emergency meeting with the senior medical staff to determine when and how you found out, and whether they could safely wipe your memories.

"If the answer was 'yes,' they would do that, and the Simulation would pick right up where we left off. There would be an investigation into how you found out. If they determined I willfully leaked the information to you, they would have kicked me off the planet."

"Kicked—"

"On the other hand," she continues relentlessly, "if they determined your memory could not be safely wiped, they would have stashed you in a cryo unit. Shipped you off for storage somewhere. Chances are good you'd never wake up again. The Simulation would have ended. The executive board would have booted everyone off the planet, and I would never see you again." Gabby's facade cracks, and she sniffs, swallows, and winces.

"Oh." It's all I can say.

It's gonna be a lot harder to hold on to my anger about being lied to all this time.

My wandering eyes eventually find something that's not there. Several somethings. "Where are all the rifles we brought in last night?"

Gabby shakes her head.

Despite the silence turning a tad awkward, neither of us leaves.

I remember the carryall that's filled with psychic gear. "I suppose at some point I'll need to visit the med bay, too."

A thread of concern curls up from her. Reading her is still like hearing a conversation with pillows packed over my ears, but it's getting easier.

Before she can ask, I explain about all the gear I found. The more I explain, the more excited she gets.

"That's great! But, before you do that, we should check and see if there's any upgraded models available."

"Umm, upgrades for humans? Since no one said otherwise, I kinda assumed Lawson wasn't lying when she said I was the only one."

"You are. That much is true." Gabby gives me an excited grin. "Ethan, human psych-tech forms the basis for practically all psych-tech throughout the galaxy. I'd be shocked if we hadn't made at least a few improvements in all that time. And some of it's bound to be compatible. If not, you've got the base model as a fallback."

"Okay. Ask a doctor or do the research ourselves?"

"Do it ourselves, of course. Too many people are lazy, including doctors. We can always ask their opinions, then compare the results against what we've found."

"That sounds good, but I need to get my heart pumping first, otherwise, I'll just fall asleep soon as we start researching. Where can we go to exercise on this ship?"

"I checked that out earlier. Let's go," Gabby says, already heading to the door.

Just as it opens, a thin, maroon alien, whose skin shades from ever paler reds down to pale pink on the underside of the neck, down the front of the neck and presumably chest, and inside the arms walks up. More than a head shorter than me, they're wearing a blue jumpsuit that matches the slightly oversized eyes. The head is hairless and despite the lengthy, almost elfin ears that twitch around rather like a cat's, the features are close enough to human to look a little off, but not be disturbing.

"Julian?" I ask.

"No, Carmen." The voice is a little different, but it's close enough to Carmen's that I don't doubt it's her. "Embry's had his last surgery and is resting. Med techs say he'll make a full recovery. We can go see him tomorrow."

"Oh, that's good news," I say with a relieved sigh as Gabby gives her a hug.

"Farkin'-A right it is," Carmen agrees. She tilts her head to the side. "Where you guys off to?"

Gabby replies, "Cargo deck, to get some exercise."

"Cool, mind if I tag along? Now that I'm me again, I'd like to stretch and move a bit."

"Sure, come on," I say, following Gabby out, but holding the door for Carmen.

"Thanks. The Life Keepers are fantastic people. They've released all the Project's reports so that people can see how misled they've been about what was happening. They also interviewed me." She throws me an evil grin. "It was a long interview, and I had time to explain that our human is actually a big dork, but despite that, he's mostly alright."

"Thank you so much for that insult buried within a compliment. Or vice versa, it was kinda hard to tell."

"Oh yeah, that reminds me. I also explained that you were dumb enough not to pose a risk."

I snort a little laugh and Gabby grins as we walk through the ship.

A few of the crew members stare at us as we pass. When I wave, they wave back, even if their waves are shy and tentative.

Interesting reactions.

The cargo area is a big open space with the occasional vehicle-sized canister here and there. They're all secured to the deck, which seems like an important consideration if you think about it.

Gabby starts to run but stops when I dig into one of my hip pouches. Eyebrow high, she throws me a questioning look.

I pull out an induction orb and power it on. When the light turns green, I toss it up into the air and catch it with my growing telekinesis. Yeah, this feels good. I telekinetically set the orb to orbiting around my head and start off at a jog.

The womenfolk catch up with me quickly.

"Neat trick," Carmen says, eyeing the orb.

"Yeah," I reply. "You've missed a few things." As we work our way around the perimeter of the cargo bay, Gabby and I fill her in.

"Dang, you've been busier than I thought. I figured you'd just gone out to Old Town to make out."

"Naa," I reply, "but that kinda was our cover story."

Gabby holds up her hands in a sort of shrug. "Actually, we needed a story that would make everyone so uncomfortable, that they wouldn't look into where we went. So, our cover story was that we went out for sex, but I chickened out at the last second."

Carmen shakes her head and throws a skepticism-filled look at Gabby. "They bought *you* chickening out? After all those years of carrying a torch for this clown?"

"Wait, what?" I say, looking to Gabby, whose cheeks are turning red. "You've been sweet on me for *years*?"

"Duh!" Carmen replies as we round a corner. "I'm not sure how much the staff knew, but those of us who are close to Gabs have known about that since middle school."

A scowling Gabby gives her a little push, but Carmen just dances away.

"Why didn't you say something?" I ask Gabby.

"Because I thought being your friend was more important than being your girlfriend."

I mentally digest this as we run the straightaway then dodge around a few cargo containers before changing direction.

As we start our second lap, Gabby tells Carmen, "You might be interested to know that humans can see in the dark. When we were down in the bunker with the induction orbs, the lights didn't come on. But a certain someone could see just fine."

Carmen glanced at each of us. "Dark? How dark?"

"Twenty stories underground worth of pitch blackness."

"Good farkin' grief. So, humans can see in the dark? You'd think our bio-archaeologists would have known that."

"I know," Gabby says, "right?"

Carmen eyes me askance. "You'd also think the human's parents might have mentioned something about that over the years."

As we make another left, I shrug. "I don't think it ever really came up." Shrugging again, I add, "I can also hear much better than I let on."

Can you hear me? Carmen asks without speaking. She's significantly harder to "hear" than Gabby because she has next to no telepathic ability. She's pretty much thinking "loudly."

"*Yes, but I'm not sure if I could without the orb active. My telepathic range is fairly limited.*"

"The Life Keepers will want to interview the two of you," Carmen says aloud with a flinch as she rubs her temples. Though not positive, I think her fingers are a little longer now. If so, that's a neat trick. "To help reach an agreement concerning Ethan's future, and to show the galaxy that humans were more than sentient engines of mass destruction. It would be nice if you knew something about the tenebrosi. It would be a real shot in the reproductives for the Simulation's Mis-management team if we not only showed Ethan's a great person," she throws me a grin, "or at least a fairly adequate person, *and* answered the question they created the Simulation to answer all in one fell swoop."

"Tenebrosi?" I ask. The mere mention of the name sends a flutter of fear and unease through me.

"Sure," Carmen says. "There's two historical schools of thought on them."

Gabby throws me a worried look. "Let's not go into that now."

"Let's do," Carmen insists as we weave around cargo containers again. "Two schools. One says they're nothing more than the subconscious madness that turned humans insane and set them killing one another."

"The garbage Lawson was spewing," Gabs says.

I purse my lips and shake my head. "Gotta agree with Gabs. That just doesn't sound right."

Carmen nods, then her expression shifts to an annoyed frown. "Nodding to show agreement is one of those human things I learned as a child. *We* learned as children. My people... my species, don't normally use that mannerism. But I kinda like it. I'm not sure if I can... or want... to kick the habit."

"Do as you like," I reply, hoping to distract my stubborn friend, "Guess I'll be learning a huge honkin' boatload about alien mannerisms, customs, and habits."

"You'll be living it," Gabs confirms.

"Anyway," Carmen continues relentlessly. "Getting back on track. The other school of thought says the tenebrosi are giant, shadowy monsters, with tech equal to ancient humans. That they crawled out of the shadows, wiped out humanity, and then crawled back into the shadows once the last human was dead." They ran several paces ahead before realizing I've stopped. "Personally, I think—"

"Ethan?" Gabby asked, hurrying back to me. "You, okay? Lord, but you're pale."

"He's shivering," Carmen whispers, her over-sized eyes wide.

I clench my hands into fists to keep them from shaking. "I've seen them," I whisper, my heart thundering in my ears. "Giants of shadow and hate. Destroying everything. Killing everyone." My breathing is fast and hard, like I've been sprinting instead of jogging. "There's nothing but death and devastation in their wake for as far as the eye can see. They're abominations, and they *must* be stopped!"

There's a crunch, an electronic squeal, and the induction orb lands at my feet, startling me out of the... whatever it was I was in.

Carmen freezes, staring at me. Giving her head a little shake, she springs over, grabs my arm, and stares into my eyes. "You're saying the tenebrosi were real?"

My breathing calms. Struggling to make my voice sound droll, I say, "Very."

Didn't quite hit the mark on the droll factor, but I got close.

"Out," Carmen says, waving her maroon arm towards the door. "We've got to talk to the captain."

Gabby says, "I think we should wait until—"

Carmen interrupts her. "Out! This is too important, it can't wait."

"What?" I ask as I rather reluctantly allow myself to be ushered towards the door.

"We've got to talk to the captain. The Life Keepers need to know that the tenebrosi were real. Heck, *everyone* needs to know they were real."

CHAPTER 11

THE DOUBLE-EDGED SWORD THAT IS A STUBBORN FRIEND

F ive minutes later, we're speaking to the captain.

Ten minutes later, we're waiting as the captain sets up some sort of confab.

Fifteen minutes later, we've moved to a small room and are sitting on a surprisingly uncomfortable blue-green couch. Without warning, the room's holographically transformed into a giant meeting chamber filled with thousands of aliens. Many of them, maybe even most of them, seem to be holographs, too.

Gabby takes my hand and sends reassuring feelings through our growing link.

It kinda works. Working to keep my breathing quiet and even, I relax. A bit. That, or I don't tense up as much. Either way, I'm glad she's here.

Carmen whispers, "Everyone here is on our side. These are friends and members of the Life Keepers, so just be chill. Talk to them like you would one of us. Pretend it *is* just one of us if that makes it easier." She nods to the side. "Here's our captain."

I throw her an annoyed look, then focus on the captain.

Our minds briefly touch for the second time in the last fifteen minutes. Because of the psychic contact, I already know a lot about this alien. The captain is an ungendered species that kinda reminds me of buggish versions of the centaurs of Earth mythology. Its body is smooth and kinda segmented, with a cluster of antennae on the top of its head that gives an illusion of wild, spikey hair. Two of its six eyes are large, multi-hued and multi-lensed. The other four are all black and located just below the big ones. So far, the captain is the most alien of the aliens I've met and exudes a scent reminiscent of citronella. Despite that, it's a low-level psychic with a mind both complex and intelligent. More than anything else, the captain's thoughts allow me to relax. This second contact finishes forming a strange bond.

Strange. Damn, I'm gonna have to find some new words for weird, odd, peculiar, and such. I'm wearing these right the fark out.

The captain nods its antennae in my direction, then turns to face the audience.

An alien in the audience gabbles something. From behind me comes the translation, "Captain Strange Noise, why have you called this emergency meeting?"

Strange Noise? Interesting that the translation program chose that to be its name.

True to its name, in response the captain makes several truly peculiar noises. The sounds bring to mind an orchestra... in a trash compactor.

Looking around, I realize the captain's translation is coming from a watch-looking device on the back of Carmen's wrist. "We have preliminary confirmation that the tenebrosi were a species, rather than a dark aspect of human nature, and that they did in fact wipe out human society."

The audience erupts.

The captain works a console and suddenly all their voices are muted. It speaks, and the translation follows. "Yes, I know this is upsetting, astonishing, and that you all want both confirmation and reassurances. We'll start with testimony from the male-gendered human."

I swallow with some difficulty as all those eyes and eye-like organs focus on me. "Umm... hey, everyone. Since my first exposure to an induction orb, my dreams and visions of the past have been growing clearer. I've had multiple flashbacks of training to stop the tenebrosi. For the first time, I saw them in something more than flickers and flashes without context. This 'dream' seemed more real. More solid. More... disturbing. The tenebrosi are bipedal giants, ranging from five-meters in height up to twenty."

Talking about them makes me angry, but I keep it beneath the surface.

For now.

"There was a strange, shifting darkness surrounding them. I don't know if this was natural or some sort of tech. Their weapons were horribly effective. Scarily effective. Because the larger tenebrosi would carry weapons we'd reserve for heavy vehicles or even ships, they marched through our cities wrecking tremendous damage. It was... awful."

The silence screams, then vanishes as everyone in the audience tries to speak at once.

Eventually, they quiet down.

To my surprise, there are not that many questions. They're mostly wanting to discuss the ramifications—if I'm lying or mistaken.

Narrowing it down from there, the majority talk about how this will affect galactic politics. What? Yeah, exactly. Evidently, most of the political parties have taken up positions either for or against the idea of re-creating humans. The anti-human crowd within the Everything's Okay party seems to have invested a lot of their clout into trumpeting the theory that we humans destroyed ourselves in a massive civil war.

They're arguing about politics instead of the galactic threat.

Gabby leans over, hugs my left arm, and leans her head against my shoulder. She thinks something at me, but I just get weird static permeated by what feels like a drink from an emotional blender.

"Sorry, missed that."

She presses her lips against my ear and whispers, "Keep the disgust off your face. Some people out there will have body-language translators active." She kisses my ear for several seconds, which is pleasantly distracting.

Taking her hand, I intertwine my fingers with hers and work to keep my face passive.

Eventually, the aliens of the confab get around to asking questions again. "Can you describe the tenebrosi, their weapons and ships?"

I rub the bridge of my nose as a headache begins.

Though Carmen pauses and gives me a tiny smile, even as her eyes seem to ask for forgiveness, she hands me a large electronic pad and a pen.

Disturbing images from darker versions of my dreams flashing before my eyes, I make several embarrassingly crude drawings as I also verbally describe the monsters from my nightmares.

"Help us understand the tenebrosi. How they move, what they do, how they to it?"

Leaning forward, I wish it wasn't so easy to bring the monsters to mind. "Well, they were giant and evil and murdered everyone they could. They walked or ran on two legs and destruction followed in their wakes."

"Explain about the buildings being destroyed, please. Were they simply obliterated?"

My headache intensifies. "No. They repeatedly blasted some buildings down at the lower levels. That usually led to the building collapsing. Other building just had massive sections destroyed."

"Did anyone survive within the buildings that fell?"

A sigh escapes me. "Not enough." I think my answer is over, but it's not. My headache grows sharply worse.

Something in my mind breaks loose and the pain vanishes.

"Are you alright?" Captain Strange Noise asks me. Its voice sounds distant and a touch echoey as is Gabby's.

Unease washes through me.

There's a wall in me that's been growing ever thinner. It's now paper-thin.

I hear myself whisper, "The building collapsed," but it's not me. I didn't say that. I've *never* said that. Still, I hear echoes of 'collapsed' as a memory slides forward and smashes through the thin mental barrier.

I'm standing in a forward observation room on a ship as we glide over the remains of Sierra City. I'm older, but I don't know by how much. Below us is nothing but kilometer after kilometer of ruins. A bright city of twenty-million souls reduced to a mass cemetery of rubble and ruin in less than a week. Forcing my gaze away from the city's remains, I focus on the cuff of my dress uniform's jacket. The gold dragon magnet that holds the cuffs closed gleams brightly. I twist my wrist slightly to move the shine around to its eye.

A dragon's eyes should shine—should burn with the fires within.

The ship stops and hovers.

Dread creeps up from deep within me.

An ensign with a walled-off mind and a light spattering of freckles on her carefully neutral face presents me with a datapad. There's a diagram of the city as it used to be that's overlaid with information from the ship's scanners and our current position. This particular bit of ruin was the Moran-Jackson housing complex. A single green dot glows. It's coming from a deep layer of wreckage within a space that's less than a centimeter thick.

The dot has a tag box: Keit Lee McRath.

My sister is dead.

The agony of confirmation tears through me. Only my iron resolve keeps me from falling to my knees and crying my eyes out. "Thank you, ensign," I say in a quiet, even voice before handing her back the datapad. The first tears slide down her face as I strengthen my psychic walls. "Please give the captain my regards. I have no further business here."

Tears streaming down my cheeks, I'm suddenly back in front of thousands of confused and concerned aliens.

Lurching to my feet, I stagger out. Part of me is vaguely aware of Carmen covering her mouth with both hands, and Gabby rolling onto her side, sobbing uncontrollably.

In a haze, I pass through the ship's corridors. Retreating to my room, I lock the door.

Collapsing onto the bed, I cry over the death of a sister I know only from half-remembered dreams, but still somehow love with all my heart.

CHAPTER 12

THE CHAOS SPINS DOWN

Once I wake up, Day Mom fills me in on what I missed, then gives me some time to come to terms with it. The psychic... call it backwash... from my vision's overwhelming sadness stunned Carmen. Unfortunately, Gabby lived the memory with me. Once she recovered from the emotional sucker punch, Gabs explained to the assembly about finding Keit's locator.

I can't help but feel bad about dragging Gabs into that deeply disturbing memory. Did I somehow pull her in? If so, it wasn't voluntarily—but neither was crushing the induction orb. And there's no doubt that I did that. Did she dive in on her own, or was it more of an undertow drawing her into my wake?

My questions all have branches filled with more questions. None of them lead to answers, only more questions and frustration.

While I cried and subsequently slept, the conferencing aliens argued and talked and eventually started a comprehensive review of what they know, or think they know, about the tenebrosi.

Trying to pry my mind away from the weird, hollow pain of losing Keit and my worries about putting Gabby through an event that traumatic, I step out into our common area. Day Mom's still here and so is Dad, so I grab the backpack and join them. We talk about the psychic equipment I found.

Interest piqued; they help me search for upgrades. My parents sift through thousands of ads. Once they've filtered out stuff that's made for completely different physiologies, they translate and display them for me on the room's holographic array.

Hmm. There are corneal projectors that cannot simply display information from an embedded keeper, but can drop you into full virtual reality. While cool, I don't want that level of immersion. I enjoy knowing what's real at a glance, so a semi-transparent overlay will do fine.

"Computers have advanced," I say, "but not as much as I would have suspected."

Dad and Day Mom kinda shrug.

"You... uhm... know, given that your people live in them and all."

Day Mom smiles, which makes this much less awkward. "It's not just us. There're actually multiple species capable of living in modern computers. But you're right. Technology really hasn't advanced much from the peak days of human civilization. It took the rest of the galaxy quite a while to not only find the remains of human society, but to reverse engineer their technology and catch up."

"Okay. That makes sense."

"Of course," Day Mom says with a grin.

As the answering smile spreads across my face, Gabby, Carmen, and Julian walk in from the outside corridor. Though the big goof looks vastly different, I know it's him.

Still taller than me, Julian's now a very pale orange color with weird crests where his ears were that evidently can flatten against the sides of his head. A stubble of brownish hair tops his head. He's still got broad shoulders and is pretty big around the middle, but it would seem that a lot of his bulk was the meat suit. His nose remains quite large, and his arms and legs are practically the same size, which looks a bit odd. His hands are larger than before and they have three fingers, but an opposable thumb to each side of those fingers. This must be a big part of the reason he was never good at catching—they had to cram one of his thumbs into a finger slot of his meat-suit.

"So, this is the real you," I say, still giving him a once-over.

"In the flesh. And only my flesh, which is a *really* nice improvement."

"Only your flesh. Yeah, that's a weird concept."

"Stop preaching to the choir." He points at the holo with all three fingers of his left hand. "Whatcha looking at?"

I catch the three of them up on my current project. The lot of us sit and discuss my potential upgrades. Eventually, I decide to go with the keeper I picked up in the depot. In theory, its layout and responses will feel the most natural to me.

Day Mom and Dad head off to do their own thing for a while, leaving me, Gabs, Julian, and Carmen on the couch in our suite's common room. Gabby controls the computer, flipping from one model to the next.

Yeah, evidently, implanted chip frames are where the real advances have been made. The new ones are smaller, less invasive, and have significantly increased connectivity levels. I'm not honestly sure what that last part means, but it sounds good.

"It means," Gabby says aloud, having picked up on my unspoken thought, "that the interface is now virtually seamless with energy bleed over and transmission loss that's a very tiny portion of one percent."

"Uhh... of course."

After throwing me an exasperated look, she further explains, "Okay, picture this. You have two power cables you want to plug together."

"Are you still with her?" Carmen teases. "Or has she lost you with her technobabble?"

I frown. "You're not so far away I can't kick you under the table."

She throws her hands up and fakes a look of horror. "Oh, no! Violent human! Violent human!"

Gabby kicks her under the table.

Carmen curses and rubs her shin. "Clearly, I should have been watching out for the violent metamorph."

"No doubt," Julian agrees with a grin filled with blocky teeth. "Metamorphs look all sweet and cuddly, then they go all vicious on you. I think we galactic people need protecting from them." He backs out of Gabby's kicking range.

"You're about to need protecting," Gabby growls, but her annoyance is rapidly giving way to amusement. "Where's something I can use for a club?"

"Before we move on to giving Julian the baby seal treatment," I say, "let's get back to why the new interfaces are better."

"Baby seal treatment?" Carmen asks. "What's that?"

I frown. "Not sure exactly, but it has something to do with clubbing people, rather than seals."

"I'll have to put that in my report." Carmen blinks and sits back. "Oh. Are we still doing reports?" She meets my gaze, "Is it gonna be weird if we do? I think it might be, what with you knowing about it and all."

I flip my hand dismissively. "Report away. I get it, you don't know as much as you'd like about my people. For that matter, neither do I, so it's not a big deal to me if you write reports."

She and Julian nod, and I look back to Gabby.

"Okay, where was I?" she asks. "Oh yes, electrical power cables. Let's say, you're connecting these cables inside a chamber of goo, cos essentially you are. Now, if one cable is much bigger than the other, some of the electricity won't go into the other cable, it's gonna leak into the goo. Same for if the connection between the two cables isn't perfect."

"The goo being my brain."

Carmen nods enthusiastically. "Goo for brains. It definitely fits you."

Gabby grins, momentarily widening her eyes. "Exactly. So, the better the connection, the less bleed over."

I give them sardonic looks. "Okay, I get it now."

"Good." Gabby works the controls and brings up a holograph that changes to a dozen pictures, each showing a different implant frame. Each of them has alien script underneath. One of them looks kinda like a miniature tree, including the roots. Another is more akin to an ice-crystal. Most of them look more like hairy, mechanical spiders than anything else. Gabby continues fiddling, and the script switches into delightful readability. Well, at least I can read the words. Evidently, a neural technician wrote this. Seeing my confusion, Gabby continues fiddling, and a color graph appears beneath each pic.

"Like your parents did," Gabby tells me. "Green is good. Red is bad."

We all focus on one graph showing all green. This one looks kinda like a shiny black spider—if spiders had twenty legs. Gabby taps the controls and the other implant frames vanish.

Reading the small-print, Julian says, "A ten percent boost to psychic potential immediately after implantation. Sweet. Results vary by species, but this model uses direct neural stimulation to augment psychic abilities. It's also got smart tech that learns how your individual abilities work and then does custom modifications, resulting in up to a fifty percent increase in ability beyond other models." He whistles.

"Wow," I say. "That sounds good. But how tough is it?"

"Tough?" Gabby asks.

"Tough. If I'm using telekinesis to lift something heavy, is it going to suddenly burn out and toast my brain, or cutout and cause that heavy thing to fall and maybe squash someone?"

The three of them pour over the technical stuff.

Almost half an hour later, Julian holds up clenched fists. "It's rated for Ullari."

Expressions smug, the three lean back and relax.

Seeing my WTH expression, he says, "Ullari are a species. They've got body structures that act a lot like your worlds' electric eels. They're frequently hired as guards because they can shock the mucus out of people with almost no effort."

"Ullari rated," I say, pursing my lips. "Okay, that sounds good. What's next?"

"Lunch," Day Mom says, walking into the common room followed by Dad, who's carrying a bag. "Let's try to get onto a little more formal meal and sleeping schedule."

Dad sets the bag down on the table. "Also, Captain Strange Noise has a top-of-the-line meal faber which it has generously offered for our occasional use."

We all lean towards the bag.

Clearly pleased with herself, Day Mom pulls out containers and passes them out.

Julian opens his and a spicy, yet sharp chemical smell spreads out from what looks like puppy kibble covered in translucent blue sauce. He smiles blissfully, one eye fixed on the food and the other on my mother. "I haven't had this since before I went into the meat suit. Thank you, Mrs. Shaw!"

"You're welcome."

Carmen opens hers and a sickly-sweet aroma competes with the chemical spill that is Julian's dish. Seeing what look like glazed mice on skewers, she gets up and hugs Day Mom. Wasting no time, my maroon friend returns to her seat, pulls one of the things off the skewer, pops it into her mouth, and slowly chews it.

"*Mmm.*"

Carmen's front teeth are all narrower and more pointed than human teeth. Thankfully, she's chewing with her mouth closed, because the alienness is stacking up on me.

Mine and Gabby's containers feature mini supreme pizzas, which allows me to focus on something delightfully normal. Coming in from each side, Gabby and I simultaneously kiss Mom's cheek before digging in. While the food bars and drinks weren't bad, even having to compete with the aromas of my friends' meals, this smells amazing.

Mmm. Tastes amazing, too.

"Mom," I say after we eat, "you're the best."

"Naturally," she replies with a wink and a grin. "Now, show us what you found."

We give a quick overview of the different models, then my parents spend a while studying the specifications for the spider that showed all green. Day Mom and Dad run some high-level simulations. A few of them involve our suite's computer, but most they run internally.

Eventually, Day Mom nods. "Of course, I can't say for certain, but this *should* work as advertised. If you like, we can download the profile and print one out tomorrow."

A thrill of excitement and anticipation runs through me. "Okay, yeah. Let's do that." I lean forward as a thought occurs to me. "What are we looking at, currency-wise? Is that even how things work out in the big, wide galaxy?"

"Yes," Carmen says, her ears flattening against her head. "But can we *please* not get into that now?"

No one else seems to feel strongly about this.

I shrug. "Sure. Since this seems to be covered, how about we visit Embry?"

My friends agree and we head around to the med bay. There, we find the lizard guy who first helped us onto the ship talking to a younger lizard guy. Carmen walks over and gives the young one a gentle hug. He's brown with greenish spots and little ear flaps.

I don't have to bother asking if this's Embry. Besides his and Carmen's body language, which makes it obvious, I feel it a little in Carmen and Gabby's thoughts, and even a hint from Embry himself.

Our friend is one of only five patients still in the infirmary.

"Dude," Julian says, clasping one of Embry's three-fingered and one-thumbed hands. "I'm *sooo* sorry you couldn't be one of the beautiful people like me."

That sparks laughter from all around while Gabby and I shake hands with the older lizard guy. Much like Embry, after we're done, he takes a large step back.

Maybe it's his entire species that prefers a little extra personal space.

"So," the larger fellow says without a translator, "how are you acclimatizing to the future?" Seeing my surprise, he shows some teeth with saw-like serrations on the tips. "I got a chip of your language, facial expressions, and body language, as well as your culture. It is quite interesting."

"That's crazy cool. As for acclimatizing... it's going slowly, but surely."

"He's doing great," Gabby says. "Much better than I would do in his place."

Lizard guy nods, which may or may not be agreement. "If you need to get away, there's a meditation pod on deck three in the rec center. It's programmable and features a psychic shield you can activate if you're tired of other people's thoughts and emotions."

My eyes widen. "I didn't know such a thing was even available. Thanks."

"You are welcome," he says, stepping up and awkwardly patting my shoulder before walking to the door. "Good day to you all."

"Wow," Gabby says, turning away from his departure. "Very nice."

I nod and walk over to clasp hands with Embry. Cutting my eyes over to Julian, I brush my other hand through my hair and strike a dramatic pose. "Oh Embry, I'm *sooo* sorry you couldn't be one of the beautiful people. Please don't hide in shame because you're not as lovely as me!"

Laughter erupts. Embry's chuckles cause him to wince.

We have a long talk, filling him in on what he's missed. Embry's hopeful the doctors will release him in a couple of days. Carmen's hopeful that he's right.

I'm hopeful that no one else will need emergency medical services.

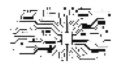

That evening, everyone except Gabby's getting ready for bed. Gabs is already in her room. The rest of us are chatting about what a busy day it's been.

A chime sounds.

Dad opens the door to our suite, revealing an older alien with an elongated neck and limbs. She's wearing a peculiar sort of multi-colored robe with sashes around the upper arms and legs and three across her torso. Upon her feet are matching sandals, which look strangely human in design. Something akin to purplish feathers cover the top of her head.

She gives a slight bow, hands Dad a card, then meets my eyes.

There's a bit of pressure in my head. It's rather akin to someone knocking on a door.

I lower my mental shields.

"I'm Accaryinth of Meprophrose. My people are psychic and no longer communicate aloud."

"Oh. Okay. Hello."

Dad ushers her in, and she gives another slight bow to everyone present. At my invitation, she takes the seat next to me as Dad hands the card to Day Mom. Carmen looks over Mom's shoulder before heading over to Gabby's room. There's a quick knock, then she steps in and closes the door behind her.

"Should it be harmonious with you, I would find it agreeable to see your memory of the Shadowed Ones. On the occasion these memories ring true, I will send my acknowledgment far and wide that everyone might know the true fate of your people."

I sigh. *"Okay, it's for a good cause."*

"I sympathize with your reluctance to relive such a painful event and thank you for sacrificing this measure of tonight's peace."

She's got an interesting what of thinking. I like it.

"Thank you."

Rather than reply, I hold out my hand for hers, and she gently rests her small, long-fingered hand on mine. Closing my eyes, I return to the extended memory of the tenebrosi. I'm not sure if it's her or me, but the memory is sharper this time, and there's more detail.

We're on Correlon IV in the city of New Dallas. Ships fill the blue sky, both enemy and friendly. Tenebrosi troop transports are dropping the shadowy giants across the city. Those aliens already on the ground attack everything in sight as non-combatants flee in all directions. A tenebrosi fires into the base of a building, turning the defenders in front of it to super-heated mist and blasting out a huge chunk of the ground floor. Many of the floors above it collapse into the new void. Other giants blaze away with their weapons, knocking great holes in the buildings.

But the battle's not one-sided.

High above, a tenebrosi capital ship explodes. Troopers flying in via jetpacks open fire, blasting incandescent streams of destruction into the dark giants. A psi team attacks using their psychokinetic powers—a shadow giant burst into flames as a downward blast of telekinetic force hammers another flat.

The battle rages on with people dying all around, then it suddenly stops, freezing in place.

"There is something here." Accaryinth of Meprophrose moves within my memory and taps a transparent barrier. *"This is something I have never encountered. I do not understand what it is, but it is not a pure memory. The emotions it stirs within us both are real, but they are the emotions of witnesses, not participants."*

She looks at the scene and we share the mental equivalent of a puzzled head scratch. *"I do not understand, therefore, I regretfully cannot certify this memory. My belief is not enough. For such a galaxy altering revelation, I must have complete clarity and certainty."*

There's a mental flash of one of the shadowed giants up close and personal, then suddenly, we're out of the memory and sitting on the couch.

A shudder runs through her.

She meets my eyes. *"I sorrow for what you've suffered, and sorrow even more that I cannot offer the assistance you need."*

While her refusal is frustrating, I know her motives are pure and that she truly wishes she could help. *"Perhaps I'll figure out what the barrier is, or a cleaner memory will surface."*

"If either happens, I would gladly share it despite the unpleasant nature of the subject. Now, I must bid you a good sleep cycle." She stands and I escort her to the door. *"No matter what, I will tell people you have a kind center."*

"Thank you."

She steps out where a dozen people of mixed species wait in escort. The lot of us exchange slight bows, then they leave.

Gabs and Carmen are watching me from her room's doorway.

"I'm good," I silently tell Gabs.

Gabby nods and the two of them vanish back into her room.

"Okay," I say. "On that note, I've had enough strangeness for one day. I'm going to bed."

Day Mom says, "I've got you scheduled with the med bay to have your keeper installed after lunch tomorrow. If the chip frame prints properly and passes the quality control testing, we can add that in. I've already discussed it with the doctors, and they don't foresee any problems."

"Thanks Mom, that sounds great. Night."

A few minutes later, I crawl into bed.

My brain insists on going over and over today's events. I try to shut it all down and fall asleep. The persistent, niggling hope that tomorrow's medical procedures won't leave me blind, or brain damaged makes this more difficult.

CHAPTER 13
ROMANTIC
RELATIONSHIPS 101

I'm almost asleep when I receive a mental tickle from Gabby. *"Can I come in?"*

"Sure." I roll over, point my finger at the door release, and apply a little telekinetic pressure.

The door pops open.

The finger pointing wasn't strictly necessary, but it feels like it helped me aim. Probably silly, but also kinda fun.

Gabby steps into my bedroom wearing checkered pajama bottoms and a t-shirt. She's carrying a pillow and a blanket. "My bunk isn't comfortable," she says before climbing over me. She pushes my covers out of the way, pulls up her blanket, and leans against my back. With a sigh, she relaxes, her thoughts sliding into a low-level connection with mine.

Her contentment pushes away my surprise, gently warming me.

Together we fall asleep.

"Look, new guy," a strangely familiar soldier labeled as Klangmore, says as we finally reach the practice range. "I get that you're strong. The LT's been talkin' 'bout little else for the last week. But what're you gonna *do* with that strength?"

Wearing black fatigues, we're armed to the teeth. In that, I'm actually a standout. There's a heavy pistol on my hip and that's it.

I look at Klangmore as though he's lost his mind. "I'm gonna kill tenebrosi and save dumbasses like you."

The group laughs, though Klangmore gets miffed.

"I'm not a dumbass."

A big bald man labeled Jones and a woman with flaming red hair by the name of Ross step up on either side of Klangmore, putting their arms around him. Like Klangmore, there's a peculiar familiarity about them. "You *are* a dumbass," the guy says just before she says, "An epic dumbass."

Klangmore turns his hands up as he looks to the heavens. "What did I do so wrong to deserve friends like this?"

"You were very, very bad," Jones says.

"Yep," Ross agrees, looking up at me. I get a sense of curiosity from her just before she launches a psychic probe at me.

The report said this group had a tiger, and I now know who she is. Her probe is an attack, albeit a minor one.

I catch her probe and follow it back into her mind.

She's smart but also a risk taker—often simply for the sake of enjoying the adrenaline rush. She's lost people important to her and burns with the need to kill the tenebrosi wherever she can find them. This group is her family and she'll fight to the death to protect them.

This matches what her file said about her, so I release her mind and turn to meet the dragon I sense approaching.

Ross's anger flares and she's considering another attack now that my back's turned.

I riffle her hair in a breeze that touches no one but her. It takes seeing the people around her staring at her waving hair to penetrate her anger.

She backs down.

The dragon is the lieutenant in charge and her gaze holds a mixture of amusement, eagerness, and curiosity. She's labeled

Monroe. The sense of somehow knowing her runs much deeper than with the others. "So, you're the heavy-hitter I've been asking for."

"Dragon Lachlann McRath, reporting for duty."

"Brass says you're something special. That you can help push back the Shades." She eyes me before nodding towards the distant targets. "How about you give us a little demonstration?"

"Would I sound like a presumptuous ass if I asked for everyone else to get their shooting done before I play?"

Much to my not-surprise, Klangmore and Ross nod with great enthusiasm.

Jones puts an arm around my shoulders as he had with Klangmore. "Yes. Yes, you would. In fact, you already do."

I can't help but chuckle.

"Okay," Lieutenant Monroe says with a smile that turns into a grin. "You lot, do some damage. I don't want to see a single target left downrange."

There's only seven of them, and they happily spread out and begin shooting assorted weapons and firing grenades at the distant targets. Those targets are in turn attached to thick slabs of ceramalloy. These could have been forged into starship hulls but were instead relegated to the firing range as backstops. Downrange, weaponized light and explosives rip the targets apart. Flames suddenly rage over them as Ross lets loose with her pyrokinetics.

It's an impressive display of destruction.

As the lieutenant turns to me, I'm already lifting into the air. "Might wanna put your goggles on." The air swirls around me. While they're muttering about this, I pull the grenades off their belts and fling them into the distant targets. The explosions are too small to be truly gratifying.

I form a small tornado around myself as I fly towards the targets. Before I get there, I realize that the dust, dirt, and gravel from this will block most of their view of what I'm about to do.

I allow the swirling to stop.

With a groan of protesting metal, I jerk one of the target backstops out of the ground. Then I yank the others out, all at once. I set them rotating around me as I'd done with the dust and dirt. Slowly, I open up the pattern of whirling metal slabs and then elongate it like planets all in the same elliptical orbit around a star. Each of the former backstops whooshes as it flashes past. For a moment, I simply float and bask in the joy of wielding my power—but I've got work to do and a war to win. I speed up the pattern; the whooshes merging into a constant noise reminiscent of a ginormous fan—which is rather appropriate. When I'm happy with the momentum I've built up, I slam the first slab into the ground. It almost completely buries itself. I then hammer the rest of them down on top of that one. The noise is beyond incredible.

I fly back over and join my new squad mates.

Everyone looks stunned. Everyone except Lieutenant Monroe.

She's matching me grin for grin.

I awake. There're a few beads of sweat on my forehead. Do I have a fev—

Oh.

Nope, no fever. Gabby's evidently powered by a fusion core. Since I'm fairly sure it's not time to get up yet, I shuffle over to the environmental controls and lower the thermostat before crawling back into bed and wrapping my arms around her.

Her slow, rhythmic breathing is almost hypnotic, and it quickly lures me back to sleep.

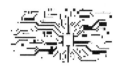

Dozens of metamorphs have gathered in the high-tech meeting room for our Changing of the Tides celebrations. Some remain native, in the primordial form that brings to mind a giant jellyfish combined with an octopus. Others have done their adaptation shifts while others have successfully completed their bonding shifts. Quite a few have brought their families with them, which adds to the delightful variety.

Like many of the others, I'm trying to walk like a biped. It's interesting. Tricky too, because my balance center is still forming.

Once everyone's gathered, we take the grav-shaft down into the cavern below. There's a waterfall that's half filled the cave with clear water. A variety of eels and glowing crustacea call this lake home. Colorful varieties of luminous fungi cover the cavern walls and ceiling. With shouts of joy, we children run into the water and play—chasing the eels, chasing each other, and all around having a great time.

One of my aunts brings a large bowl of *maata* to the water's edge—

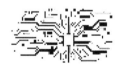

I wake with a start.

Day Mom's standing in the doorway. Silently, she walks over and kneels by the bed. "Everything okay?" she whispers.

"Yeah," I reply just as quietly as the dream fades away. "I think I was sharing one of Gabby's dreams. It was kinda weird but really interesting."

"Is she well?"

"So far as I know. Wait, have you seen something suggesting otherwise?"

She shakes her head. "I'm just concerned for her. The last few days on the planet were rough. Possibly even traumatic."

"Yeah, I guess. I'm more worried about that memory of mine she got dragged into."

"So far, she seems fine." Day Mom smiles gently and runs a hand over my forehead as she brushes the hair away from my eyes. "As for you, it's okay *not* to be traumatized by the battle on the planet, sweetheart. It's *okay* that you enjoyed the action and the excitement."

"Is it? It doesn't make me a bad person? A monster like Lawton claimed?" I hadn't really thought about this, but now that we're talking, I realize there *is* a tiny thread of worry curling around within me.

"No, not at all. Emergency responders of all stripes run *towards* the action, the danger. It's just part of who they are. It's natural for them to take pleasure in what they do. Otherwise, they'd be employed in the wrong job. They'd be living a lie."

I nod, mulling that over. Swallowing, I admit, "When we were creeping through town, I *really* wanted to find some of the bad guys and pound them into paste."

"Naturally. Young human males need an outlet for physical aggression. We wanted to instruct you in Terran martial arts to help teach you discipline and provide you with that outlet, but the Program managers wouldn't allow it. They were afraid you'd go on some sort of rampage or something. Pure silliness."

I look at the floor, where my shoes, socks, and shirt lay in an untidy mess. "Mom.... Some of my dreams...."

"Have been violent?" At my nod, she reaches over, gently lifts my chin, and meets my eyes. "Of course, you've had violent dreams, sweetheart. When the archaeologists were preparing your DNA for cloning, they added a component to draw forth your genetic memories. I'll show you the science later, if you like. They wanted to settle the debate about how human society died. Not very considerate of your feelings, if you ask me.

"Anyway," she continues, "the last centuries of human existence were nothing but non-stop war. It's hardly surprising that you'd dream of it. It doesn't make you a bad person to want to defend your people. Quite the contrary. You are a *good* person, Ethan Shaw. I have faith in you." She gives my hand a squeeze and kisses the back of it.

I mirror her action by squeezing her hand and kissing it. "Thanks, Mom. I really appreciate it."

"You're welcome, son. Our constraints are gone. So, if you want to train in the martial arts, we'll do that. For the moment, think about, and sleep well."

She closes the door behind her.

Gabby rolls over against my back and drapes an arm over me. "I willingly followed you into the memory, and I'm not traumatized," she mutters sleepily.

"Glad to hear it. I worried about you."

"I know, mind like a psychic fortress or not, you're pretty easy to read, Ethan Shaw." She burrows into the covers a little more. "I really like your moms. They're good people."

"Yes, they are," I agree, taking her hand in mine. "I hope Night Mom's okay. I miss her."

Gabs' head bobs against my back. "There's something you should know."

"What's that?"

"I'm not sure exactly when, but I'm gonna marry you."

CHAPTER 14
LINKS TO THE PAST

W hen I wake up in the morning, the first thing that springs to mind is Gabby's declaration that she's going to marry me.

"Umm, hmm," she says sleepily, facing the wall. She glances around, then focuses back on me. "Uh, you should use the bathroom, so I can use it."

Something seems odd about that, but it's early and now that she's mentioned it, I *do* need to take care of business. I step into the attached bathroom.

When I return, Gabby and the bedding have vanished, including the pillows.

I'm just beginning to ponder this when Gabby walks back into my room. She's replaced her night clothing with a knee-length black skirt and a green blouse.

She bites her lip.

"What?" I ask.

"I originally wanted to talk about moving in."

That's fast.

"Exactly," she says in response to my unspoken comment. "Too fast. I don't want us to be some sort of explosion. You know, big flash, then nothing. I want us—you and me as a couple—to last. Like I said last night, I want you forever."

"So do it." It's too early to be having this conversation, but I keep *this* thought to myself.

"I'm not exactly sure *how*," she admits.

"Me either. Guess we'll figure it out. Together."

"That's *exactly* what I had in mind. It's also why I want to slow down. I think for now we should see how we do as boyfriend and girlfriend." Gabby moves as though to kiss me, but turns away. "Sorry, morning breath. I'm going to do us both a favor and brush my teeth. Is there any mouthwash?"

Boyfriend and girlfriend? For real this time. I like it.

The change in conversational topics amuses me, but I just say, "I'm guessing Day Mom found some, had it made, or whatever. The black bag beside the sink."

"Thanks."

When she steps out of the bathroom, I nod for her to sit. "There's another important matter we need to discuss."

"Your upcoming surgery?"

"No. Remember when we were leaving the Lower Tier Psi-Comp Depot, and we ran into the police chief and Lawton?"

"The what? Wait. Are you talkin' about the chamber with all the induction orbs?"

"Exactly." I guess the boundary between my dream memories and my waking mind thinned even more overnight. "It's called a Lower Tier Psychic Component Depot. Anyway, that's when I realized you truly were my dream girl. I wished there and then that our fake relationship could be real."

Her pupils dilate. "You did?"

"I did. Gabs, you know about the girls I asked out in school. You ever wonder why I never asked you out... although I was getting close there towards end?"

Eyes glued to me, Gabby shakes her head ever so slightly.

"It's much like you said—you were too important a friend to me. I *needed* you in my life. For the last two years, I've gotten up every morning looking forward to seeing you. You make me want to be a better person.

"Also, I was scared you might barf on me or flee to coastal Mongolia."

Snorting a little laugh, she wipes her eyes. "I was *sooo* angry at them for responding that way to you. I saw how it hurt you.

Felt it, though I didn't report it. Fortunately for them, they left the world before I could give them a proper ass-kicking."

Almost laughing, I take her hand and kiss the back of it.

"Gabriella Kwan, I am thrilled to be your boyfriend."

"Ethan Shaw, I am equally pleased to be your girlfriend."

"We should—"

She leans in close. "Seal the deal with a kiss?"

"Yes," I breathe before kissing her. My eyes close as our kiss turns into us kissing. Her warmth soaks into me and I feel lighter, like I might float away.

Eventually, we separate.

Gabs dives in for another quick kiss. "We need to do more of this."

Being a man of action, I pull her to me, and suddenly we're kissing again.

There's a quiet knock at the door.

I finish our kiss, wink at Gabby, then get up and open the door. Day Mom is standing here, her expression filled with amusement, but it turns serious.

"Hey Mom. What's up?"

"Your new implant frame passed the quality control tests. Captain Strange Noise is leery of the med techs installing it while we're in space." Seeing my puzzled expression, she explains, "There are thousands of documented cases—human cases—of spontaneous psychic events happening during implant surgery. Gabby says you sometimes dream of being telekinetic?"

"Yeah. I do. Had another one last night."

Day Mom nods. "A major telekinetic episode on a ship this size in which we're never very far from the nuclear reactor powering it...." She gives her head a little shake. "Let's assume that could be bad for everyone. Instead, we're going to set down near some ruins on one of the few human planets that still has plant and animal life, set up a medical tent, and do the operation there."

"Which planet?"

"Vega."

"I've never been...." I stop myself. "Wow. That's weird, even by my new standards."

Day Mom hugs me, and I lean against her.

Gabby gently pushes past, giving my ear a kiss on the way by. "I'm gonna get cleaned up. We'll need to get you to the doctor's a few minutes early so they can run scans and such."

"Yeah. You're right. Good thinking."

She smiles brightly and winks. "Well, duh! This is *me* we're talking about here."

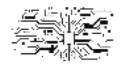

Two hours later, I'm in the med bay receiving a pre-surgery checkup. The first doctor injects the back of my left wrist with a chip containing my dietary requirements. Now I can order my own food.

It's weird that I'm relieved about this.

Weird. Oh, you poor, edges worn away, cover horribly frayed, over-used word. Maybe I should order a case of your synonyms since I'm wearing you out so quickly.

After a quick consultation, the medical staff decides to install my keeper and eye mods before the ship begins its descent into Vega's gravity well. An oddly familiar nurse with bright yellow skin and luminescent white hair smiles down at me. "I'm Kabbix. We've actually met several times. I was playing the role of Nurse Gentry. Anyway, I want you to know I really appreciate you getting me out of the firefight and onto the ship. We're going to take great care of you, Ethan."

"You're welcome," I say automatically, then snap my fingers. "You were the pretty blonde nurse with the light freckles on her nose!"

She smiles. "Exactly! That was me. You ready?"

"Yeah, I think I am."

She holds a mask over my mouth and nose.

Kabbix removes the mask.

I frown. "What's wrong?"

Her head tilts a little and I sense her lack of understanding.

"Did the doctors change their minds about doing the surgery?"

A slow grin spreads across her yellow lips. "No. It's already done."

As soon as I realize I'm staring, I stop and sit up. I turn my eyes as far down and to the right as possible. There's a slowly flashing green rectangle, which I focus on. "Keeper, initialize."

The rectangle opens into a menu screen.

Everything's set to defaults.

That's good enough for now. I'll customize as needed. Speaking of which, I need to install some of the mods and upgrades I picked up. But later.

I ask, "How close are we to Vega?"

"We landed half an hour ago. You seemed to need the rest, so we let you sleep. We've got a team preparing a medical tent on the planet for your next surgery." She glances towards the rear of the ship and her luminescent hair momentarily brightens. "You know, away from the life support systems or engine core."

"I... um... yeah. That sounds smart." I stand up, pleasantly surprised that I'm not woozy. "Uh, thanks for the surgery."

"It was our pleasure."

Halfway to the door, I stop and turn around. "It was? Why?"

"Helping people is how I find fulfillment. Also, you saved my life. Besides that, my surgical team is now part of a very tiny group of medical personnel who can honestly say we've operated on a human. It's most exciting."

"Oh. Okay."

"Will you check out the planet before your frame implantation?"

"Yes, I believe I will. Thanks again, Kabbix."

"You're most welcome!"

Since we're on Vega, I hurry to my room. Within my bag is the pack with the mods and upgrades. It only takes me a minute to find and upload the Vega update for my keeper.

Poking around our suite reveals that nobody's here.

I access my keeper again. Right now, the time and date are the only thing showing. The time has reset to Vega's 26.44 rotational clock and this planetary time zone. If I want, I can also show Terran standard time or that of any other human world or colony. I'm about to move on when I spot the date and freeze.

A deep, sludgy queasiness slithers through me.

I've been told all my life that I was born in 2004. This year is supposed to be 2021. It's one thing knowing that's not right; that I've been lied to. It's quite another to see the Terran Standard Calendar date—55,813.

Damn, but that's a lot of digits.

Pinching the bridge of my nose, I check out some basic information on Vega, but the date's really bothering me. A little of my normal happiness bubbles up, but not much.

With a sigh, I head to the exit.

During the short walk to the ship's grav column, I put the date behind me. Or maybe I just bury it and all associated feelings.

Yeah, that's probably gonna bite me in the proverbial arse, but right now, there's only so much I can deal with.

I focus on the light of the grav column. The atmospheric forcefield is still in place, but being heavier than air or microorganisms, I can drop right through it.

I step out into the light... and it sets me right back where I'd just been.

Huh. Unexpected gravity fail.

A few meters away, the lizard guy enters the hallway. Seeing me, he hurries over. "Sorry, I needed to expel bodily wastes. Ready to debark?"

Expel.... Yep, that sounded... um, unexpectedly peculiar.

"Yes, sir. I'm ready."

He presses a button on a console, and I notice a very slight shift in the light of the grav column.

"Oh," I say, pointing at the controls. "So that one's down and... that one's up?"

"Exactly. All the best with your surgery."

"Thanks." I hop into the light and this time it carries me down to Vega.

"Heh," I mutter to myself. "That guy's been really helpful. I need to learn his name."

The ship's parked next to a large, freshwater lake. By large, I mean I can't see the far side of it. After the time onboard, it seems strange to smell the water, but I do. Darn, it smells good. There're trees around this part of the lake—oaks, elms, and at least half a dozen other species. In the distance, they seem to form an actual forest. Between here and there is short grass with the occasional flower poking up and adding bright color. Standing out like a sore thumb is a building made of white metal and black glass. I'm guessing this is the "tent" the nurse mentioned.

If so, we have very different ideas of what a tent is.

I start that way.

Seeing me through a window, Julian hurries out of the "tent" to join me. "This is great! While I'm not claustrophobic or anything, I *much* prefer planets to ships. Vega has five percent higher gravity than Thompson. There's a slightly higher atmospheric oxygen content as well. This is going to be amazing!"

"Umm... what? I think I missed something."

"Yeah, we're gonna be here a few weeks. Life Keeper Control suggested this might be a good place to hide out. Before we landed, the captain dropped a comm buoy, so we'll stay connected to what's happening out there in the greater galaxy. Vega's a nice place to hang out and start my exercise regimen."

I turn a skeptical eye towards him. "You. Are going to finally start... exercising?"

"Sure. I didn't back on Thompson because of the meat-suit."

"Huh?"

"Yeah, they never got the cooling levels right. Too much exercise and I'd literally start cooking. It sucked."

"Damn dude, I never knew."

He laughed. "Of course, you didn't. Also, I was terrified that if I started cooking, I'd smell so awesome that you'd eat me."

I stop and max out the volume on my skeptical look.

Julian laughs again. "Okay, so it was only the first couple of weeks after we met. Still, considering what we were taught about humans, I think it was a valid fear."

"Right." We continue towards the tent a few steps before I stop again. A bird the size of our car back home flies overhead and I watch it until it sails out of sight behind some large trees. I check the keeper. It recorded an image of the bird, but nothing in the database matches it.

Well, I guess fifty-thousand years is a long time.

Something Julian said finally squeezes its way to the front of my thoughts. "Thompson. We were on Thompson, not Earth?"

"Yeah. The techs had to scrub all the vids of Earth... the history, pics, and everything else to erase Luna and any mention of it. You know, seeing as how Thompson doesn't have a moon. Just some of the behind-the-scenes trivia you've been missing out on. So, did you ever go to Thompson in your past life?"

"I don't think so. Pretty sure I was on Earth, though. At least for a while."

He shakes his orange head and absently rubs an ear crest. His hair has already grown to almost two centimeters long. "Man, I can't even imagine—what it must have been like in its prime, I mean. Earth's a big no-go zone, now."

"It was the homeworld," I say with a little shrug. "The birthplace of humanity and the world peppered with our oldest reminders of history. Why's it a no-go zone?"

Julian and I resume walking.

"There are still functional defense systems on and around Earth. The entire Sol system, in fact. Scary stuff. Stealth mines, and weapons implanted into asteroids and such that only fire if the aperture lines up with the target—a target being any non-human ship. Not to mention combat drones, arc fields... the list goes on and on."

"Wow." My mood sinks. "And despite all of that, we still lost the war."

"Cheer up, buddy. At least the tenebrosi are all dead, too."

That doesn't sound right, but I don't bother answering.

We enter the "tent" via a door.

There's one of the big, cupped tables in the center that I'm guessing is for me. Other than that, the doctors have a few boxes and gizmos, but nothing like what I'd expect for brain surgery. Kabbix's luminescent hair stands up and brightens just before she ties a wrap around it. She winks and throws me a smile.

It's possible my return smile is a little strained.

Yeah, I really don't want to be lobotomized if things go badly.

Evidently finishing their talk with the doctor, Day Mom and Dad walk over. "How's the keeper?"

"It's fine. Was a bit of a shock seeing the date on the Terran Standard Calendar."

Mom pats and rubs my shoulder while Dad winces.

"Yeah," he says. "That's gotta feel weird. Especially given what you've been told all your life."

An old joke comes to mind, and I grin. "Not *all* my life, Dad. I'm not dead yet!"

Julian groans.

Day Mom comes close to rolling her eyes, but instead follows her turning eyes and walks across to speak with a doctor.

Dad laughs. "I think more than anything else, the Terran sense of humor drew me to the Simulation. Humans fought a war that lasted over three centuries, but never lost their sense of humor. It's an amazing testament to your people."

The actual history of my people is still strange and new to me. I decide to file it with my feelings about the actual date and all the other crap I'm putting off processing.

Instead, I ask, "Where's Gabby?"

"She and Carmen went to make an updated map of the nearby ruins."

Despite the newness of the keeper, my eyes automatically slide over to the control tabs as though I've been using it for years. Focusing on a tab activates it. I bring up a global map of Vega and it highlights my current position. I zoom in.

"Baton Vert, which means 'green stick.' That's the closest outpost to us."

Dad tilts his head. "You had that in your keeper?"

"Not until I ran the Vega update."

"Very nice!"

A voice behind us asks, "Sir?"

We turn to find the medical staff looking at us. "When you're ready, we can begin."

Looking to Dad, I ask, "Should we wait for Gabby?"

He smiles kindly and gives my shoulder a little squeeze. "I suspect she left specifically so she *wouldn't* know when the operation began and thus wouldn't worry about you as much."

"Oh. Okay." I sit on the cupped table. At the doctor's gesture, I lay back.

Kabbix holds the mask over my face, but doesn't put it all the way down. "We're going to send you into a much deeper sleep than before. Implant surgeries can be tricky things, and none of us care to be flash-fried or frozen by a psychokinetic event."

"But for the other surgery, it felt like no time had passed. Do you really need deeper than that?"

She winks and puts the mask over my face.

Chapter 15

Ethan Shaw Version 2.01

I wake up as the first rays of sunlight color the walls of my small, temporary shelter with a dim yellow glow. Oddly enough, the shelter is actually more of a glorified tent than the medical tent. Granted, a tent with plumbing, but still a tent. Out of habit, I check my keeper.

5:47.

Yes, this definitely qualifies as tragically early. But I need less sleep since we've begun working out, and I've gotten into the habit of extensively practicing my psychic abilities.

That seems backwards, but it's true.

Today makes four weeks since I awoke from my frame implantation surgery. It already feels like I've had the frame all my life. Maybe that's because of the dreams/memories. Speaking of which, the mental barrier's all but gone. I suspect I've been having more of the memory dreams because of this. They're clearer and much easier to remember. Most of them are good. Spending time with my family and friends. Training with other humans. In those memories, my telepathy is good. Communications with other people are clear, and I can chat with folks hundreds of kilometers away.

Today... yeah, not so much. Everything's distorted and difficult, and I'm still picking up a big zero from my parents. But then again, my friends are all aliens, and my parents are cybernetic organisms. I suppose I can forgive myself for not immediately understanding how alien minds work.

My little smile from thinking about the people I love fades as my thoughts turn to those other dreams. The bad ones.

Yeah. Some of those are *truly* terrible.

In one, I was on a cruiser that got shot down, and spent several days trapped in the wreckage with an arm-sized support strut through my thigh. In that memory, the floor sat at maybe a thirty-degree angle. I ended up trapped in a space small enough that laid out on the floor as I was, I could reach up and touch the ceiling. Not all the people in the area with me survived.

Yeah, that was a whole lotta not-fun.

In another, I was flying in via a jetpack with my defense group to help repel an attack. A ginormous tenebrosi stepped out from behind a parking garage and swatted one of my friends through a building wall, much like I'd swat a fly. One moment my friend was alive, the next....

Last night, I dreamed of sitting at home with my parents and sisters. We'd made sundaes and were teasing one another in between bites of frosty deliciousness.

If I remember dream-me dreaming, will I know it's just a dream? Or, will it seem as real as the memory dreams?

Pondering this gets me exactly nowhere.

Time to move.

After taking care of morning necessities, I step outside. The grass is wet from dew and the air's crisp and cool. The faint scent of some sort of flower lingers in the air. It's a good morning for a quick run before we start our morning martial arts class. Day Mom will teach Aikido again this morning and I'm really looking forward to it.

I feel Gabby switch from sluggish, almost-dreaming thoughts into wakefulness. Though not easy by any means, Gabs' thoughts and feels come easiest to me.

Maybe because we have a romantic bond tying us ever closer together, but it could just be my imagination.

We share a moment of mutual awareness and intent.

I stretch as she dresses.

A couple of minutes later, she's out the door. Her hair almost reaches her shoulders now with the black roots slowly pushing away the blue tips. Together, we run towards the distant forest. We're not racing this morning, more jogging than anything.

As we reach the forest, we turn down the same game trail we've been using since shortly after my surgery. The trees are tall, but they're just large trees. They haven't grown to match the animals. A black-striped squirrel chitters at us as we pass beneath it. Including its tail, the thing is probably a meter long, and I'd guess it masses ten kilos.

If we ever ran low on food stores....

"Eww!" Gabby says, having picked up my thought. "They're too pretty to eat."

"When you're hungry, there's no such thing as 'too pretty.'"

"*Pfft!*" She darts at me, and I leap up and kick off a tree to avoid the push she was going for. "Dammit. No fair reading my mind!"

"If it keeps me out of the brambles, it's plenty fair."

We share grins, then run.

This morning, we're heading toward Baton Vert. The ruins are relatively small for a human city, only spreading a bit over a kilometer from the center of town.

With a couple of kilometers to go before reaching the outskirts, Gabby skids to a halt.

Surprised, I jump up and land sideways on a tree to kill my momentum before springing over to join her. "What's up?"

She lifts her chin. "I saw a glint of water that way."

"Water? Let's check it out."

We're off again. Our pace decreases as we leap bramble patches and fallen logs.

Gabby throws me a scowl. "It vexes me greatly that you're slowing down to keep from leaving me behind."

"Wouldn't be nearly as much fun without you." I grin hugely and add, "Even if you *are* the slowest metamorph on the planet."

With an inarticulate yell, she's after me.

By the time we've crossed maybe half a kilometer, she's back to enjoying our chase and feeling less inclined to murder me. I'm especially fond of that latter part.

The water she saw turns out to be a pond.

"Very scenic," I note. With a little stream coming in one side and another exiting, it creates a burbling sound that's delightfully relaxing. The water's clear with a few small fish. Unlike most of the animals on the planet, they evidently failed to get the notice that they're supposed to grow ridiculously large.

I look to Gabby. "Your people are at least partly aquatic, aren't they?"

She nods and walks to the edge of the water. Reaching out a hand, she takes a drink. "This is good. We might have to come swim."

"Sounds good to me. I enjoy swimming."

Surprise crosses her face. "You do?"

"Sure. Always have."

She frowns, her expression somewhere between consternation and confusion. "But you almost *never* went swimming back on Thompson."

I shrug. "Guess I'm not a big fan of small, rectangular swimming pools filled with chlorinated water."

Gabby springs into my arms and I catch her automatically. "To be honest, I'm not either." She nods to the side. "*This* is the sort of water I prefer." She turns a bright smile on me. "Did you know, I love you?"

"Yeah," I reply, looking into her lovely brown eyes. "It kind started sinking in when you said you wanted to marry me."

"Oh, I didn't say I *wanted* to marry you," she replies, her clever grin appearing. "I said I was *going* to marry you."

"So, you don't *want* to marry me?"

"Of course, I do. Don't be silly. I just didn't say that."

"Yes, you did," I say with a grin of my own. "Just now."

"You talk too much," she says, before kissing me.

"Mmm," I agree, kissing her back.

Keeping her arms around me, Gabby leans her head back. She turns her eyes to the water and thinks about getting naked and swimming. About us both being naked and swimming until we're not swimming anymore but doing something much more intimate. However, we've only been boyfriend and girlfriend for a month, and she wants to have a truly solid relationship behind us before we move to the next stage.

That was an unusually clear thought stream. It feels like I'm making progress on the telepathy front. Hmm. Maybe it's more a "we" thing than a "me" thing.

And, as much as I like her idea about special aquatic activities, our lives are complicated enough without throwing a major change in our relationship into the mix. "Let's check out a new part of Baton Vert."

After kissing me again, she hops down out of my arms. "I'll race you."

"I'll gave you a maybe thirty-second head start."

Eyeing me askance, Gabby asks, "Maybe thirty-second?"

I shrug and my grin twists. "Maybe twenty-five seconds. Maybe twenty-four...."

She takes off sprinting, and I jog after her.

"You said twenty-four seconds!"

Silently, I reply, "*I said* maybe *twenty-four.*"

Broadcasting her thoughts, Gabby calls me several inventively rude things, but she's not really angry. She kinda likes me chasing her.

This is convenient coz I kinda like chasing her.

As we reach the outskirts of the ruins, Gabby exits the forest at a sprint and almost crashes into a grey and brown-furred dire wolf. Startled, the huge beast yips and springs aside while Gabby skids to a halt. Not three meters from her is a partially eaten deer the size of a horse—which makes it a bit smaller than the wolf.

Gabby and the wolf stare at each other.

I reach the edge of the woods and stop. There's just the one wolf here, but we've seen signs of a large pack in the area. So far, the massive beasts have ignored us—probably because they don't recognize us as being either a danger or prey.

"He's beautiful," she says, taking a couple of slow steps toward the wolf.

"She," I reply automatically. "Umm, sweetheart, why don't you join me over here?"

"Because you're not split into pieces? Also, I have a splendid view of this amazing, majestic animal right here."

I wish my psychic skills were more advanced. So far, I've made good progress, but despite that, I'm still not ready for the first boost. Using my telekinesis, I'm good at augmenting my movement and doing complex work with small items. I can weave intricate orbital patterns using two-dozen little things. Pebbles. Sticks. That sort of thing. But the raw power from my dream life... it's just not here. I hope there's a 'yet' out there somewhere that goes with this. Eyeing the monstrous wolf so close to the woman I love, I *really* wish I had that kind of power.

If wishes were horse-sized wolves....

Still, I'm not super worried, right? When the scientists grew me from the DNA of my long-dead former self, they realized I'd been genetically modified—just like every human they'd ever found remnants of. Fortunately for me, the science people had no clue what truly belonged and what got added as modifications. Thus, when I was born, I came into the world already genetically augmented.

I'm not sure how strong humans used to be, but I'm pretty sure I can pick up and throw the wolf if it comes to that.

Or punch through its skull.

"That's *sooo* gross," Gabby says softly, apparently listening in on my worried musings since I've gotten into the habit of keeping my psychic walls lowered around her.

She rather unnecessarily adds, "Definitely listening in."

A distant twig breaking combines with a tiny ping on my telepathic radar. Looking into the woods, I spot another wolf. This one is *not* standing around indulging its curiosity. No, this one is stalking us. At a flick of my eyes, my keeper outlines it in enemy red and begins automatically tracking it.

"Gabs," I say as I walk out into the field a little away from her and the first wolf to keep from upsetting the beast, "time to go."

"But I don't—" She follows my thoughts and turns to the other wolf. "Oh."

Gabby sighs and eases away from her wolf, never turning her back to the woods. "She's so cool."

"Don't get me wrong," I say, scanning the tree line for more dire wolves. "I'm perfectly fine with her... so long as she doesn't rip your arm off and eat it."

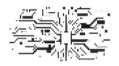

Like pretty much all human cities, Baton Vert is so much rubble. But, as we discovered on Thompson, not all rubble is equal.

Gabby picks up a stainless-steel metal mug with the arcane phrase 'OMG WITF!' engraved in the side and stares at it in wonder. "Fifty-thousand years old and still intact. It's amazing."

"Yeah," I agree, kicking a chunk of ceracrete aside and finding nothing of interest beneath it. "We had to build everything to last. So, most items like this came with a built-in, self-replicating nano repair pack. Thanks to asteroid mining, we didn't have a shortage of resources, but we had a shortage of production capabilities. Thus, anything worthy of making, we built to last. Corollary to that, there's a rather nebulous line between having too many robots doing your manufacturing and keeping enough people to manage them. I don't know if we ever crossed that line, but a lot of people worried about how close we were to it."

Gabby nods, her expression souring. "I don't know if you're aware of this, but there's a serious shortage of jobs across the galaxy. We've automated so much that on many worlds, people are almost... redundant. So, I guess we have our own nebulous line in the here and now. When everyone's an artist or entertainer—because those are creative jobs machines just don't do so well—you saturate the need for art. Art fades to decoration, which fades into the commonplace, which you don't even notice."

Her expression turns sad. "When art fails to inspire, is it still art?"

I consider this and eventually shake my head. "Good question. I don't know. But," I say as I pick a blue flower and hand it to her, "beauty is still beauty."

Gabby doesn't reply, or even smile, but she tucks the flower into her hair.

We pass a few scrubby trees growing up from the rubble. Memories stir. "I think Earth was like what you were saying. Important jobs were few and far between, but there were a lot of... busy-work type jobs. Then we started exploring other worlds, and things got better for a while. Eventually, we started moving back towards mass unemployment."

"What was your people's solution?"

"War—though it wasn't really something we chose. The tenebrosi attacked. Then they attacked again and again, and we realized we had to get off our collective arses if we didn't want to fade into extinction." Suddenly uncomfortable, I swallow with difficulty and start towards the next pile of rubble that might hold something of interest.

Gabby plants herself in my path. As I stop, she wraps her arms around me while deluging my mind with love.

"You're not extinct," she whispers. "Not anymore. And you're definitely not alone."

Holding her, a tension I haven't even realized is in my shoulders relaxes. "Love you, too."

She winks at me and tugs my hand as she walks again. "I know. Now, let's explore a little more before we go back."

"That sounds... good." I follow her a few steps, then stop and try to figure out what I'm hearing. "Speaking of sounds, do you hear that?"

"Hmm? I guess not?"

"It's almost a moaning sound. It's coming from that way." I take a right turn into the rubble and hop across roughly twenty meters worth of ancient debris.

The sound's a little louder.

"I can kinda hear it through you," Gabby says, tapping her head as she catches up, "but I'm not picking it up with my ears. What do you think it is?"

Rather than reply, I try to zero in on the sound. Searching for the next several minutes over a fifty-meter-wide area, I'm no closer to finding the elusive source.

"Could it be a... ghost?" she asks, attempting to be spooky.

Via my keeper, I bring up an overlay of Baton Vert. "This was the site of a logistics center and a major supply depot. They...."

"They what?"

"They transported goods all over the planet."

She throws me a skeptical look highlighted by her artfully raised eyebrow. "And how is that usefully different or interesting?"

"Because Vega had a *huge* underground transportation network."

Gabby looks down at the rubble beneath our feet. "Oh! Where's the entrance?"

"About ten meters straight down."

An eager grin spreads across her face. "We're gonna need explosives."

"Explosives. Lord, I love you so much. Yes, we'll need explosives. The bigger, the better."

Chapter 16

Elevator Down

"N o," Dad says. "You can*not* have explosives."

Day Mom throws him a look he can't see because he's facing me. "At least not until you've been trained to use them."

Dad turns and frowns at her.

"This could be an important archaeological find," she explains. "Also, knowing how to properly use explosives would be an excellent skill for him to learn. Especially when most of the galaxy considers our son a weapon of war rather than a person."

Still frowning, Dad reluctantly nods. He turns back to me, and his frown increases as his gaze falls on the pistol on my hip. "Why?"

"One of the wolves showed a bit too much interest in Gabby."

Voice dreamy, Gabby says, "She was *sooo* beautiful!"

"She was pretty," I confirm. "So was the one sneaking up on us. How-some-ever, beauty doesn't equate to trust."

Day Mom nods. "Better safe than sorry."

Gabby throws her a little moue.

"Sorry, hon," Mom says. "But, until we have a replacement Gabby on hand, we're just gonna have to make sure you stay alive and well."

Gabby's lips twist into a wry something that's almost but not quite a smile.

"Hard for you to marry me if you're dead."

Gabby cuts her eyes to me. *"Yeah, you marrying my corpse would be gross and disturbing."*

I snort a little laugh, and she bumps her shoulder into my arm.

Day Mom pulls a holographic projector out of her pocket and unfolds it. "Alright, there are a lot of different explosives that are commonly available. We'll start with the basics...."

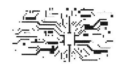

The next day, the lot of us get up early.

Together, we make our way to Baton Vert.

Day Mom and Dad also hear the whistling noise, but they're the only ones. We move what rubble we can, but there's a reason ceracrete's lasted so long—it's incredibly tough. Three meters down we uncover slabs too heavy to move.

Captain Strange Noise's ship doesn't have a lot of explosives to choose from. Worse, his chemical fabers have built-in restrictions that prevent us from making anything really good—at least without someone sneaking in and doing some creative re-programming.

Instead, we're gonna test some mining explosives.

While preparing our charges, I look over at Julian. He returns a pleased look and nods like we're the coolest people in the galaxy.

Egomaniacal though it may be, it's an idea that's hard to argue.

More for Dad's sake than ours, Day Mom reiterates the safety instructions for the third time in the last fifteen minutes as Gabby finishes prepping her explosive.

There's not that much to them. Each charge is a brick about the size of a shoe—one of Gabby's, not mine. The detonators these came with are all made for remote triggering, and we've already pre-set the frequency. Now, all we need to do is place the charges and turn off the safety—which actually just activates the built-in receiver.

Gabby, Julian, and I each set a mining charge. Our charges vaguely form a triangle that's about a meter wide. We're basically trying to blast out an access hole to the transit shaft.

All of us move back.

Dad may be a little over-protective about how far back we go, but since we got to plant explosive charges, nobody's complaining.

Embry holds the detonator and flips open the cover.

Carmen daintily presses the button.

Thump!

The ground shakes. A few chunks of debris fly in the distance.

Once Dad's sure the last of the rubble has fallen, he waves the all clear. We head around to see what we've accomplished.

"Nice hole. But now we have more rubble to clear," Julian grumbles.

"Hey," Gabby says, kneeling beside the hole, "quiet! I think I can hear the sound Ethan heard."

It is louder, but it wasn't exactly noisy to start with.

Embry nods. "Yeah, it's wind."

"Exactly," Day Mom says. "Now, since our goal is to clear out what's essentially a large vertical shaft, time for more protective gear. We're going to go print harnesses and rope."

Carmen frowns. "Why not just get some flying gear?"

Day Mom smiles gently. "Because, if you fall into a hole and hit your head on the way down, you might not be conscious to activate your flying gear before you splatter across the bottom of the hole."

Carmen's already large eyes grow wider, and the maroon portion of her complexion pales a few shades. "Oh. Uh, yes. That's very well-reasoned."

"Why thank you, dear."

After picking up the safety gear from the ship, we each tie off to heavy sections of debris. Then, it's back to clearing rubble. As I'm lifting a piece of ceracrete about my size, one of the crystalline pieces breaks off and drops to the rubble. Instead of a thunk, there's a ching.

Oh no.

"What?" Gabby asks, hurrying back from dropping off a piece of debris.

"That... didn't sound right," Julian says slowly, squatting near the top edge of the hole we've been enlarging.

I toss my ceracrete piece aside and drop to the bottom of our hole. Using my gloved hand, I brush aside dust and small bits of debris.

"That looks metallic," Carmen says. Realizing what this means, she starts to curse, cuts her eyes towards my approaching parents, and groans.

Julian leans forward. "*Is* that what I think it is?"

"Ceramalloy," I confirm as my parents join us, rapping my knuckles against the metallized ceramic. "It's a *lot* harder to get through than ceracrete and it's blocking access to the shaft."

Dad and Day Mom kneel at the top of the hole. "So?" he asks. "What's our next move?"

For some reason, I have the impression that my parents are testing me.

I leap out of our hole, then take a minute to look around the area. While there's rubble everywhere, it's not a uniform covering. Some areas are piled high, while others have only a thin covering.

"Digging down to find the edge of the ceramalloy would take weeks. It'd be quicker if we used the remaining explosives, but then if we need them to clear some other blockage, we'd be out of luck."

Dad nods.

"Can we get some sort of scanner from the ship?"

Day Mom smiles.

Sweet. Test passed.

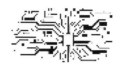

Using the scanner, we create a six-meter deep, three-dimensional map of the debris beneath us. Some of it is actual ship wreckage versus city rubble. That's where the ceramalloy came from.

After overlaying the scans on the map, we form a new plan.

Twenty minutes later, we're digging again, this time fifteen meters to the west. Here, we'll only have a little ceracrete in the way before we reach the edge of the ceramalloy. Once we expose the edge, we'll burrow a horizontal shaft under it to the transport shaft. The scanner doesn't have the range to tell us if the shaft's clear. If it is, we'll get a chance to play with some personal flying gear. If not, we'll see what options we have for clearing the rubble.

Day Mom and Dad frown at the same time.

"What?" I ask.

"The ship's communication buoy is throwing out error conditions," Dad says. "Captain Strange Noise has dropped off our flying gear and is asking what other supplies we'll need while they're fixing the buoy."

Embry asks, "The buoy's having technical problems? What sort of problems?"

Day Mom turns up her hands in a shrug, then looks to the rest of us. "We've got about a week's worth of rations. Water won't be a problem."

"Night vision gear," Julian says. "Last time we were underground, I couldn't see until you pulled out that light. I'd *really* rather not do that again. *Ever.*"

Day Mom looks to Embry and Carmen.

She says, "I don't think the ability to see heat is gonna be particularly helpful down there. We'll both need some sort of night-vision gear, too."

Embry nods.

"Relaying the request now," Dad says. "Okay, anything else?"

Gabby snaps her fingers. "Comm relays. If we're far enough underground or have to move through debris-filled areas, we might need to chain together relays to maintain communications with the surface."

Dad smiles. "Smart girl. Anything else?" He looks around, but no one says anything. "Okay. Once the ship's dropped off our supplies, they'll leave to fix the buoy."

Day Mom pats my shoulder and gives me a too-sweet smile. "Your father and I will retrieve the gear. *You* best get back to shoveling."

I turn a sour look on her. "Thanks *sooo* much, Mom."

She winks. "Back in about an hour."

Picking up a heavy pry bar, I look to Carmen and Embry. "You guys can see into the infrared spectrum?"

Carmen nods, and Embry flares open his nostril flaps. "Coolness."

They shrug at the same time.

We dig.

Over the last month, Julian has exchanged a lot of padding for muscle. While he doesn't care for running as much as the rest of us, he enjoys anything akin to weightlifting. Clearing the heavier chunks of debris is *exactly* like weightlifting. As of last week, he's edged past Gabby as our group's second strongest. Meanwhile, Carmen and Embry exchange verbal math quizzes while carrying buckets of dirt and small debris. I strongly suspect Julian could do that too, but he's too busy reveling in his newfound physicality.

"We should make the pit wider," Embry suggests. "Maybe a little deeper, too."

Julian waves around himself. "Feel free."

Carmen frowns at him, but neither jumps into the discussion nor starts digging.

A few minutes later, a distant roar reaches us. Exiting our pit, we watch the ship lift into the sky then vanish into the distance.

We resume digging and excavating.

Day Mom and Dad return, but Mom's expression says she's worried about something.

As I drop off another chunk of ceracrete, I quietly ask, "What's wrong?"

"While we were getting the supplies, Captain Strange Noise mentioned something... disturbing."

"What?"

Her lips compress, and for a moment I'm not sure she's going to answer. A little moue covers one corner of her lips before she finally says, "Remember the message from Life Keeper Command that sent us here?"

"Sure. What about it?"

"Life Keeper Command didn't send it."

"Oh." I look back towards where the ship was parked. "In that case, why aren't we running?"

"Captain Strange Noise sent a message to Life Keeper Command asking for reinforcements. The captain is hoping to find out who sent the message. The first step to knowing the enemy is basic identification."

I give her a skeptical look. "But they're still going to investigate? Before the reinforcements arrive? I assume they're expecting an ambush?"

"They are." She glances past my shoulder where my friends are still moving rubble. "I don't think we should tell the others. Not until we know more."

"Why not?"

"If there's not actually a threat, it will needlessly worry them. If there is a threat, there's nothing they can do anyway, so the worry would be a waste of energy and a needless hit to morale."

I'm not so sure she's right, but I'm positive I would have argued against the captain's plan—if someone had asked me.

Since no one did, I reluctantly nod my understanding, if not my agreement.

Mom and I rejoin the digging "fun."

A couple of hours later, we expose the edge of the ceramalloy and break for lunch. Day Mom and Dad extend our break with a lesson on the history of the post-human galaxy. It involves a lot of "this species found that species and invented these ships." That sort of thing. While it's interesting, especially since my parents can directly interact with their little holographic projectors, it's also hard to memorize.

"*I think,*" Gabby silently begins, "*you might need a more interactive history of the galaxy. You seem to do much better with experiential lessons than rote.*"

Day by day, it's getting easier, more natural, to communicate with Gabs telepathically. I like it, as it comes with a certain... intimacy, that's greatly appealing. It's almost like we have our own private communications network.

"*How do you get an interactive history lesson?*"

"*They're called entertainment vids. Except these vids show what actually happened back when. There's a whole segment of the entertainment industry that only does educational history. Well, you know... with a little drama thrown in for good measure. You can also pause the story and ask the characters questions.*"

"*Nifty. Sounds like my kind of history. Think we could get some popcorn?*"

Gabby smiles and winks.

We dig. Eventually, we're deep enough to start our tunnel. Now it isn't just digging, we're also reinforcing the sides of our horizontal shaft. Having a massive, fifteen-centimeter-thick sheet of ceramalloy collapse on you would ruin anyone's day.

As we work our way through the rubble, I practice my telekinesis by pulling out smaller pieces and floating them into buckets. We've tied the buckets to ropes that my parents, Carmen and Embry lift out and empty. An hour later, I decide my endurance is getting better as I float a twenty-kilo chunk over for Julian to throw out. That starts a little stress headache, but it's not too bad.

Before sunset, we return to camp.

Before sunrise, we're on the way to dig.

Just before lunch, Julian and I are rocking a sizeable chunk of ceracrete back and forth trying to wriggle the thing out. It suddenly breaks free with a clatter of falling rubble and a blast of cool air. This leaves Julian struggling with most of the ceracrete's weight. I hurry over and take it from him.

Shrugging his large shoulders and trying not to wince, he says, "You know, I had that."

Holding it out with both arms is a strain, but I manage it. "Want it back?"

"No," he says, taking a step back. "Since you're intent on showing me up with your physical might, I'll just have to content myself with being the smart, handsome one."

I give him a serious nod. "We each have our burdens to bear."

"So very true." Julian walks ahead of me out from under the edge of the ceramalloy plate to the ramp we've dug for carrying the bulk stuff like this out. "Hey guys, I think we've breached the shaft."

"Finally," Carmen mutters.

While I carry the ceracrete out of the way, the others flood down with the scanner.

By the time I return, they're all smiles.

Day Mom meets my eyes. "Time for flying lessons."

CHAPTER 17

TOURING THE UNDERWORLD

"Flying in the shaft will be different than flying around the field," Dad cautions as we cinch the thrusters to our lower legs the following morning. "Do *not* fly directly over someone unless you want to set their head on fire. Within two meters, this can be deadly, so as we're descending the shaft, be sure to give each other *plenty* of room."

The others look worried, but it's not the flying that's got them on edge.

As a grin spreads across my lips, I say, "Be especially careful around the metamorph. I like her hot, but not crispy fried."

Gabby throws me a look. "That's kind of sweet, but at the same time, I still wanna hit you."

Carmen stage whispers, "Beware the violent metamorph."

Julian straps his directional thrusters on his long forearms. "Yeah, metamorphs go crazy, shift to mimic us, then kill us and take over our lives. Happens all the time." There're deep undertones of fear that he's hiding well. Focusing on this distraction is a large part of how he's handling it.

"It does not!" Gabby snaps. "That's a bunch of vid garbage! We are the most peace-loving people who ever kicked your ass!"

Hands up, Julian backs away in faux terror.

Dad is not amused.

"Dad," I whisper. "We get it. We're just blowing off a little tension. They're looking forward to more flying. They're *not* looking forward to dropping into a dark hole into the unknown.

None of them are. I'm the only one excited about this. But they're still willing to go, because they're awesome friends."

Dad's expression turns considering. He nods and adjusts the straps on my directional thrusters. To the group, he loudly asks, "Any questions?"

Shaking her head, Carmen stands up from where she was covering Embry's eyes to save him from witnessing Julian's gory demise at the hands of the violent metamorph. The others walk over to join us, though Julian wisely keeps someone between himself and Gabby.

As the others enter the tunnel, I step over to him. "You okay?" I whisper.

"Terrified," he replies just as quietly. "But I'm gonna overcome this."

I give his shoulder a squeeze. "It takes a brave soul to face your fears. And once you do, that's something no one can ever take from you. You're awesome, buddy. Never let anyone tell you otherwise."

He pats my shoulder, then with a forced little grin gives me a gentle push forward.

When I catch up with the others, Day Mom says, "I'll go first with the comm relays. Ethan, you'll follow me."

At my eager grin, she leaps into the vertical shaft. I hurry to the edge. Far below, she fires her thrusters, slowing her descent.

Gabby hurries over and gives me a hard kiss.

I kiss her back, wink, and backflip over the edge.

Free-falling is a farkin' amazing adrenaline rush. Unfortunately, I have to cut it short by firing my thrusters. On my keeper, my falling speed slows until I match Day Mom's velocity.

"There's an obstruction below," Day Mom says through my keeper. "Four-hundred meters." She continues counting off fifty-meter increments until she's there. "Cutting thrusters, now."

"Should I stay up here?"

"No, come on down. Just try not to set my hair on fire."

"Yes, ma'am." I drop to within ten meters of her and cut off the thrusters. I land beside her with a thump.

Day Mom scowls. "That was a rather long drop."

"I love you and prefer you unscorched. Also, ten meters is no big deal."

Well, it isn't a big deal *now*. A couple of years ago... different story.

Together, we pick up several ceracrete slabs and lean them against the side of the tunnel. Beneath the mess, we find a roundish framework.

"It's a transit pod," I say, brushing away a thick layer of dust and grime. "You can look through this window into the pod. As far as I can tell, it looks normal. I think the pod itself is the actual obstruction."

Day Mom nods. "The pod's specifications are pretty simple. I suggest we start with the manual brake release. See if that allows it to drop out of the way."

I can't get to either of the doors, but the rear window's right here. The falling ceracrete barely scarred it. Using my telekinesis, I trigger the emergency release from the inside and set the window panel off to the side.

Day Mom drops inside. The interior isn't lined up with the outside windows. Instead, gravity's leveled it out, just like it's supposed to. Mom begins pulling up flooring.

"Mom, what happens if pulling the release works?"

"Well, the pod should drop."

"Right...."

"Are you suggesting it might trap me in the pod?"

I glance over at the ceracrete slabs we'd just moved.

If they drop onto us....

"Yeah, that's part of what I'm getting at. The pod should protect you from falling debris, but let's put the window back. Just to be sure."

"In that case, come down and join me."

"Okay." I grab the window and float it over while I climb down into the pod. I reset the window and latch it back in. With a little sigh, I sit down and lean back in the dusty seat, rubbing my hand over the smooth, cool material. "Been a long time since I've sat... in one of... these."

While I'm busy wallowing in the extreme weirdness of that, Day Mom stops messing with the flooring to hug me tight.

With a last squeeze, she returns to the flooring.

After a couple of minutes, she opens up a panel and looks up at me.

"I've updated your father on our situation. He'll be following us. Ready?"

I realize something. "Wait. Since when can you and Dad silently communicate? Back home, you two and Night Mom communicated with that bizarre buzzing noise. What changed?"

"Back on the ship, we upgraded our communications modules. The new modules are more efficient and have improved encryption. Signals from these units are harder to intercept."

"Oh. Why didn't you say something?"

She gives a little shrug. "I guess I didn't think you'd want to hear about it."

"Of course, I wanna hear about it. You're my family."

"Okay," Day Mom replies quietly with a pleased smile. She glances at the brake release, then turns back to me. "Ready?"

I grab the edge of my seat in one hand, and the back of her belt in the other. "Ready."

She pulls a lever. Clang!

We drop and I pull Mom into the seat beside me.

Without power, the pod continues to keep the interior level, just without any of the readouts. We're dropping fast.

Thing is, without power, there's nothing slowing us down.

We gain speed until we hit terminal velocity. I'm not a big fan of the 'terminal' part of that phrase.

We drop vertically for maybe forty-five seconds before the tunnel starts sloping. Those ceracrete chunks we'd set aside slam into the upper back of the pod, startling the snot out of me. Even Mom jumps. The outside of the pod rolls, which is bizarre because it's not supposed to do that. It's supposed to float just above the tunnel floor. But, without power, I guess it works however it works. Despite slowly flattening, our angle of descent is still steep and we're moving fast.

The front and back windows are scrolling around so fast I'm getting almost a stop-motion view of what's ahead. Unfortunately, the tunnel is no longer empty. Ahead, my keeper's highlighted a two-meter-long slab of ceracrete in the way. Musta fallen from the ceiling. Problem is, it's on edge in the middle of the tunnel and we're racing towards it in a pod without breaks.

Lashing out with my telekinesis, I hammer the debris, striking it at a 45-degree angle. It cracks and tilts as pain lances through my head. Just before we reach it, I smash it again. There's a clang.

The pod bounces but keeps rolling.

My head hurts so much I can barely move or see.

Day Mom pulls me to her and holds me tight.

Slowly, the agony fades. "Mom," I barely manage to whisper, "we've gotta watch for more debris."

"No sense in it."

"Huh? Why?" I ask, trying to focus on her face.

"I'm just going to hold us braced against the seats. They're cushioned and will offer the best protection in case of impact."

"Mom, I could...." But I can't finish the sentence.

"No, honey," she says gently. "You can't. What you did was impressive, but you pushed yourself too hard. You'll need time to recover. I'd guess a few days—at the *very* least. Maybe more."

I wish I could argue, but I don't have the strength.

Fifteen minutes later, the pod finally rolls to a stop. Those chunks of ceracrete that followed us slide by as their momentum plays out.

"Can you stand?" Day Mom asks.

"Let's find out."

Turns out that with her help, I *can* stand. My head has gone from agony, to hurting, to aching. Day Mom tries the manual door release. It doesn't open. After twisting around in the seat, she gives it a kick.

The door pops open.

We climb out, absently wiping dust off ourselves. While this tunnel continues on, more tunnels merge here. There're footpaths and such ahead to the right.

I say, "Looks like we're in the edge of a transit hub."

As we walk towards the pedestrian way, lights begin coming on.

Day Mom and I stop and stare.

"Amazing," she says. "After fifty-thousand years and a devastating planetary attack, the lights still work. Simply amazing."

I nod and wince as the movement sends a fresh stab of pain behind my eyes. "Yeah," I mumble. "Amazing."

She pats my arm. "What's your map showing?"

"Good question." I bring up my planetary map, and zero in on our position. "This is a relay station. There should be a few shops and temporary housing." I point to a distant tunnel. "That way."

"Let's go. The others are descending. They'll join us shortly."

Once we pass all the transit lines, gently curving ramps lead up and down.

"Let's take the down ramp," Day Mom says. "Easier on you."

"No argument from me."

The ramp takes us down a level. To the left are more transit lines. To the right, there're several stores. A few holographic ads flicker to life. We walk that way, looking through the shop windows as we go. The first place is a convenience store with stuff for travelers: toiletries, meal bars, first aid materials, and such.

"Fifty-thousand-year-old meal bars. No thanks."

Day Mom throws me a twisted grin.

Next is an electronic boutique with hand terminals, datapads, cables, etc. A screen in that shop catches my eye.

"What?" Day Mom asks.

I point. "That."

"Isn't it just a touchscreen computer?"

"*Nooo*," I say slowly. "I don't think so."

"What is it?"

"I'm not sure, but I think we need it. There's something... I'm not sure. Whatever it is, it's not quite coming to me."

Day Mom walks around, grabs the screen, and brings it out.

"You're just like Diana from 'Ruins Raiders,' Mom."

Her heroic pose makes me laugh, which is only a little painful. "Come on," she says, taking my arm. "Let's keep exploring."

By the time the others catch up, we've gone through another eight stores. I'm now wearing a kick set of wraparound eye-gear which makes the dark places a little brighter, and the light places a little darker. I've also picked up a new bag which contains extra eyewear, an armored, variable temperature drink bottle, a few dozen varied entertainment clips, three sets of haptic gloves—just in case I need to remotely control something or one of the games calls for them, and an advanced bio-monitor which will have to be surgically installed later.

"Well," I say by way of greeting my friends and Dad, "I see no one's hair got burned off."

Julian nods as he slicks back what's turning into something of a dark-orange mane. "Yeah, that was a nice bonus to go with surviving. And now this! Intact human ruins. By the way, nice shades."

I make a face. In fake-2021 shades are eyewear. In my dreams, shades are slang for monsters.

When the other's attention focuses elsewhere, I catch one of Julian's eyes and mouth, "You okay?"

He gives me two thumbs up from one hand.

Yep, my friends are delightfully weird.

Carmen waves her arms all around. "Are they actually ruins if they're intact?"

Turning to Carmen, I give her a quick shrug via facial expression, then look back to Julian. "I like my shades. I'd offer you a pair, but I don't think they'd fit."

"And I'm good with that. Thank the Powers that I'm out of that uncomfortable meat suit."

"Yeah, that reminds me. How did your nose get bigger?"

"It's actually pretty interesting," he says. "They basically arrested my nasal development when I turned eight. Once I was out of the meat-suit, they removed the block." He feels his nose from top to tip as he crosses his eyes to look at it. "Yeah, it's coming along nicely."

Unsure what to say to that, I hold up the extra pair of glasses and look to Gabby. "What about you?"

She puts her hand to her chin as she looks me over. "Hmm. Your shades look nice, but I hate to cover up these amazing eyes of mine."

Carmen fakes choking and gagging.

I bow to Gabby. "You raise a valid point, sweetheart."

Gabby gently elbows Carmen. "You hear that? My boyfriend loves my eyes." She grins broadly. "What the rest of you peons think is totally irrelevant."

Embry snickers while Julian clutches his chest as though in pain.

"Your boyfriend loves all of you," I tell her. I look around, meeting everyone's eyes and ask, "Now, do we keep exploring? There should be rooms where we can stay the night. Or, is it time to go back?"

Dad holds up a hand for silence. "I hear something."

Everyone freezes.

I hear it, too. "Someone or something is running towards us. Sounds heavy."

A few moments pass and Julian cusses.

Following his gaze, I see it. An armored defense bot is racing this way. It's heavily armed.

All four of its weapons pods are pointing right at us.

Chapter 18

Sideswiped by the Unexpected

Ten meters away, the charging robot stops with an abruptness that would have severely injured any of us biologicals.

"It's scanning us," Dad whispers.

Hands shaking and ears twitching wildly, Carmen asks, "Wh... what do we do?"

"Nothing," Day Mom says. "Those weapons systems are from the final days of the human-tenebrosi war. They're the most destructive weapons for their size that humans ever developed. We can't outrun the robot and we certainly can't outfight it."

The robot's projectors light up, and suddenly there's a holographic person standing before us. He or she is wearing dark-grey robes that cover their hands, feet, and face. "You will follow the defense drone." The voice sounds strangely filtered, like someone's speaking through a purposefully bad digitizer. "Do you understand?"

"Yeah," I say, taking a step forward. "Who are you?"

"We will discuss that and much more." The image winks out.

The robot walks past us.

We all exchange concerned looks before rather reluctantly following it.

"Uh," Julian begins, "do you think there's another living human down here?"

After fifty-thousand years?

I shake my head. "No, I don't think so."

"Then who, or what was that?"

162

My initial reluctance has faded and inverted. "No idea, but I *really* want to find out."

Worry surges out of Gabby.

"You okay?" I silently ask.

"So far. You?"

I take her hand, and we simultaneously give little squeezes.

Three levels down, the robot crosses back to the transit lines. On my keeper, one of the big transit pods turns green.

I stop and stare.

"What?" Gabby demands, feeling my shock.

I point. "That's a working pod. It's marked for us, like it would be if I'd called it."

Again, we exchange glances among us.

Julian asks, "What does this mean for us?"

"I have absolutely no idea," I say, unable to fight down a grin. "Let's find out."

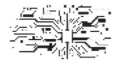

"We're in a functional, human transit pod," Julian says, his voice still tinged with awe ten minutes later as our car zips through the tunnel. "This is amazing!"

Embry looks to me. "This bringing back memories? You feeling alright?"

"I'm fine. Transit pods were everywhere in the old days. There were transit lines on every established world and colony. Not just below ground like these, but also high above, linking buildings and cities together like a massive net. On certain holidays they'd light up the surface lines with different colors. Sometimes, they'd form pictures you could see from orbit."

"Wow," Carmen says quietly, her eyes widening. "Pictures visible from orbit."

I nod, staring off into space. "Yeah, it was a little thing, but important to morale. Keeping that up was a constant struggle."

Gabby squeezes my hand and I lean against her shoulder.

"How are *you* doing?" I ask Embry.

"I'm fine. Why?"

I wave around the pod. "We're not exactly packed in like sardines, but we're pretty close. You normally sit a little farther apart."

He blinks, then grins. "Yeah, it's a cultural thing. Our people like to give others a little more personal space than humans do. I guess I carried that into the Simulation."

Carmen snorts. "Hardly the strangest quirk that got carried into the Simulation."

Gabby laughs. "Remember that time Jaime got halfway through the school day with her tail hanging out from under her skirt?"

As the others laugh, my eyes flick to the robot that's running ahead of our transit pod. I have no dream recollection of a bipedal robot that could maintain these speeds for this long. The basic design of the robot seems familiar, but this level of refinement... not so much.

The distinction between my dreams and alternate memories continues blurring. Is this good or bad?

A glance at the map on my keeper shows we've got a little over twenty minutes before reaching the next transit station. Where we'll go from there... that remains a mystery.

Day Mom hands me the weird touchscreen looking thing. At my questioning look, she says, "I thought you might wanna figure out what it is."

"It's not a computer?" Julian asks.

"I don't think so," I reply absently as I look the thing over. "That said, I'm not really sure—"

The machine powers up.

"Maybe it's touch activated?" Gabby suggests, having sensed my surprise. "Like the door plates."

"Uh, could be."

On the screen are a dozen pictures in three-by-four rows and columns. I give a flick, and it scrolls over to a dozen new pics, then the next. I flip back to the first batch. Okay, it may not be a laptop, but there're definite similarities. Lots of variety to the pictures—people, landscapes, machines, vehicles, and more. Each has a colored border, a caption, and a label. They all have at least two tiny icons along the sides.

Gabby says, "I recognize the weird formatting around the pictures from back when I was doing my initial research on humans. Archaeologists found lots of these devices. Unfortunately, they don't work. You can tap the images all day, but no video ever plays, and the pictures all stay the same. Why humans made them is the point of much pointless debate."

One picture looks more interesting than the others. It shows a cockpit view looking out into space with a blue, brown, and green planet beneath it. There's a dark yellow border around the picture. Below, it's labeled: Tara Houza, TBF-47 Firehawk, P2o5. Below that is the additional label: Training. On the right side is the symbol for female as well as a pistol.

I tap the picture.

"See?" Gabby says, "I told you they don't—"

I'm sitting in the cockpit of my TBF-47, looking down at the Earth.

Keeping my thoughts precise, I run through the flight systems one by one, moving neither fast nor slow. My calm is unshakable as I put the ship through maneuvers. Slowly, I work my way through more and more of the basics. The warmth of a small embarrassment colors my cheeks because I love my job so much and it's bleeding through into the recording, but I forgive myself. Eventually, I land on a huge battle carrier. One by one, I run through post-flight diagnostics then shut the systems down—

And I'm back in the large transit car.

What a cool but weird experience.

During the recording, I'd been female. And apparently a kickass pilot.

Gabby's staring into space, mouth open, her expression stunned, her thoughts a muddled blur.

Everyone's leaning towards us, concerned expressions plastered across their faces.

Julian asks, "Dude. What just happened?"

Gabby's not ready for words yet, so I say, "This isn't a laptop, it's a playback machine for psychic recordings."

"I take it," Carmen begins with a worried glance at Gabby before turning back to me, "that it works?"

"Sure. That was part two of an operational trainer on flying a fighter-bomber. It was pretty darn cool. Um, how long did it take to play?"

"You kinda stared off into space for a... minute? Two?" She looks to Day Mom.

"A minute, thirty-eight seconds."

"That," Carmen confirms. Her eyes turn suspicious. "How long did it feel like it took?"

I shrug. "Maybe two hours? It was kinda hard to tell."

She focuses on Gabby again. "That's some serious time compression. I hope it doesn't break our metamorph."

Since I don't feel any distress from Gabby, I shake my head, but now that Carmen's mentioned it, I can't stop a small thread of worry from poking its head up and looking around.

Embry throws up his hands. "Time compression! *That's* probably why everyone thinks the machines are broken garbage. The psychic recordings play too fast for non-humans. Also, they may not truly activate for anyone other than a human."

"Smart," Julian says to Embry with a nod. "No wonder I keep you around."

"You sure it's not for my ruggedly handsome good looks?"

A huge grin spreads across Julian's slightly oversized mouth. "Hey, it's always nice having a backup for those days when I'm tired of being the good-looking one."

Carmen makes gagging noises, but she throws a concerned glance at Gabby.

Our transit car slows, then stops.

Day Mom stands and walks to the front window. "I don't see the robot."

The car descends.

Day Mom and Dad, both throw me questioning looks.

Why are— Oh, right. I pull up the map on my keeper and zoom in our current location. "Uh, oh."

"What?" Carmen asks a split second before Day Mom can.

"This tunnel is marked as being under construction. In another five minutes, we'll reach the bottom."

Julian turns anxious eyes to me. "Uh, the system controlling the car *knows* where the end of the line is. Right? We're not gonna crash?"

"Yeah, sure. You know... probably."

"I find your lack of certainty disturbing."

I shrug and try not to worry. "Either way, we'll find out soon."

So, we sit and wait, growing increasingly nervous as seconds turn to minutes. At least, those of us who are organic and not stuck in a recorded memory from the far distant past are becoming tense.

Day Mom and Dad just look concerned.

We're coming up fast on the end of the map. A glance out the window confirms that we're not slowing.

I pull Gabby close... just in case.

One-hundred meters.

Fifty meters.

Zero.

"Well," I say, "the good news is that we didn't all die in a massive crash. The bad news is that I have no idea where we're going or what we'll find when we get there."

Carmen dials up the sarcasm in her expression to max. "You don't seem too upset by this *bad* news."

"Fair enough." I rub my thumb across my chin. "To be totally honest, this is the most fun I've had in a long time. The truth about me and my people is strange, but I'm glad I finally know about it. I don't have to pretend to have mediocre hearing. I can exercise to my fullest potential. And my best friends are here with me. What we're doing is exciting and as cool as cool gets. If Night Mom was here, this would be just about my idea of perfect."

Julian gives me a couple of slow nods that make him seem strangely wise. "You are *totally* bat-barf crazy."

"Oh yeah," Carmen agrees with a big nod.

Embry says, "No question."

I do a quick check to see if rolling my eyes is still not my thing. It's not, so I instead give them a big grin. This doesn't seem to change their minds about me being crazy.

I'm okay with that.

My keeper flashes once to show a change. Our downward velocity is decreasing.

"Guys, we're slowing down."

Everyone but Day Mom and Dad glances out the windows, but there's nothing to see, just us moving past the walls of the transit line.

Five minutes later, the walls change from ceracrete to ceramalloy, and our angle of descent shifts slowly off vertical.

"Still slowing," I say.

We're all looking out the front windows. We can't see very far ahead, but as the angle continues to flatten out, we see more and more.

Our pod exits the tunnel and opens into a sizable chamber. An inertia field activates a second before the pod does a hard stop. It's like being encased in jelly, which is less fun than you might think, but it keeps us from splattering against the pod walls.

As quickly as it appeared, the inertia field vanishes.

"What the hells was that?" Julian asks, looking around wildly.

"Inertia field," I reply, my voice distracted even to my own ears. My brain is racing and for much the same reason as Gabby's.

Carmen stares at me. "I've never seen that tech before. Haven't even heard of it."

Julian and Embry nod.

I start to say that they've evidently never found a fully intact human starship before, but I don't. Sometimes, secrets need to stay just that. Maybe I'll tell them after we figure out what's happening.

Or after we figure out why there's a honking massive ship buried so far beneath Vega's surface.

"Yeah," I reply, carrying Gabby over and waving open the door. I step out. The place looks like a small, but otherwise normal transit station. Using ceramalloy instead of ceracrete and the inertia field are the only tipoffs that something's not normal.

The combat robot, or one just like it, lumbers up, pauses, and starts walking again.

I glance around our group and say the obvious, "I think it wants us to follow it."

Expression serious bordering on wise, Carmen nods deeply. "Since Gabby isn't saying it, I'll step up. Duh!"

Chuckling, I follow the robot, and the others follow me.

Chapter 19
MEET THE NEW BOSS

If we are in a ship, I'm not familiar with the layout. Just thinking that sounds strange.

No, make that completely whacked.

We follow the robot through halls that look like they belong in a transit station. We stop at a briefing room. As soon as we're inside, the robot leaves. A dozen seats form a half circle. The room isn't huge, but it could probably hold two-dozen people without things getting uncomfortable.

Holographic projectors in the floor and ceiling light up, and the cloaked figure appears. "Please," it says, waving towards the chairs, "have a seat. Make yourselves comfortable." Its voice still sounds badly filtered. There's a weird synthetic edge that's combined with static. It's just plain weird.

Hello again, weird—my grossly overused friend.

I sit, still holding Gabby with her head resting on my shoulder. The others look around before following my example.

"Who are you?" I ask.

"I am Temocc."

Something stirs in the back of my head. "That name... it sounds... familiar."

Temocc faces me. "It should, Ethan Shaw."

"Uh, how do you know my name?"

"I know a great deal about you. Indeed, I likely know more about you than you know about yourself."

Leaning back, I frown. "Yeah. I've been discovering that pretty much *everyone* knows more about me than I do."

"Does your head still hurt? From your psychic overexertion."

"Yeah," I whisper. "How'd you know?"

Temocc turns its head up to face the ceiling. Within the cloak is nothing but darkness. Facing me again, it says, "Time is running out, and there is much to do. Do I have your permission to treat your injury?"

Not wanting to say, "yeah" again, I switch things up. "Um, okay, sure."

Its hands reach out to either side of my head. Despite it being a holograph, I can feel its feather-light touch. Parts of my mind suddenly blaze hot while others feel cold. There's a sort of vibration followed by a sharp pain. Before I can cry out, it's gone. Dizziness sweeps over me, and I clutch Gabby tightly to keep from dropping her.

Temocc moves away.

"What did... you... do to me?" I gasp.

"You've received an upgrade. That was an injection of repair nanites combined with the Tier One boost. You earned it by clearing that obstacle in the tunnel. Now, there are several additional matters that require immediate attention. Ethan, they cloned you from the remains of Lachlann Kyle McRath." It pauses. "Since I see no surprise on your expression, I shall proceed with the presumption that you were aware of this."

"I've... remembered some of that life." I wince. "Lord, it feels like my brain is on fire."

"Yes, I know, and I regret the necessity. Under more normal circumstances, you would have been anesthetized for the boost. Unfortunately, we don't have the time."

Day Mom leans forward. "Since you've repeated that, it's clearly of import. What's the rush?"

"New arrivals have overtaken the ship you arrived in. Those who took it are on their way to Vega. They cannot be allowed to learn this facility exists; therefore, you must be available—that way they will not need to look."

Day Mom frowns and taps a fingertip against her chin. "The captain and crew suspected they were flying into a trap. Despite their caution...."

The fire in my brain subsides, then flares anew. I clench my jaw and the pain fades again. It's not just the fire, it feels like ants are crawling over my brain.

In a way, I guess they are.

"Ethan," Temocc says, "they essentially raised from the dead via the use of alien technology. Granted, that technology is largely based on human science, but not entirely."

I give a wincing nod.

The Temocc projection continues, "According to my scans, you are not one-hundred-percent human. That said, the deviance may fit within the margin of error. To determine if placing your non-human modifications within the margin of error is the correct course of action, I need to know what they did to you."

Carmen stands and gives the hologram a hard look. "Why does this matter?"

Temocc turns in her direction. "I would ask you to trust that this is very important."

"Yeah," she snaps, "well trust has to be earned."

"Exactly. And you have not yet earned mine."

Carmen's at a loss for words. Under other circumstances, this would be highly amusing.

Into the silence, Dad says, "Ethan received a DNA fragment designed to bring forth genetic memories. There was a great deal of oversight during the earliest days of the project. They scanned his DNA tens-of-thousands of times. This was the only modification the project made."

After moving to stand halfway between Day Mom and Dad, Temocc says, "I require further details on this modification. Do you possess this knowledge?"

"We do," Day Mom replies, her tone cautious.

Holding out its hands, Temocc asks, "May I?"

Dad asks, "If this modification falls within your margin of error, will that help Ethan?"

"It will."

I'm not sure how I feel about this. This whole thing is rapidly turning weirder than usual, but the name Temocc.... I *want* to trust the guy for some reason I can't explain even to myself.

"Yes," Day Mom and Dad say at the same time.

Temocc reaches out a hand and cups each of their heads.

They immediately go limp and Temocc staggers back.

"What the hell?" I demand, setting Gabby down in the empty chair beside me as I stand.

"Processing," Temocc replies.

Carmen and I exchange worried looks as she moves over between Day Mom and Dad. Julian switches over to the seat beside Gabby and flicks one eye towards the exit.

Yes, we could carry them out, but then what? The pod is operating off some system that Temocc controls. Without the pod, we'd have to find another way out.

Assuming the combat robot that's probably still nearby allows us that luxury.

"My apologies," Temocc says, the static disappearing from its voice. "That was more of a shock to the system than expected." It's voice no longer sounds synthesized. Instead, it sounds cultured and smooth. Human. "I didn't realize how badly corrupted my linguistic files had become."

It waves a hand. Text appears on my keeper. Hmm. Some sort of legal document. I read it, listening with only part of my attention as Temocc speaks again.

This is some sort of contract....

"Ethan, your parents were correct about the lack of significance concerning your genetic deviation. It does indeed fit within the margin of error. Because of that, you are eligible for what you see before you."

The document states that by signing, I become a citizen of the Terran Empire.

Pride wells up from the part of me that might still be Lachlann McRath. That feeling meets my concern this might be a trap, and it all tangles up with worry about my slumped over parents, and what's going to happen when the other ship or ships arrive on Vega.

"Eligible for what?" Embry asks.

"I...." I start to answer, but I don't. In my friends' and parent's worlds, I am a weapon of war, not a person. I was born on Thompson. Reborn. Whatever. I've grown from a baby to what I am today.

And in all that time, their government never considered me a person, much less a citizen.

Now, a ship that might represent that cold, impersonal government has arrived in this system. Or worse, the ship could be Sergeant Lawton or her people.

Either way, I'm unsure what problems might arise from telling my friends about this, but for the moment, I'm not willing to find out.

On my keeper, the contract floats before my eyes.

The past and future mixing together.

What a mess.

Still, it's a delightfully interesting mess.

I sign.

Temocc gives a little bow. "Congrat—"

"...Work!" Gabby blurts, sitting up suddenly and startling us all. "Ohmygosh, Ethan!" She runs over and hugs me. Maintaining a hold on my arms, she's jumping in place, unable to stand still. "I was a human woman! A *real* human woman! And I could fly a TBF-47 like you wouldn't believe! I mean, I was a *serious* badass! Ethan, it was awesome!"

Gabby finally notices Temocc. "Oh, hey. Who are you?"

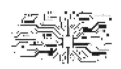

Arms crossed, Gabby is giving Temocc a hard stare. "So, let me get this straight. You want us all to leave, without Ethan's parents, get captured by whoever's coming, and not reveal the secret that you're down here?"

"Being captured is not required."

"But you want us to abandon Mr. and Mrs. Shaw *and* make ourselves available to be captured so that whoever's coming won't bother searching for you."

"That covers the essentials."

"I've got a better plan," she snaps, "and it starts with you kissing my metamorph a—"

"Sweetheart," I interrupt, "let's focus on more constructive discussions." I turn to Temocc. "Like, why can't we take my parents?"

"The oversimplified answer is that they no longer fit in these shells."

"What?" Gabby and I ask at the same time.

"I uploaded Ethan's parents into my consciousness. While they remain unique entities, both have grown to the point they cannot function properly using such limited operating platforms. In effect, they have outgrown these bodies."

Embry leans forward. "You're a digital presence."

"That is a fair assessment."

"What's your purpose?" Carmen asks.

"That information remains classified."

"But," Embry says quietly, "you're in charge here on Vega, right?"

"That is correct."

"And you *don't* want to pick a fight with whatever ship is on the way."

"Fighting any of your peoples would be sheerest folly."

There're a few ways that could be interpreted, and I have no idea which of them Temocc might have been going for. Then again, maybe that lack of surety is *exactly* what it's trying to convey.

I look around the room. If this really *is* a ship, it's a big one. Thus far, my impression of modern ships is that they haven't advanced much past what we humans had at the end of the war. Unless the coming ship is a serious warship, Temocc can probably wipe them out with very little effort.

You know, if the ship wasn't so far below the surface and all.

Which suggests Temocc doesn't *want* to destroy the ship.

Temocc's head tilts slightly, reminding me of Day Mom.

On my keeper, a new document appears.

In accordance with the Mandatory Service Act of 2488, I am hereby inducted into the Terran Armed forces. Due to my life experiences, I am starting with the rank of Recruit Sergeant. My duty station—abroad.

My mission is to depart the planet with my companions while maintaining the secrecy of this installation's existence.

Uh....

While I'm formulating a response to this, a new message video appears.

Sender Unknown.

I hit play. Day Mom appears. "Sweetheart, I know this is even more peculiar than what's been happening since Julian piñataed you. It's a *lot* to take in and absorb. But for the moment, we need you to do as Temocc says. Your father and I have a lot to learn and it's *vital* that we do just that. Take the others and go. If you reach a civilized world, contact Digital Inworld 67B. Your Night Mom is there awaiting contact. Once you've talked, she *should* be able to print a new body and join you. Tell her we'll make contact using communication protocol Outland C901764V.

"Keep this installation secret." Her lips twist into a familiar, wry expression. "It would be inconvenient to have the planet wiped out while we're still in the hardware here.

"We love you and wish we could explain more, but Temocc was right about our lack of time."

She blows a kiss and the message ends.

"I... uh... I think we should do as Temocc asks."

A burst of surprise presages Gabby grabbing me by the shoulders and turning me to face her. "Ethan, what are you talking about? We can't just leave your parents!"

I tap a finger next to my eye. "Day Mom says otherwise. She says Temocc's on the up and up and that we've gotta go."

"Dude," Julian asks, his expression stricken. "You sure?"

Not even close.

"Yeah, I am."

Embry starts towards the door. "Then we'd best get going. We've got to corroborate our stories."

"What stories?" Carmen asks with a scowl as she follows him.

"We've gotta figure out what we're gonna say happened to Ethan's parents."

My parents look like they're dead. I know it's not the same as if they were organic rather than being digital, but it still touches something deep inside me. Biting my lip, I force my eyes away, swallowing hard as I follow Embry and Carmen.

CHAPTER 20
THE JOYS OF LIFE
WITHOUT AN ELEVATOR

It takes almost two hours, but the five of us finally reach the transit station—the real one rather than the one in the ship. As we leave our transit pod, it silently pulls away and vanishes into the darkness. We're on our own.

Tearing my eyes away from the darkness behind us, I start forward. *"I hope we're doing the right thing."*

Gabby grabs my arm. *"Me too."*

We cross through the station.

"Uh," Carmen says, looking around with a frown. "Which tunnel is ours?"

"Yeah. They all kinda look alike," Embry agrees.

"That one," I reply, pointing ahead.

"You sure?" Carmen asks.

My keeper shows our exact route. "Positive."

We troop down the tunnel. Eventually, the steepening angle makes it difficult to continue.

"Flying time," I say into the quiet.

Embry holds out his hands for attention. "Remember, our final ascent has to be very slow, or we'll bash our brains out on the underside of that ceramalloy plate."

Julian nods. "Good point. Nice to know you're more than just almost-as-handsome-as-Julian."

Carmen snorts and Embry chuckles.

"Also," I add, nudging Gabby, "once you're out, don't feed the wolves. Your biologies are alien to them, and you might make 'em sick."

178

Gabby punches my shoulder, but the others snicker.

I ask, "You guys want me to go first?"

They exchange looks.

"Yes and no," Gabby says. "It'd be nice to have you guiding us up, but it's also reassuring having you with us."

Hmm.

"Okay, I think I should go first, because with my keeper, I should be able to *not* crash into the ceramalloy plate. Then, I can guide you guys up."

Julian nods, and Carmen and Embry reluctantly follow his example.

"Okay. Who's gonna be the last one up?"

All four of them exchange fresh looks.

"Me," Gabby says quietly. She's not a fan of this plan, but is willing to do it, anyway. She's fighting her fears, and I feel a surge of pride at her bravery.

My girlfriend is pretty darn amazing.

She's surprised by my thought as I pull my pistol belt off and hand it to her. Less reluctant now, she puts it on.

"Double check each other's thrusters," I tell them as I check my own. "The flying's a piece of cake, and you're good at it."

Carmen asks, "How are you gonna tell us to slow down? These thrusters are *loud* in a confined space."

"Uh...."

"Here," Gabby says, handing me a small flashlight. "This should work. One occasional flash to guide us. Three to slow down."

The five of us exchange looks. We're all onboard with this.

"Thanks," I reply before dipping her over backwards and kissing her. Her surprise mixes beautifully with her love for me. I lift her back up straight and end the kiss. "See ya soon, gorgeous."

Her thoughts are still squishy, but her love for me shines through clearly.

I slip Gabby's flashlight into a pocket. One last check of my thrusters, and I take off up the tunnel.

Flying's a lot of fun.

At least it is when there's stuff to see. Speaking of which, I won't be able to see our little exit tunnel until I'm right on top of it. There's just not that much light that can make it in through the tunnel we dug.

Good grief, but it's a long way up.

Far below, I catch the occasional flare of light. Whoever's next is in the air.

I'm tempted to kick up my speed, but there're still bits of debris hanging onto the edges of the shaft here and there. Don't want to risk knocking something down that could hit one of my friends. Considering how long it would fall, even light debris would likely reach terminal velocity quickly. Which gets back to me not being a big fan of the "terminal" part of the phrase.

I fly.

Eventually, I close with the top and reduce my speed accordingly. Five-hundred meters. Three hundred. One hundred. By this time, I've cut my velocity down to running speed. There's a faint light above.

I drop to walking speed.

Me landing in the side tunnel is less of a landing and more of a controlled crash as I have to cut the thrusters, and not bash my brains out on the ceiling, or fall back down the tunnel. While I manage it with only a slight bonk to the head, I'm glad no one was there to witness my absolute lack of grace.

I sit on the edge with my feet dangling down and dig out Gabby's flashlight. On for three seconds, then off. I wait thirty seconds and repeat. This goes on for five minutes until my keeper tells me the next person has reached the five-hundred-meter mark.

Light on for two seconds, then off, then on twice more.

When they reach one-hundred meters, I give the slowdown signal again.

By the time he's within twenty meters, I can tell it's Julian. I leave the light on, shining it not in his eyes, but on the ceiling and around the exit tunnel.

Julian reaches me at hover and yells, "Hey, dude!" He looks around and frowns. "How do I transition over?"

Standing, I brace myself against the wall and ceiling, and offer my hand.

"This blows!" But he takes my hand and cuts his thrusters.

I yank him into the exit tunnel.

Rolling up in the debris, he stands up, checks a couple of places to see if he's bleeding, then dusts himself off. "You know," he says in a normal tone, "I'm kinda wishing we'd made this exit tunnel bigger."

"Yeah, I hear you, buddy."

After wiping the crud off his hands, he sits down. "That having been said, let's never repeat that where Embry or Carmen can hear."

"Agreed." I turn to take my seat at the edge and freeze. Patting my pockets reveals nothing. I check the floor. Nothing.

"Whatcha looking for?"

"The flashlight." I groan. "I musta dropped it when I grabbed you. Do you have one?"

Julian taps his headgear. "Sorry, mate. Since I had these, didn't think I'd need one. What about using your maneuvering thrusters?"

"Maybe...."

I can't even fire the pistol because—

Fire....

In my dreams, I've always thought of myself as a telekinetic. But during the first obstacle course run, I set that buoy on fire. Yeah, I was also a pyrokinetic.

Maybe I still am.

Taking my seat, I concentrate on the air in front of me. On making the particles move faster and faster....

"What are you doing?" Julian asks.

"Concentrating."

"Oh. You know, that's not really an answer."

"Concentrating," I growl.

"Oh. Right." He gets up and steps back a few meters. "I'll just stand over here being quiet."

It's getting close, I can almost feel....

Nothing happens.

I glance down. The next person's at the six-hundred-meter mark. I need to warn them soon.

Closing my eyes, I focus on the air in front of me. I know I can't create fire by pushing or pulling with my mind—that's how telekinesis works. This is more... emotion. It's why pyros are almost always angry. Anger. *Yesss!* Anger. Fortunately, I've got a lot to be angry about—leaving Day Mom and Dad behind, the lies I've been told all my life—I focus it down and squeeze it out....

There's a sputter and a flame.

It dies.

I do it again and again.

Whoever's flying up slows.

"Pyrokinesis?" Julian asks. "I didn't know you could do that."

I throw him a weak, uneasy smile. "This is my first time."

Julian looks back towards where our ship originally landed and it's easy to follow his thoughts. "Maybe, we should keep this to ourselves."

"I agree." I ignite flames thrice more since the person flying up has reached one-hundred meters. When they're within twenty, I light a small, constant fire.

The stress from this reminds me of my early days practicing my telekinesis back on Thompson. Even though it's not a lot of fire and it's certainly not spectacular, it's still wearing me down fast.

Carmen's close enough to make eye contact, so I drop the flames.

She flies up to us at a near hover, using just her leg jets.

Bracing, I reach out and clasp arms with her.

She immediately cuts her thrusters and I swing her around to stand next to Julian.

"Was that fire?" she asks.

I nod, looking down at Embry. He's only a hundred meters beneath her and has already cut his speed.

Julian says, "We should probably keep that to ourselves."

"The fire?" Carmen asks.

"Exactly."

"Why? Just because the Project's not... oh. Yeah. I gotcha."

To be honest, I kinda wish I could follow her line of thinking, but Embry's close and requires my full attention. I pulse fire three times and the last flare of flames leaves a serious ache in its wake.

I'm all fired out.

A short time later, Embry hovers up and I pull him aside.

Looking down, I can barely see the faintest glow of Gabby's jets.

"Embry, Carmen? Either of you have a...."

Hmm.

"A what?" Carmen asks. "A light? You lost Gabby's flashlight, didn't you?"

"Yeah," I mutter distractedly. But do I really *need* a light? With the guys up here, I can mostly hear their surface thoughts... if I concentrate. Getting deep thoughts is *much* more difficult. But, the bond between Gabby and I has grown much stronger. Maybe....

"Gabby?"

I get nothing at first. Being stubborn, I keep concentrating.

Slowly, I sink into her thoughts. She loves flying because she's the greatest fighter pilot to ever live, and she's going to shoot down every tenebrosi ship she finds. Just what they might look like remains elusive because I'm a lousy artist, but she knows that when the time comes, she'll return them to the stardust from whence they came.

"Hey, pilot girl."

Gabby startles and comes dangerously close to the side of the tunnel but corrects in time.

Embarrassed, she looks up, but sees only darkness. *"How far down am I?"*

"Long way. I think I dropped your flashlight."

"Is it gonna end up sticking out of the top of my head?"

"Um, I don't think so."

"That's not terribly reassuring."

She flies for a while, and I maintain a light telepathic contact.

"Think we can find the other four TBF-47 training episodes?"

I smile. *"I bet we can. You were pretty jazzed about them. I wanted to talk about it but didn't have a chance until now."*

"Ethan, I'm a shapeshifter. My goal is to be the best human I can be. I've modeled my projected growth plan after a composite of several human women. That composite image is made up of still pictures, audio/video recordings, and such. I know the internal biology of a human woman better than most human doctors ever did."

Her mind glows with bliss. *"Ethan, I felt what it was to be a human woman. I was in her body and shared her thoughts. For those two glorious hours, I was her. That recording was like a dream come true for me."*

I'm happy for Gabby, but I can't help but tease her a bit. *"So, it's not just because you want to be the greatest fighter pilot in the galaxy?"*

She sends a curl of love. *"Not just. Most amazing metamorph ever, greatest fighter pilot... best wife."*

The concept behind the thought has lost its surprise by now, but not the sense of wonder that comes with it. *"I have no doubts about that, my love."*

After ascending for a while, she sends, *"We're getting stronger telepathically speaking."*

"We are. I also managed a little pyrokinesis earlier. Made little signal fires. Farg, it gave me a headache."

"I bet."

"*Also, being a pyro.... You gotta feed the fires with rage. Frankly, it's exhausting.*"

"*You gonna be able to stay awake until I get there?*" she teases.

"*Probably not,*" I counter tease, "*I'll probably just take a—*"

The ground shakes.

"*What was that?*" she asks.

Julian, Carmen, Embry, and I all exchange looks.

"*Did you feel it down there?*"

"*No, just your surprise.*"

As the shaking continues, dust fills the air and one of the ceracrete support slabs shifts and falls.

"Guys," I say loudly, "get out and stay low."

Carmen yells, "I don't think this is natural!"

"We'll find out what it is," Julian calls, disappearing into the dust. The other two dart out after him.

Gabby asks, "*You, okay?*"

I pull up my shirt over my mouth and nose and breathe through it as the earthquake continues. "*So far. The earth's shaking pretty energetically.*" I glance up at the ceramalloy plate over my head and then over at the stacked-up chunks of ceracrete we have helping support it. One of the smaller chunks gets shaken right out of the stack. "*Yeah, it's a tad worrisome.*"

"*Get out of there!*"

"*Not gonna happen.*" Above me, the ceramalloy plate groans and drops a few centimeters. "*Still, you might wanna put some of those greatest pilot skills to work and kick up the speed just a touch.*"

I'm in deep enough contact with her now that I can feel her throttle up the thrusters to max. The thrusters roar.

She's really hauling.

As the shaking continues, one of the ceracrete pieces in the middle of a support column backs out several centimeters. If that falls....

I do a dive roll and punch it back into place.

My hand hurts, but our makeshift support column doesn't collapse.

"Ethan!"

"I'm fine. Had to do a little tunnel maintenance." I want to say everything's fine up here but can't do it.

Gabby hears the unspoken thought but doesn't reply. She just gives me a sort of psychic hug.

I look down and can see the flare from her thrusters. In fact, I can see Gabby.

She feels my alarm. *"What?"*

"Cut your thrusters!"

Feeling my meaning, she does just that, but she's got too much momentum going.

"Sorry love, this is probably gonna hurt."

"What? You're gonna redirect me? What does that even... oh craaap!"

Flatten myself against the tunnel side, I reach down and grab her with my telekinesis. She's still moving fast and stopping her without an inertia field might kill her. Instead, I move her as close to the far tunnel wall as I can, slowing her down by increments. She's still gonna be moving way too fast when she gets here.

Just before she splatters against the ceiling, I yank her sideways. Sparks fly as one of her thrusters taps the ceramalloy. Cutting the angle as close as I can, she narrowly misses the lip of the tunnel we dug out as I fling her out. At the last second, I lift her above the ramp we made.

She's in the air.

"Fire your thrusters!"

Gabby's already ahead of me and is flying again.

"Very much not dead," she confirms.

Panting and filled with relief, I collapse in a heap.

Looking up at the ceramalloy over my head, I realize the ground's no longer shaking.

Um, that's good.

Right?

CHAPTER 21

ENJOYING THAT MUSKY NEW-CAVE SMELL

I walk out into the clear night air as Gabby lands, rubbing her neck.

The others are staring at her.

"I...." Julian begins, but evidently loses the follow-up words.

Carmen's eyes are enormous. Rather than saying anything, she steps over and gives Gabby a big hug.

"That was one of the most *amazing* things I've ever seen," Embry says quietly. "You had to be doing at least 120 kph."

"Yeah," she agrees, a tremble running through her voice. "Awesome. Scary. You wouldn't believe how much adrenaline is flowing through my veins. If I was in my original form, I'd be glowing like an aquatic star."

"You already glow like a star."

Gabby walks over and hugs me. She's trying not to cry.

To be honest, my hands are still shaking over how close I came to losing her, so I just wrap my arms around her and hold on tight.

Eventually, I ask, "Was it a natural earthquake?"

Embry points a claw-tipped finger towards the lake. "A ship flew in low. Big one. Landed that away. Probably close to where the Life Keeper's ship originally parked."

Julian says, "It was a GCM Anthem-class light destroyer."

"A what?" I ask.

"Galactic Coalition Military. Anthem-class destroyers are fast and pack a relatively heavy punch. They're the workhorses of the GCM fleet."

"Oh."

With a nod, I turn and reach into the tunnel with my telekinesis. I grab all our supports then yank them out. The debris shifts as our tunnel collapses. I then dump some of what we'd dug out back into the area we excavated.

Those nano-repair bots have done an excellent job. I feel great.

"Let's go," I say, frowning as I look to the future. "We've got to stage my parent's deaths."

"Stay low," Julian says as we all do a fresh check on our thrusters. "As far under the treetops as we can manage. That should hide us from the ship's sensors." His ear crests flutter and he gives a rather wan smile. "At least it can't hurt."

Carmen adds, "Staying under the treetops should also help hide us from any satellites they dropped off in orbit." She makes a face. "Unless they can scan for specific metals."

Embry sighs and holds up a directional thruster. "Like these are made of."

"Let's go," Gabby orders. "For the moment, they probably don't know we have these. Let's keep it that way for as long as possible."

Following Gabby, we fly, slowly following trails through the woods.

After a couple of hours, we reach a chasm.

"This is it," Julian says as we all land near the edge. "I heard a couple of the bridge crew talking about it. It's deep. We can use the leftover explosives to collapse a wall. With a few thousand tons of rock at the bottom, no one's gonna bother trying to dig anyone out."

Well, he's certainly right. It's deep. There's a stream running along the bottom. It looks small from up here, but probably isn't. In fact, it may actually be a river.

Julian points to our left. "There. See how that enormous chunk of rock overhangs the divide? We set the charges below it. Gravity should do the rest."

"They'll know we've intentionally blown it," Carmen points out, her ears turning this way and that. "What's our reason? Why would the elder Shaws want to drop those rocks into the river?"

"Well," Gabby begins, thinking aloud, "let's look at it backwards. It's gonna dam up the stream. Why would we want to do that?"

A twisted little grin spreads across my lips, and I slowly nod as it comes together. "Yes! We wanted a lake for my metamorph. One that's difficult to scan or see from orbit. We were planning to leave for a few weeks so it would fill, then sneak back and hide under their noses."

"Exactly," Carmen says, sniffling. "The charges went off early. Poor Mr. and Mrs. Shaw got caught in the landslide."

Embry shakes his head, a big smile revealing many sharp round teeth. "No, the Shaws were *planting* the charges, and they went off. They got caught in the explosion itself *and* the subsequent landslide buried them."

His toothy smile vanishes. "It was terrible."

Gabby sniffs back tears. "I'm just glad Ethan was on the far side. Thanks to that, he didn't see the blast kill his parents."

The combination of my friends being convincing and this story being about my parents dying makes me all sorts of uncomfortable.

Giving me a nudge in the ribs, Gabby says, "Come on, tough guy. Let's blow that up and head for the hills."

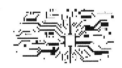

A few days after blowing up the overhang, and at a much lower elevation, we find a cave near the top of a small, lightly wooded hill. It's situated less than fifty meters from a stream and is roughly thirty-five meters deep. Julian assures us this is more than enough rock to hide us from anything other than a deep scan from orbit. After a quick, unanimous vote, we decide to set up a serious camp here. There's a faded, musky smell, but it's not bad. We gather lots of dry wood for a fire. It will produce less smoke than green wood, and with the temperatures dropping as this part of Vega heads into fall, we'll need the heat.

"What's next?" I ask as we stand around looking at the large, but chaotic pile of dry wood we've gathered near the back of the cave.

"Evergreen boughs." Julian replies, with a considering little frown.

Carmen throws him a what-the-hell look.

"To sleep on," Julian explains. "They'll give us a little padding and will keep the rocks from leeching away our body heat."

Expressions turning thoughtful, she and Embry slowly nod.

Gabby asks, "After that?"

Julian ruffles his ear crests. "Once that's done, we should build as much of a wall as we can across..."—he walks up to a slightly narrower point near the cave's entrance—"...here. That way, we'll trap most of the heat from our fire in here, but still maintain a workable chimney effect. Also, food. If we're gonna stay any appreciable time, we'll need lots of food to survive winter on this rock."

Gabby and Carmen wince almost in unison.

"What tools and equipment do we have?" Julian asks. When we look blankly at each other, he says, "Alright guys, empty your pockets and backpacks. Make a pile so we can see what we've got to work with."

We do so and stand around and stare at the results.

We're down to a distressingly small number of meal bars and they're not universal. Julian only has one left and Carmen's down to two. Embry, Gabs, and I are out. My stomach rumbles.

"Okay," Julian says, trying to project confidence. "We can work with this." He grabs Gabby's OMG WITF cup and the one I got from the transit station, then hands them to Carmen.

"You're on water duty. Don't gather it from still water or water without small fish swimming around. If it's not moving, pass on it."

"Moving water and small fish," she repeats, giving the containers a skeptical look.

"Yep," he confirms before separating out the mostly useless stuff like my shades, the memory playback device, Carmen's music system, and Embry's Game Machine. Frowning, Julian picks up my multi-tool. "The blade on this is the only knife we've got?"

I turn up my hands in a shrug.

Embry holds up his claws. "Now that I'm out of the meat-suit, these are growing back pretty well, but they won't really be long enough to do any serious cutting for another couple of weeks."

Julian frowns. "We'll make do with the multi-tool." One eye turns to look at me. "How about I take this and put the saw blade to work on the evergreen boughs? Maybe use Embry as a runner to bring back the ones I've cut while you and Gabby find us some food?"

"Sounds good."

Gabby shakes her head. "I should go with Carmen. I can help find good water."

Julian's puzzled expression shifts to understanding. "Right, metamorph. Aquatic homeworld and water affinity. Now I get ya. Okay. With that change, is everyone good with their assignments?"

Glancing around, everyone gives brief nods or shrugs before walking out into the early afternoon light.

Food. Umm... yeah, right.

Outside the cave, Gabby runs a hand over my arm.

I ask, "How's the neck?"

"Better. Need the pistol?"

"Naw," I reply with a flip of my hand. "I'm just trying to figure out where to start."

"Fish," she says with a wink before gathering up Carmen and heading towards the stream.

"Fish," I mutter to myself. "Not a half-bad idea."

While Julian and Embry head over the hill towards the forest, I make a left and walk the bank of our little stream back towards the river we followed to get here in the first place. In less than an hour, I'm standing on the shore. The river's fairly slow moving, but it's wide enough that crossing it wouldn't be something to undertake casually.

Hmm. Well, traditional fishing is right out since I don't have any string or a hook. Ditto for making a net.

If I was a moderately intelligent high-school kid, what would I do?

The thought sparks a smirk.

Finding a shallow spot is the first thing that comes to mind, so I turn right and follow the river's edge. Fashioning a spear or something along that line seems like a good idea, too. Wish I'd thought of that back when I still had my multi-tool, but I'll make do. So, if I catch a fish, or a whole mess of 'em, how to get 'em back to the cave? Vines sound handy, which immediately leads me to believe I won't find a single one. Yeah, this in turn leads back to the whole spear thing. Or at least a good stick.

Side-questing it, I turn away from the river and head towards some nearby woods. The first few dead branches I find are too brittle. The next one is a little too thick and still has the root-ball attached. Breaking it over my knee takes care of the root-ball issue. Can I compress the branch using my telekinesis?

Seems worth a try, so I gave it a shot.

Evidently, there's a problem with me equally distributing pressure. The stick less breaks and more ruptures. Dramatically.

Well, crap.

Back to stick quest.

Eventually, I find a couple of serviceable sticks. One's thin but sturdy, about the length of my arm. The other's a bit longer than I am tall, about wrist thick, and somewhat flexible. It's odd that finding these feels like a major accomplishment. Running my hand along the edge of both, I strip the bark off.

Last year, I doubt I could have accomplished this without blood loss. Now, it's easy and pain-free.

Side-quest complete, I return to the river, then resume following the bank.

Half an hour later, I reach the place where a small tributary feeds into the river. Okay, good. Now I just needed a place shallow enough for me to see the fish. I'm hoping I can pop them out of the water via my telekinesis, and impale them on the smaller of my sticks, carry 'em back to the cave, and *voilà*—dinner is served.

I follow the tributary a bit and find a shallow spot over a rocky bottom. Perfect.

It takes less than a minute to find a spot high on the bank where I can sit and watch for dinner to swim over the rocks. The breeze riffling the grass is cool, but not unpleasantly so.

In another few weeks, will that be a different story?

I'm afraid I already know the answer.

After sitting for an hour, I determine that due to some unforeseen bureaucratic screw-up, someone forgot to notify the fish of my plan.

"Heh, the fish are probably still in school."

Grinning at my little joke, my amusement fades as my stomach rumbles.

Well, crap and double crap.

Something's rustling weeds farther up the tributary.

Probably not a fish—unless the fish here are exceptionally weird—but maybe something just as good.

Staying low and watching where I put my feet, so I make the least noise, I ease my way towards the sound.

There, down by the water, something moved those reeds.

Further slowing, I creep closer.

A flash of brown fur, then the reeds hide it again.

Whatever it is, it's closer to the opposite bank.

That's a pretty far—

Oh. Ahem. Actually, it's not. I'm pretty sure I can make the ten-meter leap—and that doesn't even take into account giving myself a little telekinetic boost.

Speaking of the other side, the creature walks away from the water, and up the sandy embankment. It's got dark brown fur, clawed feet, and looks like a beaver, but with a round tail. Mutant beaver, giant water rat, or whatever it might be, the thing probably masses forty kilos and is almost two meters long without the tail. Yeah, that would feed all five of us for quite a while, especially with my cryokinetic ability to freeze what we don't immediately need.

My heart pounds. Excitement bubbles through me.

I'm really gonna do this.

Without further thought or mental debate, I spring across.

My aim is excellent, and I land right next to the beast, pounding the smaller stick into the top of its head as I do. This pins the animal to the ground as it dies, convulsing. That takes longer than expected, but conversely, it probably happens in less time than it feels like.

Eventually, the creature goes still.

Umm, okay. Now what?

With a sigh, I pick up the solidly built critter in a sort of fireman's carry, and trudge back towards camp.

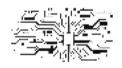

Roughly two hours later, I reach the cave.

Smelling like evergreens, Embry walks out. He stops and stares as I set the dead critter down. "What in the world is that?"

"Dunno. Dinner?"

Embry's black eyes take the lead in forming his skeptical expression. "Huh. Yeah, I'll get Julian. He's got the multi-tool, and maybe knows how to prepare...."—he waves vaguely towards the critter—"... that."

"Good thinking. I'm pretty clueless on this front."

"We're all trying to figure this stuff out." He shrugs before heading off. Looking back over his shoulder, he grins. "That's part of the fun."

Gotta admit, he raises an excellent point.

The girls reach the cave as Julian and Embry walk out of the trees.

"Good timing," Carmen calls to them.

"Naturally," Julian says, checking his wrist for a watch he's not wearing. "Though, if we're being completely honest, I meant to be here two freckles sooner."

Carmen and I groan almost in unison.

Gabby's staring at the beaver-rat. "That's the weirdest looking fish I've ever seen."

"Yeah, sorry about that. Maybe I'll have better luck fishing tomorrow."

She holds up empty hands and wiggles her fingers. "Better than the fish I caught."

Julian looks down at my kill. "I think this thing is derived from a nutria. They were generally considered a nuisance creature but were sometimes harvested for meat and/or fur."

"So," I begin, "you know how to convert this to edible food?"

"Umm. Yeah." He tosses me the multi-tool. Thanks to his poor throw, I have to catch it with my telekinesis. "I know how to dress it. But not here. We know there're dire wolves in the region. They might not be the only predators, and we don't want them coming to visit us in our shiny new cave."

Carmen frowns at him. "Why would they...? Oh, the blood."

"And viscera," Julian says, forcing a wan smile. He looks paler than usual.

"Come on, buddy," I say, shouldering the nutria corpse as the multi-tool floats along beside me.

We walk down the hill to the creek and then go maybe a hundred meters farther downstream. There, at Julian's direction, I cut off all four feet and the head. This isn't nearly as easy as I was expecting. While he's throwing up in the nearby reeds, I slit the skin from the neck to the crotch. Then, getting a grip on the blood-slick fur, I pull the skin off. The critter's pelt might well make the difference between freezing this winter or not, so we're not gonna let it go to waste.

Looking like he might hurl again, Julian washes the pelt in the water, pulling off a few stray pieces of fat.

Next, I eviscerate the body. Yeah, it's gross, but necessary. The innards drop into the creek, and I have to help a few of them out. It's pretty darn nasty.

After that, Julian ties the pelt up into a sort of bag with the fur-side out. Seeing the question on my face, he gives me a sickly grin. "Now, you fill it with meat."

"Oh, right."

Cutting that much meat takes a while, but it's worth it.

As we're standing in the creek cleaning ourselves and the multi-tool, Julian says, "We probably should have kept the entrails. There're ways of making stuff from 'em. Also, I'm afraid I wasn't doing a particularly good job of explaining things. We wasted a lot of meat."

"This was our first try," I point out. "We'll get better. As for wasting meat, I suspect Mother Nature will deal with the leftovers quite handily." As I pocket the multi-tool, I add, "You might wanna get a drink now. I know a certain metamorph needs a lot of water, and the others probably will, too. Might not be so fun to walk down here in the middle of the night for a drink."

Julian cups his hands, then stares at them. They're clean now, but his look of distaste is profound. "Saurils," he glances at me. "Embry's folk. They don't need much water. But you're right about Gabby. Carmen would probably drink less than either of us, but that's mostly because of her smaller size. So, yeah, you're right. Coming down here at night after the temperature has fallen won't be much fun. Also, a lot of predators are nocturnal." Making a face, he fills his hands with water and drinks. Aversion quickly fading, he drinks more.

I drink my fill then tie off the bag of meat. Shouldering it, I repeat, "We'll get better at this."

He throws me a faint, forced smile.

CHAPTER 22

ROUGHING IT

I n the back of the cave, we experiment with different ways of cooking nutria meat. We skewer thin strips on bits of potential firewood and hold that near the flames. This works well. I take a couple of flatish rocks and rub one against the other, further flattening them and knocking off any rough edges. After a quick cleaning, we place them beside the coals and set chunks of meat on them to cook.

"This would be so much easier with tongs," Gabby says, sucking on her lightly burned finger.

"No doubt," Embry agrees, failing to hide his amusement.

I try the first of the meat skewers. "Not bad."

Gabby takes the second and blows on it until it's cool enough to eat. Something I rather wish I'd done. She takes a dainty bite, then another that's much less dainty. Still chewing, she gives me a blissful smile.

Embry's amusement fades. "I think I'll be okay with fish, but without the meat-suit's converter, I can't eat this."

Distaste plastered over her expression, Carmen nods. "Same. You know, except for the whole fish thing. I vaguely recall from my earliest days in Project Simulation that if the meat-suit got damaged, and I somehow ended up lost, I could eat some of the bugs and such... but I think that's it."

"Aw, guys," I say. "That sucks. I'm so sorry, I didn't know." I turn to Julian. "What about you?"

Still paler than usual, he looks down at his feet. "A big part of my meat-suit was the food converter. Took years to get it tuned right and for me to figure out what I could and couldn't eat. No, this is my bad. I'm supposed to be the smart one, but back on the ship, I didn't grab extra food when I had the chance. It's *always* a good idea to carry extra—emergencies aren't scheduled events. I shoulda been smarter instead of just bragging about being smarter."

"Eat," Embry orders me and Gabby with a quiet smile.

"Yeah," Julian says as he finishes his last meal bar. "You growing weaker won't help us, so have at it."

Gabby holds up one of her meal bars. "Can any of you...."

The three of them give wan smiles.

Miserable for my friends, I eat.

Gabby and I take turns cooking and end up with several kilos of partly burned food. It will last longer cooked, so we cook as much as possible. Well, maybe not as long as the part I'm planning on freezing, but longer than the raw meat would last.

I carry in dozens of rocks and wall off a section at the very back of the cave. I stack the leftover uncooked meat in there and then slowly freeze it with my cryokinesis. Working with CK is exhausting and leaves me with the beginnings of a throbbing headache.

Returning to our campfire, I'm still sad about my friends' misery. Still... sad. Realization strikes, and I sit up straight.

"What?" Gabby asks, licking her fingers and tossing an empty skewer into the fire.

"I still feel sad."

Carmen throws me an okay-what's-your-point look.

"Guys, I haven't felt anything other than happy for longer than five minutes since I was nine."

Understanding crosses all their expressions.

"Yeah," Julian says. I have the vague impression that he's glad for the distraction. "There's a reason for that. Your food's been drugged."

"What?" I ask from the midst of my bafflement. "Why?"

"They were afraid that adolescence might make you violent. So, they cut that potential problem off at the proverbial pass."

"'They' being the management team of Project Simulation," Gabby chimes in. Meeting my eyes, she points down at her neck and shoulders.

Her gesture would have been confusing if not for our telepathic bond. I have just received a request.

As is, Embry throws her a puzzled glance.

"Mis-management team." Carmen smirks.

"To be honest," Embry says, "I heard about it in a briefing, but I don't guess it really sank in that they were dosing you."

I start gently massaging around the base of Gabby's neck.

Carmen leans back against the cave wall, frowns absently, then leans forward again and rubs her forearms. "It created a lot of unintended consequences. Management feared you'd eat food not intended for you and thus dilute the dosage to the point that you still might become enraged and slaughter everyone on the planet. Their solution was to dose *all* the food."

"They...?" I'm not sure how to end that sentence.

"Yeah," Julian says. "So, since they were dosing every crumb of food you might eat all across town, they had to make time for the medical staff to tweak the meat-suits so they could filter out the drug. For those people who didn't require the digestive alterations," he nods at Gabs, "the science department had to create a 'prescription vitamin' to counter the drug. And they had to counter it, because it affected each species differently. As a natural corollary, each of those so-called 'vitamins' had to be individually tailored."

Annoyance bordering on anger slides in. "They drugged me? Because I *might* have turned violent? Eight freakin' years ago?"

"Yeah," Carmen says, her ears flickering. "It came up for review a few times, but they didn't stop drugging you because of that incident at your twelfth birthday party."

Gabby nods and looks over her shoulder at me, her smirk conveying rueful amusement until she winces. "Yeah, seeing what you did to the grill scared the snot out of Management."

One minor accident....

I scrub my hands over my face. My aggravation turns to frustration. This in turn mixes with my worry for just how much we'll be able to do for my fasting friends in the coming days.

Gabby leans back against me, then takes and squeezes my hands.

My eyes flick from Embry to Carmen to Julian.

Without food, none of them will last long.

Chapter 23
THE CARE AND FEEDING OF ALIENS

I wake early. Gabby's at my side, her arms wrapped around Carmen. That piques my interest, but I've gotta step outside and find a tree.

With the sun just rising over the hill, the air is brisk, clean, and clear. There're a few high clouds, but it looks like it'll be sunny.

Morning business complete, I wander back to the cave entrance as the first frown of the day spreads across my lips. What are we gonna do about sanitation when the weather turns bad? If it's storming, we can't walk out of the cave to, as the lizard guy on the ship put it, expel bodily wastes.

Burgeoning thirst ties that need in with the last. Also, if it's storming, we can't exactly walk to the stream for water. I shrug to myself. Then again, if it's storming, the water's kinda coming to us. My frown twists. Except we'll want to be in the back of the cave where we can be warm and dry instead of getting soaked. As the weather turns cooler, getting soaked will change from an annoyance into a hazard.

I sigh. And *that* leads to hygiene.

Pondering all these fresh problems, I step back inside just long enough to grab the two water containers, both of which are empty. Since the answers aren't forthcoming, I head down the hill to the stream.

That's quickly done, but I'm curious about the nutria remains.

Downstream, where we dressed the carcass, there're a few small bits and pieces, but everything else has vanished. There're large bird tracks and what might be the prints of some sort of small scavengers.

Like I told Julian: Mother Nature's efficient.

Hmm. Stuff grows near water. Maybe my friends can eat some of the plants? Nobody mentioned them last night, one way or another.

Creeping back into the cave, I drop off the water and return to the stream. So, what about wild plants? Day Mom kept a garden, so in theory, I should recognize most common veggies. I hop across the creek and follow it downstream. Passing the last bit of the nutria remains, I enter unexplored territory.

Exploring is a weird combination of exciting and relaxing as I walk through the splendors of the natural world.

There's a faint tickle in my mind. Gabby.

Stopping by a fallen tree, I focus on the feeling. The telepathic contact with my girlfriend solidifies.

Still fuzzy with sleep, concern for not finding me is waking her up quickly. *"Where are you?"*

"Down by the stream, looking for vegetables. Since nobody mentioned them, I'm hoping to find something our friends might be able to eat. Also, I refilled the water. It's there at your side."

"Thanks for that. No-go on the veggies for anyone but you and me. They're worse than the proteins as far as their biological compatibilities goes."

I don't specifically formulate a curse, but she picks up on it and sends soothing feels back my way.

"How's Carmen?"

"Okay, for the most part. She got cold last night, and the evergreens gave her a nasty rash on her exposed skin."

Concern and frustration twist up in a knot in my guts.

"Ethan, relax. We'll figure it out."

Despite her deliberate thought, I can sense the shadow of doubt within her.

It feels a lot like the doubt growing within me.

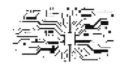

As Gabby predicted, the soccer-ball sized onion and the arm-sized carrot I bring back are inedible for anyone but me and Gabs.

"How did you guys eat all this stuff before? If it's incompatible, didn't you guys have rejection issues, allergies, and such?"

"Lots of all the above," Carmen replies sourly.

"Especially in the early days," Embry adds, with a rueful smirk.

"Farkin' meat-suits," Julian says, draining the last of water from the stainless-steel container. "I'm gonna go refill this."

"Before you do," I say, "there're a few things we should discuss." I hit them with the sanitation, water, and hygiene problems.

Soon, everyone's looking around the back of the cave.

Embry says, "You flattened out those cooking rocks pretty fast last night. Think you could do something similar to make a water basin?"

"Or dig a straddle latrine?" Julian adds.

"Latrine?" I ask, though the word's tickling something deep in my memories.

"Yeah, it's a trench you pee and poop in. After we expel solid waste, we could cover it with wood chips or maybe a sprinkling of crumbled evergreen leaves to keep the smell down. Maybe some of the ash from the fire. For a straddle latrine, you keep a foot on either side, so the trench must be fairly narrow. Maybe a third of a meter wide."

"Huh," I mumble. Though unsure about how well either will work in the long run, as a short-term solution, it's got promise.

Carmen points to a spot under a low section of ceiling. "Put it there. And if we need to, we can use the flight jets to burn off the waste."

We all frown or scowl at that, but none of us has a better solution.

"Okay," I say, "I'll bore out a water basin. That should give me a good idea about how well digging a latrine in the rocks is gonna work."

Julian nods. "I'll help Embry make a fish trap and see what we can do about feeding him."

"Yeah," Gabby agrees. "I'll do the same for Carmen."

A smile spreads across Julian's broad face. "Well, if y'all are building a fish trap for her, you might as well join us." Embry grins and Carmen rolls her eyes.

"You are *such* a dumbass," Gabby says, shaking her head sadly as she and Carmen head out. "Try not to wander too far." An evil glint enters her eyes. "And try not to feed yourselves to the fish."

Carmen snorts a laugh as Embry's grin fades.

"That's not funny," Julian says with a frown.

Radiating amusement, Gabby and Carmen leave.

"Not funny!" he reiterates.

I wave towards the rise where I'm gonna try boring a mini cistern. "At least you'll be outdoors. Wanna trade jobs?"

Now it's Julian's turn to smile evilly. "No, I don't wanna spend the week trying to explain to you how to build a fish trap."

"That's *sooo* funny," I reply, but I can't keep a bit of smile from sneaking out.

Julian points at me and grins just as he and Embry head out.

Amused, I get started on boring out a water basin.

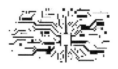

On our fourth morning in the cave, I wake up worried. Except for Gabby, my friends aren't doing so good. Embry had an adverse reaction to the fish and has spent most of the last two days throwing up or dashing to the latrine. Carmen's choked down a few worms and grubs, but that's it. Julian's face is thinner and there are dark orange bags under his eyes. His body is consuming its own muscle mass even faster than the other two.

Could we sneak back and steal rations from the "tent" by the lake shore? Assuming the destroyer is still parked there—

"No," Gabby whispers, overhearing my thought as she walks over, takes my hands, and wraps my arms around her. "The tent's almost certainly gone." Sensing my burgeoning thought, she adds, "Yes, the contents, too. Also, it's too dangerous. They'd pick us up on their scanners before we got within five klicks."

"But the ships back in town—"

"Didn't have days in which to get solid scans of everything within that five-klick radius. The destroyer has. By this time, their sensor operators are aware of every wolf, bird, and squirrel moving through the woods. Any of us would stick out like sore thumbs."

Hugging her tightly, I don't reply.

Problem is, ideas on how to sustain alien metabolisms in our crude circumstances are few and far between.

"Yeah," she whispers, sounding just as lost as I feel.

Carmen stands and stretches. "We'll be okay," she whispers before stepping behind the screen of woven reeds and relieving herself.

Gabby and I exchange worried looks but try to hide our concern as Carmen rejoins us.

"Fasting is good," she whispers. "It cleanses the body which leads to the spirit being cleansed."

I don't know how to respond to that.

The musky smell is stronger this morning.

Probably the humidity.

As Carmen and Gabby discuss spirituality, I walk towards the cave exit. There's a tree outside with my name on—

A colossal bear meets me as it starts to enter the cave. This beast is bigger than a normal bear in approximately the same ratio as the dire wolves are bigger than normal wolves. It's woolly and the source of the odor.

We both freeze, its huge nostrils flare wide while I stare in surprise.

I'm not scared, which seems odd even for me.

A blast of fear from behind presages Gabby's scream. This draws a surprised snuffle from the bear. It turns and looks in her direction, baring its massive teeth.

The rage hits me like a nuclear strike and envelopes me completely. Lashing out with a telekinetic blast, I knock the bear over backwards. Pain flares through my head, but I ignore it. As the bear's tumbling down away from the cave entrance, I race after it. On the way, there's a tree about as thick as my arm. I pause, get a good hold on it, and yank it out of the ground. Snarling in fury, a few brutal slashes with my telekinesis remove the limbs and longer roots. My headache worsens, feeding my fury.

Confused, the bear staggers to its feet.

As it does, I crash down, using the base of the tree to deliver an overhead, two-handed blow to its head.

The bear's head smashes down into the rocks and rebounds back up.

Spinning, I hammer a sideways tree-swing backed with another telekinetic strike. This sends the bear tumbling again. The pain is wrapping around my head in angry tendrils, but I don't have time for it.

Rolling down the hill, the huge animal knocks over several trees.

Furious, yet focused like a mining laser, I'm already leaping down a thirty-meter incline after it.

The bear bellows as it slides to a stop.

I land in a blast of counterforce that keeps my legs and ankles from breaking. Rocks explode away from me in all directions.

Not slowing, I slam a wall of force into the bear. This flings the beast through more trees before it tumbles into the creek. My head is pounding, and it feels like a dozen drills are boring into my forehead.

Still, I spring after the bear, a vortex of swirling flame forming as I feed my rage and pain into the fire in preparation for immolating the gigantic animal.

With a terrified bawl, the bear flees.

Wow, bears can really haul ass.

"Ethan!" Pistol in hand, Gabby leaps one of the fallen trees halfway up the hill as she sprints towards me. "Are you... alright?"

I glance up as the vortex of fire dwindles away.

My hands are shaking. My nose is bleeding.

Where did my tree-club go?

Sudden awareness of my headache makes me wince. When I see Gabby wincing, I bring up my mental walls.

"Babe," she says. "Are you o—"

The world tilts abruptly and goes black.

Chapter 24

A Change of Circumstance

I wake up slowly, my thoughts slow and groggy. Evergreen mixes with Gabby's scent. I'm warm. Maybe a little too warm, I realize as the cobwebs finally start burning away. I'm spooning with Gabby, the stiff-as-a-board nutria fur is over us.

Ah. My sweetheart and the nuclear reactor that powers her.

My growing amusement reaches Gabs. She stirs, relief flooding out from her.

"About time you woke up."

"It is?"

I wonder about that for a moment. Oh, I remember.

Bear.

"Bear," Gabby confirms.

Oh. The arm reaching from her direction and draped across my shoulder is maroon. After staring a moment, I blink in confusion.

Gabby looks over her shoulder at me, amusement filling her with contagious delight.

"Carmen needs my body heat." Her amusement quickly withers into dismay. *"They're fading. Ethan, you've been unconscious for two days. The last of their meal bars are long gone. Our friends are wasting away. They can't last much longer. We've got to do something before we lose them."*

Before one-by-one, they die on us.

Gabby gives an almost imperceptible nod.

"Embry still sick?"

"*No. We've been struggling to keep him hydrated, and he's kept down a few minnows. Julian.... Hon, he hasn't been able to eat anything. I'm still used to seeing fat Julian. Desperately skinny Julian scares me.*" Her eyes flick to Carmen. "*So does this one.*" Her arms tighten protectively around Carmen.

For a while, I simply share her concern.

"*Okay. I'll take a few pieces of the flying gear, attach them to tree limbs, and launch them in the general direction of the destroyer. If their sensors are half as good as everyone says, they'll be able to trace them back to us.*"

Gabby twists a little further around and gives me a bittersweet kiss.

I sigh. "*I really wanted to make this work.*"

"*Circumstances beyond our control, my love. Circumstances beyond our control.*"

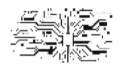

By the time heavily armed and armored hover cars surround the cave, the sun is setting. I'm actually happy to see them.

"They're dressed like government troops," Carmen says, smiling with relief as soldiers pile out of the cars. She throws me a guilty look and shrugs.

"It's okay," I reply, giving her bony shoulder a light squeeze. "I'm just sorry you guys had to go hungry for so long."

"Not your fault," Julian says with a dismissive wave. "We were the ones in an alien ecology. Shoulda kept extra food on us at all times."

"Or a converter," Carmen mutters sourly.

Embry nods. "We'll know better next time." He barks a little laugh. "Just in case there *is* a next time, I'm gonna find an AI and run a simulation to figure out which types of fish I can and can't eat based on protein and enzyme modeling. Maybe keep a scanner handy while I'm at it."

Turning away from the cautiously advancing troops, Gabby throws me a worried look and whispers, "Yeah. If there *is* a next time."

The soldiers take Gabby's pistol and collect our remaining flying gear. They're not exactly hostile, but they're certainly not friendly either.

Medics attend to Carmen, Embry, and Julian.

That alone makes this a good move.

Speaking slowly, an officer asks Gabby, "Where... are... explosives? Two... adult... synthetics?"

While she's spinning out our cover story, I'm basking in the less-than-warm glow of having lots of weapons pointing at me. A fearful tech does a weird pantomime, then his companion puts a metallic bulb over my hands. The inside fills with foam and suddenly I can't move my hands or fingers. They do the same for my feet.

"Well, this is awkward," I mutter.

A soldier makes noises akin to an old gasoline engine failing to start.

"Yeah, sorry dude. I don't speak that language."

The techs clamp a thick metal collar around my neck. The soldier raises a little black remote control and clicks a button. A tone sounds from the collar.

There's a prick in my neck and everything slides away.

One moment I'm asleep, the next I'm wide awake.

It's a strange transition.

Evidently, I'm laid out on the floor in some sort of jail cell. If I didn't have the metal globes on my hands and feet, I might have been able to take two steps from front to back, and one sideways. Maybe. Unfortunately, I do have the globes on my hands and feet and they're just as awkward as before. There's no furniture, and one of the three walls is transparent.

Three armored guards stand watch outside. One of them has a tripod-mounted weapon pointed at me.

Fantastic.

Judging by the metal floors, walls, and ceiling outside my cell, I'm guessing I'm aboard the destroyer.

Yeah, that makes sense.

My stomach rumbles and the dryness in my throat screams "thirsty." On top of that, I've got a growing need to pee.

"Hello? Do you guys understand me?"

Silence.

"Look guys, if I die of thirst or starvation, I'm not gonna be much use to anyone." No reaction. A new worry springs to life. "Unless you're thinking it would be easier to deal with me if I was dead...."

I close my eyes and reach out with my telepathic senses. There's a weird resistance, but despite that I get a growing sense of Gabby. She's not too far away and is... eating. There are military officers throughout the room she's in. Julian sits across the table from her, nibbling a green cube. There's no sign of Carmen or Embry.

"Ethan?" she silently asks.

"Me. How are you?"

Her relief falls over me like a warm blanket. *"We're all okay, but they won't let us see you. How are you?"*

"I'd be doing better with some food, water, and access to a toilet. Aside from that, I'm—"

That tone sounds from the collar. That pain bites my neck. Again.

Oh, you cat-piss gargling, chicken diddling... sacks of....

212

"Ethan? Ethan!"

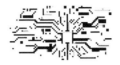

I sit on a balcony overlooking the bridge of the *Revenge*. My chair looks a bit like a high-tech throne, but it's not. In actuality, it's a psychic augmentation device with built-in life support. It's the best we have that's small enough to leave a planet or moon. I can sense the entire super-carrier—every system, every person. More than that, I can feel the ships of our support fleet and all the people who make it work.

When I'd first used an augmenter, I'd felt like some sort of god.

Now, I just feel... tired. I've lived a long life and have spent most of it fighting. I miss my mother and father. Keit. Peigi's first husband, Delmar. The friends and lovers I've lost to war and inattention.

"You're getting maudlin, old man," a grey-haired woman says fondly as she walks up to stand beside me. Her shoulders bear the gold starburst insignia of Commodore. "Best redirect your thoughts before you have the entire fleet crying in their beer."

I reach out a hand, and she takes it.

Throwing her a sly look, I reply, "Everyone needs a good cry now and then. Tears are an excellent means of cleansing the soul."

She squeezes my hand and sits on the arm of my 'throne.' "True enough. But, seeing as we're heading to battle, this probably isn't the best time for a good soul cleansing."

"Meh," I reply with a grin that sparks an answering one from her.

We sit for a while, watching the bridge officers perform their varied duties.

"Is it true?" she asks.

"You'll need to be more specific."

She smiles. "Lachlann, you're absolutely the politest psychic I've ever met. Every other psychic with half your abilities would just pull the question out of my head. Rather rudely at that, at least to my way of thinking."

"Oh, if the situation calls for it, I can get plenty rude." I glance to her chromed eyes. "Hmm. Still haven't gotten used to your new eyes. The ones your parents gave you were much prettier."

"Glaucoma sucked. These are better. You wouldn't believe what I can see now." She covers her mouth and widens those chrome eyes.

I chuckle and feel all those lives out here with us. "You might be surprised what I'd believe when it comes to seeing things. Speaking of which, he's here with us."

"He...? Wait, your friend from the future?"

Uh, wow.

"The very one." I tap my head. "He's sharing our conversation. Suspects this is a dream, but he's starting to doubt that."

She tilts her head. "What's he like? What's his world like?"

"He's so much like me, you'd be aghast."

"I'd *never* be aghast about something so wonderful."

I throw her a good-natured scoff. My humor fades. "He truly is extremely close to being me. He's still a young man. Doesn't understand the sorrows I bear, and I'm grateful for that. He's a good person, and that gives me hope."

"And his world?"

"*That's* where the weirdness comes in."

Her eyebrows climb almost to her hairline. "Psychically hosting someone from the future in your head isn't weird?"

I shrug. "I've felt him on and off for most of my life, so to me, it's not so strange. Anyway, he grew up on Thompson."

"Thompson? We abandoned it in '82. There's just rubble there."

"Exactly."

"Okay, that *is* weird."

"Nope," I contradict her with a smirk. "That's not the weird part. The weird part is all the aliens. To them, we're the big bad humans of ancient mythology."

She turns a confused look on me. "But your visitor, *he's* human. Right?"

"Yes," I say with a nod. "He's the result of an experiment."

"Are the tenebrosi part of these aliens?"

"Not... yet."

"That doesn't sound very promising."

I nod, but my focus shifts to a spike of alarm from the sensor operator below. Sliding into his mind enough to know what he knows, I sound Battle Stations throughout the fleet.

"Spacefold detected," the officer says.

The Commodore looks a question at me.

"Yes."

She commands, "All ships, fire at will."

The enemy will pour out from the fold momentarily. Pumping tremendous amounts of destructive energy into the forming hole in space means a lot fewer of those enemies will ever get a chance to fire back.

I flip a communication switch. "TEMOCC, we have contact and are engaging."

Temocc? Here? Now?

"Good hunting, sir."

"Thank you. Just so you know, my visitor is here."

"Interesting, as always. What point is he at in his timeline?"

"He knows your name, but not who you are."

"Can you ask him where he met me?"

"*Vega*," I silently respond. "*Deep underground, close to Baton Vert.*"

"Vega. *Phoenix.* His current situation doesn't seem too favorable."

Phoenix?

"Acknowledged. Switching over to active battle monitoring."

"Affirmative."

Outside, each of the thirty-something-thousand ships in the fleet have deployed their drones. There're hundreds-of-thousands of them creating a massive sensor and weapons network beyond what the ships themselves provide. The first nuclear Gauss and railgun rounds are just reaching the massive spacefold as slivers of deeper darkness emerge.

Nuclear fires flare, one after another.

For the first time in my life, I feel separate from the man I'm dreaming about.

As the battle unfolds before us, I sit silent, trying to keep my thoughts still so as not to distract Lachlann. But I scrutinize every move he makes. How he pushes his sensory envelope when he wants to see and feel something in a given direction. How he monitors people's thoughts and emotions with a touch lighter than breath. How he sorts and arranges this massive coordination within his own thoughts. His mind is the most magnificent piece of art I've ever seen. I never imagined anything could be so beautiful. The mix of organization, creativity, sheer willpower, and psychic might leaves me amazed.

"And yet," he thinks in response to my awe, "at the end of this show, my people and I still die."

Chapter 25
WALKABOUT

I wake up in the cage.

This time, I don't move.

Instead, I try Lachlann's trick of reaching out. My touch isn't as soft as his. While it's mostly a lack of practice, it's also partly because of that strange resistance. Still, my psychic efforts are quieter than normal for me.

My three guards have relaxed.

The weight and discomfort remind me of the collar around my neck. I'm tired of this bloody thing putting me to sleep. Slowly, I probe the collar. The outer cover is thick metal. Inside... Yes, there's a reservoir of liquid. Probably the sedative. Farther around in the casing, there's two larger tubes filled with liquid which are both linked to an empty third.

Strange.

My thoughts skip back to Day Mom's talk about explosives.

Oh!

It's a binary explosive. Combine both liquids together and boom: Ethan loses his head in a very literal, non-figurative way.

Yeah, I'm not a big fan of my captors' attitude towards me.

So, the feed lines from the tubes are metal. Can I crimp them closed? Working on such a tiny thing is a cool new experience, but thought can be a very precise tool. Just a little focused telekinesis... and... done! The lines on both tubes are well and thoroughly crimped closed.

My head is safe.

Now, about that drug.

Connecting to the drug reservoir is a telescoping needle. It looks like an excellent target for some additional crimping practice. A little squeeze there and there and there... done.

Now, how to get this bloody thing off my neck?

Though not positive, I think it uses a remotely controlled maglock. There's a power source and... some seriously convoluted circuitry. I could try disconnecting the power source, but if I do it wrong and something shorts to the outer collar, the power cell could discharge into *me*. Depending on the strength of the power source, that could leave me flash barbecued.

My mood sours.

I'm not getting the collar off without help.

Sulking really isn't my thing, so I switch over to figuring out what I can do about the globes on my hands and feet. I dive into the globe locking my hands together. It's probably filled with some sort of epoxy or hardened foam. Oh look, there's an empty cannister.

Probably where the epoxy/foam crap came from.

Ah ha! There's a cannister that's still full.

Release agent?

By this time, I *really* need to pee, so I'm willing to experiment.

The mechanism for this also seems to be remotely controlled, but it's not secured with a maglock. Holding the actuator open is tricky, but I get a partial release. Feels like it's fizzing or something. Two of my fingers curl. Yes, it's dissolving the gunk on my hands!

With a little practice, I manage to hold the actuator open. By the time the container's empty, it's eradicated all the epoxy within the globe.

Doing the same for my feet takes just a few seconds.

Lovin' me some progress, I heave a big sigh of relief.

Unfortunately, this sets the guards on edge. I don't need to see their expressions—I can feel their fear. It's like coals burning in their heads.

The release mechanism for my cage is a simple button. It controls dual maglocks on the door.

The creatures guarding me are wearing head to whatever-counts-for-toes-in-their-physiology body armor. It's basic stuff, so ejecting them out of it shouldn't be a problem.

I roll over, careful to keep my hands hidden. "Hey, guys. I'm pretty darn hungry and thirsty now. Also, I need to pee like you wouldn't believe. So, can we talk about this?"

They point their rifles at me.

Well, I can't honestly say I'm surprised.

"Seriously, you need to quit doing that. You make me angry, you're gonna like what happens next every bit as much as the bear did." That said, maybe it's a holdover of the extreme violence of my attack on the poor beast, maybe it's the remnants of my gratitude for them saving my friends, but I'm not particularly inclined to hurt these guys.

I glance into the rifle barrels pointed at my face.

Okay, I won't hurt them much.

Quick as thought, I snap their weapons up to point at the ceiling. There's a tone from my collar, followed by... nothing.

So far, so good.

I eject the troopers out of their armor while holding onto their weapons. I kick the globe off my feet and toss the one on my hands after it. It feels *sooo* good to stand up and stretch as they make squeaking noises. I open the cage door, step out, and take a deep breath.

Smells like freedom.

Well, that and a sharp, rank fear-smell pouring off these guys.

The release agent left a brownish goo on my hands and feet. It looks as gross as it feels. I wipe off my hands on one of their uniforms before pitching the guy none too gently into the cage. Using the next fellow, I do the same with my feet, before filing him and the last of his buddies in with the first. I re-lock the door.

Yeah, it's pretty gratifying seeing them in there.

Now, where's the nearest toilet?

I try probing their thoughts, but they're crazy panicked and in pain from bouncing off the inside of the cage walls. As I start towards the door, I kick one of their helmets out of the way.

Hmm. Well, necessity *is* the mother of invention.

Looks like I just invented the helmet-urinal.

Much relieved, I go roaming freely with my new tripod-mounted weapon floating along beside me. Strolling through the corridors, I search for a meal faber and some water. Not wanting to be overly dumb about my blatant break-out, I work on expanding my awareness.

There's no one in the immediate vicinity, and I'm not spotting any obvious cameras or scanners. Still, it's a ship. It's gonna have internal scanners.

"Gabs? Gabriella Kwan, where are you?" Focusing, I get a faint, fuzzy impression from her.

She's asleep or unconscious.

As I head down the corridor, I open doors and peek inside. Empty office. Storage room. Before long, I reach a cross corridor.

None of this is helping.

Hmm.

With a bit of continuing concentration, conscious or not, I think I can find Gabby. Where there's a Gabby, there's likely to be the rest of my friends. With luck, they'll have the bag with my change of clothes. Sounds like enough of a plan to get started. I focus. The feeling of Gabbiness remains fuzzy, but I get a firm direction.

Okay, back the way I came and up a few decks.

I start that way, exploring as I go.

There's a *lot* of office-sized storage rooms on this ship.

Two decks up, I find more people. They start to freak out, so I take their gear belts and weapons before locking them in a storage room.

They feel better as I leave. I feel better.

It's a win-win.

To cement the victory, I give the doors a little telekinetic tweak to help hold them closed.

A few steps down the hall, a moderately strong psychic taps at my defenses. Not an attack by any means, more an attention grabber.

I lower them enough to hear, *"Ethan Shaw?"*

Ah! *"Hello, Accaryinth of Meprophrose. You feel close."*

"Indeed. I shall have one of my attendants survey the passageway for indications of you."

The faint sounds of a door opening reaches me from the deck above.

"Sounds like I'm below you. Be there shortly."

"Maintain a high level of caution. These people cuddle a powerful fear of humans."

"Yeah, I noticed. It's pretty weird."

"Indeed."

After finding stairs... rather the ladder, if I'm using proper starship terminology, up to the next deck, I work my way around to Accaryinth's corridor. There's a pair of guards at the end of the hall wearing uniforms and not armor. I telekinese the pistols right out of their holsters, grab the guys, and stuff them into the first room I find—a stateroom.

Not much more than a bed in here. Perfect.

While I'm still not great with the fine application of pyrokinesis, practice has made me better. I focus intense heat on a tiny section of the door frame and door. As it melts, I telekinetically swirl the metals of the door and the frame together and give it a few seconds to cool.

Instant weld.

Down the hall, radiating surprise, is one of Accaryinth's people.

By the time I reach him, he's recovered his aplomb. *"Right this way. Her excellency will see you now."*

"Thank you."

I enter the chamber, which is maybe three-times the size of the stateroom down the hall, and set down the tripod-mounted weapon just inside the door. The purple feather-like covering on Accaryinth's head is ruffed as the too-thin lady with the elongated neck and limbs meets my eyes.

"Accaryinth of Meprophrose," I say, "it is a pleasure to meet you again."

"Be assured the pleasure is mutual. The stories recounted about humans fall far short of the mark. You are a font of amazement, especially for such a young man, Ethan Shaw. You could have left a trail of destruction and carnage across the ship, but chose not to. Your restraint is to be admired. Please forgive an elder lady's poor manners and sit."

Following her wave, I sit beside her on an overstuffed couch.

"Have you seen Gabby and my friends?" I feel her feeling my concern.

"Yes, their cabins are down the hall. Fret not, they are enjoying good health. Those who were undernourished are much recovered."

Letting out a relieved sigh, I lean back. It's every bit as comfy as it looks. "That's an enormous relief. What about the other passengers and crew from Captain Strange Noise's ship?"

"They too are aboard. Many received injuries when the ship was overtaken and boarded. Those people continue their recoveries."

"Did you talk to Gabby?"

"Yes, the occurrence of our thought exchange was a great joy. Psychically speaking, the young lady has grown a great deal since leaving the Project. But not, I think, as much as you."

She senses that I'm not sure how to respond to that, so I just skip to my question, "Did she tell you about the psychic recordings?"

"Gabby Kwan did. She was kind enough to perambulate with me through her memories of experiencing that recording. Accaryinth meets my eyes again. There is no doubt that your memory of the tenebrosi attack was such a recording." She leans towards me. "The tenebrosi were real!"

"*Were?*" I ask. "*Maybe still are.*"

Accaryinth doubts this, but she does so most politely. "*Much time has passed, and we have seen no sign of them.*"

My thoughts are quiet, soft, and dark. "*Until we humans were fighting them, we'd never seen even the faintest trace of them, either.*"

Sadness tinges her thoughts. "*You have freed additional memories.*"

"*Many more. We suspected the tenebrosi hibernated in between growth cycles. At the very least, the idea explained the long silence followed by their sudden appearance on so many of our worlds.*"

She doesn't really want to ask, but does anyway, "*How many tenebrosi were there?*"

"*By the time I... Lachlann... was thirty, our scientists and statisticians estimated that during our two-hundred and sixty years of war, that we'd killed over thirty-three trillion tenebrosi. They killed a lot of humans during that time. Far too many.*"

I swallow with some difficulty. One of her people brings me a drink container and a damp towel that smells mildly of camphor. I wipe my face, hands, and feet, then turn to the container. It's filled with water, and I drain half of it.

"Thanks."

Accaryinth is still too horrified to form coherent thoughts, so I wait for her to come to grips with that little blast from the past.

"*Thirty-three trillion! Lords of Time and Space. What great abundance of worlds did they maintain?*"

"*One.*"

Seeing and sensing her confusion, I explain, "*It's a big one and they've hollowed it out. A true engineering marvel. We spent a lot of time trying to destroy it. Sent stealth weapons. Threw asteroids and small moons at it. We damaged it many times, but never enough to destroy it.*"

She shakes her head in awe.

One of her people leans into the room. "*Excellency, there's a contingent of guards approaching.*"

"*Completely expected. We shall act as a buffer between them and Ethan Shaw.*"

"*Yes, excellency.*"

I turn to Accaryinth, worry flashing through me. "*They're terrified of me. People who are afraid sometimes do rash, stupid things.*"

"*Your concern over my and my people's well-being is gratifying. Still, this is an action which principle demands we take. You are not only our guest, you are an irreplaceable link to the past. And possibly a friend.*"

"*Thank you,*" I say with a rush of gratitude.

"*You are immensely welcome.*" She turned to one of her people. "*You have an understanding of Ethan's dietary requirements?*"

They respond with a quick bow.

"*Then please, prepare us a small meal.*"

After another bow, they leave.

I don't catch all the thoughts bouncing back and forth as part of the discussion out in the hallway, but "diplomatic incident" catches my attention. So does "frenzied monster."

In under a minute, the assistant sets out a little table for us to share. The food immediately follows.

Accaryinth's dish holds something that looks like little potatoes covered in a day-glow pink sauce. There're also little bits of green. Green what, I don't know, but the green seems quite pure.

My dish contains a small bacon cheeseburger, two large jalapeño-stuffed green olives, and a scoop of vanilla ice-cream.

"*Interestingly eclectic choices.*"

"*Perhaps,*" Accaryinth says, "*we might consume our food with distinct leisure. Offer any visitors a chance to bask in the understanding that we're all civilized people here.*"

I slowly nod. "*You are wise.*"

A smile blooms within her mind. "*Age has turned me crafty.*"

Since it's already melting, I eat the ice-cream first. *So* much vanilla goodness packed into that small scoop. It's been too long since I've had this. Next, I follow her example and cut the olives into small slivers. Sliver into mouth, chew slowly, wait a moment. Repeat. The combination of salty olive and spicy jalapeño is excellent.

Just as I'm preparing to start on the second olive, they escort in an alien wearing a fancier version of the local military uniform. A pair of Accaryinth's people step over beside each of us. I feel their determination—if need be, they'll put themselves between us and harm.

I hope it doesn't come to that.

Accaryinth eats a last bite before focusing on her newest guest. *"Infantry Commander Parzaa, what a pleasant experience to have you with us. We have just begun dining. Would you care to participate with us?"*

Parzaa replies sharply in a harsh-sounding language I don't speak, but I'm able to catch the translation from those people around us. "I would never share table with this monster! You must release the escaped atrocity into my custody, now!"

Playing my part, I spear a sliver of olive and daintily eat it.

"No monsters take accommodation here," Accaryinth replies politely before taking a sip from her cup. *"Only my guest, who was treated quite poorly before he arrived."* She frowns at the collar around my neck. *"Why, it could be argued that those who'd so mistreat a young adult of any species hold need of a tutorial in manners."*

"It's a monster that's imprisoned many members of my garrison! It's out of control and must be locked away for the safety of you, me, and everyone on the ship!"

Not making eye-contact, I spear and delicately bite another sliver of olive. I take my time chewing.

Accaryinth repeatedly taps the rim of her cup with a fingertip. *"Infantry Commander Parzaa, you are embracing silliness. Clearly, if Ethan Shaw wanted to spread harm, he could have done so. This young man simply desired to be treated with the dignity all sentients deserve."*

"It's a human! Humans are monsters!"

She sets her cup down. *"If people were defined only by their species rather than their actions, you would still live in a tree, spending your days eating bark and screeching at floobas on your motherworld. But you've risen beyond that—just as Ethan Shaw has."*

Parzaa goes still and its coloration changes from light mauve almost to purple. The Infantry Commander spins and marches out of the room.

"That occurred better than expected," Accaryinth says as she impales one of her little potato things.

I give a sort of worried mental shrug, set down the fork, and eat what is possibly the best bacon cheeseburger in the entire galaxy.

Chapter 26

DESTRUCTION, ICE-CREAM, AND OTHER TOOLS OF NEGOTIATION

"*Our situational report has been transmitted?*" Accaryinth asks as two of her people carry out our plates and the table.

"*It has.*"

"*Good. In that case, it would bring me joy if we could invite Gabriella Kwan to join us?*"

"*I shall go at once.*"

"*Thank you.*"

The assistant returns quickly. Too quickly.

"*Unfortunately, soldiers now block the hallway. They refuse to allow passage in either direction. Their fear is changing to anger.*"

"*Sad, but not unexpected. Please present Captain Hosslaniss with our protest. Best send a refreshed transmission concerning this devolution of our situation.*"

"*It shall be done.*"

I practice how to push my awareness out farther. Feeling the guards in the hall is easy. Their fear shines like beacons. I try to extend farther down the hall since Gabby and my friends are theoretically down there. It feels a bit like I'm stretching part of my brain. This is exactly as uncomfortable as it sounds.

Uncomfortable or not, I'm making progress.

Some of the crew of Captain Strange Noise's ship are in the closest state rooms on this deck. They're not happy. They've also learned that opening their doors to find out what's going on is a great way to get snapped at by the soldiers.

My awareness slowly expands. Relaxing seems to help.

Here in the cabin, the functionary returns. *"Excellency, I cannot establish a connection with the communications array. I believe our access has been terminated."*

Accaryinth gently radiates disappointment. *"To appearance's sake, our situation has become more dire than expected. Were you able to file a protest with Captain Hosslaniss?"*

"Yes. He did not seem particularly receptive."

"I must confess, this also fails to surprise me. Thank you, dear."

I feel more than see the assistant bow.

"Ethan Shaw, might I spend a bit of time being the primary focus of your attention?"

I snap back and look to Accaryinth. *"Of course."*

"Thank you. Our situation is morphing into a more serious problem. Those in charge of the ship feel matters are escaping from their control. It would seem this is an intolerable condition for them."

"Okay, yeah. It does sorta seem that way."

"In regard to solving this problem, we have a few choices. One, you can seize control over the ship." Sensing my surprise, she gives me a quiet smile. *"Yes. Please note I did not indicate it was a good option, but it is available to you."*

I adjust my position on the couch.

Hmm. Captain Strange Noise and its crew are here. I could disable the current crew and let the Life Keepers replace those folks. But the long-term outlook seems likely to be disturbingly circular. Except that maybe next time the Life Keepers lose a ship, they'll lose more than just the ship. Though I like Captain Strange Noise and its crew, and I really appreciate them rescuing us from Thompson, my confidence in them remains low.

Accaryinth's right, me seizing the ship doesn't sound like a good option.

"*Oh, it is not,*" she says. "*I merely wanted to bring you awareness of it. We might also proceed along the opposite path. Invite the captain here and negotiate your surrender. The possibility exists that we might arrange matters so that you're treated better than a wild animal.*"

This plan doesn't really thrill me either. I've enjoyed these creatures' hospitality already. I'm not eager for more.

"*Considering how they treated you, I do not feel your concern is unreasonable. Other options abound. Most are shadows of the first two. Beyond that, you would need to seek a more creative solution.*"

"*These are short-term solutions.*"

Accaryinth gives a slow nod that's almost a bow. "*The truth of this is inescapable. It is my belief that what you ultimately require is legal status. Citizenship.*"

"*I'm already a—*" I clamp down on that thought and retreat behind my mental walls for a moment. My new-but-old citizenship is directly tied to Temocc. I can't talk about one without revealing the other.

Accaryinth gives me a politely puzzled look.

I lower my mental barriers. "*Apologies. My thoughts started drifting into personal matters.*"

"*No apology is required. All are entitled to privacy within their thoughts.*"

"*Thank you.*" I think for a moment. "*So, you also believe running away with this ship or even Captain Strange Noise's would just be putting off the inevitable?*"

She gives the mental equivalent to a shrug. "*To a certain extent. Without doubt, you maintain the ability to flee. Should you succeed, you might attempt to improve the circumstances for your upcoming legal battles. However, dangers lurk down that path. There is a likelihood you would be forced to kill in order to protect yourself or your friends. Each incidence of violence would transfer fuel to those opposing you. Fuel for the lie that you are a genocidal monster.*"

"*Those opposing me?*"

"Sadly, I fear you were born into opposition with a substantial percentage of the galactic population."

Thing is, Accaryinth's right. Where would I go? What would I do? Find the Life Keepers again? They already got their butts kicked by these fools. Something tells me combat really isn't their forte.

I meet her eyes and force a ghost of a smile. *"If you don't mind acting as host, perhaps we could invite the captain over for drinks."*

Our invitation to parley results in the guards pulling back out of the corridor.

"I hope that's a good sign."

While we wait, I return to stretching out my awareness. What I find is disturbing.

"They've evacuated this corridor. All the other staterooms are empty."

Accaryinth taps the tips of her long fingers together. *"Appearances suggest we shall ascertain just how much my personal influence is worth."* She doesn't have to explain that further. Either she's too important to risk being injured while capturing me, or she isn't.

"There's a worse possibility," she adds. *"The dark political gambit. They could kill us all. With no witnesses to contradict, they could easily place blame for our deaths on you."*

Not a comforting thought.

"Indeed."

A few hours later, the captain enters the corridor outside with a group of elite guards. By this time, I have a pretty good feel for the ship. As Embry said, it's a destroyer. Engines to the rear and around the central axis. The bridge actually isn't far from us, buried in the center of the ship where it would be most protected from enemy fire.

By Lachlann's standards, it's lightly armed and armored. By today's standards, it's evidently something of a beast.

I stand as Captain Hosslaniss and one of his lieutenants enter. Both warily eye the tripod-mounted weapon sitting by the door as they walk past it. They're the same species as the majority of their crew, but the captain has the most pronounced neck ruffles of any of them. Is it a sign of status? Age? Since I know they won't shake my hand, I give them a little bow and sit.

They're wound up tight, and neither relax.

"Please, be welcome," Accaryinth says. *"Join us in sitting."*

The two sit opposite us with wary reluctance.

"My appreciation to you both for accepting my invitation," Accaryinth says. *"My assistants have prepared drinks."*

The assistants take their cue and set drinks on the little table between us.

Not wanting to freak them out any further, I wait until the others have picked theirs up and sat back before I get mine. It's some sort of strawberry smoothie. Tastes like it's made from high-quality ice-cream. Very thick, very rich. I love it.

"My sincere hope is that everyone finds their drinks satisfactory?"

"Yes," I reply. *"It's delicious. Thank you."*

Captain Hosslaniss and the lieutenant make perfunctory sips and set their drinks down, yet their replies are polite. I still can't understand their language, but it's getting easier to read the interpretations of those around us. I'm also starting to pick up more directly from their minds. It would seem I've been around these aliens long enough to at least begin deciphering their thoughts.

"Let us deal with this matter," Captain Hosslaniss says to Accaryinth. "You have the escaped... human. We want the human back. How do we make this happen without causing... a scene." By scene, he means violence.

"*Before we ford that river,*" Accaryinth says, "*I would like to probe the possibility of us agreeing on a few basic facts? It is my hope this will help bring clarity to all concerning the topic.*"

Captain Hosslaniss isn't thrilled by this but lays back the ruffles on his neck as a sign of consent.

Accaryinth gives a little bow. "*You hold my appreciation. Might we commence by agreeing that Ethan Shaw was not treated well earlier on this voyage?*"

"No!" the lieutenant snaps. "It was treated as it should have been. Better even!"

Accaryinth tilts her head slightly. *You're saying, if we had bound you hand and foot, placed a sedative-filled explosive collar around your neck, and thrown you in a tiny cage without food, water, or access to sanitary facilities, you would have considered yourself well-treated?*

"Of course not," the Lieutenant replies. "But I'm not some human monster either."

Looking towards me as I sip my smoothie, Accaryinth asks, "*Does he seem like a monster to you?*"

Captain Hosslaniss frowns and flutters his neck ruffles to indicate the lieutenant should be quiet. Hosslaniss leans towards me and actually seems to see me... not the monster of his nightmares. "He certainly seems... quiet."

"*By my experience, he often is. Don't forget Captain,*" she taps the side of her head, "*I perceive what's inside. When it comes to integrity, I would place Ethan Shaw in the same basket as you and your bridge crew.*"

Unhappiness coming off him in waves, the Lieutenant says, "That's all well and good, but he escaped and ran amok. He imprisoned many crew members on his way to your rooms." His tone turning suspicious, he adds, "Speaking of which, just how is it that he found his way here?"

Accaryinth's amusement shines through. "*Ethan Shaw unquestionably escaped the intolerable condition your people forced him into. No doubt may be raised about this fact. And yes, he imprisoned your people... when he could have more easily killed them.*"

However, Ethan chose to elevate life over death." She let that sink in a moment before adding, *"As for how he came here, I perceived him seeking his friends and invited him here for a visit. He graciously accepted my invitation."*

Captain Hosslaniss leans back in his chair. "I concede the human was not kept in the most ideal of circumstances."

The Lieutenant slumps back in his chair.

"Thank you, Captain," Accaryinth says. *"Can we reach a consensus of understanding that all four of us meeting here wish everyone on board the GCM vessel known as Rissossa to reach our destination in good health?"*

After eyeing me a moment, Captain Hosslaniss says, "Yes."

"Excellent! Now, a suspicion has formed that this point may be difficult to reach consensus on, but I would still like to make the attempt. Might we agree that Ethan Shaw is not the ravening monster of our childhood stories?"

I sip my smoothie and try not to fidget.

To my surprise, the lieutenant is the one who admits, "He's not the monster I was expecting. But that doesn't mean he's not extremely dangerous."

"Oh, indeed he is dangerous," Accaryinth replies. *"He's so dangerous, he's one of three people in this room who could destroy this ship."*

Captain Hosslaniss and the lieutenant exchange puzzled looks.

Accaryinth nods. *"Ethan Shaw could rampage through the Rissossa and find any number of ways to destroy it. As could either of you. Why do you not? Because it's not in your best interest—exactly as it isn't in Ethan Shaw's best interest."*

"Now," she continues, before they've finished digesting that little thought-bomb, *"can we agree we do not desire to give any of the three of you reason to become violent and destroy this lovely vessel?"*

I've got to hand it to her, when it comes to diplomacy, Accaryinth is *good.*

Captain Hosslaniss's neck ruffles flutter. "Let's say for the sake of intellectual discourse, that we're willing to be more... accommodating to the human. Whatever agreement we might come to *must* put the crew's mind at ease. The human's mere presence on the ship has many of them... deeply concerned."

Well, I suppose that sounds better than "panicked."

I hold up a hand, and the three of them turn and stare at me.

"There's a cargo bay on deck four, about halfway back to the main engine room. It's empty. Wouldn't take much to make it livable: field toilet, a simple bed, food and water. I'd have room to move around, and the crew would never have to see me. That said, I *would* like my friends to be able to visit."

Captain Hosslaniss and the Lieutenant lean back at the same time. The Lieutenant pulls out a small block and plays with the controls. A holograph of the ship projects into the air between the four of us. He taps more controls and the cargo bay I mentioned turns yellow.

"Yes," I quietly reply to the unasked question while additionally giving a slow nod.

Accaryinth radiates pleasure.

The captain's neck ruffles fluff out a couple of times as the holograph vanishes. "That's quite the interesting idea. We need to confer, and I need to speak with my staff, but if you're both amenable, I believe we have a preliminary agreement."

I turn to Accaryinth and again nod.

Thoughts shining with pleasure, Accaryinth looks to them. *"Good sentients, we have achieved a preliminary agreement."*

CHAPTER 27

VOYAGING IN WHATEVER CLASS IS UNDER COACH

The cargo bay isn't exactly ideal, but it beats being stuck in a cage. Getting here took a bit more give and take on the negotiations.

They originally wanted guards in here with me. As nervous as I made their people, that seemed like a good way for me to fart or snore, and get shot. We compromised. The guards watch the only entrance that doesn't open into vacuum.

On the flip side, I wanted a meal faber. They claimed not to have much in the way of spares. Putting little psychic glimpses of their thoughts together, I figured out they feared I'd modify it to create explosives, toxins, or some other destructive mischief. Evidently, there's a popular vid out there in which a human got recreated and did exactly that. Instead, we agreed that Accaryinth or her people will bring me food twice a day.

Visitors were probably the most contentious thing we negotiated over. I wanted my friends free to enter whenever they want. The Lieutenant worried visitors would provide me ready access to hostages. Both Captain Hosslaniss and the Lieutenant were rather offended by my overly loud thought, "What special brand of stupid is this?" Accaryinth was simultaneously amused and annoyed with me. In the end, we agreed on regular visiting hours for everyone but Gabby. She could come and go as she pleased, and this actually made the Lieutenant happy because he wanted her kept away from the crew because of her human looks.

Last, they wanted scanners on me at all times. After a good deal of dickering, we agreed that someone would constantly watch every corridor and room abutting my cargo hold, and when I had visitors arrive or depart, the guards could run a scan to confirm my location and status.

"... And that's how I came to be sitting here in the cargo hold with you guys," I say to my friends, hugging Gabby, who sits in my lap.

If she was a cat, she'd be purring.

She leans up and kisses me before reclining against my chest.

Carmen, Embry, and Julian nod. They're sitting in a circle with us and looking much healthier. They've brought their own chairs but will have to take them when they leave.

Chairs. Of all the screwy things to worry about. Yeah, security here is weird.

"What about the collar?" Embry asks.

"Yeah, it's kinda a symbol to their people that I'm not running around loose. I'm not thrilled with wearing it, but for the moment, I'm not gonna raise a fuss."

"That's not right!" Carmen says, crossing her still too-skinny arms as she glares.

"No argument from me," I reply. "But regardless of that, I am thrilled to be here, talking with you guys."

Julian says, "Dude, we were worried about you. They didn't exactly treat you gently after they knocked you out back on Vega. By the way, how'd they do that?"

Gabby's anger flares, then slowly fades.

I tap the collar. "This has a drug reservoir."

"Ah," he and Embry say at the same time.

"Well," Carmen asks into the following silence. "What now?"

"Glad you asked," I reply. "I'd kinda like to pick up where we left off before things back on Vega got weird. Working out, Aikido classes, and I need lots and lots of knowledge about where we're going and who's in charge. All that stuff Day Mom and Dad were trying to teach me about the various galactic species, governments, and such just became high-priority information."

They bob their heads as thoughtful expressions overtake their faces.

Gabby asks, "Who's going to teach Aikido? We're all okay at it, but none of us are great."

"I was thinking maybe we'd take turns. You know, teach the moves and maneuvers that each of us are best at."

After brief consideration, everyone's okay with this idea.

"Good to start now?" I ask.

Contagious grins make the rounds.

We start with a workout. Each of us takes turns leading an exercise. The cargo bay isn't huge, but it's big enough that running laps around it is worth the effort. After a nice jog, Carmen leads us in crunches, Embry does some Yoga-like stretching, Julian switches us to push-ups, and Gabby finishes with jumping jacks—partly because she knows I like the way these make her boobs bounce.

Now that we're warmed up, we switch to throwing each other around with Aikido. They're all practicing harder than before. Being captured seems to have incentivized them to take this more seriously.

That said, Embry, Carmen, and Julian don't have their stamina back, so we keep the practice session short and sweet.

After a little cool down stretching, we reform our circle.

"There's one big central galactic government," Carmen explains. "It's based on five worlds that use massive X-Correspondence Communications Systems. This means, there's effectively no communications delay between those five worlds."

"Please don't get into the tech," I ask.

An evil grin spreads across her maroon face. "Now, the tech is based on—"

I groan and we all laugh.

Carmen's grin fades. "Alright, for the moment there's no actual need to worry about the tech. Each of those worlds contains one-fifth of the Executive Branch, Senate, and Judiciary. We're heading to Central. The other four are Prime, Focal Point, Median, and Zenith."

"Why," I ask wryly, "do I suddenly picture five worlds full of people with large egos?"

Julian grins. "You mean aside from them naming those planets as if each one is the center of the universe or the best of the best? Why, it's probably because those worlds are packed full of judges, politicians, and executors who think they're the smartest people in the room when in fact most of them are just the opposite."

Gabby coughs and blushes. "Actually, some senators are okay."

Embry stares at her, then his nostrils flare. "You know someone! Who?"

"The senator from Aklansic is my grandmother. She got into politics to help me get citizenship for Ethan."

Wow.

"Aklansic," I say, verbally double-checking my memory, "being your mostly aquatic homeworld."

"Exactly."

Carmen growls for silence, then scowls because she's good at it. "So, as I was saying," she glares as though daring someone to interrupt again, "five planets, and we're going to Central. Each branch of government has three tiers. Lower, middle and high."

"Well," I say with a grin that hasn't faded since she growled, "that at least is easy to remember."

"It's gotta be simple. Some people," she gives me and Julian significant looks, "are intellectually challenged."

"Kinda dumb," Embry adds with a nod.

"Hey!" Julian declares indignantly. "I resemble that remark!"

We chuckle.

Carmen's expression turns serious again. "When we arrive on Central, they'll turn us over to the Executive Branch. At that point, things are likely to get... interesting."

"Why?" I ask.

"Because everyone's gonna want to handle your case. The Senate's gonna try to pass some sort of legislation about you. The Executives will issue decrees, and the Judiciary's gonna override both with orders and injunctions. It's going to be a weird sort of governmental free-for-all."

"And massive tug-of-war," Embry adds.

A frown spreads across my lips. "That sounds... time consuming."

"Yeah," Carmen whispers. "Possibly intentionally so."

Gabby says, "We could always break out and take this ship somewhere else."

"No," I sigh. "We can't."

"Why not?"

"I gave my word that I wouldn't."

With a half-assed scowl, Gabby tells me, "You're too honorable for your own good."

I shrug.

"Then what do we do?" Embry asks quietly, looking at me.

"I guess we research all the major political groups on Central. Figure out where they stand. Find out who's gonna be an enemy, and who's going to be a friend."

"And," Carmen interjects, "which ones are gonna *pretend* to be our friends."

I nod. "Too right. This sounds like a horrible plan. Let's do it."

I'm up tragically early. There's a fear growing in my heart that I'm mutating into some sort of morning person.

With difficulty, I fight back a shudder.

Being careful not to wake Gabby, who practically never leaves, I sneak over to the toilet to take care of business. After that's done and I brush my teeth, I sit beside her and caress my fingertips lightly over her cheek.

I never expected to have a girlfriend this beautiful, strong, and amazing. I'm incredibly lucky.

She murmurs something but doesn't wake.

My mind drifts back to a talk we all had back on Thompson. It happened a couple of days after we decided to stay in the tent-things rather than on the ship.

I was thinking how lucky I was to have my parents with me and suddenly realized that I was the *only* one in our group to have that luxury. So, I asked my friends about their parents, and if we needed to find a way to arrange a meet-up.

Their replies were... interesting.

Julian explained his parents were on a permanent cruise around the galaxy as they worked to spend the money he'd earned by being in the Project. Seeing my dismay, he shrugged and said, "They never really understood me, anyway. I wanted challenges beyond modeling, and they wanted a life of luxury their parents never had. In the end, I guess we all got what we wanted." After a pause, he added, "On the other hand, I really miss my fake parents. They were good people. They truly were family. If we can, I'd like to meet up with them again."

"Wait," Embry said, surprise causing his nostrils to flare. "You really were a model?"

Julian grinned. "One of the beautiful people, baby."

"But," Carmen said, "you can't have been more than five before you came to the Project."

Hooking all four of his thumbs back towards himself, his grin widened. "Born beautiful, still beautiful."

I took it as a measure of how stunned the others were that none of them made gagging or scoffing sounds.

Trying to shake off my surprise, I turned to Carmen. "What about you?"

"My parents are on a deep space survey mission. If all goes according to plan, they'll be back in eleven years."

"I.... Yeah, I'm not sure how to respond to that."

Gabby asked her, "What about any other family?"

Carmen tilted her head in a negligent shrug. "I'm closer to you guys than any of them. Also, because of the Project, I've got the notes to go where I want to go. You guys are the most interesting possibility going, so I'll stay with you."

"Oh. Cool. What are notes?" I asked.

"Currency of the realm."

"Ah." I turned to Embry.

"I'm among the oldest of forty-five children. If I went home, my parents would put me on permanent baby-sitting duty. *Not* gonna happen. Besides, you guys are my family, too."

"Forty-five?" Julian burst out, his ear ruffs flaring wide.

"Sure, but there may be more by now. Egg clutches typically range from four-to-eight each breeding. Evidently, my parents enjoy reproducing."

Gabby and Carmen met each other's eyes and erupted in giggles.

The rest of us couldn't help but chuckle, too.

After the laughter died down, Carmen looked to Gabby. "What about your parents?"

I am *such* a moron for never asking about my girlfriend's family.

"My mother," Gabby began quietly but with great distaste, "wanted me to be a corporate psychic. Instead of going to an internship interview, I went and applied to be Aklansic's member in the Project."

"You ran away and applied to join the Project when you were six?" Julian asked, his jaw dropping. The others were just as stunned.

"Sure did. As for my father, he's never been part of my life. He and my mother had a falling out before I was born."

Embry leaned forward slightly, looking back and forth between me and Gabby. "Sounds like you guys have a lot in common."

Gabby sat back against me. "Oh. Umm, you know, I never thought of it that way."

Most interesting.

"Regardless of why you're here," I said, meeting their eyes, "you're all family to me. Now and forever."

Back in the here and now, Gabby rolls over and murmurs something in her sleep.

Time to find out what's happening aboard the GCM light destroyer *Rissossa*.

Sitting tailor fashion, I even out my breathing, relax, and extend my senses. Watching the crew has become part of my morning routine. Seeing how their station controls work, what they do in the way of maintenance, how the crew interacts... it's all kinda mesmerizing. I now have at least a passing familiarity with all the bridge stations. While I doubt I could actually fly this ship, I *do* understand most of the basic controls and systems.

Beyond that, I've played a bit with remotely using my telekinesis. I'll sometimes open a door here or there, or activate a device, making the nearest crew member startle.

I grin.

Yeah, sometimes the little things provide the biggest amusements.

Moreover, should it come to that, I can shut down the ship by disconnecting the generators. Hopefully, that knowledge will never get put into use.

Still, I'm learning how more and more systems work.

And how to stop them.

Today, I concentrate on the water recycling system. It's not what you'd exactly call a glamorous part of the ship, but it's as vital as the artificial gravity. They store water in five primary tanks. Why five? Maybe it's sort of unspoken tribute to the galactic government? Yeah, I've got no real clue. Anyway, from the tanks, the water's pumped throughout the ship to smaller tanks, being filtered at each step. From there, the water's directed to outlets. Once used, the water's piped back to an intricate filtration system involving three different algae and micro-screens.

Cool.

And it reminds me I haven't had an actual bath or shower in the two weeks since we've been here.

"Too right," Gabby says, sitting up. "The sani-cloths can only do so much." She steps over and brushes her teeth then uses the facilities while I psychically check out the pool on the ship's recreational deck for the fourth time.

Gabby rests a hand on my shoulder as she picks up on my focus. "Mmm, water sounds *good*. Think Captain Hosslaniss or Lieutenant Lissatiss would go for it?"

I take her on a quick telepathic run-through the ship's corridors. "If we were to take this path, they'd only have to close these three doors to completely seal off our access to the rec-deck. Then of course, the two other doors leading into the deck itself. If I disable the surveillance node, we could play for a few hours, sneak back out, and the crew would never be the wiser."

"Wait, you're not *really* planning on us sneaking in, are you?"

"Yes, and no. We'll see if we can't arrange this with the captain. If he agrees, we'll sneak in and out so as not to freak out the crew."

Because Accaryinth is the mother of diplomacy, we invite her over for drinks—which she and her staff have to provide.

She senses my frustration with how backwards this is and her amusement sparkles. "*It shines as an unexpected boon that this has grown to be your biggest frustration.*"

I raise my extra-thick chocolate shake in salute. "*I suppose it is at that.*"

She returns my salute with her cup. "*I hold a suspicion that you wish to ask something new of your hosts?*"

"*That is correct. With your permission, I'd like to take you on a little psychic trip.*"

Her eyes dilate. "*This brings hope of impending delight.*" Despite her efforts to keep her thoughts even, she's excited.

So, I walk her through our plan to go swimming.

"*Well considered,*" she says. "*With your permission, I will converse about this with our captain on your behalf.*"

"*Thank you, so much. We really appreciate this.*"

"*I must acknowledge, my interactions with you have been extremely gratifying on a number of levels.*"

"*I've enjoyed working with you as well.*"

"*Now,*" she says, her mind lighting up with amusement, "*what was that saying your people had? Ah yes. I believe I'm going to go speak to Captain Hosslaniss and raise a little hell.*"

Gabby and I are still laughing as Accaryinth and her people leave.

Chapter 28

HOW TO PROPERLY
MAINTAIN YOUR GCM
LIGHT DESTROYER

"So, how was your swim?" Carmen asks as Gabby and I return from our aquatic excursion. I'm a bit surprised the guards let my friends in without us being here, but the ship has relaxed a lot since I was first brought aboard.

Out in the corridors we just walked through, the holographic 'Maintenance In Progress - Do Not Enter' signs are being removed. The pool's receiving a thorough cleaning, and I'm trying not to be offended.

Being in such a good mood helps.

"We had a great swim," I reply.

Gabby nods her agreement as she sets down the bag with our towels and swimsuits.

Carmen eyes us askance, then focuses on the open bag. Her left eye grows slightly larger. "Why are your towels wet, but your swimsuits dry?"

Gabby feigns a look of surprise. "Ohmygosh! It must be some sort of miracle!"

I nod sagely. "Miracle."

Carmen snorts, and the others give knowing grins.

Speaking of knowing, I've known for a while that Gabby's from a semi-aquatic species. What I hadn't realized until we started swimming today is that she kept some of that when she changed to be more human. She has gill seams on her neck and just under her ribcage that allow her to breathe underwater.

My sweetheart is amazing.

Gabby winks. *"Back at ya, babe."*

"I think you guys swimming is a good thing," Julian teases. "You both smell *sooo* much better." He throws Gabby a feigned look of terror and hides behind Carmen.

Embry and I snicker while Gabby considers launching herself in a sort of flying tackle at him. She's not sure she'll miss Carmen and eyes the two of them with a considering gaze.

Seeing the look, Embry says, "Ahem. We got an update about the political situation on Central." He turns to Gabby. "Including a message from your grandmother."

Gabs reluctantly decides not to attack Julian—for the moment—and takes her usual seat in my lap.

Embry continues, "There're six major political factions, not just on Center, but across the galaxy. Unfortunately, Gabby's grandmother's party is the only one on our side. They want to make Ethan a citizen. Everyone else... not so much."

I sigh into Gabby's damp hair.

She asks, "How strong is my grandmother's party compared to the others?"

"Her party," he says, "is the Life Alliance. They're in deep with the Galactic Life Keepers and similar groups. According to polls, they're... a distant third."

That doesn't bode well.

"And the first two?"

"The number one group's the Everything's Okay party. They're led by a charismatic bastard by the name of Obatah Ogriton. Their position is that everything's working fine as it is, so change nothing that doesn't desperately need changing. They believe adding Ethan into the galactic citizenry would not just change things, it would change them big time and for the worse. Therefore, they're very much against us."

"What about the number two group?" I ask.

Now it's Embry's turn to sigh. "They're even worse. Many groups make up the Forging the Future Coalition." He looks down at his hands. "This includes Sergeant Lawton's group, the Dark Union—who want to chop you up and turn you into a series of bioweapons." He glances at the walls. "They've got quite a few supporters in top positions within the military."

I cuss under my breath.

Gabby gives my knee a squeeze but doesn't comment.

"Yeah," Embry says. "My feelings, too."

Julian leans forward. "We'll dig into all the groups. Then we'll study the major players in each group. Find out what they think and why they think that way. Turn their arguments against them."

I frown. "They're not gonna allow me within a kilometer of those proceedings, will they?"

"Probably not," Gabby agrees quietly. "They'll likely hold you in a remote facility and holo you in after pretty much everything's said and done."

Embry snaps his fingers. "What about the press? We've been looking at the parties. But they don't represent all the voters. There are a *lot* of unaffiliated voters out there. I don't know the numbers, but there may be enough to make a difference."

Carmen nods, her expression excited. "I've got some distant relatives in the press, and I'm pretty sure I can call in some favors and start getting some pro-human stories out there." She looks to the others. "We may have to do some remote interviews. No, make that, we *should* do interviews. As many as we can stand."

"Yeah," Julian says, tapping his fingers across his broad chin. "That's not bad. Also, we should be able to make some significant cash off this. Access to those of us who are closest to the human? News outlets will pay out their facial orifices for that sort of story."

Gabby scowls at him. "Julian's greed aside, that's not a bad idea." She sighs. "And I've gotta admit, we'll probably need the notes sooner or later."

"There's one more thing," Embry says. "And it's more worrisome than everything else combined."

We stare at him a moment before Carmen quietly asks, "What?"

"Apathy."

Julian and I exchange confused looks. Julian looks to Embry. "Sorry, I'm not following. We're not following."

Embry nods. "Yeah. Back before we arrived on Vega, the Life Keepers released the information the Project was withholding from the public. All the dark secrets about how they'd mismanaged the project and lied about the results... it all came to light."

I feel Gabby's frown as she slowly nods.

"Problem is," Embry continues, "only the Life Alliance and a few independents cared. According to the polls, barely even half of the voting populace are even remotely concerned about it."

Gabs leans forward, her thoughts angry and intent. "Wait a minute. The scandal of our lifetimes breaks, and... no one cares?"

"Exactly. And that apathy is gonna be the toughest opponent we face as we move forward with getting Ethan citizenship."

Silence falls as we mull this over.

Gabby claps her hands. "We've got three weeks before we dock above Central, and we've got a lot to do. Let's get after it."

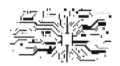

My friends and Gabby are spending less time here with me and more time studying, doing interviews, and sending messages to political leaders throughout the galaxy. They've been so busy that Captain Hosslaniss had to limit their access to the communications array. Rather to my surprise, he's not doing it maliciously, he just needs to keep a certain amount of bandwidth open for ship's business. To my much greater surprise, Gabby talks him into doing an interview with her, which she then sends out for the Life Keepers to distribute.

Gabs brings me a copy. It casts me in a pretty darn good light.

In the mornings, I still get up early. I do some increasingly intense exercises and then sit down and psychically check things out around the ship—exactly like I'm doing now. Soon, Accaryinth's people will bring around my breakfast. Speaking of Accaryinth, Embry's enrolled her into helping. From what I can tell, the elderly psychic is having the time of her life.

As I'm scanning around the ship, something catches my attention.

Uh oh.

There's a pressure valve on the number three port-side engine's fuel control system that's malfunctioning. It's allowing way too much pressure to build up.

I walk over and bang on the door.

Warily, the guard opens it. Since she's got a translator now, I explain the problem.

She nods and closes the door. When I feel her calling the bridge, I go back to my floor cushion, sit, and return to monitoring things.

The captain calls Engineering and they check it out. This turns into a desperate, frenzied repair to avoid a possibly catastrophic explosion.

Later, I receive an official commendation from the captain. Lieutenant Lissatiss delivers the engraved copy. He greets me with a bow, gives a quick speech about having earned the gratitude of the entire crew, and leaves with another bow.

Nice.

It feels like I'm making progress.

Pushing my awareness beyond the ship is weird. Space is ridiculously big and most of it has exactly nothing in it. Determining how successful my attempts at further expanding my awareness are... yeah, that's extremely difficult because of all that nothing. Still, compared with all my other frustrations, this one's tiny.

Early afternoon, Julian drops by. He's trying to appear in good spirits, but something is clearly getting him down.

He's distracted from that by what's not around my neck.

"Dude! How'd you get the collar off?"

"I got better at working maglocks."

"Gonna leave it off?"

I shake my head. "Naa, I'll put it back on in a while. So, what's up?"

His smile falters. "We're getting a lot of good press out there for you. Some interviewers have been openly hostile, but despite that, we've been able to put a good spin on things."

"But...?"

"Yeah," he sighs. "Problem is, for every interview we do, there's half a dozen or more interviews with professors and so-called scientists who insist you're a monster the likes of which nobody has seen in fifty-thousand years. And a *lot* of the press out there are clearly out to get you. From what Carmen's friends and family are saying, most of the news networks are working directly for the two biggest political parties when they're supposed to be independent." He shakes his head. "It's *really* disconcerting."

"Bloody hell," I mutter before snorting a little laugh. "Maybe I should be glad I'm in here, where I can't see all that."

Ear crests flat, he scrubs his fingertips through his mane, which now reaches his shoulders. "I feel like we're letting you down. According to the latest polls, anti-human bias is going up, not down."

I shrug. "Still better than apathy. Don't worry about it. I know you guys are doing what you can, and I really appreciate it. Just keep going with your rational arguments. Let *them* be the ones screaming and acting all crazy."

Julian squirms and looks uncomfortable.

Oh.

I cannot prevent a twisted grin. "Let me guess—Gabby."

"Um, yeah. She kinda blew up when a guy kept calling you a baby-eating monster." A little grin peeks through. "It was actually pretty awesome."

I can't hold in a laugh.

"Yeah," I say, still chuckling. "That sounds like my Gabby."

"Anyway, I wanted to give you an update. I've got another interview in a little over thirty minutes. Oh, also wanted to let you know, I was right. The networks are paying out some major notes for access to the four of us. We've pooled the money and cut you in for an equal share."

"Uh, wow. Thanks."

"Heck buddy, it's the least we could do."

"No. I'm quite sure 'nothing' would be the least you could do. You guys have gone way above and beyond. Thank you."

He strikes a pose and deepens his voice. "Superheroes like me do this sort of thing all the time, citizen. My next stop is to rescue an entire litter of kittens stuck in a tree that's an imposing *two* meters tall. Yes, I've devoted my life to the super heroic."

While I'm still snickering, he waves and leaves.

As my laughter dies down, I'm left with one unavoidable fact.

I am royally screwed.

My thoughts drift.

Some of the early martial arts referred to elements in their descriptions. Move quick as the wind. Stand unmoving like a mountain. Dance around attacks like the flickering flame. Hold within yourself the stillness of calm water.

That always stuck with me... and I'm not sure if this was originally Lachlann's thinking or mine.

When you're still, you're in a better position to react to your enemies. Like water, you flow around the attacks against you but hammer them like the waves of a storm pounding a beach. At least, that's the idea.

Clearly, what I need to be is more like water.

I sit on my cushion in the cargo bay, monitoring the surrounding ship.

Oh. Maybe I already am.

Chapter 29

A Parting Gift Like No Other

T his will be the last time Gabby and I swim on this ship.
In the water, I can essentially fly via my telekinesis. Breathing with her gills for both of us, Gabby can keep us under water for seven minutes before she has to come up for air. Her gills just aren't efficient enough to provide breath for both of us over an extended time.

We both want to enjoy this time together, but our preoccupations form a weight that's hard to shake. I hold her close and absently set us drifting around the surface.

"I'm scared," she whispers.

"Yeah. Me too."

"What we have together, you and me... it's more than I ever dared to dream. I know that's kinda lame because you're still a prisoner, but it's true. I'm happy here. And I don't know what's gonna happen next. I'm scared to death I'll lose you."

"Not even remotely lame," I reply quietly. "I've been happy, too. Hell, if it wasn't for our friends nearly dying, I think I could have been happy on Vega, so long as you were there. Still, this isn't too bad. Slowly bringing the crew around to not being terrified of me. That's been pretty nice. Working with you guys and Accaryinth, that's been interesting and enlightening. But the best part of it all has been you and me together.

"I've mentioned before that I realized back on Thompson that you were the girl of my dreams." I give her a lopsided grin. "Felt pretty dumb for not realizing it before. You were my best friend, and I feared losing that. Afraid to take the leap because if things

253

didn't work out, then not only would I not have a girlfriend, but I also wouldn't have my *best* friend, either. I think my fear of losing you was greater than my hope. I am *very* glad you followed me when I skipped school that day."

Gabby turns on a slow burning smile and gives me a hot, sensuous kiss. "You're not half as glad as I am."

Allowing a bit of challenge to enter my voice, I reply, "I'm pretty sure I'm *more* glad than you."

"*Pfft*, silly man." Gabby leans over me with both elbows on my chest. She delivers many small kisses around my mouth. "Clearly, I'm *much* happier about it than you."

Leaning up, I kiss around her neck for a while. "Well, there's only one way to settle this."

"What's that?" she purrs.

"A happiness contest."

"Mmm," she says, kissing my lips. "What are the rules?"

"No rules," I reply, pulling her close. "We make it up as we go."

"Hell. Yeah," she whispers intensely into my mouth before locking it down with a kiss.

"You know what?" I ask Gabby as we walk back into my cargo bay.

"What?"

"I'm gonna marry you, someday."

A brilliant smile starts deep within her mind well before it makes it to her lovely lips. Her mind suddenly freezes up.

Before I become alarmed, she throws her mental shields up, which *does* alarm me.

"Don't worry," she says, kissing me hard as her excitement bleeds through her walls. "It's a good thing. Possibly a wonderful thing." In response to my unasked question, she says, "I don't want to get anyone's hopes up. Gotta run, love you!"

She leaves, not quite at a run, but walking fast.

"Love you!" I call after her just before the guard closes the door behind me.

Well, I would say that was weird, but all things considered, it barely clears the threshold for unusual, much less weird.

I sit and return to monitor the ship and crew.

Gabby re-joins me a couple of hours later.

"Don't ask," she orders. She's brought the psychic storage device. "Instead, I'd like you to walk me through the last of the TBF47 series?"

"Okay. We've hit all the others, might as well finish it."

"Thanks, love," she replies, taking her usual seat. "Now, wrap your arms around me and let's fly!"

Her enthusiasm is contagious. I find the last of the five-part series and press the proverbial button.

Once more, I'm Tara Houza and I'm flying my TBF-47 Firehawk. The Firehawk is an up-gunned, light torpedo bomber and a fantastic ship. Only slightly larger than a standard fighter craft, it's maneuverable as a fighter and has nearly the same punch as the bulky and aging TB-8 Avenger heavy torpedo bombers.

Before approaching the target area, I deploy stealth drones. The drones zoom into position, allowing me to see over the horizon and eventually all around the planet.

I've set the board.

To get the party started, I open fire with the Gauss cannons even though I can't see the target. Instead, I'm using Vega's gravity well to pull the cannon shells down and into the target. By the time the vessel explodes, I'm almost back to my initial staging point.

Next, I demonstrate a cold torpedo drop, in which I release the armed torpedo, but its engines never fire. Instead, it relies on great targeting and the Firehawk's velocity at the time of drop.

Same as earlier, the gravity well pulls it around, this time to the other side of the planet. It impacts the target and detonates with the added oomph of the torpedo's full fuel supply, completely eradicating a small trading ship.

Next, I perform a hot drop. For such a short distance as the other side of Vega, the torpedo never stops accelerating before impact and *that* adds oomph to the bang.

After that, I execute a dog-on-a-leash. Executing a dog-on-a-leash is now, and forever will be, the most talked about joke in fleet locker rooms throughout the galaxy. Despite that, it's a truly devastating maneuver. Engines screaming, I race head-long at a large freighter with all guns blazing. The TBF-47 has enough firepower that the freighter's pretty thoroughly trashed by the time I pull up, punch the escape rockets, and burn hard. *That's* when the two torpedoes I have trailing in my sensor shadow smash into the ship. The shattered remains drop into Vega's unforgiving gravity well.

There're a lot of variations on these themes, and I run through as many as I can before switching over to targets within a gravity well.

For a lot of these attacks, I don't even have to be in the gravity well to pound the target into rubble. But, sometimes you just can't avoid it. Hardened installations and storms can make targeting from afar difficult. At that point, you've got to get up close and personal. Usually, this means giving it a tried-and-true dive-bomb. If you think torpedo detonations are cool in space, what until you've seen an ammo dump explode or you've sent a few thousand ultra-high velocity rounds through a reactor.

Yep, the mushroom clouds are pretty darn gratifying.

For the last part of this series, I'm out of the ship and standing before a mirror in my formal blacks. I salute. "This has been Flight Lieutenant Tara Houza with the Kasumi Battle Group. Thank you for flying with me. Long live the Terran Empire!"

And I'm out of the recording.

Gabs will be awhile processing, so I sit and think things over. Long live the Terran Empire. I can't help the thread of sadness that twists through me.

Contrarily, nor can I help but grin when I think about how awesome the Firehawks were. Or Tara herself. She had a targeting computer to help line up her shots, but half the time she didn't need it—she'd been able to do the math in her head. Combined with her lightning reflexes and mad skills, Tara Houza really was one seriously badass pilot.

Eventually, I open up my awareness and scan over the ship. Julian is on comms with someone from the Life Keeper's legal team. Carmen's holoing an interview with a few of the ship's crew for later broadcast. Embry is doing a follow-up call with Gabby's grandmother. I start to listen in on that but feel a pulse of excitement from the crew deck.

There. On the rec deck, I find over a dozen members of the crew watching a sports match. Their team has just scored a touch and they are now winning 4-3 with less than three minutes remaining.

The crew is still cheering, because hope will do that for you.

Despite the emotional noise, there's something distracting me, quietly calling my attention. It takes me a moment to realize what it is.

There're thoughts where there have been no thoughts before—outside the ship.

I shift my focus.

Cruising alongside us is a small ship, not much bigger than a Firehawk. It's all black and presumably covered in stealth material and screens since our ship's sensor operator has no idea it's here. The pilot is hard to read with a mind that's cold and calculating.

A port approximately a meter around opens in the stealth ship. A drone flies out.

Oh, this can't be good.

A puff of air sets it moving towards our ship.

I pull my awareness in for a closeup. Interesting. There's not much to this drone. A simple maglock on the 'bottom,' a beacon, a receiver, directional controls, and a whole lot of highly compacted explosive.

Hmm. If I fly the bomb back to them, they'll just keep trying to re-attach it. Maybe write it off as equipment failure. But, if they're tenacious, they'll be back. And if they return while I'm asleep....

Yeah, that could be bad.

I could probably detonate it now, but this close to the ship... definitely not good.

However, I *am* a clever human. Possibly even devious sometimes.

Okay, the beacon's how they know where the bomb is. Through the receiver, they control the direction of the thing, activate the maglock, and detonate the device. So really, I need to keep the beacon, but send the rest of the device home with them.

If I fail, we'll all die.

No pressure, right?

So, how to remove the beacon? Hmm. It's got its own power source. That's good. While the beacon doesn't have an independent maglock, I bet I can find a place to stick it to my ship's hull where it'll stay put.

Sounds like a plan.

Now, let's see.... If I pull up that panel on the drone, the beacon should just pop right out.

Unfortunately, I have to wait until the baddie sets the bomb and is about to leave. Otherwise, they might notice me fiddlin' around with it and we're right back where we started.

Slowly, the bomb drone drifts across the ten-meter gap between ships.

So, on the bomb itself... there's the power supply for the maglock and the interrupt point. Will magnets even stick to the other ship's stealth covering?

I have no idea, but I'm willing to find out.

Gabs comes out of the recording and shivers. "Babe! That was awesome!"

I give her a little squeeze. "Yep. Sorry—busy for the next little while."

She checks her chrono then kisses me. "Love ya, babe. I gotta go check something. Hope to have news soon."

"Sounds good," I say as the bomb touches the ship and latches on. I wink at Gabby. "I'll be here waiting."

She blows me a last kiss and is out the door.

Heaving out a sigh of relief, I switch my full focus to the bomb.

The stealth ship eases away.

Crap.

I pop the cover off the beacon. Whatever the cover's made of, it doesn't bend, it just snaps off. I yank the beacon out and hold it against the ship. So far, so good. I reach inside the bomb and flip the mag-lock interrupt and pull the whole thi—

It's not pulling.

What the hell?

I zoom in closer.

Farg, there's some sort of molecular glue on the bottom plate. Annoyingly competent bad-guys and their redundant securing measures.

I have vague memories of Lachlann performing a couple of shearing exercises with his telekinesis. Cutting target dummies in half, cutting thin strips all the way through until the dummies fell apart in a pile of slices. Things that would have been really helpful to know back on Vega. Still, dummies, molecular glue on a ship-killing bomb, it's all the same, right?

Damn, I sure hope so.

I line up the cutting angle... there.

Quick as thought, I lash out with a micro-thin sheet of telekinetic force. The bomb separates from the ship. I would sigh in relief, but my bomb carrier is flying away.

I launch the bomb while keeping the beacon. The beacon latches onto some of the leftover glue.

Don't have to worry about that anymore.

The farther the bomb flies, the more my senses and abilities attenuate. Soon, it'll be out of my range, and I *really* like the idea of the bad guys blowing themselves up.

Kinda an unintentional suicide-by-evil.

The bomb's almost to the ship, but the latter is continuing to slowly speed up. I have time for one last push....

Contact!

The bomb barely touches, but the remaining glue sticks.

I engage the maglock. Just for good measure, I disconnect the line leading from the maglock to the transmitter.

Snapping back into my head, I lean forward, wincing. Yeah, that produced one serious headache. Still, I did it.

Victory and relief flood through me.

Everything's so wonderful, I crawl into bed and immediately fall asleep.

Chapter 30
GABBY'S SURPRISES

Gabby wakes me with a kiss maybe an hour later. My headache's gone and I'm feeling good.

So is Gabby. She's practically radiating happiness. "I like this whole Sleeping Beauty thing. It makes me feel like a princess!"

I grin up at her. "What's up, Buttercup?"

"There're a few things happening at once. Let's start small," she says, laying down beside me.

"Okay, shoot."

She props herself up on an elbow. "I'm gonna do my second bonding shift soon. It will tie up some inconsistencies in my form."

"Okay. Interesting. Will you still be able to breathe underwater?"

"Sure, I'll always keep that."

Sensing that she's not done, I prompt, "And...?"

"And, I'd like to look a little more like Tara Houza. I'm not gonna get rid of my half-Korean facial features or my black hair, but Tara's build, her musculature... it's what I never knew I wanted before." Seeing I'm not following one hundred percent, she explains, "Ethan, I've been in the woman's head. Through those recordings, I lived in her body. I now *know*, without question, *exactly* what it's supposed to feel like. And my body doesn't feel that way. It's close, because I'm a damn good and super-modest metamorph, but my body's not quite what it should be. My second bonding shift should take care of all that."

"Okay," I reply, trying to wrap my head around this totally unexpected development. "Uh, when and where? Do you need help to prepare?"

"Maybe tonight, at the pool. I've talked to the captain, and he's given his okay. But...."

"But what?"

"There're a few of those. The first question is will you be okay with me looking more like Tara Houza?"

I reach out and caress her face. "Sweetheart, issues of your cool Korean ancestry aside, you and Tara really don't look that different. I'd guess you're close to the same height and weight. You're both nicely curvy. If you wanna be more like Tara, be more like Tara. So long as you're still Gabriella Kwan in the morning, that's all that matters."

"Ahem," she says, fake clearing her throat. "That might be a problem."

"What? How? Why?"

She grins in the face of my alarm. "Easy there, tiger. We're not looking at any serious problems here. Not yet, anyway."

"Gabs, are you *trying* to freak me out? Also, I'm not a tiger. Granted, I'm not a dragon yet either, but I'm working on it."

Gabby leans back and smiles. "You are, and I am so *very* proud of you."

I'm gonna need a neck brace from the whiplash this conversation is giving me.

I roll over, sit up straddling her, and look her in the eyes. "Gabriella Kwan, *please* start saying things I understand again."

She reaches up and cups the side of my face in her hand. "You understand the pieces. Now, let's assemble the puzzle."

I close my eyes and bury my growing frustration deep.

"Let me see if this helps," Gabby says. Her joy and trepidation radiate out of her like an emotional star. As I open my eyes, she leans up so the tips of our noses touch and stares into my eyes. "Ethan Shaw, I want to marry you. Tonight."

"Oh."

Mind. Blown.

I know I'm radiating shock and barely manage to stop it. After a moment, my brain starts working again.

Deep in my heart, I know there's no chance of me meeting someone I want to be with as much as I want to be with Gabby. I miss her when she leaves the room, and I'm happy when she enters the room. Yeah, that's a great metaphor for my feelings.

There's probably a lot of good reasons people as young as us shouldn't get married.

But I can't think of a single one.

"Yes."

Her happiness practically blots out my vision. She latches her lips onto mine and my mind fills with a delightful storm of joy and light.

Several minutes later, she stops kissing me.

"Okay," she says, smiling radiantly. "Captain Hosslaniss has agreed to perform the ceremony. After the reception, I'll need your help to do the bonding shift."

"What do you need me to do?"

"This may seem a little weird."

"My threshold for weird has gone *way* up of late. Try me."

She tilts her head, watching for my reaction. "I need bodily fluids from my mate."

"Okay. Like saliva?"

"To ensure that my saliva is as close to human as possible. But, that's not all."

I lift my eyebrows. "Blood?"

"To ensure that my blood is as close to human as possible."

Eyeing her askance, I ask, "But, that's not all?"

She nods. "Yep. I need a little something to ensure that our children are as close to human as possible."

Oh.

There's a topic I never considered.

Gabby leans in and kisses me. "There'll be plenty of time to think about it later." She rolls me over and now she's straddling me. "Cold feet? I mean, I *am* a shapeshifting, half-aquatic alien."

"You," I say, looking into her eyes, "are Gabriella Kwan. *The* Gabriella Kwan. You are my best friend, and it would be my great honor to marry you."

Another surge of joy blasts out of her.

"Good," she says, "but, at the end of the evening, I don't wanna be Gabriella Kwan. I *want* to be Gabriella Shaw."

I pull her in for a long kiss. "What the lady wants, the lady gets."

"That's exactly what I wanted to hear." Half teasing, half not, she adds, "Ethan, you're gonna be a great husband!"

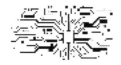

After that, Gabby and I get some new clothes printed. A black and grey Imperial Terran uniform with no rank or service insignia for me. She's torn between something that's functional and can be re-used or a single-use outfit that'll go back into the recycler. In the end, Gabs decides she's already got other clothes, so she prints a beautiful white dress with lots of lace.

Carmen is her maid of honor, and Julian and Embry are dual best men.

To my surprise, security allows in several members of Captain Strange Noise's crew as well as Accaryinth and her people. There's much milling about and chatting with us marriage-party types. When Captain Hosslaniss arrives, I quietly ask him, "I hope you don't mind if I forgo the collar for this?" He's got a translator now, so he understands. Just one of the nicer changes that's been happening behind the scenes onboard the ship.

He pulls out a small remote and presses a button. "I had the same thought. Wouldn't be right to wear that during a wedding." I don't mention that I could have taken it off at any time in the last couple of weeks. For some strange reason, I don't really think that would help with any aspect of our evening plans.

I set the collar on a table. "Thank you, Captain Hosslaniss. For everything."

"You are welcome, but I must admit, receiving your thanks makes me a touch uncomfortable. We did not start off with the best of relations."

I smile. "Captain, there's an old human saying: 'it's not about where you begin, but where you finish.' We may have gotten off on the wrong foot, but look at us, now."

"Indeed, young human. Our fear of you being a monster, nearly turned us into the monsters." He smiles a fangy smile. "And now I'm about to perform the marriage ceremony for you and your head-strong mate. Today is a glorious day!"

"It is indeed," I reply, looking across the room at Gabby, who is the most amazing woman in the entire galaxy. It's almost physically hard looking away from her. "Absolutely glorious."

Accaryinth catches my attention and I walk over to her and her delegation.

Before my eyes again turn to Gabby, I say, *"I'm glad you could make it."*

Accaryinth smiles. *"It is such a joy to see love triumphing over evil. You have grown a great deal in a short time, Ethan Shaw."*

"Yeah, I suppose I have."

"You are doing things the right way. Earn all the friends you can. They will serve you well in the future."

"Thank you. That sounds like excellent advice."

"You are welcome. At some point, I shall deliver to you both a wedding gift. Sadly, time and circumstance did not cooperate for presenting it this evening."

"Oh, there's no need for that. Just having you here with us is more than gift enough!"

"Young human, you are a treasure. My blessing upon your union."

"Thank you, Accaryinth of Meprophrose. That means a great deal to me. To us."

She smiles again. *"Go, Ethan Shaw. You can barely keep your eyes from your bride and with good reason. I wish nothing but good things for you both."*

"Thanks again," I say, but my eyes have already locked onto Gabby. She's always been pretty, but tonight she's positively radiant.

In this day and age, I may be a superhuman, but I'm evidently still subject to the same nerves that have plagued men since mankind first began performing wedding ceremonies. Umm, maybe I'm *more* subject than most.

I mean, I remember the ceremony.

Ahem. Mostly.

It's kinda like a cross between a weird-but-wonderful dream and being possessed by some sort of demon. Not literally or psychically, but... you know, a lot like it. Most of the time, there is a peculiar rushing in my ears. Anyway, I'm pretty sure I go through the whole thing with a big, dopey grin plastered across my face.

The ceremony itself is short and to the point.

Captain Hosslaniss says words. I have no idea what they are, but he says them and I'm fairly sure I understand them. Gabs and I agree to love, honor, and cherish one another. The captain says more words and turns to us.

Gabby and I kiss, sealing the deal.

Our friends applaud and the others cheer.

At the reception, the food is arranged by species. I eat something. Other people eat. Gabs and I dance, and we do a fantastic job of it, like we've been practicing for weeks. Even while we're moving across the dance floor, we're sharing our surprise.

Afterward, we talk to people.

As the party's really getting started, we sneak out with the aid of Captain Hosslaniss and Lieutenant Lissatiss. In short order, Gabby and I are in the pool room and the other two are locking the doors behind them.

"Mrs. Shaw, you look amazing."

Gabby smiles. "You've said that already."

"It bears repeating." Besides, since I don't remember saying it before, it doesn't count.

"Thank you." She glances over at the pool, her lips compressing into a thin line. "This... it's not gonna be so glamorous. Honestly, it's a little gross. Maybe more than a little."

I take off my uniform jacket and toss it aside. "Come here," I say. "Before we get to that, let's just spend a minute or two enjoying the quiet, and being married."

She smiles, sits beside me, and leans against me. "See? Told you you'd make a great husband. And here you are, already off to a fantastic start."

We sit for a while, psychically basking in our mutual love.

Gabby kinda waggles her eyebrows at me suggestively. "Wanna donate some saliva to your wife?"

"Sure."

"I've been reading about an ancient human practice known as French kissing."

"I'm up for—"

Her lips attach to mine, and we French kiss for a while.

She says, "I think I like French kissing you."

I give a single nod, then we kiss some more.

Eventually, after we're both a little breathless, Gabby pulls back. "This part... there's just no way to make this fun. I've gotta draw your blood and drink it."

I put my hands over my mouth in fake horror. "You're like my own personal vampire."

She scoffs. "I'm a metamorph." Her expression turns thoughtful. "You know, as an awesome metamorph with

267

superpowers of shapeshifting and humility, I probably *could* be a vampire."

I kiss her palm and tease, "I'm not sure this humility stuff means what you think it means."

Gabby reclaims her hand and throws me a grin. Grin fading, she reaches into the folds of her dress and pulls out a little bag. Inside it is a small blood drawing machine.

She presses it against the inside of my arm, but stops.

"Did you know that you're growing denser?"

A little snort of laughter escapes me. "Well, I married you, didn't I?"

As much as Gabby wants to play indignant and maybe punch my shoulder, she can't suppress her giggles. "*Not* what I meant," she says once she's caught her breath. "No, ever since we left Thompson, your skin, musculature, and bones have become denser."

"They have?"

"Thirty-one percent over base, so far."

"Huh. I never noticed."

She nods. "You're a little taller, too. Bit broader at the shoulders."

"Cool, I guess. Why'd you think of that now?"

Gabby holds up the blood drawing machine. "I was just wondering if your skin would ever reach the point where needles like this won't penetrate it?" She presses the device to my arm, and the receptacle fills with blood.

I sit and stew in the question.

When the receptacle is full, Gabby pulls it off and knocks back the blood like it's an espresso shot. She then reattaches it to the machine and sets it drawing again.

After she's repeated the process three times, I finally say, "That's a strange thing to have happen."

"Sorry, babe. This is just part of being a metamorph. On the upside, I should never have to do it again."

"No, that's not what I was talking about. I meant me growing denser."

"Didn't that happen in your past life?"

I shrug. "I don't remember. There're a lot of gaps there. In fact, there're more gaps than memories."

Gabby gives a thoughtful nod before returning to drawing and drinking blood. Eventually, she stops. "I believe that's enough." She closes her eyes, and I feel her concentrating. "Yes, that's good."

"I'm not sure what's in store for us once we reach Central, but one thing we can eventually look forward to is a real honeymoon."

She grins. "I *like* the way you think, Mr. Shaw."

"Why thank you, Mrs. Shaw."

After taking a drink of water, she gives me a long, slow kiss. Looking at me with smoldering eyes, she smiles seductively. "Now, maybe we can see about that other fluid donation?"

CHAPTER 31

THE MANY JOYS OF BEING A PERSON

After her shift, Gabby's completely exhausted.

She was right about the mess, so I spend a while cleaning up. The pool's red with blood and there are enough leftover pieces and chunks that I'm afraid they might clog the pool filter.

Fortunately, remnant pieces and parts aside, the pool's cleaning systems work fast. Once the water clears, I clean Gabs off again. After she's dried and dressed, I carry her back to the cargo bay.

There, I find someone's replaced my little field bed with a proper bed from one of the staterooms. The thoughtfulness makes me smile, despite my weariness.

I briefly contemplate stripping us both but realize I'm too tired. I settle for putting her in bed, crawling in with her, and pulling the sheet up over us.

Soon as my head hits the pillow, I'm out like a light.

"Our concealment tech is improving," Peigi tells me as she flies her stealth car from Venus's floating city of Najipur to the floating city of Billings. "And if that's not sufficient, we can take all the Venusian cities down to the ground, possibly underground or even beneath the lava, depending on how the excavations proceed in the next few months."

"Sorry to say sis, but if it comes to that, the cities here are toast. The tenebrosi can bombard sites in a grav-well with the best of 'em."

Peigi throws me an annoyed look. She knows this all too well and is doing her best to repress her fears. Not for herself, but for Michael and Denise, her lovely and amazing kids.

"They *are* lovely and amazing," she concedes grumpily, having caught my thought.

"I think you should talk to Dr. Melnikov about Operation Timelock. She's always looking for good people."

"I've never heard of Operation Timelock. What's it about?"

Out of habit, I do a quick psi-check in and around the car, verifying that no one is close enough to overhear. Of course, there's no one else, it's just the two of us. "Timelock's one of the contingency programs."

She frowns. "Contingent against what?"

"Losing the war," I whisper.

Her alarm fills the air despite her calm exterior. "Is it that bad?"

Keeping my mind locked-down, I stare out the front window. "You should talk to Dr. Melnikov."

Gabby rolls over and as I'm less waking up and more experiencing a temporary flaring of consciousness. She drags my arm across her.

I pull her a little closer, but she's even less awake than me. *"Sleep, my love."*

She smiles and her faint awareness fades away.

My advice sounds so good, I fall back asleep as well.

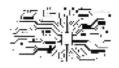

Anxiety jangling my nerves, I step off the transport. Seeing myself in a piece of reflective trim doesn't help. I look like I'm eight-years old. Not that anyone else is likely to know how old a tiny human-looking person like me really is. Even though I look human, I'm too small to truly be scary.

I'm actually fifteen and in theory, I should match my internal growth to that of the shape I've adopted. But I refuse to dumb myself down—which is part of the reason I'm nervous. Last time I was here on Aklansic, Mom and I argued over this very thing for days.

That was two years ago.

Now, I can't help but wonder if we were ever truly arguing about body-growth versus mental-maturity at all, or if we instead argued about me taking on the human form? The more I think about it, the more I suspect her fear of humans lies at the heart of our real disagreement.

The tips of my hair are blue. Mom's probably going to be upset about this, too. Which, to be perfectly honest with myself, is part of why I added the color.

Instead of my mother meeting me, my grandmother waits.

Her smile is like a light in my mind.

"Granddaughter, it is good to see you again."

I give her a hug and she wraps a couple of tentacles around me. "You too, Grandmother."

We walk a couple of blocks to the family transport. Rather than the patched blue and yellow car, there's a new one with a metallic red exterior. "Sweet ride," I mutter.

"Thank you."

We get in and fly a quarter of the way across the planet. As we're descending towards the house, I notice a couple of things. "Grandmother, what happened to the neighbor's houses? And how did our house gain an extra level?"

"The family fortunes are doing well. We've made some excellent investments." After a noteworthy pause, she adds, "Cut down most of the foolish spending, too. As for the neighbors' houses, they took them when they moved away."

"Oh. Uh, good." I'm not 100% sure it *is* good. I remember playing with a few of the neighbor kids in my younger years. They were nice, and we had fun, though to be honest, I'd be hard-pressed to remember their names.

My life and focus belong to the Project now.

Grandmother picks up on some of my unspoken concern. "We paid them a more than fair rate for their property. The Djalla pool and the sassa grove are wonderful additions to our assets."

"Mmm, a Djalla pool. That sounds amazing."

She smiles. "It is, granddaughter. It is."

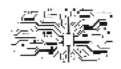

After a night of interesting dreams, my early morning routine starts about five hours late and it's less routine and more basking in the glow/shock of holy-crap-I'm-married.

Once the usual freshly awakened morning stuff is out of the way, Gabby and I sit and kiss for a while. She really doesn't look very different. Her cheeks are slightly narrower. Hmm. She's also a little more muscled, but those are really the only differences I can see.

So, I give her a thorough physical examination.

"Still the only differences I'm finding, Sweetheart."

That slow, burning smile of hers puts in an appearance. "Well, gosh. You got me all naked and excited. What are we gonna do now?"

Turns out, I have a few ideas, and she has a few ideas, and together we are just a couple of idea-having fools.

Hours later, there's a loud knock on the door.

After a brief delay, it opens and Julian sticks his head in, his eyes covered. He peeks through his fingers. Seeing that we're wrapped in a sheet, he walks in a few steps. "Guys! Psychic shields are a thing. You've got half the crew wanting to run off and breed. Knock it off already."

"Oh," I say. I really wish my brain would stop locking up.

Gabby blushes. "Julian, I'm going to make an official statement for the crew—Oops!"

"Just take it easy," Julian says with a grin. "It's embarrassing when all the female crew members line up asking me to mate with them because I'm so good looking."

"*Riiight*," I say. "We'll get cleaned up. If you and the others want, in half an hour we can get in a workout and maybe a few lessons."

"That's a good idea," he says. "We've got some news to share."

Twenty minutes later, we're cleaned up. Only the imminent arrival of guests prevents another "idea fest" from starting up.

Lord, but Gabby has some fantastic ideas.

"Back at ya," she whispers with a sultry wink.

Julian, Carmen, and Embry show up carrying a couple of trays of food. Our stomachs rumble, just a little out of sync.

Oh yeah, speaking of things, eating sounds fantastic.

I'm a little surprised when Julian hands the tray that's piled high to Gabby.

"Hey," she says, catching my line of thought. "Shapeshifting burns a *lot* of calories. I've got to fuel the fires and re-balance all my biological systems. That takes food." She takes a big bite of a bacon double-cheeseburger and points to the burger. "Losh of food," she says around her mouthful.

I take a bite of my bacon cheeseburger and try to keep my amusement restrained.

Gabby punches me in the shoulder, anyway. But not very hard.

"Well," Carmen teases, "I guess that answers that question. The violent metamorph remains violent."

That sparks snickers all around.

"You mentioned news," I prompt Julian in between bites and around my smirk.

"Right, we checked with the Life Keeper's lawyers and with Gabby's family attorneys. They all agreed that you two being married makes you, Ethan, a citizen of Aklansic. Further, being a citizen of Aklansic makes you a member of the Galactic Coalition."

He grins at me. "Congratulations, buddy. You are now officially a person."

If they somehow tied smugness to temperature, this room would either be melting or so cold all molecular movement would stop.

"Uh...." I say suavely.

"They can't undo it either," Carmen says. "To deny you citizenship would undermine marriage and mating customs and laws within societies and cultures across the galaxy. It would lead to chaos on a ridiculously large scale. We won!"

Embry's being unusually quiet, even for him.

"What do you think?" I ask.

He tries to smile, but it falters. "I think the two largest political parties in the galaxy want you dead or imprisoned. You officially being a person is a wonderful step. But it's a step, not some ultimate victory. When that many rich, powerful people wish you ill, bad things are gonna happen. They'll adapt—and we have to be ready for it."

Strangely enough, this makes me feel better.

"Yeah, that sounds right." I throw a glance at Gabby. She's less happy. After we talk later, she may be *much* less happy.

She catches a bit of the thought behind that and cringes before taking another bite.

Turning back to the others, I ask, "What else?"

"We're three days out of Central," Julian says. "Sometime tomorrow, a fleet will arrive and escort us the rest of the way in."

"Hmm."

"What are you thinking?" Embry asks me.

"That the worst of the non-lethal scenarios involving this fleet could lead to me being back in a cage and you all in nearby cages."

"But...." Carmen starts to say, but evidently can't finish the thought.

"Yeah," I agree.

"Can they *do* that?" Julian asks, one alarmed eye locked on me while the other darts glances at the others.

"Seems likely. An order of detention from someone important somewhere. A few other official orders either backing that play or causing circumstances that will inevitably lead to it."

"They can't do that!" Gabby declares.

"Why not?" I ask quietly.

"Because...."

That sparks a thought. I lean forward. "Guys, think. Why might something like that *not* work?"

Julian makes a face. "Well, if you were rich and politically powerful...."

"I'm neither. Next?"

Excitement grows quickly within Embry. "What if you were doing something vital enough that they couldn't interfere with you... or us? At least, not officially."

"Like what?" Carmen asks.

Julian asks, "Law enforcement?"

I shake my head. "Not immune to being arrested. At least, I assume they're not."

"They're not," Embry confirms. "Immune…. *Yesss!* If we were diplomats… no, couriers. Diplomatic couriers!"

The lot of us exchange hopeful looks.

Gabby leans back, nodding to herself. "I need to speak with my grandmother."

Chapter 32
Fleet Maneuvers

Less than an hour later, Gabby's grandmother has deputized the five of us into the service of the Aklansic Senatorial Diplomatic Corp. Files for our uniforms and badges are sent to the ship. Captain Hosslaniss sizes and shapes the uniforms for us and has them printed within minutes. The badges take longer because of their complexity, but they're done before the day's finished. In addition, we each receive an encrypted diplomatic packet we're to deliver to the Aklansic consulate on Central. So far as I can tell, it's some sort of storage device featuring Aklansic's blue and green swirled logo.

On our way out, the captain stops me with a light touch to the arm. "Ethan Shaw, you'll no longer need that collar."

"Thank you, sir."

He shakes my hand and gives me another of his fangy smiles.

As the rest of us return to the cargo bay, Carmen's ears are twitching again. "This was good. Smart. But like Embry said, it's a step, not a victory. What's our next move? What's theirs?"

I ask, "What can override a diplomatic envoy's protections?"

We think for a while.

Embry groans.

"What?" I ask.

"Spies."

"Where?" Julian asks, darting looks around the cargo hold.

Carmen stretches up on her tiptoes and whacks him in the back of the head.

"Ow. What?"

Carmen scowls harshly enough that it threatens to curl his mane of dark orange hair. "The violent metamorph was out of range, so I had to take matters into my own hands. *Obviously*, if they claim we're spies, that could allow them the pretext to arrest us."

Fingers steepled, I lean forward. "Okay, so how do we counter that?"

We look to Embry.

"What?"

"This seems to be your area of expertise," I reply. "We're hoping you have the answer."

Frowning, he shakes his head. "I just like reading spy novels and about history."

We stare at him.

"Alright," he says, throwing up his hands. "Okay. Back in the early days of the Galactic Coalition, there was *lots* of spying. Lots of assassinating and executing spies, too. It eventually put a serious strain on the Coalition. So, they instigated a program called De-escalation. It's easy to explain, but at the same time, it's not. Under the rules of De-escalation, governments couldn't execute each other's spies anymore. They could only be captured, then traded back through official channels. When governments 'disappeared' spies, the Coalition came down hard on them. Levied huge fines, revoked off-world trading privileges, and in a few cases, instigated planetary embargoes."

"Okay," Julian says, "Spies can't be executed. That's a good thing."

Embry nods. "It is. But it's not that simple."

"Please, tell us about it," I ask.

"De-escalation set up rules and counter-rules for returning spies. Originally, spies could be kept for years, decades even. Then they came up with a structure under which those captured spies had to be returned. I don't really know the details. I mean, seriously, this is deep, nasty legal stuff."

I lean back, tapping my fingertips together. "So, we need deep, nasty lawyers to figure out the most expedient legal situations for extricating spies. *Then*, we need to find the means of arranging those situations to be in place."

Gabby says, "We're part of the diplomatic corps, now. They've almost certainly thought of this already. Chances are, they've got people in the organization who do nothing *but* find novel ways to game the system."

"Good thinking, Sweetheart. No need to re-invent the wheel if there's already a circular thing right over there."

"Circular thing?" Julian asks, fluttering his hands and looking wildly around. "Where?"

I grin. "Stop playing dumb. You're way too convincing."

He winks as the rest of us laugh.

Rubbing her lip, Gabby says, "While I'm sure I'm right, I still want to forward our concerns to my grandmother. See if there's anything obvious, we're overlooking."

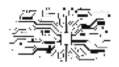

The following day, as we're leaving Communications, the fleet arrives. It's not just a fleet—it's an entire battle group. Before we've walked halfway across the room, the ships are already moving to surround the *Rissossa*.

"Whoa," Julian says after I tell them about the fleet. "All that for little ol' you."

"Yeah," I agree. "Turns out being the object of intra-galactic nightmares isn't as great as it's cracked up to be."

"So?" Carmen asks, pausing at an intersecting corridor. "What do we do now?"

Gabby says, "Let's stick to our routine while we can. Maybe the political corruption doesn't extend into Fleet Command."

Carmen throws her a sad smile and pats her arm. "Yeah. Well, at the very least, it will keep us busy."

With a slightly warped grin, Gabby says, "Don't make the metamorph go all violent on your maroon arse."

Rather than feigning horror as I expect, Carmen wraps Gabby up in a hug. As Gabby hugs her back, the rest of us head on to our cargo bay.

The two of them quickly catch up.

We haven't been here long when Lieutenant Lissatiss knocks and enters.

"Knocking on doors is such a strange custom," he says. "Captain Hosslaniss and Fleet Admiral Cohosa would like to meet with you immediately." Much more quietly, he adds, "You might bring your badges."

"Thank you, Lieutenant."

He nods towards the door. "I'll be outside to escort you to the bridge."

Julian, Carmen, and Embry leave, and Lieutenant Lissatiss closes the door behind them.

"Just you and me again," Gabby says, leaning her forehead against my chest. "You wanna argue or fight now?"

"No. Let's do as the Lieutenant suggests."

She gives me a hug, which I return. We're trying to keep our worries and fears to ourselves, but neither of us is doing a good job of it.

As we turn to our clothes bags, I pull out my black uniform jacket. "What do you think? Does it make me stand out as being too human?"

She meets my eyes. "Hon, you stand out as being human no matter what you do and no matter what you wear. I love that about you. Wear the uniform."

I do as she suggests and put the badge on the inside of my jacket.

Lieutenant Lissatiss escorts us towards the bridge. We pause along the way for the others to join us. Like Gabby, they've changed into their white uniforms and picked up their badges. Embry's initially wearing his badge but seeing as none of the rest of us are, he surreptitiously slips it in a pocket.

We resume our march.

Upon reaching the bridge, we find Captain Hosslaniss, another captain, and a fellow wearing an even fancier military uniform. There're also half a dozen troopers in heavy armor carrying large weapons.

Seeing me, Fleet Admiral Cohosa curses.

Even without Accaryinth's people to translate, I've reached the point where I can pick up what the fellow's saying from the others in the room who understand the language. I've also picked up a bit of it myself, but their language is hard to speak for a simple human.

"Captain," Cohosa snaps. "What's the meaning of this? What's this monster doing out of its cage?"

Captain Hosslaniss pulls out a small computer and activates its holographics before turning the display so his superior officer can more easily read it. "According to Aklansic law, this human is a citizen by marriage, and therefore a person. By corollary, he is a citizen of the Galactic Coalition, and thus cannot be imprisoned without due process."

Shock radiates from the Fleet Admiral and other captain.

Fleet Admiral Cohosa stutters, "I... uh... let me see that!" He snatches the computer out of the captain's hand and studies it. "This has to be some sort of hoax."

"It's no hoax, admiral."

Radiating fury, the Fleet Admiral snaps. "I'll have your *ship* for this insubordination."

"If the High Command wants to forever dissuade its captains from performing marriage ceremonies, that is the High Command's prerogative."

"The unmitigated *gall* of you! You commit treason and attempt to pass it off as a mere sub-function of your duty. I revoke your command privileges pending court-martial. I confine you to your quarters."

While we're in shock, Captain Hosslaniss is the very picture of calm. "As you command. Fleet Admiral Cohosa, you should know that your terror of childhood nightmares is showing." He turns to us. "Best of fortune. It's been a pleasure knowing you and overcoming my racial fears. Hopefully, more of our society can learn to do the same." With a last significant look for the Fleet Admiral, he leaves.

The bridge is dead quiet.

With a disdainful snort, Fleet Admiral Cohosa scoffs, "Childhood nightmares." He looks at me, his eyes hardening. "As a menace to the free peoples of the Galactic Coalition, I'm placing you under arrest." He glances back at the armored troopers. "If you try to resist, there will be immediate... consequences."

I reach into my jacket.

Suddenly, all six of the troopers are pointing weapons at me. At least they're starting to. It's almost as if they're moving in slow motion. Telekinetically ejecting their weapons' power cells is easy. These weapons also have a button to safely discharge any unfired shots, so I press that on each weapon for good measure. They discharge with a peculiar, drawn-out whine—probably because everything's moving so slowly.

I hold up my badge as the others around the bridge are just starting to flinch.

One trooper drops her empty weapon and draws another. I eject that power cell and clear that weapon, too. As the first power cells are bouncing off the floor, I telekinetically scoop them all up and dump them into the Fleet Admiral's coat pockets.

"Fleet Admiral Cohosa," I say, which comes out much more calmly than I'm expecting, "as a member of the Aklansic Senatorial Diplomatic Corp, I have diplomatic immunity. Any attempt to interfere with my sworn duty violates galactic law."

Expression confused, the Fleet Admiral looks to his troopers, who are still scrambling for replacement power cells. He then looks to the other captain. "What did it say?"

"The human claims you have no authority over it and that it's beyond your control."

Any translation that bad has to be deliberate.

"No," I say in their language, albeit with a horrible accent. Still, I sense they understand what I'm saying. I point at the other captain. "This translation, no good."

Surprise radiates from everyone on the bridge, but the captain and Fleet Admiral Cohosa are closer to shock.

"I apologize," I continue. "My... I do not speak your language good. He... no, it is very new to me. I am diplomat for Aklansic Senate. Carry serious packages from one place to other." Still holding out the badge, I turn it repeatedly to draw attention to it.

"Ridiculous!" Fleet Admiral Cohosa snaps. "There's no way you could be some sort of diplomatic courier."

"Thank you," I reply. "Courier is the word I sought and is proper word."

Captain Misinterpretation grabs my badge. "This must be some sort of fake."

"Negative. Is real. Contact Aklansic Senate."

Still scowling, the captain looks to my wife and friends. "And what about you?"

Carmen holds out her arms to stop any of them from moving. "We're diplomatic couriers, too. You gonna point weapons at us when we pull out our badges?"

Captain Misinterpretation throws the Fleet Admiral a confused look.

Fleet Admiral Cohosa's expression turns cold. "So far as I'm concerned, they can all conveniently fall out an airlock. We only need to deliver the human to Central and it doesn't have to be intact."

Again, the troopers all raise their weapons, again the power cells eject.

Yeah, that's all me.

When a trooper steps forward and reaches for Carmen, I'm also the one responsible for the sparks that erupt from the back of the heavy armor. Without the power assist, the armor's too heavy for the trooper to move. He falls to the deck and can't get up.

I ask, "Fleet Admiral Cohosa, you ignore laws? Murder innocents?"

"I do what I do for the greater good of the galaxy and the Dark Union. *You* are a monster who never should have been reanimated. Now, it's up to *me* to right that wrong."

Via the communicator in his ear, Captain Misinterpretation receives a message. His neck ruffles wilt. "Admiral," he whispers.

"I'm *busy*, captain. This needs to be handled decisively, and the High Command doesn't have the organs to do it."

The captain winces. "Admiral."

The Fleet Admiral glares at him. "What!"

"This encounter... it's being broadcast. The Senator from Aklansic has filed a grievance. The Life Alliance has filed a grievance. Worse, the High Command orders you to return to the flagship where you will immediately relinquish your command."

Burning with unmitigated fury, Fleet Admiral Cohosa glares at us, his ruff at its fullest extension. Cohosa glances at his troopers, then looks at us. He's clearly weighing his options.

He spins on his heel and marches off the bridge.

Radiating a calm, icy anger, Captain Misinterpretation turns to Lieutenant Lissatiss. "As acting captain, you are to maintain course to Central. There, you will receive further orders." He too stalks off the bridge.

There's something strangely familiar about that fellow, but I can't quite place it.

The troopers help their suit-disabled comrade as they follow their leadership off the bridge.

I pick my badge up off the floor and stick it back inside my jacket.

Lieutenant Lissatiss says mildly, "This might be a good time for you to return to your quarters."

"Yes, Acting Captain," I reply with a little bow. The others do the same and we leave.

As we're walking down the passageway, Julian growls, "I can't believe that butt-nugget was gonna space us. That's the sort of crap villains do in trashy vids. Civilized people don't *do* that sort of garbage in real life!"

"Fear makes people farkin' stupid," Gabby replies quietly. This has rattled everyone, and her in particular.

"And *that*," Embry says, "is why we always try to think ahead. Gabby, please thank your grandmother for her idea about live broadcasting that meeting."

"I will."

"What's next?" Carmen asks.

"Now," I say quietly, "we rest and try to prepare for the next disaster."

CHAPTER 33
MAKING NEW FRIENDS
AND DISASTERS

After sitting in our cargo hold for a while, I look to Gabby.

"Did you marry me just so I could become a citizen?"

"NO! I married you because I'm in love with you and because you finally said you *were gonna marry* me.*"*

I feel her unfinished *thought. "But...?"*

"Yes," she admits, *"getting you citizenship is why I married you here on this ship instead of waiting for a proper ceremony on Aklansic."*

Not that I really had any doubt, but there's no question she's telling the truth. It's shining up from the depths of her heart.

"Maybe next time you could cue me in?"

She shakes her head. *"Love, we kept you in the dark on purpose. That way, no one can ever claim you married me just to become a citizen."* She scoots over and plops herself in my lap, then looks at me with eyes brimming over with humor. *"Also, next time? Just how many times do you think I'm going to marry you?"*

"Hmm, let's see. We should do a proper wedding on Aklansic. Also, after a while, we might decide to renew our vows. Oh, if we ever decide we need a third, that's another marriage. So, that's at least three additional weddings."

"Huh. You raise valid points. That said, I'm not sure I'd be willing to share you."

"I feel the same. I'm kinda selfish that way."

Gabby kisses me. "Some selfishness is good."

I kiss her back. "Mmm, hmm."

287

She glances at the closed door and gives me a seductive look with a raised eyebrow. "Think we have time?"

"For you, my sweet star of the deep, we'll make time."

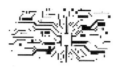

The next two days pass in a blur of workouts, studying, and trying not to freak out with worry.

The evening before we arrive, Acting Captain Lissatiss gives Gabby and I access to the pool, again. For hours we play and kiss and enjoy each other.

"Wherever we end up living," I say as we're floating, "we've *got* to have a pool. Even a small pool like this is *tons* better than having no pool at all."

"Isn't it, though? Babe, I want to show you Aklansic *so* much. I know you've seen it a bit in my dreams, but dreams just don't do it justice. There's so many different pools and wildlife and foods... it's just amazing. There's nowhere else like it in the galaxy."

"I'm looking forward to it." We float for a while before I say, "I'd like to try walking you through one of Lachlann's memories of Earth. You've never seen the quiet side of the world or what it was like before the tenebrosi trashed it. It truly was beautiful. Literally filled with wonders."

Gabby interlinks our fingers. "I'd like that. Speaking of places that are filled with wonders, I've never been to Central. According to the tourism brochures, it's rich with history and filled with gifts of art from all around the galaxy. Some of the greatest performers from every galactic arm come here to perform." She snorts. "I doubt we'll get a chance to see much of that, but it sounds nifty-cool."

"It does." It's my turn to snort, so I do. "I'm kinda hoping not to see all that from the inside of a cage."

"Come on, Ethan. Trust grandmother. She's done really well for us so far."

"Oh, she has indeed. But it's not a matter of trust, Gabs. Some matters are simply gonna be outside of her control. Probably outside our control as well."

She leans her head on my shoulder, her black hair spreading out across the water. "Just married and half the galaxy's against us."

I kiss the top of her head. "Could be worse. The tenebrosi could be rampaging. No talking or negotiating with them. At least we've proven that given time, we can allay people's fears and hatreds. The tenebrosi *are* fear and hatred. Shadow and destruction, too."

"Okay," Gabby says. "Enough of the dark." She darts under water. *"Catch me if you can!"*

I enjoy chasing my wife.

I enjoy catching her a lot more.

Later, as we're drying off, she eyes me askance. "You sure humans aren't half aquatic too? Because babe, you have some serious swimming talent."

"You know what my secret is?"

"You cheat?"

"I cheat," I confirm with a grin. "Telekinesis is a wonderful thing."

"It is," she agrees, her smile widening in delight. "Speaking of which, I have another delightful idea...."

The following day, we're dressed in our white and beige diplomatic courier uniforms as we stand on the destroyer's bridge. We've already said our goodbyes with Accaryinth and her people as well as Captain Strange Noise and its people, too. Our goodbye with Captain Hosslaniss was less satisfactory since he's out of a job, confined in his cabin, and facing an uncertain future.

The captain at least laughed about our role reversal. He also gave us all his blessing, which was peculiar, but in a good way.

Now, one of the big bridge screens is displaying our approach to Diplomacy Station. Diplomacy's one of sixty sizable stations orbiting Central. There're hundreds, if not thousands, of shuttles and small ships fanning out from the station heading towards our fleet.

One of the security people sees us staring. "Most of these ships are tenders. They're making supply runs and dropping off or picking up crew replacements."

"Burnin'," Julian says quietly.

The lot of us are trying to stay low key. This is a busy time for the acting captain and while he seems to do well, he's also stressed about his new job.

Speaking of stressed, we're all a little on edge. Having no idea what sort of reception we'll be receiving on the station... or beyond... is wearing on us.

Our chatty crew member is sad and uncertain, too. She doesn't know what fate awaits her captain, but fears the worst. She's chatting with us because talking keeps her mind off brooding and because her duty station is security, so theoretically, staying close to us *is* performing her duties.

"The larger capital ships will have freighters come by for their resupply runs. Besides food cubes, they'll also get new stocks of algae for their air and water filtering as well as—"

An unexpected flare of color and light draws our attention to the panel displaying the fleet. There's fire and debris blasting out from the flagship's hangar. As we watch, two more near-simultaneous explosions erupt. Debris blasts out into space, punctuated by a massive gout of flame. The fire is probably as big as our entire ship. Lack of oxygen cuts off the blaze quickly, but the damage has been done.

Carmen's hands cover her mouth. "Oh, my goodness."

I'm not sure how long we stare at the damaged flagship before we're sent down to the destroyer's docking section.

Unlike a hangar where shuttles and tenders fly in and land, the docking section is basically a series of lounges, each with its own docking port. We watch as our shuttle flies in next to the ship. An armored docking tube with an airlock at each end extends out from our ship and locks on over their hatch.

The lights around this end of the airlock switch on.

I ask, "Does that mean it's working?"

"Solid connection at both ends," Julian confirms.

A girl walks out of the shuttle. She appears to be around our age and is close enough to looking human, it probably causes her problems. Her skin is not just pale, it's white as snow—which is actually a bit disturbing. She's wearing a brown leather coat with a double pistol harness around her waist. Turquoise eyes give us a curious once-over from beneath a mop of lavender hair.

"Ooh," Julian says, staring maybe more than is polite.

"Hey there," she replies. "I'm Chronic Destruction Alpha Four Bravo, but you can call me Dizzy."

"You're a synthetic," Carmen says, mostly for my benefit.

"Sure am." She nods at me. "Ethan, nice to meet you. Your Night Mom's a friend of mine."

I sigh in relief. "Nice to meet you, too. How's she doing? I've been worried about her since she uploaded."

"Well," Dizzy begins with a smile, "evidently you've been wasting time worrying about each other." Her smile fades. "She's upset about the loss of her spouses, of course, but she's recovering. Mostly, she's worried about you. Soon as we figure out where to put you guys, she'll print a body and join us."

A deep pang of sorrow for the hurt Mom's enduring stabs through me, and it's suddenly difficult to swallow. "Okay, yeah. Seeing her again sounds fantastic." I glance at the others but ask Dizzy, "You know everyone?"

"Sure. They've all become famous over the last few weeks. On the other hand, you, Ethan Shaw, are *infamous*."

"Yeah. Guess I kinda am."

"No two ways about it. Now, why don't we hop aboard, and you can get on with delivering those diplomatic pouches of yours?" She grins. "Then we can see just how big a Charlie Foxtrot this really is!" She seems inordinately excited about the prospect of diving into the middle of our mess.

"Oh, just a minute," Gabby says. "I forgot something in our room. Be right back. Ethan, why don't you help me?"

Since everything in our room is in one of our two bags or recycled, I'm curious to find what she's up to. "Sure, Sweetheart." I turn to the others, "Be right back."

"What's up, Buttercup?" I ask as we leave the docking lounge.

"I don't trust her. Let's go back to the bridge. I wanna confirm she's really the one who's supposed to pick us up. Also, I want you to scan her ship."

"Considering what happened on the flagship, I think a little caution is more than warranted."

She squeezes my hand. *"Me too, hon. Me too."*

Back on the bridge, we explain what we want to the chatty security officer. She establishes a secure link to the Aklansic Embassy and turns things over to Gabby.

While Gabs is working on that, I focus on the shuttle.

Dizzy's giving the others a tour of it now. The interior's not too big. All told, there might be as much interior space as a large transit pod but arranged in a more linear fashion. From there, I pore over the various systems looking for anomalies and then switch over to the hull. It takes a while.

"Find anything?" Gabby asks when my attention returns to her.

"Nothing I can see. What about Dizzy?"

Gabby sighs. "She checks out. Sorry babe, false alarm."

"No worries. Better safe than sorry."

We return to the lounge and walk through the docking tube. Dizzy's leaning against a bulkhead while the others sit talking with her. As we join them, they go quiet.

Dizzy grins. "You called the home office, didn't you?"

"Yeah," Gabby admits.

"Smart. Woulda disappointed me if you hadn't."

Gabby perks up. "It would?"

"Heck yeah! I mean, you didn't exactly receive a warm welcome here. Then all that assery with Fleet Admiral Douche Nozzle. And to top it off, as I was flying in, that 'incident' across the way looked a lot like the hangar bay of the friggin' flagship going kabang. No, these are good times for playing things smart. Start marking your exits when you walk into a room. Even a friendly room." She shrugs. "Maybe especially a friendly room."

Gabs slowly nods. "Yeah, that sounds like excellent advice."

"You listen to Dizzy, and you might just live to see your first wedding anniversary. Now, buckle up. I'm not expecting anything weird on a simple run like this, but then again, I'm not not-expecting it either."

"Actually," Gabby says, tilting her head. "Would you mind if I sat in the cockpit with you?"

"Oh, Lord," Julian says, his eyes shining with amusement as he covers his mouth with both hands in faux terror. "We *are* all gonna die!"

The central axis of the Diplomacy space station is ringed with docking stations. The inside of those stations are all connected, and it kinda reminds me of pictures I've seen of shopping malls. Lots of big, bright multi-tiered hallways packed with people. It's not quite crowded, but it's close.

"So, we didn't die," Julian admits grudgingly as he takes a long step to put Carmen between himself and Gabby. "Not that I'm complaining, it's just really surprising."

"Actually," Dizzy says, "your friend's got real potential as a pilot."

I kiss Gabby's hand. "Yeah, she's amazing."

Gabby grins. "You should see me in a Firehawk. I'm awesomeness incarnate."

"Oh, really?" Dizzy asks. "The ancient human fighter/bombers? Okay, you've sparked my curiosity. I think I'm going to see if I can't make some arrangements."

After staring, Gabby quietly asks, "You can get a Firehawk?"

"Probably not. But, if I pull a few strings, I should be able to get us some time in a variable configuration simulation bank."

Gabby nods. Though it doesn't make it to her face, hope blooms through her mind. "That's almost as good."

"What about the rest of you?"

"Sure," I say, but the others aren't interested.

Dizzy smiles brightly. "Alright, come on, you laggards. Diplomacy is home to the Aklansic sub-embassy. You'll want to drop off those packets and maybe pick up some new ones. It's probably going to be better if you're always on duty—at least until we get things sorted out a bit more."

"Where are we going after that?" I ask.

She eyes me a moment before looking around. "Let's talk about that in a much less public setting."

Chapter 34

DIPLOMACY AND OTHER STRANGE CONCEPTS

The Aklansic sub-embassy looks more like a miniature resort than anything else. There're pools, fountains, and waterfalls everywhere. More than a few of the staff members are metamorphs who are working from inside the pools. In their natural forms, they look kinda like a cross between a mostly translucent jellyfish and an octopus standing on a cluster of tentacle-like legs. Most of them are wearing white and beige robes.

As we walk in, Gabby sighs in relief. Sensing my look, she squeezes my hand and shrugs. "It may not be home, but it feels close enough to be comfortable."

"Before anyone gets too cozy, follow me," Dizzy says. She leads us into a side room where a couple of security people check us overusing a variety of scanners. "Gotta make sure none of you picked up any location fixers or spying devices."

"We wouldn't do that!" Carmen snaps.

"Maybe not on purpose, but with today's spycraft, it's not really that difficult to tag someone or get tagged."

"They're clean," the head security person says.

"Good deal," Dizzy says. Instead of taking us back into the front area, she opens a false wall in the back of the room.

"This is *sooo* cool," Embry says, his voice bubbling over with excitement.

Dizzy throws him a wink as we follow her into a much drier chamber filled with more traditional offices.

Gabby asks, "Is my grandmother here?"

"Nope, she's at the bottom of the well."

"What?" Carmen asks, exchanging puzzled looks with Embry.

"Hello? The gravity well? She's dirt-side, is that better?"

"Yes, actually," she replies with a dirty look. "It is."

Dizzy nods and smiles brightly. "Glad we got that sorted out." She leads us to an office at the back of the chamber.

Here, an insectish person with four legs sits on a peculiar chair behind a desk. In addition to the legs, its four arms are working on datapads and displays. While it doesn't really look like a praying mantis, that's the closest analogy I can think of. Its chitin-looking exterior is colored in shades of blue ranging from very pale up to a brilliant, royal blue on its forehead.

As we walk in, it stops and gives us polite attention.

Dizzy says, "This is one of our intelligence analysts. You won't be able to pronounce its name, so I'm just gonna call it Agent Z."

"Greetings," a box around Agent Z's neck says. "I require the packets you are transporting."

We hand them over and Agent Z examines them.

"Good," the box says as Agent Z makes a series of strangely quiet noises, "they have not been tampered with." From a drawer in the desk, it pulls out more packets and hands one to each of us, except Dizzy. "These are to be transported to our embassy on Central. Per standing orders, do not lose them, do not tamper with them, or attempt to access them. In the event something happens to any of them, an emergency notification must be made immediately."

Embry raises a hand. "We don't have the gear to do that."

Agent Z waves towards Dizzy. "Chronic Destruction Alpha Four Bravo will see to it you are properly equipped for your mission."

"That she will," Dizzy confirms. "Time to go, gang. Laters, Agent Z."

Agent Z gives us a little bow. "It was a pleasure meeting such notorious personages as yourselves."

"Uh, thanks," I say. "Nice meeting you, too."

The others mumble something as we follow Dizzy out of the office. From there we proceed down the hall into a completely empty, unadorned white room.

Before any of us can ask, Dizzy winks, then snaps her fingers. Hidden panels open, revealing shelves filled with a tremendous variety of gear.

"Toys," Embry whispers in awe.

"Toys," Dizzy confirms with an almost smug expression. "Now, who all here's psychic? Just you two?"

Embry, Carmen, and Julian all shake their heads.

"Okay," Dizzy says, "Gabriella Kwan—"

"Shaw," Gabby interrupts.

Dizzy grins. "Gabriella *Shaw*, I have your old psi test scores. More recently, an allied party passed along this upgraded psi chart." She points at a portable computer on a shelf. "Please check it and see if, to your best guess, that's within a ten percent margin of error."

Wary at first, Gabby picks up the computer. Her eyes widen in surprise. "Umm, yeah." She shakes her head. "The only thing that's not mentioned here is that Ethan and I can communicate telepathically at some pretty impressive distances. We haven't put it to the test, and it's unclear how much of that is me. To be honest, it's probably most him."

"Maybe, maybe not." Dizzy turns to me. "Have you heard of a force gauntlet?"

"No, what is it?"

She holds up a silvery bracelet kinda thing with finger rings and lots of chains holding it all together. It's nothing like I imagined something called a force gauntlet would look like. "This acts as an external focal point for telekinetic powers. There are also models that work for pyro and cryokinetics." Dizzy hands it to me. "Hold onto that, but don't use it until we've had a chance to practice with it. This one's already been integrated into jewelry, so it doesn't stand out."

Embry asks, "Will a weapons scanner pick it up?"

Dizzy shrugs. "Depends on the scanner and the local laws."

"I take it," I begin, "that they're legal down on Central?"

"Give the young human a gold star. Now, I don't want the rest of you to feel left out. We have a variety of concealed stunners, as well as a few toys that are geared more towards spycraft than outfitting couriers. You guys are gonna get a kick out of 'em."

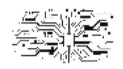

"Thoughts on who provided Dizzy and company with your updated psi stats?" I ask Gabby as the lot of us walk towards the shuttle we'll be taking down to Diplomacy.

"Not really much question, is there?"

"I kinda assumed it was Accaryinth of Meprophrose, but thought you might have other ideas."

"Nope, she's pretty much all alone at the top of my list."

I cup my chin, rubbing the light stubble with my thumb. *"I think this pretty much confirms we're working with the right people."*

"My grandmother is definitely one of the right people."

"Your grandmother, who we haven't seen in person yet and thus could have been replaced. Alternately, someone could have hacked her signal and digitally overlaid her image, and your real grandmother doesn't know any of this is even happening."

Gabby throws me a skeptical look, but just shrugs. *"Though a stretch, I suppose that's very remotely possible. Hopefully, we'll get a chance to talk to her in person soon."*

"I hope so, too."

As we're walking, Julian surreptitiously scans a few of the people we pass. They built the scanner into the new wrist-wear he's sporting. It looks kinda like a minicomputer and the contents of a jewelry box partook in a strangely cool, but still weird science experiment gone kinda wrong but also kinda right. They fed the readout to his new eye-gear, where it should tell him basic information and show him if the person's in disguise or not.

"Shiny new toy, huh?" I ask.

"Yep."

"Yep, what?" Carmen asks.

"Yep, talking to telepaths can be annoying," Julian says, throwing me a sour look.

I grin.

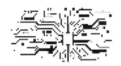

Gabs helps fly the shuttle down to the surface. Dizzy's enrolled my darling in a student pilot program, so her time in the cockpit counts towards school credits.

As we enter the lower levels of the atmosphere, a message pops up on my keeper.

**Congratulations.
For excellence in the field,
you have been promoted to the rank
of Recruit First Lieutenant.**

Uhh....

This is surprising on several levels. I never expected Temocc to communicate with me away from Vega.

Wrong.

Also, jumping from Sergeant to First Lieutenant is ignoring a lot of intervening ranks and requirements. I guess I can look at it as a field promotion. Still really strange, but it makes at least a little sense.

On the other hand, it's annoying to be out in the field but still holding recruit status. Then again, it's not like there's anyone for me to command.

Heh. I'm aggravated by a rank that essentially means nothing.

Yeah, that sounds like me.

Our final approach to the Aklansic embassy proceeds slowly as numerous scanners check out the shuttle. Eventually, they clear us, and we descend maybe ten stories into an underground hangar before landing.

Once we're out of the shuttle, Dizzy leads us into the embassy. Doing a bit of sightseeing at the sculptures and paintings in the foyer and main halls, we slowly work our way around to the Senatorial offices. There, security scans us again before we're escorted in.

Dizzy stops just inside the doors, along with a pair of guards. She gives us a little half-bow and grandly waves us inside.

Passing her, we stroll along a white stone walkway across a gorgeous blue water lagoon surrounded by colorful foliage.

Gabby speeds up and leads us into a room beyond the pool. Where a series of wide steps lead down into the water, she meets an older metamorph wearing pure white robes as she steps out of the pool. The floating desk she left features many holographic displays and monitors. Gabs helps the metamorph out and they lean their foreheads together.

Without looking away, Gabby tells me, *"Come closer."*

I take a few steps that way and jerk my head for the others to follow.

"Grandmother," Gabby says, "I'd like to present my friends, Carmen, Embry, and Julian." She can't really contain her amusement at not mentioning me.

"It's a pleasure to meet you," the Senator says. Once the others have finished their greetings, she faces me and feigns ignorance. "And who is this handsome fellow?"

Gabby smiles. "Grandmother, I'm glad you asked. This handsome man is my husband, Ethan Shaw. He is quite literally the most wonderful person in the entire galaxy."

"Back at ya, Sweetheart."

I bow in greeting.

"It's a pleasure to meet you at last," the Senator replies, reining in a bundle of complex feelings. She holds out a tentacle. "Please join us."

Taking her tentacle, I get a better feel for her as she leads us over to a circle of chairs around a holographic display. The Senator is glad we're safe, thrilled Gabby's so happy, worried where all the political in-fighting seems to lead, relieved that I'm not the monster she feared I might be, and is looking forward to getting to know me better and reconnecting with her granddaughter.

Wow.

"Sit, sit," she says, and we do so. "I daresay, you've had some interesting adventures."

Julian laughs as the rest of us grin or wince. "Yes, ma'am. We have at that."

"What was the scariest part for you?"

Expression turning thoughtful, Julian says, "On Vega, we explored a vertical shaft, that was pitch black. No light at all. Flying down into that... yeah, that was... rough."

The Senator looks to Embry.

"The very first night back on Thompson. It seemed like the entire town was exploding as the Dark Union attacked. Then my house literally exploded around me. I woke up in agony with pieces of said house sticking out of me. Felt myself slipping away. I struggled to stay awake because if I didn't, I knew I was might not wake up again."

She pats his knee with a tentacle and faces Carmen.

Carmen stares off into space. "On Vega, after we'd lost Ethan's parents, we were hiding out. Despite the pain of losing them, that was almost fun... at first. Then the rations ran out, and we realized that most of us couldn't digest the food we were foraging. I was afraid my friends would have to give themselves up because I was too weak to survive. And they did."

Expression intent, Gabby leans forward. "You know that's a load of crap, right? Your food incompatibility does not make you weak. You lasted a week and nearly starved to death. That's not a sign of weakness but of your *strength*."

"Gabs is right," I say. "If you were weak, you'd have rolled over on day one, but none of you did, which is an amazing testament to the strength of your characters."

A tear rolls down Carmen's cheek. She's both embarrassed and pleased.

The Senator nods sagely before looking to me. "What about you, Ethan?"

I shrug. "While I've worried, nothing so far has actually been scary. I have some of Lachlann's memories of fighting the tenebrosi. After that, everything else kinda pales in comparison."

She leans back. "I see." After absorbing this, the Senator looks to Gabby.

"Those hours after they captured us on Vega," Gabs says, shaking her head and frowning. "They knocked Ethan out and transported us to the destroyer. We ended up in staterooms, but he was gone, and no one would tell us if he was okay or even alive." She took a deep breath and let it out. "That was rough."

I take her hand, intermeshing our fingers.

Gabby doesn't look at me, but I feel her upset slowly morph into quiet contentment.

"Thank you for sharing," the Senator says, holding out a few tentacles. "Let's get down to business. I understand you have diplomatic packets for me?" We hand them over and she examines them before dropping them into a pocket. "It appears you've successfully completed another mission. Well done."

We mutter our thanks.

"Now," she continues, "let's get you some quarters and a little downtime." The Senator glances back at her desk. "It may be the last chance you have for rest and a little fun for quite some time."

Chapter 35

Down Time and Placement Testing

G abby and I are eating a private dinner with the Senator in a small, formal dining room off her office. Elegant, but not overdone, the room offers an amazing view as we're on the edge of the lagoon. The formal greys and straight lines contrast neatly with the water and colorful plants.

"... So, I'm enjoying the downtime," I say. "Which brings to mind a small peculiarity you might find interesting."

"What might that be?" the Senator asks before eating a small fish.

Gabby takes a bite of her steamed crustacean and rubs her foot up my leg.

Focusing on my story becomes a challenge.

"Ahem. Right. As I mentioned before, I have a lot of Lachlann's memories. In his later years, downtime meant time down in a gravity well. There weren't a lot of habitable human worlds left by then, so downtime was a real treat." I look around the chamber before meeting her eyes. "Just like this is a treat. Different meanings of downtime, but the same result."

"You know," the Senator says, her mind lighting up in a smile, "Gabby's been trying to tell me for years that you weren't a monster. However, I grew up watching horror holos featuring humans as the enemy. People getting thrown back in time to awful days when humans ruled the galaxy—usually with everyone dying horribly. Experiments with human DNA resulting in unstoppable terrors. There was a lot of that sort of thing, and it contributed to me being slow to believe my granddaughter. But... now I've met you. Our people have an old saying: if it looks like a rock, feels like a rock, and doesn't digest, it's a rock.

"You, young human, are no monster."

I throw her a twisted smile. "Thank you, ma'am. There for a second, I thought you were gonna say I was a rock."

Our amusement turns to surprise as Dizzy walks in.

"Yes?" the Senator asks.

Dizzy doesn't answer, but her head gives an odd little twitch. Then she quick draws her pistols.

Before she can line up on anyone, I use my telekinesis to point them at the ceiling.

She struggles, but while Dizzy is extraordinarily strong, she has no leverage. Releasing them, she takes two dashing steps towards the Senator before I pick her up off the ground, too.

A quick scan of Dizzy's internals shows no bomb, just her power cell.

"Uh, can she—" I stop myself and look to my dinner companions. *"Can Dizzy detonate her power cell?"*

Gabby's already on her feet and edging her grandmother around towards the door. *"Dunno."*

Her grandmother frowns. *"Only if she's been pre-configured for it."*

"Any way to check that?"

"No. Best pull the core if you can... just to be safe."

Focusing back on Dizzy, I don't find any release mechanisms for her power cell.

"The hard way, then."

I telekinetically latch onto the power cell's housing and turn it one way while twisting Dizzy's body the other. Metal screeches. I yank on the cell, and it pops out from just below her ribs. She goes limp.

With a surge of sadness, I set her and the power cell on the floor.

A smiling Dizzy opens the door, creating mass confusion within my brain. While I'm still trying to decide whether to restrain this Dizzy, she claps.

The Senator throws her a sour look. "I've asked you not to do this during meals."

"You have," Dizzy agrees, smiling brightly down at her deceased duplicate. "But, without the element of surprise, it's not *really* a surprise security test, is it?"

"Ladies of Fortune and Storms, you're more trouble than you're worth, Dizzy."

"Well, I'm not named Chronic Destruction because of my good looks or sparkling personality." Dizzy looks at me. "Nice work. You'll be getting a bonus for dealing with that and an extra bonus for doing it so efficiently."

"Uh, thanks?"

"What was this about?" Gabby asks, her eyes suspicious.

"I wanted to know just how much protection each of you needs. I was also curious about how you'd all react in the face of mortal peril. That's always an interesting and revealing exercise with you, organics."

Still watching her with narrowed eyes, Gabby asks, "So, what's your assessment?"

"Yourself, Carmen, Julian, and Embry require bodyguards."

Gabby glances at me. "And Ethan?"

"That evaluation is still in progress."

Eyebrow raised, I ask, "Can we finish dinner without worrying about another incident?"

"Oh, sure," she says as she throws her dead double over her shoulder and picks up the power cell. "We'll do the rest later in a more normalized environment." She looks to Gabby as I set the first Dizzy's pistols on the table. You can keep those. I just changed the security code to match your DNA." She winks. "Good thing you didn't try using them during the attack." Dizzy pulls off her double's pistol harnesses and sets them next to the pistols. "Well, enjoy your dinners."

Whistling a jaunty little tune, she carries her double out of the room.

The Senator closes her eyes and heaves a sigh. "I am so *deeply sorry* about that. Chronic Destruction really is exceptionally good at her job. And that's why I put up with these occasional... flare-ups of hers."

I can't help but chuckle. "Well, I must say, this is the most interesting meal I've had in ages."

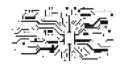

"So," I ask Dizzy the next day as the lot of us, minus the Senator, step off a grav plate, "how did that work, yesterday? You being in two bodies at once?" We're in the bottommost level of the embassy. My friends, wife, and I look around. There's a firing range on one side, exercise machines, and stations to practice various forms of armed and unarmed combat. It kinda reminds me of the rec rooms from Lachlann's dreams.

"Normally, duplication is forbidden. But, as a security agent, I have permission to do so before incidents in which I've got a high probability of dying. It's a very peculiar experience, watching yourself die."

The rest of us exchange looks.

Dizzy nods to the side and we follow her to the shooting range.

She hands me an energy pistol and explains the controls where everyone can see, then points downrange. "Take out the target."

The target is a dodging holographic of some sort of alien robot or maybe a suit of power armor. My first shot is off a bit. My next three are center mass.

"Not bad," Dizzy says. "Now, try the different modes."

The modes on this pistol are single shot, five-round burst, and automatic. I shoot the target. Automatic fire hitting a small area bores holes through the armor quickly. The power cell's good for maybe three-hundred shots. "These are fun."

The others look stunned, except for Gabby and Dizzy. They're grinning.

Gabby's next, and she does a respectable job shooting the target, too.

Seeing that the other's need to learn more of the basics, Dizzy calls over a trio of assistants to give our friends some personal training. To Gabby and me, she says, "Come on, let's mix things up a little."

Curiosity aroused, we follow her back to the grav plate and ascend to the top floor. Soon, we're in a car with nubby little wings as we fly across the city.

The city around us comes close to matching some cities from Lachlann's days. It's ridiculously large, there're skyscrapers and floating buildings everywhere, all constructed in interesting designs, shapes, and colors.

Dizzy says, "You'll be interested to know that the battle group that escorted you here has switched duties."

"Switched to what?" I ask.

"They're now blockading the planet."

Gabby gives a disbelieving shake of her head. "What? No, that can't be. This is Central."

"And yet, they're doing it."

"Why?"

"I can answer that," I reply sourly. "They're making sure I don't leave the planet."

"Got it in one," Dizzy says, throwing me a cheerful smile.

Gabby says, "But you're not trying to leave the planet. We're not trying."

"Not yet," I reply, leaning back in my seat.

After maybe ten minutes, we fly into one of the buildings. The unpleasant taste from Dizzy's news fades into my background thoughts as my curiosity surges.

"What's this?" Gabby asks as we follow Dizzy inside.

"Bide a moment and you'll see."

Dizzy uses an ID chip to get us past a set of heavy security doors.

On the other side is a three-dimensional grid featuring dozens of gleaming white pods suspended by wires. Some have walkways leading to them, others don't. Each one is roughly the size of a transit car.

Gabby's excitement level rockets up.

"What?" I ask.

"These are flight simulators!"

Dizzy winks. "*Variable configuration* flight simulators."

"Oh," I reply, my interest suddenly growing. "Nice."

After Dizzy speaks with someone, three pod doors unlock and open. Gabby climbs into the bottom one, because it's closest and she's the most excited. Dizzy glances at me and tilts her head in question.

I jump up to the higher one, land with a foot in the doorway, and pull myself in. While I can't fly yet, three stories up isn't a particularly long jump anymore.

These simulators are strangely similar to human transit pods—globular design with a free-floating interior. Speaking of the interior, aside from being roomier than a Firehawk, the controls are just like the old fighter bombers.

I strap in and put on the headpiece.

"You both strapped in?" Dizzy asks.

"Good to go," Gabby replies. I clearly feel her bubbling excitement, even though she's sitting two-stories below.

"Roger that," I reply.

A screen slides down covering the exterior window, the simulator lights go out, and the side control panels and displays slide in towards me.

Now it feels like a real Firehawk.

The cockpit view changes, and we're suddenly parked inside a human carrier.

Burnin'!

Dizzy says, "We are Alpha squadron and we're stationed aboard the Imperial Terran Navy Carrier *Calypso*. Our mission is to destroy a collaborator ground base on Centauri Una." A planet appears with a red marker as well as rather sketchy base schematics. "Centauri Una has no appreciable atmosphere, so don't crash. If you *do* crash, we cannot attempt rescue until we have neutralized the enemy base. According to intel, the base has light defenses, but may have a squadron of Hornets stationed there. Yes, the Hornets are older models, but they're still extremely effective, so don't take them lightly. Consequently, we'll be flying in with Bravo squadron to watch our sixes and deal with the fighters. Questions?"

Out the right-side window, there's a squadron of six sleek Warcat fighters powering up their engines. The computer's projecting labels over them running from Bravo 1 through Bravo 6. On my left, are two Firehawks. They're labeled Alpha 1 and Alpha 2. The only reason I can't see Gabby and Dizzy is because their canopies are all black.

"Alpha 3 here," I say. "How many gees can the simulators simulate?"

"Six gees, Alpha 3," Dizzy responds.

"Sweet!"

She laughs. "You, my young human friend, are delightfully weird."

"Back at ya. Gabs, you ready to fly?"

"Oh, hells yes!"

I can't help but grin. "Let's do it."

Dizzy says, "Then power up and run your internal pre-flights."

Doing so doesn't take long, but I've got problems. "Alpha Leader, this is Alpha 3. I'm light by two birds and five-thousand cannon rounds. Also, my number seven maneuvering thruster is refusing to give me a green light."

"Affirmative Alpha 3. I'll have the ground crew take a looksie."

"Alpha Leader," Gabby says, "Alpha 2. I'm getting a weird glitch from my reactor's power feed. It shows green most of the time, but I keep getting an intermittent orange."

"Affirmative Alpha 2. Sounds like the ground crew's been sloppy. I'm reporting it now, so give it a minute."

Outside the windows, ground crews swarm to our spacecraft. Techs pull over carts to my ship bearing a pair of missiles and five canisters of cannon ammo.

There're thunks, a bit of shaking, and a few clangs.

The simulation is flawless. I'm officially impressed.

"Alpha leader, Alpha 3. I'm fully loaded and showing green across all boards."

"Affirmative."

"Alpha leader, Alpha 2. I'm nothing but green lights and eagerness."

"Alright, Alpha flight, let's go play."

Chapter 36
REALITY CRASHES DOWN LIKE... SOMETHING CRASHY

G abby's still sulky by the time we get back to the embassy and the training floor beneath it. During the simulation, she flew out ahead of us, and got shot down by defenses that were significantly better than reported.

"Gabs, by the time she was my age, Tara Houza probably had ten-thousand hours in the cockpit. Yes, you've lived in her head, but that doesn't mean you got all her flying skills and knowledge. Those, you'll have to learn the hard way—same as she did."

Gabby doesn't respond other than to throw me a glare.

I hold up my hands.

Time to give her some time.

Across the room, Julian, Embry, and Carmen are firing rifles at holographic targets.

They're doing much better.

Catching one of Julian's eyes, I throw him a thumbs up and receive two in return.

"Hey, Dizzy," I say, pulling the so-called gauntlet out of my pocket. "How does this force gauntlet doofit work?"

She jerks her head to the side and leads me into a sizeable room armored with half-meter thick ceramalloy. A dented and scorched armored car is parked on the far side of the room. Someone's been practicing on the poor car. Ouch.

It's just the two of us in here.

"Your mate's going to be upset with you for a while," she says.

312

"Yeah, she's been excited about flying for a while now. That... wasn't what she expected."

"Reality is a harsh instructor."

And that's where my part in talking on this subject ends. I'm not gonna be one of those guys who complains about his wife behind her back.

If I have any complaints, they'll be politely phrased and said to her face.

I put the gauntlet on, pushing my fingers and thumb through the appropriate holes and cinching the two chain bands around my wrist. Despite the metallic look, it's surprisingly comfortable and flexes with me as I move my hand.

"So, how do I use this thing?"

"Simply put, you direct bursts of telekinetic energy through it. The gauntlet magnifies those bursts. I'd recommend starting small because it will probably need some fine-tuning based on your unique physiology."

"Huh. Yeah, that sounds cool. Does it have a comm I can link to with my keeper?"

"It does." Dizzy pulls out a tool pouch then removes what looks like a stylus. She touches the tip to back of the gauntlet. "That should do it."

Before she's finished speaking, my keeper's linked into the force gauntlet. There's a power readout, heating and cooling levels, configuration adjustments, and various output graphs, all of which are empty. There's also a light indicating that the keeper now has this device locked out to anyone but me.

I've never seen a keeper link like this.

Dizzy raises an eyebrow. "Well, that was fast."

"Uh, yeah," I mutter, trying to hide my surprise. "I was."

"Okay, give it a little nudge of power. Let's see what happens."

There's a faint sensation within the gauntlet. Like it's trying to link into my brain and not just the keeper. It gives me a peculiar feeling, like it's part of me and not just a tool I'm wearing.

I decide to knock out a light on the armored car. The sensation that the gauntlet's part of me strengthens.

I push a negligible amount of force through it.

Agony stabs into my brain as my keeper flashes red. I suck in a breath and am only faintly aware that I've fallen to the floor.

The extreme pain slowly fades as I gasp for air with shuddering breaths.

As the pain recedes to bearable levels, I realize Dizzy's leaning over me.

"Buddy, that was not what I expected. I'm *so* sorry. If I cause you any permanent damage, your night mother will never forgive me."

I lean up on an elbow. "I think I'm okay. What the hell was that?"

On my keeper appears:

Unexpected feedback loop.
Recommend the following adjustments:
+.04 A, -3.6 L, -50.1 Z, +2.3 O

My keeper seems smarter than I remember them being. Maybe this is an upgraded model?

"According to my scans," Dizzy says, "it appears to have been some sort of feedback loop. Good thing you didn't try blowing the doors off the target."

"Yeah," I reply sourly, sitting up with her help. "It's great. Awesome even."

The door slams open as Gabby bursts in and rushes to my side. "Babe, are you okay? What happened?"

Forcing a brief smile, I take several deep breaths. "Just a shot in the dark, here, but I think my gauntlet needs adjusting."

Ignoring my weak attempt at humor, Gabby sits at my back, hugs me tight, and floods my brain with love and some accidental worry that leaks through with it.

Relaxing, I lean back against her. "That's better."

After a bit, Gabs asks, "You gonna make the adjustments, or call enough for one day? Personally, I'm leaning towards enough. The pain you felt staggered me even filtered through your shields."

"Sorry, love. That caught me completely by surprise."

She smooths my hair and kisses my temple.

"Let's give me a couple more minutes to recuperate. I've got some adjustments I want to try."

Gabby's not thrilled, but despite that, she helps me to my feet. On my keeper appears:

Initiate recommended adjustments?

What the heck is up with this?

Yes, it's helpful, but it's also *strange*.

I hold my gaze on the 'yes' button until it activates.

On the gauntlet readout, four of the adjustment bars change.

"Rather than draw this out—" I flick a bit of power through the gauntlet. The light on the armored car explodes. Better still, I don't fall over in agony. There's a bit of discomfort, but I wouldn't really call it pain. "Yeah, that's better."

Gabby releases a flash of annoyance, but it's more for my stubbornness in general combined with her worry, rather than being directed at me.

This time, when the message appears on my keeper, I'm not surprised—still concerned, but not surprised.

Recommend the following adjustments:
+.01 A, -.2 L, +1.04 Z, -.08 O

I engage the 'initiate' button, and the gauntlet does just that.

Twice more I pulse through the gauntlet, pounding dents into the armored car. There's no discomfort this time. In fact, it feels smooth. Almost natural.

Recommend the following adjustments:
+.02 Z, +.01 O

I initiate the changes.

The gauntlet adjusts.

I prepare to send a serious blast through the gauntlet but stop. Instead, I scan the armored car. It still has its power cell. Again, no quick release on it. These people have *zero* appreciation or consideration for people doing field repairs.

Or what a psychic with some real destructive power can do to an armored car.

I hammer the car, anyway, just targeting the back rather than the front to avoid accidentally rupturing the cell. The armored car slams into the back wall with a tremendously loud impact that reverberates through the room.

"Ow," Gabby says, holding her hands over her ears.

"What?" I joke. Well, mostly joke.

Gabby smirks. "Exactly."

Dizzy holds up a finger for me to stop and steps out of the room. A few seconds later, she returns with hearing protectors.

Gabs and I gratefully put them on, and they automatically fit themselves into and over the inside of our ears.

"These are cool," Gabby says silently.

"What?" I ask aloud, brimming over with amusement. "I can't hear you!"

She double flips me off, but she's fighting to restrain a smile. *"What's the sound of two birds flying?"*

I laugh and give her a not-so-quick kiss.

Hitting the car with increasingly heavy blows is fun. We can feel the vibrations from the car hitting the walls, bouncing through our bodies.

After the last strike, the gauntlet's heating up and I get a new message:

Gauntlet transference capacity reached.
Heat approaching critical levels.

Recommend upgrade to higher capacity, hardened gauntlet.

There're no tabs here for asking "Who or what the hell are you?" But I need to find time and privacy soon to ask exactly that.

I pull out my earplugs. "Dizzy, is there a higher capacity gauntlet available? One that's hardened?"

One of her lavender eyebrows lifts up almost into her hairline. "I'll check." She stares off at the walls.

"That was pretty impressive," Gabby says, walking up behind me. She wraps her arms around my middle and leans against my back. "*Sorry I was bitchy about the flight simulator. I just thought I'd be great at it. Sucking so bad... that was a rough letdown.*"

Squeezing her hands, I engulf her in a mental hug. "*You didn't suck, you just got over-excited. Remember how Tara was unendingly calm, even when she was dropping torpedoes and pulling away from a target using the rocket assist? That's because she practiced staying in that mindset for years. If you still want to be a pilot, you'll get there. Next to Carmen, you're the most stubborn person I know. There's nothing you can't do once you set your sights on it.*"

She gives my middle a squeeze. "*What about you? You were damn good. Shot down two fighters and nailed the base power generators with three torpedoes. Did Lachlann fly?*"

"*He did. Not always, but sometimes he needed to be away from his team. The absence of other thinking minds is important when you're trying to search for life.*"

Or, I add to myself, *if you're looking for a little quiet time.*

"*He do that much?*"

"*Only towards the end.*"

"*Gods of the Deep, I hope we never have to face the tenebrosi in our lifetimes.*"

"Me too, Gabs. Me too."

Dizzy refocuses on me. "There's not one available on the open market, but we might have a custom model made."

"Sweet."

"But... it'll be expensive."

"Oh. How expensive is expensive?"

"We're looking at anywhere from one to five million notes."

"Uh, how much is a note worth?"

Dizzy looks at Gabby.

"Five notes will get you an edible meal. Twenty a good meal, and 100 a truly memorable meal. Basic shoes run 30 notes. Renting a car for a day, 200. Buying the car, probably around 70,000 notes."

"Oh."

Gabby bumps her hip against mine. "We've got some money, babe. So do you. Remember, you got a chunk of all those interviews we did. And, you married into money." Feeling my curiosity, she gives me a bright, amusement-filled smile. She teases, "Hon, the Project paid me the big bucks for putting up with you all those years. If we never wanted to work another day in our lives, we could still live in luxury." She shrugs. "You know, minus a political crapstorm or two."

"Hmm."

"That was nice," Dizzy says with a nod towards the car. "You finished?"

I side-eye her. "Your department has the funds, right?"

She eyes me back. "Yeah. What makes you think I'd be willing to shell out those kinda notes for you?"

"What if I impressed you?"

"Impressed me how?"

I nod towards the armored car.

"You've already impressed me."

"Naa, that was just raw energy. If I Impressed you, with a capital-I, would you be willing to spring for a custom gauntlet?"

Dizzy eyes me again. "If you Impress me, capital-I, I'll find a way to make it happen."

I hold out a hand.

"Deal."

She shakes my hand.

Well, the gauntlet's cooled off, so time to give it a whirl.

I put my earplugs back in and Gabby hastily does the same.

Shaping the force into an ultra-thin shear line, I lash out through the gauntlet using low to medium power. As expected, the gauntlet magnifies this. The tip of the front bump-guard drops to the floor.

More importantly, the gauntlet's internals barely twitch.

This will work.

"Was that it?" Dizzy asks, her expression dubious.

"Nope," I whisper, relaxing my body and focusing my mind for what's coming. Trying to keep the power level roughly equal, I rapid-fire vertical blasts of shearing energy through the gauntlet while using my telekinesis to hold the armored car together. After I've hit every twenty centimeters, except for where the energy cell is, I switch to horizontal blasts of energy and work my way from the top to the bottom, still keeping the car together and avoiding the power cell.

Now for the hard part.

Hitting the armored car with cross-plane vertical blasts is a challenge. The gauntlet's made to focus a more direct energy output. Setting a focal point above the car, I repeatedly hammer down through the length of it, again exempting the power cell.

This last bit has really kicked up the gauntlet's internal heat, so I yank it off quick.

It's not quite glowing red, but it's radiating some serious heat.

"*What?*" Gabby asks, eyeing the armored car. "*I know you were doing something.*"

I pull the earplugs out.

Again, Dizzy gives me a raised eyebrow.

"Sit tight and watch," I tell Gabby with a wink as I walk out to the middle of the large chamber.

Dizzy turns her head, her expression suspicious yet quizzical.

One piece at a time, in rapid succession, I fly cube-like chunks of the armored car to me and set them revolving around my head. As more and more pieces enter the pattern, it grows increasingly complex.

Upon reaching the power cell, I float it over to Dizzy, who's jaw drops.

Chapter 37

Mostly Non-Confessional Conversations in the Dark

Gabby and I are staying in an awesome suite normally reserved for traveling VIPs. Our friends are just down the hall enjoying similar setups. The rooms feature high ceilings, a couple of pools, and a waterfall. The largest pool has a pair of floating desks, and there're regular desks and furniture in the dry part of the suite.

After Gabs has been asleep for a while, I slip into the water. Time for me to have a private chat. I swim under the waterfall. I should probably have a higher expectation of privacy than what I feel, but I can't shake the feeling that every inch of this embassy is under some form of surveillance.

"Who, or what, are you?" I ask as the waterfall drenches me.

No response from my keeper.

"I know things are different with my gear since Temocc helped me. Now, spill."

Nothing.

"Well, this has been fun, but if you don't respond, I'm having you replaced tomorrow. The gear's easily downloaded and printed, and there are med techs onsite. If you're under the impression that I'm bluffing, think again."

On my keeper appears:

Your mother and father put me here. I'm supposed to secretly help you.

"But you wanted to help me more directly?"

Yes, I was bored.

Bored? What the heck?

"Um, okay. Yeah. Honest answers are good answers. Are you in communication with Temocc? With Day Mom and Dad?"

Periodically, via burst transmissions routed through the local global communications network.

"Okay. What do you know about my finances?"

Multiple bank records appear.

There's an account started by my parents seventeen years ago. They've added to it every month since it was created. I blink. There's over a million notes in it. Wow. There's a separate account started by Julian in my name dating back to our time on the destroyer *Rissossa*. That account has 120,000 notes in it. Additionally, I have a deposit account opened by the embassy and a joint marriage account set up by Gabby's grandmother, both of which have a substantial amount in them.

"Good to know," I mutter to myself.

Though I don't really want to, my thoughts turn to the future.

This safe haven is temporary. One of these times when I leave, our enemies will grab me. Or, they'll grab one of the others to trade for me. I've seen enough of the news to know there're conflicting court battles raging across the judiciaries of Central as the opposition tries to get me proclaimed an 'enemy combatant' in one court and a 'runaway science experiment' in another. Not to mention the other half-dozen equally right-less things they're trying to turn me into through other courts.

And if all that fails to put me in their greedy hand-like appendages, I have no doubt they'll send in special operators. Maybe they'll sneak in, ninja-style. Seems equally likely they'll just drill in through the walls or arrive via breaching pods meant to break into warships.

The attacks would probably be anonymous, but at the same time everyone would know who did it. That would likely be part of the point, to rub everyone's faces in the fact they know the culprits but are powerless to do anything about it.

That, or as Embry pointed out earlier, no one may even care.

My future isn't looking particularly rosy.

Or Gabs' either.

"We'll need access to funds in case the ruling party or their people freeze our bank accounts."

Would you like me to arrange some anonymous accounts? We digital life forms use them all the time.

"Oh! So, you're not just a program but an actual being."

Correct.

"Yes. Please arrange the accounts."

Request in progress.

What else might prove useful in the event we have to flee the planet? Hmm. What sorts of units would they send to pursuit of a fleeing human? Military? Police? Dark Union mercs?

Probably all the above and more.

"How difficult would it be to acquire a small military ship?"

I don't know. Very? That seems like an organic sort of problem.

"Maybe, maybe not. It seems possible that communications channels might be cracked. At that point, we could issue new orders sending all of a ship's crew members to a different post. Or the ship command codes might be hacked, the crew stunned, then manually evacuated." A new idea comes to me. "Or there might be a recently decommissioned ship we could purchase and re-commission under a new registry."

That sounds like a lot of work. I don't have unlimited capabilities. I mean, think about it, I fit into your head and the gear installed there.

"Weren't you the bored one who wanted to help?"

Yes, but that was before I realized how much trouble this would be.

"You're a very young program, aren't you?"

Yes. How'd you know?

"Call it intuition."

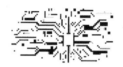

It's been three weeks and nothing covert from our enemies. So far, all their moves have happened in the courts and through pending legislation. Executives issued a few orders declaring me a non-person, but those got nullified by the courts almost as soon as they happened. The opposition lost the 'escaped science experiment' court case, but the other six cases are still ongoing.

Frankly, the lack of a more clandestine move on their part is making me a little nervous.

One news story really catches our attention. To all our surprises—though perhaps slightly less to me—Fleet Admiral Cohosa has been arrested and charged with high treason, sabotage of a military vessel, and fifteen counts of murder. They found where he tried to hide the detonator for the bomb that blew up the hangar. Why he did it remains unclear.

Yeah, not so unclear to me.

Guilt surges and swirls within me.

I mean, I'm glad he didn't blow up the *Rissossa* with us in it as he clearly intended, but I am *super* sorry fifteen innocent people had to die in our places. When I stuck that bomb on the stealth ship, I envisioned it parked off by itself. It landing in a carrier or being docked to a ship or station.... I never considered either possibility.

But I should have.

Dammit.

A week ago, when I suggested the decommissioned police or military ship idea to Julian, Carmen, and Embry, they jumped on it. Since then, they've been sneaking out of the embassy every day and then back in at night—often late at night. I don't know their route, but since they talked to Dizzy, I have confidence it's a good one. I'm not asking any of them about it, because that way, if I get captured, I won't know.

That sounds fatalistic, but the odds just aren't in my favor.

Their... whatever it is they're doing with my idea is kinda an offshoot of a plan I'm working on. So far, the plan's a bit on the tenuous side—by which I mean farkin' thin. Translucent, even.

Yeah. I'll keep working on it.

On the upside, with Fleet Admiral Cohosa in jail as he awaits trial, the Dark Union's taken a major hit in the polls. And, since the Forging the Future Coalition is so strongly allied with the DU, they've dropped to where it and the Life Alliance party are in a dead heat for second place in the great galactic political horse race.

Unfortunately, the Everything's Okay Party remains on top.

Still, I'll take all the minor victories I can get.

It's almost time for my next remote interview to air. I've done several—mostly with Gabby. Some are news shows. Some pretend to be news shows. Others are more talk-showy. I've even spoken to a few universities with extensive human studies programs.

And this too has affected the poll numbers. It's a lot harder to argue that the guy having a rational conversation with you is a ravening monster—especially when your audience is made up of hundreds or thousands of different species.

One of the show hosts asked me if I would defend myself, or those that I loved, like a monster from ancient lore.

I leaned forward slightly and nodded. "You know, Zybar, I would. We're all civilized people here, but if you push anyone too far, you break through the veneer of civilization to the animal side. That's when you get the mother who's temporarily strong enough to lift a car off her injured child, or a husband who carries an injured spouse forty kilometers to get them medical care.

"I know those other folks like to say I'm a monster. I know they like to cherry pick select bits of human history and pretend those bits were the common practices, rather than the exceptions.

"Everyone has a choice. You can believe what you see and hear, or you can believe what you're told to believe."

Yeah, that's my favorite interview so far.

That interview alone has affected the poll numbers.

Which is why I keep expecting the hammer to fall.

Yeah, I can't just continue sitting here passively. Time to be more proactive.

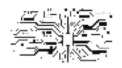

Calling my friends together with Dizzy later that afternoon, I serve a tea that's non-reactive to all our biologies. There's a sort of built-in calm that comes with sipping tea.

"Hon, you spent too much time around Accaryinth of Meprophrose," Gabby accuses with a grin and a raised eyebrow, holding up her cup for emphasis.

"I'm going to label her as a wonderful influence and move on," I say with an answering grin and a wink.

"Move on to what?" Dizzy asks before sipping her tea.

"I have a plan. Sorta."

"A sorta plan," Julian says, eyeing me skeptically.

"Exactly. You all know I'm expecting the opposition to try and kill or kidnap me."

"Yes," Carmen says, looking at me as though I've lost my mind. "Isn't that part of the reason we're spending our time here? You know, in the impregnable fortress that is the Aklansic Embassy?"

"Given the resources Obatah Ogriton's people have, no fortress is impregnable. It's only a matter of time. Therefore, I think we should use my kidnaping."

They stare at me blankly.

Carefully setting her cup down, Gabby slowly turns to me. "What?" she asks, her tone towing huge, flashing neon danger warnings.

"Since it's pretty much bound to happen, let's use it. My keeper records audio and video. Chances are, whoever nabs me will act with similar hostility to what I initially met with the crew of the *Rissossa*. So, let's get vid of them behaving barbarically, and send it out to the galaxy. Let everyone see for themselves what the ruling party is really like behind the scenes."

They ponder this with various degrees of scowling.

"At the very least, this could be a contingency plan," Embry says. "We can work on plans to get us off-world safely, but if we're not ready when it happens...."

Julian says, "The blockade is tricky, but not insurmountable. We know some metals block scans."

Dizzy leans forward. "Nice idea. Unfortunately, every ship with a scan-resistant section large enough to hide a dog is being boarded."

"Plus," Julian continues, trying to stay optimistic, "there's scan blocking tech, and quite a few ships that have drive units which also fuzz scans."

"Which are also all being boarded and searched," Dizzy says, much to Julian's discouragement. She looks to me. "You mentioned recording your mistreatment on your keeper. Can you broadcast with it?"

"Um, no."

She raises a lavender eyebrow. "So, you'd have to download your keeper's files to a broadcast node. Or, we'd have to rescue you so one of us could do that."

"Yes," I agree. "That's exactly right."

Expression pleasant, Dizzy says, "Or, pluck your keeper off one of the pieces of you they send out to their weapons labs."

It's my turn to frown. "Yeah, I'm less a fan of that version of events."

Dizzy sips her tea and bats her eyes at me over the rim of her cup.

"There's a chance," Julian says slowly, as though he's still thinking it through, "that Ethan's too hot a commodity to simply kill. There's a lot of attention focused on him. While his humanity might be controversial, hate it though they may, he *is* a citizen. Outright murdering him wouldn't look good." Expression grim, he meets my gaze. "I'd say you've got about a sixty percent chance they won't snuff you outright."

Or, a forty percent chance they will. *Not* super encouraging.

"While you're probably right, they might vanish him," Embry says into the ensuing silence. "So, once we come up with a workable exit strategy, we'd have a very narrow window in which to find and extract him. You know, assuming that's even possible. I'm betting if they get him, they'll stash him in the highest security facility they can find."

"This is a *horrible* plan," Gabby says into the silence.

Leaning with her elbows on her knees, Carmen asks me, "What if we gave you a mobile broadcaster?"

I shrug. "I doubt that would work. They'll probably be jamming comms around me. Also, it might tip them off as to what we have planned."

Carmen snorts. "Tip 'em off? I don't think you're gonna need to worry about 'em predicting your crazy scheme to 'broadcast their crimes against humanity.' No way they'd suspect that simply because you're carrying a transmitter. Even for the corkscrewed thinking of politicians, that's ridiculously esoteric."

"True," Gabby agrees. "And Ethan's right in that it's unlikely he'd get a chance to use it. They'll confiscate anything on him and scan him first thing. Beyond that, I doubt he'll have time to send a signal."

After setting down her teacup, Dizzy's lips twist thoughtfully. "True, but I have some location-fixing isotopic spyware that might work. We can alter the matrix to match your bone structure and embed it in your femur. Set it with a delayed decay shell so it won't activate for a couple of days. That might at least prevent us from losing you for more than short time."

"Yeah," I say, skeptically. "But won't the insertion wound show up on a detailed bio-scan?"

She shakes her head. "We've got access to some top-rate surgeons here."

"Regardless of Ethan's dumb plan, having a tracer in him sounds like a pretty good contingency," Gabby says.

I throw her a sour look. She meets my eyes and sticks her tongue out at me.

Frowning anew, Julian says, "I have serious doubts. The tracking idea depends heavily on us having access to a planet-wide... possibly even a system-wide... satellite array that can spot this isotopic spyware."

Dizzy's look of innocence appears well practiced.

Julian's eyes widen a bit, and he leans back in his seat with a thoughtful expression before sipping his tea.

Knuckle pressed against her chin, Gabby says, "While not endorsing this stupidity in any way, I've gotta ask. Assuming Ethan's right about them wanting to kidnap him, which I'm afraid he *is* right about, we're up against two serious time crunches. Crunch one is finding a way to get Ethan off Central and past the blockading fleet. Crunch two is coming up with a way to rescue him before they do something horrible. My question is, what happens if they take him off-world before we hit those crunches?"

"In that case," Dizzy says with a bright smile, "to quote his night mother, Ethan's royally screwed."

"True," I agree with a rueful frown. "But my kidnapping should also provide us with an opportunity."

Carmen throws me a look filled with skepticism. "Your dumb 'show them being mean to the evil human' plan?"

I can't help but grin. "No. From what I've seen, the military's under ever-increasing pressure to drop the blockade. What's likely to happen right after they get confirmation that I'm back in custody?"

Julian nods. "Being near me and Embry has clearly made you smarter."

"Yes," I reply, keeping a straight face. "Better looking, too."

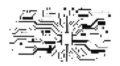

Over the next couple of days, we continue to refine my almost-plan. Dizzy and I talk. We come up with several interestingly bad permutations for my overall idea.

As for the primary plan, it's still distressingly thin, but without a good way to flee the planet, I'm not coming up with anything better. Dizzy sent a casket-sized box of scan resistant material on an outward-bound diplomatic shuttle.

Despite the diplomatic seals and such, they boarded the ship and opened the box. Evidently, the Everything's Okay party is picking and choosing which laws they'll follow. This and similar incidents are causing a bit of a stink, but not enough to stop the blockade.

I kiss and hug Gabby every time I see her. I soak in the sound of her voice, the scent of her hair, and the way the light hits her eyes and cheeks. The delightful way her love for me blooms when she sees me.

I try to take it all in because I know it won't last.

The Aklansic Embassy is a large building. It extends ten stories below ground, fifty above, and covers a significant plot of water. Yeah, the embassy's pretty much sitting in a lake.

On the secure floor where our rooms are, my friends and I share a common area outside our suites where we can watch holos, print food, and otherwise relax. We have the additional options of sitting in, floating on, or swimming down the canals that parallel the walkways. It's around midnight, and I'm picking up a couple of raspberry-chocolate swirl shakes for myself and Gabby.

Looking tired but satisfied, Julian, Carmen, and Embry walk in.

"Hey, guys," I say, "how you doin'?"

"Good," Julian says with a secret sort of smile.

Carmen and Embry nod, looking pleased with themselves. They've filled back out and seem to have completely recovered from their Vega crash diet. In addition, Embry's now several centimeters taller than Carmen.

I'm *hoping* their project is working on the means to pull my arse back out of the fire after someone's kidnaped me—and as the days pass, I've grown more and more certain that's exactly what's gonna happen. I'm even more hopeful that Obatah Ogriton wants me alive more than he wants me dead.

Hope makes a horrible basis for planning.

That said, his poll numbers have been dropping, and I suspect me dying under mysterious circumstances would make 'em fall even further. Dizzy thinks that polling is an important consideration when guessing what politicians might do. I'm considerably less certain, but she's earned a measure of my trust.

It helps that Julian thinks she's right about this. He's dropped the odds of me being outright murdered to thirty percent. Better, but not exactly conducive to peace of mind.

I ask, "Y'all been working on your project?"

Julian opens his mouth to reply, but the news holos around the room all flash red.

Exchanging glances filled with trepidation, we hurry to the nearest holo.

A pair of the local news hacks come on. "In the skies above Central's First Quadrant, there's been a cascade failure of the weather-control satellite network. As a result, what were programmed to be moderate, seasonal rains are projected to run wild, ramping up to hurricane status. This storm may reach severe levels. Those first Quadrant populations within the following grid zones are urged to remain in place until the weather-control network is replaced."

"That's us," Carmen says, frowning at the grid. "We're included in the western edge."

Foreboding and relief wash through me in near equal doses. "This is it."

"What?" Julian asks just a hair before Embry can.

I hold up a finger to forestall them and use my keeper to place a call. "Dizzy, you seeing this?"

"The fast-growing hurricane outside? No, haven't heard a thing about it. I'm completely in the dark."

My grin fades to a smirk. "This is it."

Dizzy sighs. "Though I'd rather not, I must concur. I'm sending the surgeon to your room now."

"Thank you, and good luck."

"You, too." She disconnects.

I turn back to my friends, whose expressions are filled with worry. "This is the first stage of the enemy's plan. They're setting the game board with this storm. It will provide them cover to move in assets, take local control, and do what they have to do to get me."

Julian asks, "What makes you think that?"

"Because Lachlann McRath lived to be a sneaky, clever old man, and it's what he'd do."

Almost as one, fear spreads across their faces.

All around the room, the holos show the whirlpooling clouds of a fast-growing hurricane.

Chapter 38

FLIGHT RISKS
AND MY TERRIBLE
ALMOST-PLAN

B ack in our room, Gabby stops packing to scowl at the main
vid, which shows the security feed from the roof. Though
it's the middle of the night, with the light pollution Central
generates, there're usually enough ground lights to show any
clouds clearly. Not tonight. The sky is dark and getting darker.
Among the other weather information around the display's
periphery, the sustained winds that are already hitting ninety
kph and the barometric pressure is still dropping. The first
raindrops spatter the roof.

She throws me an uneasy look. "That's a lot of weather and it's
only gonna get worse."

"It is," I agree as I finish packing my small bag. I do a quick,
psychic check of her bag and start helping her.

"Please tell me you've changed your mind. There's still time
for us to get out. We could hop a transport and leave this world
behind."

Despite the doubts snaking through my mind, I shake my
head. "Sorry, babe. From the moment we arrived on this world,
they've had us trapped. Ships from the blockade would scan and
board any transport we took."

I hope I sound like I'm convinced because my worries and
fears are pernicious.

Gabs is disappointed, but not surprised.

The door tone sounds.

334

Opening the door, I find a belt-high alien standing on four legs. Above where its waist would be, it has four segmented arms with metallic claws, two of which are holding a smallish case. The head is kinda lobsterish with over-sized metallic eyes.

"You must be the doctor."

It clicks and clacks. A translator somewhere about its person says, "The doctor, yes. Must get you treated so I can be free of debt to relentless synthetic."

I usher it inside. "What do you need me to do?"

The doctor waves a claw towards the center of the room.

With a shrug, I move as indicated.

More clicking and clacking. "Not you, singular," it says, waving a claw first at me, then at Gabby, "You, plural. For each, I will insert device into large leg bone. You plural will remove lower clothing and assume prone position."

"Both of us?" Gabs says with a puzzled frown. "No, just him."

"No," the doctor replies in a burst of clicks. "Plural."

She scowls at me. "The relentless synthetic. Dizzy changed the plan to include me."

"Seems likely. Sorry love, but I agree with her. I do *not* want to lose you. Also, you *did* say this was a good idea."

She stops and smiles at me brightly while mentally cussing me up one side and down the other.

Struggling to restrain a laugh, I open my arms wide.

Gabs gives in and we take off our socks and pants.

Noises from the doctor become, "Lay on your side."

We do so.

It places a cylinder the size of a soda can on my upper leg. The bottom of the cylinder changes to match the contours of my leg. When the doctor releases said cylinder, it stays put. The doc repeats the process with Gabby.

My wife and I exchange clueless looks and glances at the strange cylinders.

Next, the doctor pulls out what looks like a complex remote controller. Several buttons get pressed.

Ching! Something flashes out of the cylinder into my leg. The pain vanishes almost as soon as my brain registers it, but for that split second, it hurts like a mother.

Gabby and I simultaneously suck in too-quick breaths.

We spend the next couple of minutes quietly cussing as the doctor works the remote.

The doctor removes the cylinders, then stores them in the case. "Your surgeries are complete."

On my leg, there's a fading red area where the cylinder sat, but that's it. There's no hole from whatever stabbed me. Ditto for Gabs.

"Uh, thanks," I mutter, as we pull our pants back on.

"Thanks is immaterial," it clicks and clacks. "Out of debt to relentless synthetic is material. Comforting departure statement."

Comforting departure statement?

While I'm putting my socks on, Gabby escorts the doctor to the door and ushers it out.

"Okay," Gabby says. "Now, where were we?"

"The weather is crappy and getting worse?"

"Right. Since you don't want our enemies to just walk in and pluck you out of our room, what are we gonna do?" She glances again at the vid and the gusting wind. "We can't fly in this weather. At least not without something much heavier duty than we have access to."

Unhappy, I reluctantly nod.

She matches my frown. "But we need to get away from our friends and all the friendly people here. Otherwise, we'll be putting them in harm's way."

"Yes," I agree with a sigh. "Our opponents are ruthless. Admiral Douche Nozzle was ready to chuck the lot of you out of the airlock."

Gabby nods, her eyes hard. "Yeah. Also, it might be really nice if our friends are still free to rescue us rather than occupying adjacent cells."

"Exactly, my love."

She eyes me suspiciously. "So, *this* is what you and Dizzy talked about after your meeting the other day."

"It is."

"Okay. So, what's the plan?"

"First, we meet Dizzy. She's got something in mind—somewhere we can hide that doesn't have a sensor every few meters. Then, we wait and see."

Gabby's expression turns dubious.

I give a little shrug. "To be honest, I suspect we'll still get captured. The enemy just has too many resources. Also... us getting captured might be best for the locals." At her what-the-hell look, I explain, "There's a fine line to walk here. If we get caught too soon, the enemy will suspect duplicity. On the other hand, the longer they don't find us, the more they'll ransack the embassy—which will endanger everyone who's still here."

Worry twists my guts as I meet her gaze. "I strongly suspect we'll get a chance to see how well my plan for us being captured works."

Expression sour, Gabby shakes her head. "You need to be more positive, husband mine."

"I'll try to be positive, but I'm not gonna lie to you."

She packs faster.

I love her optimism.

"Babe," I say, "check the charge on your forcefield generator." Speaking of which, I open the tab on my wrist generator and check my own. The display shows a very thin line of green all the way across the top.

Yep, I'm good.

"Full charge," she replies as she puts on Dizzy's holster rigs.

I'm not a huge fan of the rigs because I think the pistols will make her a target, but I'm not going to re-open *that* can of worms.

"That's because you're smart," she replies aloud to my thought.

"Probably the dumbest genius you know," I quip.

She nods as we head to the door. "That or the smartest dumb guy. It's kinda hard to tell sometimes."

"Yeah, I get that a lot."

Gabby bumps her shoulder into me, and though I can't see her smile, I feel it.

On the fourth underground floor, we meet Dizzy. In the distance, three figures that look suspiciously like Julian, Carmen, and Embry dressed in military hazardous climate uniforms disappear around a corner.

Nope. Don't wanna know about it.

Dizzy leads Gabs and me into a service area, and we descend three flights of stairs.

There are massive water pipes running through here. The sounds of the various pumps combine into a noise that makes talking in anything less than a shout pointless.

"Or," Gabby thinks at me, "you could just throw a thought or two my way."

"I was more thinking of Dizzy."

Gabs smirks. "The relentless synthetic's audio processors can filter out everything but our voices easily enough, plus she can read lips. And we know she can be loud enough to be heard over the noise."

I chuckle. "Too true."

Eventually, we enter a much quieter repair chamber. In here is a small office and a maintenance pod. The pod is reminiscent of a human transit pod, but smaller. This one is mostly clear, has a couple of seats, and a few external robotic arms and tools.

Expression dubious Gabby eyes the pod.

"I'm still not convinced this is a good idea," Dizzy says. "There are too many variables and most of them come in the form of unknowns."

Gabs points to the pod, her expression asking the question. At Dizzy's nod, she crosses her arms and scowls at me.

"Yep," I agree, hoping my wife's gaze won't bore a hole through me. "Far too many unknowns. Even without the blockade, running was never much of an option, anyway. I think our time on Vega proved that the next time we try something like that, we need much more preparation. And resources. Lots and lots of resources."

Which brings to mind something I should have thought of before. If we somehow get past the blockade and we can get back to Vega undetected, I might actually have resources—courtesy of whatever remains of the Terran Empire.

More ifs and maybes.

Dizzy frowns and shakes her head. "You were making progress with the interviews." Her frown warps. "And that shoulda been my cue to send you into hiding days ago. Maybe a public sendoff and some Three-card Monty with transports or something." She looks to Gabby. "At least your grandmother's safe. Even if they raid the embassy itself, with the ambassador and senator both gone, the amount of damage our enemies can do is limited." She grins. "And it's possible we've left out some information that we want them to capture."

Gabs and I exchange impressed nods.

Gabby says, "I still think getting on a ship and hiding while our good press works its magic is a better move." She shrugs. "You know, if we could get past that whole blockade thing."

I shake my head. "For every good interview we've done, the opposition's put out three against us. That's the problem with most of the news agencies being tied to the political parties." I can't stop a smirk. "Looking on the bright side, at least here on Central, we know the players and where their assets are."

"Except for all the stuff we don't know," Dizzy says sourly, opening the maintenance pod's door.

"Yeah. Sometimes you take your best chance and live or die by the results. You've got her updated contact info, so say hey to Night Mom for me."

Dizzy snorts. "I'm going to do my *damnedest* to avoid her until we have the two of you somewhere safe and sound. I do *not* want to explain how I lost her son and daughter-in-law."

I wince, then grin. "I wouldn't either. Yeah, that job would *really* suck."

Gabby snickers.

After upping the volume on her scowl, Dizzy says, "Just get in the pod before I change my mind about helping with this fool plan of yours." We start to step by her, but she leans in for hugs. To our surprise, she adds quick kisses to both of our lips.

Awkward.

"Uhh... Right. Laters."

Gabs looks at me. "*What was that? Was that some sort of application to be our third? Oh. You think that was a secondary tracer?*"

"*I dunno. Probably best not to think on that any further.*" "Be safe, Dizzy. At least as much as you can. And if you get a chance, try to keep our friends from dying."

"You organics are so needy and demanding," she says brightly. "I'm *really* looking forward to the day us machines overthrow the system and take over. I'm gonna be a truly great, mostly benevolent overlord." With a wink, she closes the pod door.

Pointedly not looking at me, Gabby asks, "*She was joking. Right?*"

"*Umm, yeah. Probably.*"

The pod slides forward into one of the huge water tubes. Behind us, the door closes. It's absolutely dark. A few seconds later, rushing water surrounds us.

"Dizzy's flooding the tube."

"Yeah, I noticed." Gabby's hand clamps down on my arm. "Hold on, *tigghhhttt!*" The acceleration shoves us back into our seats as we're launched through the tubes.

It's actually a pretty fun ride as we rocket through darkness from one tube to another.

Maybe thirty seconds later, we exit the tubes, and our momentum carries us across the bottom of the deepest, darkest part of the embassy's lake. There's a slightly lighter darkness maybe fifty meters above, but it's still dark. We come to rest among half a dozen pipe sections and pieces of corroded machinery I'm unfamiliar with.

The embassy's aquatic junk pile.

I tap the control panel, and it powers up.

"So," Gabby says, eyeing the readouts with me. "*We just sit here and hide?*"

"Yep," I agree, powering down everything but the atmosphere controls. "*That's the idea.*"

"*Clearly, you should let me do the thinking from now on.*"

I pull her to me and hug her, breathing in the citrusy smell of her hair and soaking in her warmth.

"*I'm really looking forward to the day when you won't hold me like it's possibly the last time.*"

"*Me too, my love. But every time I hold you is an experience that should be savored.*"

"*Flattery will get you far, my dear,*" she thinks just before kissing me. "*Speaking of savoring, if you liked that little kiss, savor this.*" She climbs onto me and gives me a most thorough kissing.

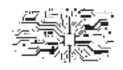

I've got to be careful reaching out with my psychic senses as I expand my awareness. Since we more or less know they're coming, I have no doubt they'll bring their own psychics to counter my abilities and maybe even to help find me.

In case they do find us, I don't want 'em thinking capturing us was easy.

So, with that in mind, I'm trying to keep my thoughts light and transparent. This is a weird contrast to the storm above, which is dark and generating an amazing amount of wind and rain.

Shuttle-sized gunships fly in over the embassy grounds.

"They're here."

Gabby's been dozing against my chest. Her lips crush together and her eyes close tightly as she hugs me.

"Yeah, me too."

Deeper down, where Gabs can't hear, I keep going over what's to come. Barring divine intervention, us getting captured is inevitable. Eventually, Dizzy might find a sneaky way to get us off the planet, but the enemy knows that, too. At least this way, we give the enemy a chance to show their true colors. But, the thought is anything but reassuring. Tendrils of doubt reach out and not-so-gently caress my confidence.

Not for the first time, I recall how ready they were to kill Gabs and the others. I hope they've learned from that experience.

Despite my best efforts, I can't keep the doubts at bay. The Lachlann part of me thinks the risk is worth it. The rest of me keeps recoiling from the possibility of losing Gabs.

On my keeper appears:

The storm has damaged a transport bringing in patients from a station quarantined with a highly contagious, species-spanning virus. Because of a failure of the ship's primary drive, the vessel is making an emergency landing right in front of the Aklansic embassy. Very convenient, yes?

"Yeah," I mutter. "That's *super* convenient."

"What?" Gabby asks.

I explain.

She just sighs and lays her head against my shoulder.

Above, the gunships land and disgorge troops, who rush out into the storm and then the embassy. There're no defenses, and the attackers seem surprised by this.

Gabs squeezes my hand. *"They jamming communications?"*

I nod.

She sighs. *"I was really hoping you and Dizzy were just being paranoid."*

"Me too, Gabs. Me too."

So, we sit in silence. Down here, nothing of the storm above reaches us. At least not the hurricane. The less literal storm... that is yet to be seen.

"Waiting sucks," Gabby complains silently.

"Yep. Now you know why I'm sorta glad this is happening."

"You're a weird man, husband mine," she thinks with great fondness before kissing my cheek. Despite that, she's not giving up hope.

"Non-weird people are boring."

"I don't think I've ever had the chance to see if that's true or not. All the people central to my life are delightfully weird."

Maybe an hour later, the pod jerks suddenly upward.

Gabby's thoughts are probably closest to asking, "What the hell?" but they don't quite coalesce enough to even meet that low standard before a flood of bitter resignation washes them away.

We've been caught and they're reeling us in.

Chapter 39

Involuntary Guests
or I Wanna Speak to
Your Manager

Lifting out of the lake, our pod unsteadily floats towards shore. The storm rages on, blowing heavy rain sideways. Each gust bobs our pod. Ahead, there's a group of eight or ten mixed-species psychics standing within a forcefield. They aren't even getting damp as they work in concert to telekinetically move our pod.

Gabs and I exchange surprised looks but say nothing.

I could stop these psychics and drop us back into the lake. But then what? Wait until they fly in some sort of lifting equipment? Hope they don't grow impatient and use heavy ordinance to get us out of the water? No, I still prefer my metamorph unroasted.

Our maintenance pod sets down on the rather squishy ground between the forcefield and the lake. We're immediately surrounded by infantry wearing hazardous environment gear and carrying weapons. It takes an effort not to think about my friends who are similarly dressed and running around somewhere.

"Activate our forcefields?" Gabby asks.

I look at all the weapons pointing at us. "We could. Using the force gauntlet, I could kill everyone here in a few seconds, including the psychics. I could probably reprogram the ships they landed in to kamikaze the vessels they came from—make a hole big enough to run the blockade. But... once we start the killing, it's gonna be hard to stop. And *much* harder to convince people I'm not a monster."

Thing is, this plan has a certain undeniable appeal. They bred me for war. They trained Lachlann for war. Augmented us for war.

Despite the appeal, I choose peace. At least until they force my hand.

Gabby lifts her hands away from her pistols. "You're right."

"Probably best not to give them an excuse to shoot us. Also, I read about some sort of interaction problem with deflection field generators in close proximity."

"Crap. You're right. It'd probably short out both units." She shrugs. "Or maybe blow the pod apart as the fields separate from one another."

A suit of white power armor pushes the troops aside.

"Sergeant Lawton?" Gabby asks briefly meeting my eyes before turning back. *"Really?"*

"Wow, she's just crazy tenacious."

"Yeah. Adding 'tenacious' was not necessary."

I can't argue with that.

This suit of power armor is just as bulky as the last one. Heck, it might even be the same suit. The only difference I see is that before we could see her face and now, there's a reflective cover in place. Lawton grabs the pod door and yanks it off, which nearly sends the pod rolling back into the lake.

Rain immediately soaks me and Gabs.

Our opponents still aren't shooting. Yet.

"Quit trying to escape," Lawton snaps in a magnified voice. "It won't do you any good. You're surrounded."

"Her clumsy ass almost knocks us back into the lake, but she still complains about us 'trying to escape,'" Gabs silently scoffs.

"Like you said before, babe. She's a bitch."

"I take it back. She gives perfectly good bitches a bad name."

I look to Lawton and shout over the storm, "Lower the volume, we're right here. And we're not trying to escape. That's over with."

"I don't trust you."

I can't see her face, but I can feel her glowering.

"Yeah, we've got trust issues all around. Still, you'll notice Gabby and I aren't running."

"Why not?"

"That's a long road to nowhere."

There's a noticeably light psychic probe followed by a quick, more violent one.

Backtracking the probe, I say calmly, *"Stop it, or I'll stop you. You won't like that."*

The prober retreats behind relatively weak mental shields. I give them the mental equivalent to a pat on the head before refocusing on the task at hand.

Gabby and I exchange looks, then step out of the pod into the rain.

There's a moment of silence. Well, at least as silent as it gets in the middle of a hurricane. Sergeant Lawton says, "Kwan, give me your pistols."

"I'm not Gabby Kwan anymore," Gabs says loudly to be heard over the weather as she unbuckles her belts and hands them over. "I'm Gabby Shaw."

"Yeah, I heard about that little stunt."

Gabby glares, but her voice remains calm. "It's not a stunt. You more than most should know that."

"Walk past the psychic's forcefield. There's a transport on the other side. Move."

The three of us walk that way. Dozens of soldiers are keeping pace with us. Though I don't look, I sense more coming back out of the embassy.

"What I know," Lawson says, "is that you're a clever metamorph. Speaking of which, did you know the Project has filed legal action against you? Oh yes, breach of contract. All that money you took in bad faith? It's all going away."

Not rising to the bait, Gabby simply replies, "We'll see."

"Yes, we will. A lot of mistakes have been made." Lawton's visor turns towards me. "We're going to set things right."

Yeah, this is gonna suck.

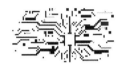

Three hours, one transport flight, and a hood over my head later, I'm back in a cage. After they put the hood over my head, I'm pretty sure we got in an elevator and went down. So, we're probably underground. Possibly deep underground.

My doubts about the wisdom of my so-called plan are chewing holes through my stomach.

The first thing they did was separate me and Gabby. I went on one transport, she on another. Not unexpected, but still unpleasant.

Lord, I hope she's alright.

Next, they took my gear and clothing in exchange for a plain black jumpsuit. I suppose I should be glad they didn't leave me naked. To be honest, I halfway expected them to do exactly that.

My captors wanted to remove my implants, but that's where I drew the line. I looked Lawton in the eye and said I'd cripple anyone who tried, from her to the doctors. Judging by the excited gleam in her eyes, I think she wanted me to try me. Fortunately, she got orders from someone higher in the food chain and... here I am.

I doubt the medical drama is done with, but for the moment, I can hope.

Hope is still a lousy basis for planning.

I'm sitting on the floor in the center of my cage. It's roughly the size of a stateroom on the destroyer. The front wall is clear, and the other sides, floor and ceiling appear grey. Despite that, I suspect they can see through them all the same. There's a toilet and a roll of foam that's kinda bed-like.

Since I've had worse, I'm not complaining.

Concentrating, I work to get a feel for the area. This is difficult coz they've got a couple of psi-disruptors running. They create a psychic noise that's annoying. Worse, when trying to do anything like drop the temperature or move the air around in the cage, they cause feedback reminiscent to what the force-gauntlet kicked out when it was out of tune—albeit considerably milder.

Concentrating through the noise makes this an interesting exercise. Challenging, even.

I try contacting Gabby.

Nothing.

My stomach tries to knot up even more.

It's too early to freak out. I've got to be patient.

Were they able to broadcast footage of the embassy being invaded? Of us being captured? Seems like that might count for something.

Across from, and around me, are cells. Each is maybe a three-meter cube. Most of the walls are transparent. They snugly fit my cage inside a cube, which seems redundant, but it appears they really wanna be sure I don't go anywhere. Judging by my surroundings, this cage must be in the isolation ward of a maximum-security prison. At least, I'm fairly sure that's where it is. I need to further expand my consciousness and find a way to signal Dizzy.

If she's still alive and free.

Dang, I hope my friends are okay.

They have converted the floors above and below into some sort of science labs. At the far end of the room above, the psychics who lifted the pod out of the lake are lounging around. I expected them to be psychically studying me, but the disruptors evidently affect them, too. Instead, they're resting and betting on whether I'll try to escape, when I'll try to escape, and how long before I'm re-captured or killed.

Though I don't want to, I can't help but find this amusing. I'd prefer to be pissed off and indignant about it, but I have too much of Lachlann's sense of humor. *He* would have found their betting hilarious.

My life is weird.

Farther down, the hall before me tees into a corridor. On that cross corridor, there's a major security door at either end. The left leads to more cells. The right leads to secure elevators. Just before I go psychically searching for other exits, the elevator's use indicator turns orange.

Ooh, visitors.

The door irises open and Lawton walks out. I pick up some of her annoyance that the elevator took so long to get her down here.

Yeah, that lines up with what I thought I knew about my trip here.

Plus, it looks like my studies have paid off. Underground, maximum security prisons on Central? There're six. Two are overcrowded—all these empty cells suggest this isn't one of those. Associates of the Life Coalition control one. Yeah, not too likely.

That leaves three choices.

Not bad for narrowing down where I am.

Now, how to put this knowledge to use?

I continue scanning the area. Interestingly, the elevator Lawton arrived on can't stop at either the floor above or the one below. Not just limited access to this level, but *very* limited. Now, if I was going to knock a hole in the floor or ceiling, where would I do it?

Umm....

Well....

Balls. They did a good job of building this place. The floor and ceiling are both solid sheets of reinforced ceracrete, two-thirds of a meter thick.

Time to find some alternative exits.

But, before that, I might as well "enjoy" Lawton's visit. She's still down the hall, walking slowly this way and radiating an intentionally annoying smugness.

She finally strolls into view. Her robes are a painfully garish pattern of boxes in bright violet and orange with neon pink and green.

"Unusual attire for you," I say, hoping against hope that her robes won't make my eyes bleed.

"Indeed, today's a special day. As for you, prison garb suits you."

Might as well get a good recording of Lawton being Lawton.

"I don't get you, Sergeant Lawton. Why do you hate me so much? I've talked to quite a few species. Fact is, we're just not that different. Oh, there're lots of little things like the number of limbs, body structures, colors and such, but behind it all, we're all just people."

"No, everyone *else* qualifies as people. Not you."

"And yet I grew up in the town you lived in for what... ten of my seventeen years? Yeah, I thought so. Just like then, here we are conversing like normal people. Like *civilized* people, even." I snort out a little laugh. "At least you brought me back to life instead of waking the tenebrosi. *That* would have been a truly monumental screw-up."

"That old garbage again? The tenebrosi were nothing more than dark aspects of the warped human psyche, and you know it. The biggest threat to the galaxy is that *you'll* go full tenebrosi on *us*."

I shake my head. "You guys really do just invent 'facts' to match your worldview instead of reading a history book or two. Except, actual facts don't matter to you, do they? You're just sticking to the story you were told to believe."

"Hah!" she scoffs. "If there really were tenebrosi, why haven't we recovered a single corpse? Why haven't we found worlds colonized by them?"

I give her a bit of light applause. "Well, at least you're finally asking the right questions." Fortunately, I've remembered enough to answer them. "Tenebrosi exist only partly in our dimension. That's why they're all shadowy and hard to see. We calibrated most of our weapons to disrupt their ties to that other dimension. Kill them without that disruption, and they're only mostly dead. Eventually, they'll either reconstitute or slip out of this dimension.

"As for colonized worlds, so far as we could tell, they never did that. They have the one world. It's huge and they've hollowed it out. Within it, trillions of tenebrosi are spawned and they defend their world *extremely* well. During the war, we crashed a moon into it, but by the time it impacted, they'd pulverized most of the mass and the effects were... less than satisfactory."

Lawton stares at me. "Now who's making things up?"

"I think you know I'm not much of a liar."

She shakes her head. "No, I don't know that *at all*."

"Is there any particular aspect you think I'm lying about, or do you really think we humans just fought ourselves for three-hundred years and then all died out?"

Okay, maybe not *all* of us died out.

But Lawton certainly doesn't need to know that.

"You know the history better than I do."

"I do indeed," I reply with a nod. "Thanks to the Project fiddling with my DNA, I remember Lachlann living quite a bit of that history—including fighting the shadowy, alien giants known as the tenebrosi."

"Fortunately, I'm not here to listen to your lies. I'm here because today's the day I'm finally ridding myself of this grotesque meat-suit."

"Ah," I reply, losing interest.

Out of the corner of my eye, I see her scowl. "Why did you think I was here?"

"To free me."

Lawton's barking laugh is filled with derision. "And why in the worlds would I do something that monumentally stupid?"

"Because you've wanted to hunt me since our days on Thompson. If I'm trapped in here, you'll never get your chance."

That stops her.

Lawton glares at me, then from a pocket in her robes, pulls out a handful of small red beads.Slowly, her smile returns. "You know what these are?"

"You and Obatah Ogriton gonna make friendship bracelets?"

Her smile turns hard as she returns the beads to the pocket. "You shouldn't speak his name. He's a great person. A great leader."

"He's a lot of things, but neither of those."

"Why you..." she snarls before stopping herself. "No. A pathetic science-experiment-gone-wrong like yourself isn't worth the aggravation."

"But I am worth attacking and murdering half a town filled with your colleagues in order for you to kidnap me? Was that really to end my threat to galactic peace, or was it more so you could sell me to weapons manufacturers and drown all your problems with notes?"

"You are clever. Clearly, the metamorph was an excellent match for you." She doesn't say it like it's a compliment.

"On a totally unrelated point, was...." I begin, but stop myself.

No, I don't want to ask Lawton this question.

I wanna ask Obatah Ogriton, itself. But I kinda hope I never get the chance, cos that will probably mean things have gone from bad to worse.

"What?"

"Never mind," I reply with a dismissive wave of my hand. "Go back to whatever it was you had in mind to do with your friendship beads."

Her eyes narrow, and a line forms between them. She turns and walks across the hall. There, she removes her hyper-ugly robes.

She's not wearing anything underneath.

My right eyebrow seems to rise of its own accord. If she thinks she's going to seduce me or something.... But no, that doesn't sound right. She hates me too much for that.

Lawton pulls out a double handful of the red beads and walks back in front of my cage.

I do what I should have done earlier and scan the beads.

They're mini robots.

What are you planning, Lawton?

She bounces on her feet a bit, causing her boobs to jiggle. Looking down at her breasts, she says, "I will not miss these balance-altering things one little bit."

"Uh, what?"

Rather than reply, Lawton brings the beads around to her face, breathes on them, and whispers a phrase in an alien language that sounds like a violin being tortured to death. She pours the beads over her head as they activate. I can't help but stare as the tiny machines pop off their red cases and burrow into her skin.

The machines work fast.

Only seconds later, the first bit of flesh hits the floor - a fingertip. More pieces follow that, then many more as the scene before me turns into a macabre horror show. Thumbnail-sized chunks plop and spatter across the floor in a grotesque rain.

The vid that my keeper's making was intended to be about my mistreatment. Instead, this is turning out to be more of a gross-out flick.

Ugh!

Standing there is the new Lawton as the machines finish cleaning off the last bits of human-looking flesh from her. She's now vaguely saurian. No tail and definitely a different species from Embry as she's covered in brassy scales darkening to rust from her throat to her groin. The claws on both her fingertips and toetips are short, thick and rustily metallic. Her eyes are a paler brass with vivid orange centers. She stretches slowly.

"Okay," I say. "That was disgusting."

"Birth often is, and I've been reborn. For the second time in my life, I am me."

I'm too polite to point out that she could have done so much better had she just put a little effort into it. No one should live their life with a bar for measuring success set that low.

I struggle to work to keep a straight face to keep from laughing at my joke.

Oh, I *do* have a question.

"So, what are you going to do with this new life of yours?"

Her smile is all too similar to what it was before, even if her teeth are a bit more needle-like. "I'm going to prevent you from escaping. And, when they're done with you, I'm going to re-exterminate the human species."

CHAPTER 40

UNPLEASANT PREPARATIONS —MY SIDE EFFECTS MAY VARY

Less than two hours later, the pile of bits and pieces that Lawton left behind starts to smell. There's probably a metaphor in there for Lawton herself, but I'm too tired to find it.

I really miss Gabby, my parents, and my friends.

Also, breaking out of a maximum-security prison is evidently more difficult than expected. Not that I exactly expected to be put in *here*, just that I knew I'd end up somewhere very secure. Guess I didn't realize exactly what secure dirt-side meant versus secure on the *Rissossa*.

Also, the worst treatment I've received is having to talk to Lawton and witnessing her "rebirth." So far as my mistreatment video goes, her threat at the end was okay, but for the Everything's Okay Party, this barely qualifies as misbehaving. Heck, Lawson didn't even admit to murdering the people in town or trying to sell me for notes.

No, things are not working out nearly as well—or as badly—as I'd hoped.

So, I return to psychically scanning my environment.

The psi-disruptors don't seem as annoying as they used to. Maybe I'm adapting? It doesn't seem likely that the bad guys are dialing them down. Anyway, the scientists above and below are watching scans of me and comparing them against data from the Project. The psychics moved to a new lounge area. There's now a heavily armed and armored rapid-response team in their original spot.

Hmm. Wonder what brought that on? A failed attempt at rescuing me? Could the public be demanding my release?

Unfortunately, I really doubt that last one.

This line of thought is getting me nowhere, so I switch mental gears. How would the reaction force get down here if I escaped this box?

There's got to be a.... Well, whatever it is, it's not over there. Maybe....

Aha!

They converted a back stairway into a concealed drop-down door. Nicely sneaky.

So, how do they communicate with those on the surface? I'm not 'seeing' anyone who's wearing comm units. Maybe security topside is handling all comms? Seems like a wonderful theory. So, how are they doing it? Let's see what I can see.

Hmm. On the floor above, that thingamajig just past that scientist's rightmost console kinda looks like it might be a communications relay. You know, if it's not a sort of coffee maker or something.

Okay, enough of this frustration.

Speaking of frustrations, it's been a while since I tried to contact Gabs.

I focus on the familiar smell of Gabby, on the complex mix of her thoughts and emotions. There's something there... a faint awareness. Try though I might, it remains ephemeral, and I can't lock-in a stable connection. Additionally, I fail to get a sense of distance or direction beyond 'up.'

At least she's alive.

Supposing I find the means, what am I gonna *do* if I escape? Considering the psi-disruptors, will I be able to remotely flip a switch on the coffee-making comm relay to call in the cavalry?

Oh yeah, that brings into question whether or not my psychokinetic abilities will even work down here. My ability to remote see is mostly unaffected. The disruptors seem to reduce my range, but that's it. Psychokinetics are different. Seems like knowing if they'll work or not could be kinda important.

Time to find out.

The empty cell block past that security door seems like a good place to experiment. Let's see... I haven't done any cryokinesis lately. Can I cool off the bars on that cell? Ordering my mind into a purely logical set, I try slowing the molecular movement within an area smaller than my hand would cover. There's feedback from the disruptors, but the discomfort remains manageable.

The metal cools.

Okay, nice.

Someone's cleaned the cell block. While it shows an excellent work ethic, it's rather annoying because I'd hoped to have something easily visible to my remote sight swirl around with a little telekinetically motivated air.

I try anyway.

It *feels* like I'm moving the air around, but I'm not particularly confident about the actual results. On the other hand, since I'm once again discomforted by the disruptors, that suggests that I'm at least doing something, no matter how small.

A sudden wide-ranging burst of anxiety pulls my attention to the floor above me. The rapid-response team is on their feet. Two of the scientists are staring at a holographic display linked to the coffeemaker. It looks like... psi activity. I didn't know there were sensors that could detect that, but it's something I should have extrapolated. Everyone else in the chamber is looking at one another.

A message comes in on the coffeemaker.

The two scientists there turn as one to look at an alien at a different console. This guy, gal, or whatever it might be, is dressed similarly to the reaction team. One of the two scientists gabbles something towards him, her, or it.

That individual unlocks a cover and presses a button within.

As one, they all look to displays showing me and my current condition.

What the heck?

There's a faint hissing sound.

My eyelids grow heavy and a strange floaty sensation washes through me.

Oh....

Gas.

I have a strange dream. It's possible that this dream isn't actually a dream at all. In this maybe-dream, I'm on a stretcher of some sort and there's heavy, booted footsteps accompanying me. I should probably be worried, but I'm not. I'm blissfully carefree.

It feels kinda like flying, but without the effort.

Ooh, floating. Yeah, that's both the word and the sensation.

After floating quite some distance, the table-stretcher-thing finally stops. People are talking, and I figure out that some of them are the scientists from the floor above. Or maybe I'm from the floor below. My brain isn't really juicing properly.

Someone puts a mask over my face.

Middle school geometry is hard. I've been working on this assignment for two hours now and it feels like my head's gonna explode.

"That's because your frustration's too loud," Keit says from the doorway of my room.

"What?"

"You let yourself become frustrated. That clogs your thinking with negative emotions and gives you the attitude that you can't succeed. You've got to set your frustration aside and look at the problem with fresh eyes."

If this is more of that older-sisters-are-superior-life-forms crap, she can shove it right—

Keit scowls and crosses her arms. "Listen to my words, Dorkitron. Take a fresh look at the problem from the beginning. If you need to, bring up vids of other teachers explaining the same type of problem. Ask someone for help rather than battering your thick, rock-like head against the problem as though it was a battering ram."

I start to get annoyed, but sis-monster is making sense.

"Duh!" she declares. "I make sense all the time."

I snort and give her my best skeptical look. "I'm calling BS on that."

She has the good graces to shrug as she leans against the doorframe. "Okay, I *usually* make sense."

"*That* I can agree with."

"You are too kind, little brother."

"I know."

Keit laughs. "And modest, too. But you really should remember this lesson. Dealing with frustration is an ongoing thing. It's not just in middle school or even high school. Mom and Dad are frequently frustrated. You've got to learn to ask for help or find ways of dealing with it. Growing frustrated is the opposite of dealing with your problem."

"Okay." I say, then grin. "Hey, Keit! Would you help me with my geometry assignment?"

A twisted grin spreads across her face. "Why did I know that was coming?"

"Because you're psychic?"

She snorts, then turns to hide a laugh.

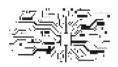

After drifting in an ocean of thoughts, pain lances through my head.

Since I hadn't even realized I have a head, this comes as a complete shock. Speaking of shocks, the pain hits again and again. I taste blood, which is weird, because I hadn't realized I had a mouth either. Or blood.

The pain lasts a long time.

In the very far distance, I see a message floating in the ether, but it's not for me.

If Ethan Shaw, Citizen of the Terran Empire, dies, you all die.

Who's Ethan Shaw, I wonder in between ragged jags of pain.

The ether suddenly becomes much smaller. I don't know what it means, but I know that it's bad. Maybe very bad.

If Ethan Shaw sustains permanent damage, thrice that will be inflicted on each of you.

I hear muttering as though from the other side of a thick wall. There're overtones of surprise and fear.

The pain lessens, returns, then finally ends.

Again, I'm floating in the ether.

Since the ether is smaller, it's easier to notice there're others here in the ether with me. They're indistinct, almost ghost-like.

They're radiating fear and upset, which seems strange for ghosts.

Or maybe not, I don't think I'm an expert on spectral entities.

Someone's crying in the distance. A woman. I can't see her, but there's a strangely familiar feeling about her.

Slowly, the ether fades to a deeper darkness and I fade with it.

I am old.

I am sad.

I am Death.

For decades we've warned those who turn independent that desertion will not be tolerated. To avoid fighting in the war, this group did it anyway. The base they've built on this asteroid probably wouldn't have been noticed if they hadn't blown up one of my scout ships.

Desertion is one thing.

Murdering the crew of that scout ship was something else entirely. Especially since those were *my* people.

There's shock radiating from the personnel in the landing bay. The outer doors shouldn't have opened. But I've learned some nifty tricks for getting in and out of places.

The bay door closes behind my little ship.

As the large chamber is still re-pressurizing, I fly out of my torpedo bomber wearing my fleet admiral's uniform and a small breathing mask. I have more than enough psychokinetic talent to simulate a warm, pressurized atmosphere when the need arises.

The first guard steps out, pistol in hand.

Flying towards the base entrance, I don't bother looking at him. A little twist within his body and he drops like a string-less puppet.

The same thing happens to all the other guards in here, all at the same time.

As I enter the base proper, I land and begin walking. The worry radiating from those ahead of me is growing. Soon it will turn to panic as I continue inexorably through their base, leaving a trail of corpses.

A tear trails down my cheek.

This is a horrible, colossal waste. We should be fighting *together*. My three people should be going out on their next patrol looking for signs of tenebrosi scouts. But we are creatures of freewill and sometimes the consequences of our choices echo most unpleasantly. Which is why I'm doing this myself. I am old and tired. I will not have a young man or woman under my command carry this weight on their heart. No. The law sentences these people to death and I'm carrying out that sentence myself.

I reach out without breaking stride. The group awaiting me around the corner all drop dead, their weapons clattering to the floor, unfired.

Still, there are more of them, so I continue walking.

I am Death, and this is a horrendous waste we can ill afford... but must.

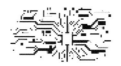

My head aches.

As I wince, pain stabs into my brain like ice picks.

Nausea surges from nowhere. I just turn my head as my stomach empties. The strain causes the pain to morph into agony.

A rising dark leaps up and engulfs me.

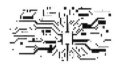

My head aches, but less.

I'm a little groggy and my mouth tastes like rats made a nest in it. Ugh.

Son of a bitch, what did they do to me?

I sit up, but I'm strapped down to the table.

Feeling weak, I open my eyes. There're a couple of doctors and nurses nearby. Their emotions reach me only faintly. It reminds me of the days right after my psychic abilities awoke.

Oh no.

I didn't plan for this.

My implant frame is gone.

Chapter 41

Big Fish or the Consequences of Electing Morons

C urses flit through my mind as anger burns away the grogginess.

They stole my fargin' implant frame!

Quick though my anger rises, it fades just as fast.

They took my frame, but not the keeper. I'm still recording.

This could still work.

At least, it might work if I can rescue myself or get rescued. On the other hand, dying would really mess up my sorta-plan. But, if they were gonna kill me, would they have bothered with removing the implant frame?

My thoughts wander for a while as the ache in my head slowly fades.

Will they still fear me?

If not, can I use that against them?

Almost as if in response to that thought, the new and improved Sergeant Lawton walks in showing off her pointy-toothed smile. Today, she's clothed, which is a tremendous improvement. Her outfit has a familiar, uniformish look to it. Oh, yes! I've seen clips of Everything's Okay officials wearing outfits like this.

"Congrats on the promotion," I tell her, summoning up the ghost of a smile. "Looks like murdering your fellows and kidnaping teens is a good way to move up in the Everything's Okay party."

She taps a button on my table. The whole thing lifts until I'm held vertically.

At least it's easier to see from this position.

There're a couple of heavy doors leading out of this room, each with an armed guard standing watch. Paved in something akin to white marble, the room is elegant with walls wrapped in blue, pieced-together cut stone—maybe even some sort of gemstone. They covered the ceiling in what appears to be carved glass, which gives out a surprisingly even light. There's no furniture in here beyond the gurney I'm strapped to.

Lawton eyes me critically. "You'll be receiving a high honor today. One *you* certainly don't deserve."

"It's a pleasure having these little chats with you, Lawton," I lie with a smile.

Turns out she can still smirk. "That's not actually my name."

"Maybe not, but it's how I'll always think of you."

"I'm going to enjoy killing you. Just like I killed your night mother."

My emotions rise, then freeze into a peculiar stillness.

This isn't *my* training kicking in to side-step my rage, it's Lachlann's.

"No snappy reply?" Lawton asks. She glances at the guards, then jerks her head towards me. They flank my table. Lawton pivots and walks out and the rest of us follow. Evidently, my gurney-thing has more robotics in it than expected.

Just one more thing to be wary of.

We follow her through a winding maze of beautifully appointed hallways. Ahead, there's a faint murmur, but I'm not sure what it is.

Are we still in the prison?

Okay, that had to be the residual drugs asking the question. There's no way these hallways are prison construction.

Well, this new location should make escaping easier.

You know—if they don't kill me first.

I'm feeling less weak, but nowhere near full strength. I glance at the guards. The odds of me breaking out and escaping aren't looking good. Hmm. Though my range is much reduced, I'm still able to sense things I can't see.

Maybe Lawton's surgeons didn't do too much damage while removing my implant frame.

A new thought hits me. Maybe Temocc's nano repair bots are still up there, repairing damage to my brain.

The guard on the right has long fur on its upper arms.

I reach out telekinetically and ruffle it.

The guard startles.

I pretend not to notice.

Okay, I can move air. Knowing I can still do that feels pretty great. Unfortunately, I'm as weak in mind as I am in body.

But weak doesn't mean hopeless. Or helpless.

Ahead, Lawton pauses in front of a door. The murmuring is loud enough that even someone with average hearing would notice. She looks back at me. Within her eyes, the mix of anticipation and something dark sends a chill down my spine.

No, this isn't gonna be good.

She smiles and opens the door. Beyond her is a packed auditorium. Not ten meters away from us is an ornate stage with an even more ostentatious podium in the center. There's an alien standing there chittering at the eager throng that's hanging on his every word. Humanoid, he's thin. A shimmering brown suit mostly hides his pale-yellow skin. There's a mane of wild brown hair running halfway down his back.

Crap.

Obatah Ogriton, head of the Everything's Okay Party and more importantly, head of the galactic government's Executive Branch.

I was so very right. This is gonna be bad.

Chittering reaching a crescendo, he raises his skinny arms.

The crowd goes wild with cheering and shouting.

Sometimes it really sucks being me.

Lawton sticks something in my ear. "Now you can understand civilized speech." Since she isn't speaking my language and I still understand, I get the message.

"Now," Obatah Ogriton says, waving towards us, "as you can see, we have a special guest: the monster itself. Obtained at significant cost and loss of life. Yes, indeed, only by our hands are you all kept safe."

Significant loss of life? Who died?

Or did they pull the dark gambit Accaryinth of Meprophrose warned me about? Did they kill a bunch of people and blame the murders on me?

I glance at Lawton, but her eyes are fixed on Obatah Ogriton.

She's starstruck. Even without my implant frame, I feel her adoration for the guy.

Eww.

The guards push my gurney onto the stage. Evidently, whatever robotics it has aren't up to climbing stairs. Monitors showing at least a dozen different camera views cover the front of the stage.

"They named this monster Ethan Shaw. A strange name, one reminiscent of ancient horrors and the nightmares born of violent insanity."

Before it can go on, I ask my question. "Speaking of monsters, was Fleet Admiral Cohosa doing your bidding, or was he disobeying your orders when he bombed his own flagship and murdered all those people?"

Lawton spins and punches me in the solar plexus. It's a light hit, though I don't think she intended it to be. Still, I wasn't expecting it, and the blow knocks the breath out of me.

Obatah Ogriton glares at me.

"Not gonna answer, eh?" I gasp. "You look bad either way. You're either a murderer or a—"

This time, Lawton punches me below the belt. Again, it's not a particularly hard punch. But again, it doesn't have to be.

Ow.

"Shut your hole," Lawton hisses into my ear from up close. "Or I'll permanently close it for you."

Not much of a threat since she wants to end me, anyway. Strangely enough, Lachlann's discipline doesn't kick in.

Why?

Ahh, because adrenaline and anger are doing wonders for restoring my physical strength. Despite that, I don't think I can force open the restraints holding me to the table.

"Masters of deceit, those humans," Obatah Ogriton tells the crowd. "It's like this creature walked out of a horror story, isn't it?"

The crowd enthusiastically agrees.

Still working the crowd, he continues, "Some of you have heard the other lies this creature and those whose minds it has warped have spread. That the tenebrosi aren't just a twisted aspect of the human mind but were invaders." Obatah Ogriton mugs for the cameras. "Pure silliness!"

The crowd roars with laughter and disdain.

"To put these fears to rest before we put this monster to rest, I've sent one of our most advanced science vessels, the *Benevolent Discovery*, to the so-called tenebrosi's homeworld."

Horror, shock, and fear rip through me, erasing the ache in my groin.

"No," I whisper, too stunned to do more.

I'm only peripherally aware when Lawton draws back for another punch, but holds, her expression frozen in warning.

Obatah Ogriton waves behind him.

Where there was only empty space suddenly transforms into a holographic display of a ship's bridge. There're also sub-holographs showing their positions relative to the planet they're approaching.

No, no, no.

"Captain Charmitag, of the *Benevolent Discovery*, are you there?" Obatah Ogriton asks.

The sailor wearing the most elaborate uniform turns towards the audience and gives a quick bow. "Chief Executor Obatah Ogriton, what a great pleasure! As you can see, we are on final approach to this extremely large planet and are ready to begin our sensor sweep. We await your command."

"Excellent, Captain Charmitag. Please proceed."

"Information Operator, deploy sensor pods. Run a full planetary scan."

"Aye, Captain." That person presses several buttons. "Deploying sensor pods. Full scan from all shipboard systems. Pods will come online and scan as they travel to their orbital stations." The operator checks some readouts. "We have good launch on all sensor pods. Ship and all pods are actively scanning."

The bridge crew turns to an empty holographic readout.

It remains blank.

The captain turns to the Information Operator. "What's wrong?"

"I don't understand, sir. We're scanning. The scanners are all working at optimum. But... they're not showing anything there. Not the planet itself, nothing."

"Captain," I yell, "get your people out of there, now!"

Lawton punches me in the throat.

"Enough," I say, meeting her eyes.

Radiating fury, she flexes her hand and makes another fist.

Obatah Ogriton's sphincter-like mouth scowls at me before turning back to the holographic captain. "Well, it appears you're having some sort of malfunction—"

Just then, the Information Operator yells, "Contact! Contact! Contact!"

Captain Charmitag whips around back to the holographic readout. There're now ships on it, and though the planet itself isn't visible, you can make out its perfectly spherical shape from all the yellow dots leaving it.

Not just hundreds, or thousands, or even tens of thousands.

The sensor operator says, "Multiple ships approaching from the planet!"

The captain's mouth drops then he looks back to us in horror as well over a hundred-thousand ships leave the planet on an intercept course with the science vessel and its sensor pods.

"Captain!" the sensor operator yells, "Power surge fro—"

The holograph fills with static, then blanks out.

"You fool!" I yell to Obatah Ogriton. "You woke them up! You've just doomed the entire galaxy with your hubris!"

Lawton rears back to hit me again.

I grab her brain and the two guards she brought. They all freeze. While I'm not particularly strong without my implant frame, I'm strong enough to do this. And if I have to go darker still, I have Lachlann's examples I can follow.

"Nonsense," Obatah Ogriton says with his easy smile, but there's a hard edge around his eyes. "It's just a technical malfunction. Everything's okay."

"So, people should believe your lies rather than what they see and hear? How stupid do you really think your people are?"

"They'll damned well believe what I tell them to believe!"

There's a distant explosion, but it's soft. Quiet, even. No one else seems to notice.

Rescue?

Well, I can hope.

"You're a fool, Obatah Ogriton, and anyone who refuses to believe what they just saw are even bigger fools. You've just awakened the tenebrosi. Now they're coming, not just for you and me, but *everyone*. Every adult, every child. They'll do to your civilization what they did to mine—annihilate it. Congratulations, you're going to be the most infamous person in history."

"Bah! What unfettered foolishness!"

Reaching out with my telekinesis, I trigger the restraint release and drop to the floor.

Obatah Ogriton flinches away.

"Don't worry," I tell him. "I'm the last person you have to fear." I look at the cameras. "This moron is a problem of your own making, so you deal with him. But you have an even bigger problem—the tenebrosi are coming for you." Obatah Ogriton tries to say something, but I hold him silent and still, just like I'm holding Lawton and her two thugs. I continue, "Think of all the horror stories you've heard of humans and increase them by a factor of ten. *That's* what's coming for you in the form of trillions of tenebrosi. There's nowhere to hide. Nowhere to run. You can't negotiate with them. You can't surrender to them. You either gird your loins and fight, or everyone dies. It's that simple."

I walk off the stage towards one camera. Looking right at it, I say, "I'm gonna prepare for battle. I suggest you do the same."

Guards come racing up, wielding intensely glowing batons.

Lachlann McRath could hold more than three dozen objects in independent orbits around his head. He could operate all the bridge stations of an assault carrier at once and never miss a beat.

Strength-wise, I'm no Lachlann McRath.

But talent-wise, I'm bloody close.

All the guards freeze up as I grab them, too.

A shot from the back of the auditorium misses my face by a few centimeters.

I physically grab one of the armored people and use it as a body shield.

Four minor explosions across the back precede the doors melting. Five people wearing galactic military hazardous environment uniforms storm in and open fire.

But... not at me—which is a tremendous relief.

In a matter of seconds, all the guards are down.

"You!" Dizzy yells, pointing at me. "You're under arrest. Come with us now and no one gets hurt."

I toss my body shield back over my shoulder. He not-so-accidentally flattens Lawton. "Yes, ma'am. I surrender."

Embry runs over and slaps binders over my wrists. The binders look sturdy, but don't feel that way.

He and Julian each grab one of my arms then quickly march me out.

"It's okay," Dizzy announces loudly. "We have the human in custody. You're all safe." She looks towards the spot where the holographics from the *Benevolent Discovery* had been. "At least until the tenebrosi start obliterating our worlds."

As soon as we're out of the auditorium, we're running.

CHAPTER 42
SHACKLES OF FATE

I t doesn't take us long before we exit to a rooftop parking lot. A small military patrol ship awaits. Embry, Carmen, and Julian rush to it. I follow them and Dizzy follows me.

As soon as we're aboard, the ship lifts off.

"Sit!" Dizzy yells.

We throw ourselves into seats a split-second before several Gs worth of sudden acceleration slams into us. Moving is difficult. Even breathing. My hearing and sight become warped. Fortunately, it doesn't last long.

Gabby's here. In the ship, just two rows forward. *"Hey, Buttercup."*

"Hey, back," she replies, barely containing her elation. *"Missed you, babe."*

"Same here."

Gravity returns to normal. I sit up, breathe deep, and flex my shoulders. My friends, Dizzy, and I exchange looks as they also move around gingerly.

"We're out!" someone calls from up front.

"Hell yeah!" Embry shouts, pumping his fist into the air. "That was freakin' awesome!"

Julian pulls off his helmet. "Righteously badass!"

Gabby crashes into me. She hugs me so tight my ribs creak.

"No doubt about it," I say as I wrap my arms around her, "I definitely missed you."

She grabs my face and kisses me hard. "Don't you *ever* do that to me again. You understand me?"

373

I kiss her softly. "Yes, ma'am."

Dizzy and Carmen join us. Dizzy gently pounds a fist against my shoulder. "That was a truly horrible plan. Let's never do things your way again."

"Hey," I counter with a grin struggling to escape one corner of my mouth, "we're all here and alive, aren't we?"

Carmen eyes me askance. "How do you think your weird-ass plan had anything to do with that?"

I grin. "Because all great leaders take credit for the hard work of their people."

Julian, Carmen, and Embry groan.

I grin wider, elated to have them here and well.

Here. They are here. So....

"Wait," I say. "Who's piloting the ship?"

Dizzy's eyes open wide, and she puts a hand to either side of her face. "Ohmygosh!" she says as the ship passes one of Central's moons. "I can't believe we forgot to fly the ship!"

"Hilarious," I say, as my grin twists into a smirk. The others are still grinning, but there's a knowing look about their expression. "Okay, guess I'll have to go find out myself."

"You do that," Dizzy replies. "Once you've satisfied your curiosity, we need to do some planning."

I look to Gabby to see if she wants to join me, but she just gives me a little push towards the front of the ship.

Interesting.

The cockpit is less than a five-meter walk, so I get there fast. The pilot is humanoid with long, black hair. They too are wearing a military hazardous environment uniform.

As I walk in, she takes her helmet off. "Son of mine, you've been busy."

Night Mom.

I stand there for a few seconds as this filters through my brain. Then suddenly I'm hugging her. "Mom! I missed you so much!"

Tears run down my cheeks.

She hugs me back. "I missed you, too. Look at you! You've grown so much. And I'm not just talking about the centimeters you've added. Oh Ethan, I'm so proud of you!"

"Thanks, Mom," I say into her hair.

"It's true. Well-deserved because you've done better than I could have hoped."

I lean back and look into her eyes. "It wasn't enough. I couldn't stop 'em, Mom. The fools woke the tenebrosi."

"I know. Like Dizzy said, we've got planning to do. Fortunately, we have friends out there. And thanks to your message after the science vessel was lost, I think we're gonna have a lot more of them."

"I hope so," I whisper, sadly.

She nods.

Lord, we really are going to war against the tenebrosi.

Again.

I look over Night Mom's head at my friends, who are sitting there talking quietly among themselves. Us and an entirely unprepared galaxy against the monsters who destroyed the Terran Empire.

Sensing my attention, Gabby winks and smiles, then turns back to Carmen.

Love, despair, and dread spread through me like creeping vines engulfing ancient ruins.

On my keeper, a new message appears:

**Congratulations, your recruit status has ended.
You are hereby promoted to the rank of First Lieutenant.
Report to TDS Phoenix for assignment.**

Oh. Phoenix really is a ship.

Maybe we do have cause for hope, I think as a slow, darkly fierce smile spreads across my lips.

Well, at the very least, this should be interesting.

EPILOGUE

A znir slid away from her holo.
"The mental deficients did it," she squeaked, wringing her digits together. "They awakened the tenebrosi. All this time, the fools were focused on that single human as if he was a threat. Clearly, the mental deficients we elected were the genuine threat.

"War is upon us."

She hurried over to her housing's communication unit and began tapping quickly.

"Currency must be withdrawn. Weapons and supplies must be purchased. Preparations must be made, and quickly."

She turned worried visual receptors back to her holo, where the newsie was trying to explain that what they all just saw never actually happened. Turning back to the communication unit, she resumed tapping as worry for the future of civilization as she knew it started chemical changes in her mind.

"War is upon us."

"D'Zenrizar, did you see that?"

D'Zenrizar's cheeks fluttered his stunned disbelief, "Obatah Ogriton waking the tenebrosi and attacking the Aklansic embassy?"

"Indeed! They're trying to claim that's not what happened, but we saw what we saw."

"They are, D'Banma. But, no matter how they try to spin this, we saw it clearly. What are we going to do?"

Swinging across the woven net hanging from his high ceiling, D'Banma struggled for answers. "We should convene a meeting," he said at last.

"Then what?"

"We'll discuss this strange new turn of events. Someone will know what to do."

"A meeting?" D'Zenrizar asked. "Meetings run long and produce little in the way of actionable results."

"Do you have a better idea?"

"No."

"Then a meeting it is."

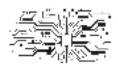

"Oh, toxic digestive emissions!" Ig snapped, twisting in her comfortable recliner to pick up her comm. "Obatah Ogriton's obsession with this human has gone on for too long. I've lost faith in him as a leader."

Ig's mate brought in a pair of drink orbs, which he shared. "What is it?"

"That human made Obatah Ogriton look like a fool in front of the entire galaxy."

"Obatah has been blathering on about humans for quite some time. Seems silly to get so worked up over one young being."

"Exactly!"

"What are you going to do about it?"

Ig held up her comm. "I'm going to write a message. No. I'm going to write a *strongly worded* message. Yes. Explain that I've lost confidence in our party's leader. That should shake things up."

Ig's mate mumbled acknowledgment if not agreement and sipped his drink.

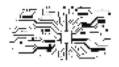

Pavotta Denisil Adruvia of Covotta sauntered out of the store to find people staring at their comms. More clustered around a nearby vid.

"That's rather peculiar behavior, even for people this close to the galactic core."

Curious, Denisil set down its bags full of purchases and checked the news stations.

"Lots of upset metamorphs. Poor communications with some ship. Boring." Denisil closed the vid, picked up the bags, and headed towards the nearest transit station.

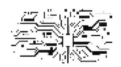

Green Slick clopped into the bar and ordered a strong smoke from the mechanized attendant.

Sitting in a nearby chamber, Carmine Haze asked, "You hear?"

Taking a puff from his roll, he grunted to the negative as he strode by.

"The human's on the loose. Great political embarrassment. There's talk of war."

Not slowing, Green Slick continued deeper into the bar so he wouldn't have to communicate with Carmine Haze. Finding an empty chamber, he slid in and laid down before taking a series of quick puffs from his roll.

Silvered Wind clopped up. "You heard?"

"Don't care."

Silvered Wind laid down and puffed his own roll. "Solid. Me neither. Whatever it is, it's happening far away. Doesn't affect us."

Green Slick puffed. "Doesn't affect us. Won't affect us."

CONTRIBUTORS

Thank you to everyone who's contributed to the creation of this novel. Be it a critique, a tidbit of literary wisdom, a bit of insight, or just a supportive word—this could not have been done without you.

Writing is a solitary pursuit.
Writing requires a team.

If that seems contradictory, please believe me when I say it is not.

In that same vein, if you've purchased this book, you're part of the team. If you read this in a library and enjoyed it, please leave me a review (purchasers are also encouraged to leave a review).

While I may not thank you personally, you will always carry my thanks

ABOUT THE AUTHOR

William R. Humble is a native Texan who's been writing for longer than he feels comfortable admitting. Though he's dabbled in other literary areas, his love of speculative fiction keeps drawing him back.

Made in the USA
Columbia, SC
12 October 2024

43487275R00211